KINSMAN

KINSMAN

Ben Bova

Methuen

First published in Great Britain 1988
by Methuen London Ltd
11 New Fetter Lane, London EC4P 4EE
Copyright © 1987 by Ben Bova

Printed in Great Britain by
Redwood Burn Limited, Trowbridge, Wiltshire

British Library Cataloguing in Publication Data

Bova, Ben, *1932–*
    Kinsman
    I. Title
    813'.54 [F]

    ISBN 0–413–18650–4

Author's Foreword:
Reality and Symbols

I HAVE RETURNED to where I started, returned to Chet Kinsman, to the character who has haunted me since I first began writing seriously.

If you have read the Tor Books edition of *As on a Darkling Plain,* you know the genesis of this book: How I wrote a very early version of it in 1949–50, a version that predicted the Space Race of the 1960s, which culminated in the American landings on the Moon. How the novel was rejected everywhere, in part because publishers were afraid it would incur the wrath of anti-Communist witch-hunters such as Senator Joseph McCarthy. How Arthur C. Clarke encouraged me to keep writing, and how eventually I was able to hand him the first copy of the first edition of *Millennium.*

When *Millennium* was originally published, in 1976, the idea of putting laser-armed satellites in orbit to shoot down nuclear-armed ballistic missiles was widely regarded as fantasy. Except by a few of us who knew better. Today the concept is known as the Strategic Defense Initiative, or Star Wars. Billions of dollars are being spent on it. Passionate arguments have been waged over it among scientists, politicians, pundits, and even science fiction writers. But in the early 1970s the only place that such an idea could be explored seriously in print, outside of classified technical publications, was in the medium called science fiction.

To the large majority of the public, science fiction is regarded as a field that deals with the fantastic, as far removed from reality as fiction can be. In truth, science fiction examines reality, and explores it in ways that no other form of literature possibly can. I must admit, though, that I am speaking now of *my* kind of science fiction, the kind that I write and the kind that I published when I was an editor. There are many other types of stories being marketed under the name of "science fiction." They may deal with unicorns or video games, barbarian swordsmen or robot killing machines. It is these types of stories, and the films and TV shows made from them, that convince most of the public that science fiction has no connection with reality.

My kind of science fiction examines the future in order to understand the present. It is social commentary of a new kind, a variety of literature that has been developed and sharpened in this century mainly by a handful of writers in the United States and Europe who are familiar with the physical sciences, their resultant technologies, and the impact of these technologies on society. Those of us who practice this art are agreed that modern technology is the major force of change in society today—and will continue to be, for the foreseeable future.

It seems clear that technological developments, from nuclear bombs to birth control pills, are the driving force in our civilization. The engines of change begin with the scientists and engineers. *Then* come the industrialists, churchmen, politicians, and everybody else. In our fiction we attempt to examine how science and technology bring change. We do not try to predict the future so much as to describe possible futures. We are not prophets warning of doom or describing utopias. We are scouts bringing reports of the territory up ahead, so that the rest of the human race might travel into the future more safely and happily.

In *Millennium,* the concept of using lasers mounted aboard orbiting satellites to protect the nations of Earth from nuclear missile attack was both a symbol and a realistic extrapolation of technology. In science fiction, such a scientific concept can be used both as a symbol and as a part of the authentic technical background for a story.

I knew in 1965 that a space-based defense against ballistic missiles was inevitable. I was working then at Avco Everett Research Laboratory, in Massachusetts, where the first truly high-power laser was invented. We called it the Gasdynamic Laser, and the first working model was built and operated under the supervision of the physicist with whom I shared an office. In its first ten seconds of operation, that crude laboratory "kluge" produced more output power than all the lasers that had been built everywhere in the world since the first one had been turned on, five years earlier.

By January of 1966 I was helping to arrange a Top Secret meeting at the Pentagon to inform the Department of Defense that lasers were no longer merely laboratory curiosities. It was clear, even then, that a device which could produce a beam of concentrated light of many megawatts power could be the heart of a defense against the so-called "ultimate weapon," the hydrogen-bomb-carrying ballistic missile.

The meeting we set up in the Pentagon was snowed out by one of the worst blizzards ever to hit Washington. If you ever want to take over the government, wait for a two-foot snowfall. You can then take all of Washington with a handful of troops—if they have skis.

In February 1966 we finally met with the Department of Defense's top scientists and stunned them with the news of the Gasdynamic Laser. Seventeen years later an American President authorized the program that the media snidely calls Star Wars. I have told the story of the history, and future, of the Strategic Defense Initiative in a nonfiction book, *Star Peace: Assured Survival,* published by Tor Books in 1986.

But long before then, I used the very-real facts about laser-armed satellites as the background for my novel *Millennium.*

I had never given up on Chet Kinsman. He was too much a part of me, too deeply ingrained in my subconscious mind. I watched my first, unpublished novel become history as the Soviet Union did indeed put the first satellites and the first human space travelers into orbit and the United States roused itself to leapfrog the Russians and place the first men on the Moon. The way *I* had written it, that first step on the Moon was not made by Neil Armstrong; it was made by Chester Arthur Kinsman.

Kinsman would not let go of my imagination. I found myself writing short stories about him. He was a dashing young military astronaut who founded the Zero Gee Club, the first man to make love in weightlessness. He fought in orbit and killed a Russian cosmonaut, a shattering experience that altered his entire life. He got to the Moon, finally, and rescued a fellow astronaut who had gotten hurt while on an exploring mission. He battled the bureaucracy of Washington, as any modern pioneer must, in his efforts to get the United States to return to the Moon.

While these stories were shaping themselves in my mind, while I was writing them and seeing them published in science fiction magazines, the outline of *Millennium* crystallized and came to life.

Once *Millennium* was published, readers reacted powerfully, especially to the ending. I was encouraged to bring together the stories dealing with Kinsman's early life, and I wove them into a second novel, *Kinsman,* a "prequel" to *Millennium* even though it was written several years afterward.

In the meantime, of course, the scientists and engineers were making steady progress in the fields of space technology, lasers, and computers. So much so that in March 1983 President Reagan announced the start of the Strategic Defense Initiative. Once again I watched my fiction start to turn into history. Nothing in the original *Millennium* and *Kinsman* has been invalidated by the events of the past few years. But now many of the details that I had to sketch minimally can be shown in much clearer perspective.

Now, in these two volumes, the whole story is played out from beginning to end. From a brand-new lieutenant on a joyride in a supersonic jet fighter plane to a man who literally carries the weight of two worlds on his shoulders. From a brash youngster who thinks of sex as nothing more than fun to a man who cares so much about the woman he loves that he is afraid of a relationship that will hurt her.

There are many differences between the original pair of novels and this new retelling of them. For one thing, the human, emotional story of Kinsman and the woman he has loved all his life is told properly for the first time. Because the two novels were originally written the way they were, many details—and some larger aspects—of the story did not blend smoothly, one book to the other. Now they have been reexamined, rethought, and rewritten. All the characters and themes now mesh properly, and you can read the story of Kinsman's life from beginning to end as a single seamless garment.

The social and political implications of building a defense

against nuclear attack, however, remain almost exactly as I originally wrote them. That is because they have not changed. The ultimate result of space-based defenses against nuclear attack will be a unified world government. There is absolutely no doubt in my mind about that. Who runs that government, what kind of a government it will be, what role the United States will play in it and what role other nations will play—all those questions are unanswered. Their answers will be the political history of the twenty-first century.

There are many symbols in Kinsman's story. I mention this mainly because most critics have been blind to them. Or perhaps they think of symbolism only in its psychological sense, where rockets are considered phallic and a wheel-shaped space station is thought to be vaginal. That is not the sort of symbolism I am speaking of.

Kinsman himself is a symbol. A young American male, full of the adventure of flying, who brings both love and death to the pristine realm of outer space. In *Millennium,* he becomes a Christ figure, and his closest friend, Frank Colt, takes on the role of Judas. Colt himself symbolizes the dilemma of the black man in modern America.

The Christian symbolism is at its plainest in the section of *Kinsman* where he rescues the injured astronaut on the surface of the Moon. In that tale, titled "Fifteen Miles" when it appeared in a science fiction magazine in its original form, the surface of the Moon becomes a testing ground, a place of ordeal and punishment. The central question is redemption: Can Kinsman save his soul, or is he damned forever? This becomes the question for all the rest of his life, and forms his underlying motivation in *Millennium.*

The technological gadgets of the story also serve as symbols. Equating Moonbase's water factory with a human being's heart and blood is obvious enough. So, perhaps, is the symbolism of a lance of light that destroys the death machines of ballistic missiles. But the idea of humankind's reach into space *forcing* a change in human attitudes on Earth, which pervades the story of Kinsman's life, has escaped the attention of most critics.

There are two aspects to this, in the story. One is the laser-armed satellites, the Star Wars system, placed in orbit to defend against nuclear missile attack. The other is weather control, using technology to tame one of the most fundamental forces on Earth. Push and pull. Negative and positive. Yin and yang. The important point is that once the human race began to extend its ecological niche beyond the limits of planet Earth, all our old ways of thinking became doomed. Most people do not realize this yet. Most are oblivious to the fact that national borders are swiftly losing their meaning in a world of communications satellites, hydrogen bombs, continent-spanning missiles, and the expansion of human life into space.

The facts are there to see, but most people are not emotionally prepared to deal with them. It is through the symbolism of fiction that we prepare our minds for these new concepts. In the truest sense, Chet Kinsman does exist, and his message of hope and peace and love is the ultimate reality.

—Ben Bova
West Hartford, Connecticut
March 1987

To Mark Chartrand, despite his puns

KINSMAN

Fear death?—to feel the fog in my throat,
    The mist in my face,
When the snows begin, and the blasts denote
    I am nearing the place,
The power of the night, the press of the storm,
    The post of the foe,
Where he stands, the Arch Fear in a visible
    form.
Yet the strong man must go . . .

—Robert Browning

Age 21

FROM THE REAR SEAT of the TF-15 jet the mountains of Utah looked like barren wrinkles of grayish brown, an old threadbare bedcover that had been tossed carelessly across the floor.

"How do you like it up here?"

Chet Kinsman heard the pilot's voice as a disembodied crackle in his helmet earphones. The shrill whine of the turbojet engines, the rush of unbreathably thin air just inches away on the other side of the transparent canopy, were nothing more than background music, muted, unimportant.

"Love it!" he answered to the bulbous white helmet in the seat in front of him.

The cockpit was narrow and cramped. The oxygen he breathed through the rubbery mask had a cold, metallic tang to it. Kinsman could barely move in his seat. The pilot had warned him, "Pull the harness good and snug; you don't want anything flapping loose if you have to eject." Now the safety straps cut into his shoulders.

Yet he felt free.

"How high can we go?" he asked into the mike built into the oxygen mask.

A pause. "Oh, we can leave controlled airspace if we want to. Better'n fifty thousand feet." The pilot had a trace of Southern accent. Alabama, maybe, thought Kinsman. Or Georgia. "Thirty thou's good enough for now, though."

Kinsman grinned to himself. "A lot better than hang gliding."

"Hey, I like hang gliding," said the pilot.

"But it doesn't compare to this. . . . This is *power*."

"Right enough."

Power. And freedom. Six miles above the tired, wrinkled old Earth. Six miles away from everything and everybody. It

3

couldn't last long enough to suit him.

Ahead lay San Francisco and his mother's funeral. Ahead lay death and his father's implacable anger.

Life at the Air Force Academy was rigid, cold. A first-year cadet was expected to obey everybody's orders, not make friends. No matter that you're older than the other first-year men. A rich boy, huh? Spent two years in a fancy prep school, huh? Well, snap to, mister! Let me see four chins, moneybags! Four of 'em!

Yet that was better than going home.

His father had refused to stop off in Colorado when he had taken his ailing wife from their estate in Pennsylvania to her sister's home in San Francisco. And Kinsman had delayed taking leave to visit his mother there. Time enough for that later, after his father had gone back East to return to running his banks.

Then, suddenly, unalterably, she was dead. And his father was still there.

Instead of taking a commercial airliner, Kinsman had begged a ride with a westward-heading Air Force captain.

If t'were done, he told himself, t'were best done quickly.

Now he was flying. Free and happy.

Suddenly the plane's nose dipped and Kinsman felt his pressure suit begin to squeeze the air out of him. His arms became too heavy to lift. His head felt as if it would sink down inside his rib cage. He could hear the pilot's breath, over the open mike, rasping in long, regular panting grunts, like a man doing pushups, and Kinsman realized he was breathing hard too. They were diving toward the desert, which now looked as flat and hard and gray as steel. The pressure suit squeezed harder. Kinsman could not speak.

"Try a low-level run," the pilot gasped, between breaths. "Get a real . . . feeling of speed."

The helmet on Kinsman's head weighed two million pounds. He made a grunting noise that was supposed to be a cool "Okay."

And then they were skimming across the empty desert, engines howling, rocks and bushes nothing more than a speeding blur whizzing past. Kinsman took a deep exhilarating breath. The plane shook and bucked as if eager to return

4

to the thinner, clearer air where it had been designed to fly.

He thought he saw some buildings in the blur of hills off to his left, but before he could speak into his radio mike the pilot blurted:

"Whoops! Highway!"

The control column between Kinsman's knees yanked back toward his crotch. The plane stood on its tail, afterburners screaming, and a microsecond's flicker of a huge tractor-trailer rig zipped past the corner of his eye. The suit squeezed at his middle again and he felt himself pressing into the contoured seat with the weight of an anvil on his chest.

They leveled off at last and Kinsman sucked in a great sighing gulp of oxygen.

"Damned sun glare does that sometimes," the pilot was saying, sounding half annoyed and half apologetic. "Damned desert looks clear but there's a truck doodling along the highway, hidden in the glare."

Kinsman found his voice. "That was a helluva ride."

The pilot chuckled. "I'll bet there's one damned rattled trucker down there. He's probably on his little ol' CB reporting a flying saucer attack."

They headed westward again, toward the setting sun. The pilot let Kinsman take the controls for a while as they climbed to cross the approaching Sierras. The rugged mountain crests were still capped with snow, bluish and cold. Like the wall of the Rockies that loomed over the Academy, Kinsman thought.

"You got a nice steady touch, kid. Make a good pilot."

"Thanks. I used to fly my father's Cessna. Even the Learjet, once."

"Got your license?"

"Not yet. I'll qualify at the Academy."

The pilot said nothing.

"I'm going in for astronaut training as soon as I graduate," Kinsman went on.

"Astronaut, huh? Well, I'd rather fly a real airplane. Damned astronauts are like robots. Everything's done by remote control for those rocket jocks."

"Not everything," Kinsman protested.

He could sense the pilot shaking his head inside his

5

helmet. "Hell, I'll bet they even have machines to do their screwing for them."

It was an old house atop Russian Hill. Victorian clapboard, unpretentious yet big enough to hold a hockey rink on its ground floor. The view of the Bay was spectacular. The people who lived in this part of San Francisco had the quiet power to see that none of the new office towers and high-rise hotels obscured their vistas.

Neal McGrath opened the door for Kinsman. His normal scowl warmed into a half-bitter smile.

"Hello, Chet."

"Neal. I didn't expect to see you here."

"He needed somebody to take charge of things for him. This has hit him pretty hard."

McGrath reminded Kinsman of a Varangian Guard: a tall, broad-shouldered, red-haired Viking who hovered by his Emperor's side to protect him from assassins. His ice-blue eyes looked much older than his years. He was barely twenty months older than Kinsman, but his suspicious scowl and low, growly voice gave him an air of inner experience, of wariness, that strangely made people trust and rely on him. Kinsman had known him since McGrath had been the ten-year-old son who helped their gardener mow their lawn. Now McGrath was his father's personal assistant, and was being groomed for one of the family's seats in the House of Representatives. He would be a senator one day, they all agreed.

Stepping from the late afternoon sunshine into the darkened stained-glass foyer of the old Victorian house, Kinsman asked, "Where is my mother?"

"In there." McGrath gestured toward a set of double doors that rose to the ceiling.

Kinsman let his single flight bag drop to the marble floor. "Is my father . . ."

"He's upstairs, taking a nap. The doctor's trying to keep him as quiet as possible." McGrath bent to pick up Kinsman's bag. "There's a room for you upstairs. How long will you be staying?"

"I'll leave right after the funeral, tomorrow."

"A lot of the family is flying in from the East. They'll expect to see you afterward."

6

Kinsman shook his head. "I can't stay."

"If it's a matter of fixing things with the Academy I can call . . ."

"No. Please, Neal."

McGrath shrugged and started toward the broad, stern dark-wood staircase, his footsteps echoing on the cool marble floor.

Kinsman went to the tall double doors. An ornately framed mirror hung on the hallway wall just before the doors, and he saw himself in it. His mother would not have recognized him. The blue uniform made him look slimmer than ever, and taller, despite the fact that he had never quite reached the six-foot height he had coveted so desperately as a teenager. His face was leaner, dark hair cropped closer than it had ever been before, blue eyes weary from lack of sleep. His long jaw was stubbly; his mother would have insisted that he go upstairs and shave.

He slid the doors slightly apart and slipped almost guiltily into the room. It had been a library at one time, or a parlor, the kind of a room where women of an earlier generation had once served tea to one another. Now it was too dark to see the walls clearly. The high windows were muffled in dark draperies. The only light in the large room was a ceiling spot illuminating the casket. Kinsman's mother lay there embedded in white satin, her eyes closed peacefully, her hands folded over a plain sky-blue dress.

He did not recognize her at first. The cancer had taken away so much of her flesh that only a taut covering of skin stretched across the bony understructure of her face. All the fullness of her mouth and brow were gone. She was a gaunt skeleton of the mother he had known.

Her skin looked waxy, unreal. Kinsman stared down at her for a long time, thinking, *She's so tiny. I never realized she was so tiny.*

He knelt at the mahogany prayer rail in front of the casket but found that he had nothing to say. He felt absolutely numb inside; no grief, no guilt, nothing. Empty. But in his mind he heard her voice from earlier years.

Chester, get down from that tree before you hurt yourself!
Yes, Mommy.
You could have a fine career as a concert pianist, Chester,

7

if only you would practice instead of indulging in this ridiculous mania for flying.

Aw, Ma.

I do wish you would be more respectful of your father, Chester. He's proud of what he's accomplished and he wants you to share in it.

I'll try, Mother. But . . .

If I give you my consent, Chester, if I let you join the Air Force, it will break your poor father's heart.

I've got to get away from him, Mother. It's the only way. I'll put in for astronaut training. I won't kill anybody. It'll all work out okay, you'll see. You'll be proud of me someday.

"So you finally got here."

Kinsman turned and saw the tall, austere figure of his father framed in the doorway.

He got up from his knees quickly. "I came as soon as I could."

"Not soon enough," his father said, sliding the doors shut behind him.

Kinsman pulled in a deep breath. They had fought many battles in front of his mother. He had been a fool to hope that today could be any different.

"It . . . she went so fast," he said.

His father walked slowly toward him, a measured pace, like a monster in a child's horror tale. "At the end, yes, it was fast. The doctors said it was the Lord's mercy. But she suffered for months. You could have eased her pain."

Kinsman realized suddenly that his father was *old*. And probably in pain himself. The man's hair was dead white now, not a trace of its former color. His eyes had lost their fire.

"I talked with her on the phone," he said, knowing it sounded weak, defensive. "Almost every night . . ."

"You should have been *here*, where you belong!"

"The Air Force thought differently."

"The Air Force! That conglomeration of feeble-minded professional killers."

"That's not true and you know it."

"I could have had any one of a dozen United States Senators bail you out of your precious Academy. But no, you were too busy to come and ease your mother's last days on Earth."

8

"None of us knew she was that close to the end."

"She was in pain!" The old man's voice was rising, filling the nearly empty room with its hard, angry echoes.

"I couldn't come," Kinsman insisted.

"Why not?"

"Because I didn't want to see you!" he blurted.

If it surprised his father, the old man did not show it. He merely nodded. "You mean you couldn't *face* me."

"Call it what you want to."

"Sneaking around behind my back. Forcing your sick mother to consent to your joining the Air Force. The only son of the most prominent Quaker family in Pennsylvania —joining the Air Force! Learning how to become a killer!"

"I'm not going to kill anyone," Kinsman answered. "I'm going in for astronaut duty."

"You'll do what they order you to do. You surrendered your soul when you put on that uniform. If they order you to kill, you'll kill. You'll bomb cities and strafe helpless women and children. You'll drop napalm on babies when they order you to."

"I'm not going to be involved in anything like that!"

"My only child, a warrior. A killer. No wonder your mother died. You killed her."

Kinsman could feel waves of fire sweeping through him. Gritting his teeth against the pain, he said, "That's a rotten thing to tell me . . ."

"It's true. You killed her. She'd still be alive if it weren't for you."

The pain flaming through him was too much. Fists clenched against his sides, Kinsman brushed past his father and strode out of the room, out of the house, out into the bright hot sunshine and clear blue sky that he neither felt nor saw.

By the time he realized the sun had set, he found himself in Berkeley, walking aimlessly along a wide boulevard, carried along by the flow of students and other pedestrians streaming past shops and restaurants. Music blared from car radios passing by. Garish lights flickered from shop-front windows.

He stepped into a bar. The sign on its window said it was

a coffee shop, but the only coffee they served had Irish whiskey in it. Kinsman ordered a beer and hunched over the frosted glass, staring blankly into its foamy head. He heard a sweet woman's voice singing, looked up into the mirror behind the bar, and saw a girl sitting on a stool in front of a microphone, strumming a guitar as she sang.

"Jack of diamonds, queen of spades,
  Fingers tremble and the memory fades,
  And it's a foolish man who tries to cheat the
    dealer . . ."

The people sitting around the bar wore shabby denims or faded khaki fatigues. A couple of suits and casual sports coats. Kinsman felt out of place in his crisp sky-blue uniform.

As he watched the night deepen over the clapboard buildings and the lights on the Bay Bridge stretch a twinkling arch across the water, he realized he had spent most of his life alone. He had no home. The Academy was cold and friendless. There was no place on Earth that he could call his own. And deep inside he knew that his soul was as austere and rigid as his father's. I'll look like him one day, Kinsman thought. If I live long enough.

"You can't win,
  And you can't break even,
  You can't get out of the game . . .

She has a really sweet voice, he thought. Like a silver bell. Like water in the desert.

It was a haunting voice. And her face, framed by long midnight-black hair, had a fine-boned, dark-eyed ascetic look to it. She perched on a high stool, under a lone spotlight, bluejeaned legs crossed and guitar resting on one thigh.

He sat at the bar silently urging himself to go over and introduce himself, offer her a drink, tell her how much he enjoyed her singing. But as he worked up his nerve a dozen kids his own age burst into the place. The singer, just finished her set, smiled and called to them. They clustered around her.

Kinsman turned his attention to his warming beer. By the time he finished it the students had pushed a few tables

10

together and were noisily ordering everything from Sacred Cows to Seven-Up. The singer had disappeared. It was full night outside now.

"You alone?"

He looked up, startled. It was her.

"Uh . . . yeah." Clumsily he pushed the barstool back and got to his feet.

"Why don't you come over and join us?" She gestured toward the crowd of students.

"Sure. Great. Love to."

She was tall enough to be almost eye level with Kinsman, and as slim and supple as a young willow. She wore a black long-sleeved pullover atop her faded denims.

"Hey, everybody, this is . . ." She turned to him with an expectant little smile. All the others stopped their chatter and looked up at him.

"Kinsman," he said. "Chet Kinsman."

Two chairs appeared out of the crowd and Kinsman sat down between the singer and a chubby blonde girl who was intently, though unsteadily, rolling a joint for herself.

Kinsman felt out of place. They were all staring wordlessly at him, except for the rapt blonde. Wrong uniform, he told himself. He might as well have been wearing a badge that spelled out NARC.

"My name's Diane," the singer said to him as the bar's only waitress placed a fresh beer in front of him. "That's Shirl, John, Carl, Eddie, Dolores . . ." She made a circuit of the table and Kinsman forgot their names as soon as he heard them. Except for Diane's.

They were still eyeing him suspiciously.

"You with the National Guard?"

"No," Kinsman said. "Air Force Academy."

"Going to be a fly-boy?"

"Flying pig," mumbled the blonde on his left.

Kinsman looked at her. "I'm going in for astronaut training."

"An orbiting pig," she muttered.

"That's a stupid thing to say."

"She's wired tight," Diane told him. "We're all a little pissed off."

"Why?"

11

"The demonstration got called off," said one of the guys. "The fuckin' mayor reneged on us."

"What demonstration?" Kinsman asked.

"You don't know?" It was an accusation.

"Should I?"

"You mean you really don't know what day tomorrow is?" asked the bespectacled youth sitting across the table.

"Tomorrow?" Kinsman felt slightly bewildered.

"Kent State."

"It's the anniversary."

"They gunned down a dozen students."

"The National Fuckin' Guard."

"Killed them!"

"But that was years ago," Kinsman said. "In Ohio."

They all glared at him as if they were blaming him for it.

"We're gonna show those friggin' bastards," said an intense, waspish little guy sitting a few chairs down from Kinsman. He tried to remember his name. *Eddie?* The guy was frail-looking, but his face was set in a smoldering angry cast, tight-lipped. The big glasses he wore made his eyes look huge and fierce.

"Right on," said the group's one black member. "They can't cancel our parade."

"Not after they gave their word it was okay."

"We'll tear the fuckin' campus apart tomorrow!"

"How's that going to help things?" Kinsman heard his own voice asking.

"How's it gonna *help*?"

"I mean," Kinsman went on, wanting to bounce some of their hostility back at them, "what are you trying to accomplish? So you tear up the campus, big deal. What good does that do—except convince everybody that you're a bunch of loonies."

"You don't make any sense," Eddie snapped.

"Neither do you."

"But you don't understand," said Diane. "We've got to do *something*. We can't just let them withdraw permission to hold our parade without making some kind of response."

"I'd appeal to the Governor. Or one of my senators. Go where the clout is."

12

They all laughed at that. All but Eddie, who looked angrier still.

"You don't understand anything at all about how the political process works, do you?" Eddie sneered.

Kinsman smiled. Now I've got you! He responded with deliberate tempo, "Well . . . an uncle of mine is a U.S. Senator. My grandfather was Governor of the Commonwealth of Pennsylvania. Several other family members are in public service. I've been involved in political campaigning since I was old enough to hold a poster."

Silence. As if a leper had entered their midst.

"Jesus Christ," breathed one of the kids at last. "He's *really* Establishment."

Diane said, "Your kind of politics doesn't work for us. The Establishment won't listen to us."

"We've gotta fight for our rights!"

"Demonstrate!"

"Fight fire with fire!"

"Action!"

"Bullshit," Kinsman snapped. "All you're going to do is give the cops an excuse to bash your heads in—or worse. Violence is always counterproductive."

The night and the argument wore on. They swore at each other, drank, smoked, talked, yelled until they started to get hoarse. Kinsman found himself enjoying it immensely. Diane had to get up to sing for the customers every hour, and they would call a truce for the duration of her set. Each time she finished she came back and sat beside him.

And the battle would resume. The bar finally closed and Kinsman got up slowly on legs turned to rubber. But he went along with them down a dark and empty Berkeley street to someone's one-room pad, up four creaking flights of outdoor stairs, yammering all the way, arguing against them all, one against ten. And Diane stayed beside him.

Eventually they started drifting away, leaving the apartment. Kinsman found himself sitting on the bare wooden floor halfway between the stained kitchen sink and the new-looking water bed, telling them:

"Look, I don't like it any more than you do. But violence is *their* game. You can't win that way. Tear up the whole

13

damned campus and they'll tear down the whole damned city just to get even with you."

"Yeah," admitted one of the girls. "Look what they did in Philadelphia. And with a black mayor, too."

"Then what's the answer?" Diane asked.

Kinsman made an elaborate shrug. "Well . . . you could do what the Quakers do. Shame them. Just go out tomorrow in a group and stand in the most prominent spot on campus. All of you . . . all the people who were going to march in the parade. Just stand silently for a few hours."

"That's dumb," Eddie said.

"It's smart," Kinsman retorted. "Nonviolent. Conscience-stirring. Like Gandhi. Always attracts the news photographers. An old Quaker trick."

"I could call the news stations," Diane said, smiling.

A burly-shouldered kid with a big beefy face and tiny squinting eyes crouched on the floor in front of Kinsman.

"That's a chickenshit thing to do."

"But it works."

"You know your trouble, fly-boy? You're chickenshit."

Kinsman grinned at him and looked around the floor for the can of beer he had been working on.

"You hear me? You're all talk. But you're scared to fight for your rights."

Looking up, Kinsman saw that Diane, the blonde smoker, and two of the guys were the only ones left in the apartment. Plus the muscleman confronting him.

"I'll fight for my rights," he said, very carefully because his tongue was not quite obeying his brain. "And I'll fight for yours, too. But not in any stupid-ass way."

"You callin' me stupid?" The guy got to his feet.

A weight lifter, Kinsman guessed. Pumps iron every day and now he wants to show off his muscles on me.

"I don't know you well enough to call you anything."

"Well, I'm callin' you a chicken. A gutless motherfuckin' coward."

Slowly Kinsman got to his feet. It helped to have the wall to lean against.

"I take that, sir, to be a challenge to my honor," he said, letting himself sound drunk. It took very little effort.

"Goddam right it's a challenge. You must be some

goddam pig—secret police or something."

"That's why I'm wearing this inconspicuous uniform."

"To throw us off guard."

"Don't be an oaf."

"I'm gonna break your head, wise-ass."

Kinsman raised an unsteady finger. "Now hold on. You challenged me, right? So I get the choice of weapons. That's the way it works in the good ol' *code duello.*"

"Choice of weapons?" The big guy looked confused.

"You challenged me to a duel, didn't you? You have impeached my honor. I have the right to choose the weapons."

The guy made a fist the size of a football. "This is all the weapon I need."

"Ah, but that's not the weapon I choose," Kinsman countered. "I believe that I shall choose sabers. Won a few medals back East with my saber fencing. Now where can we find a pair of sabers at this hour of the morning . . . ?"

The guy grabbed Kinsman's shirt. "I'm gonna knock that fuckin' grin off your face."

"You probably will. But not before I kick both your kneecaps off. You'll never see the inside of a gym again, muscleboy."

"That's enough, both of you," Diane snapped. She stepped between the two of them. The big guy let go of Kinsman.

"You'd better get back to your own place, Ray," she said, her voice flat and hard. "You're not going to break up my pad and get me thrown out on the street."

Ray pointed a thick, blunt finger at Kinsman. "He's an agent for the Feds. Or something. Don't trust him."

"Go home, Ray. It's late."

"I'll get you, blue-suit," said Ray. "I'll get you."

Kinsman replied, "When you find the sabers, let me know."

"Shut up!" Diane hissed at him. But she was grinning.

She half-pushed the lumbering Ray out the door. The others left right behind him. Suddenly Kinsman was alone in the shabby little room with Diane.

"I guess I ought to go, too," Kinsman said, his insides shaking now that the danger had passed. Or was it the

15

thought of going back home?

"Where?" Diane asked.

"Back in the city . . . Russian Hill."

"God, you *are* Establishment!"

"Born with a silver spoon in my ear. To the manner born. Rich or poor, it pays to have money. Let 'em eat cake. Or was it coke?"

"You're very drunk."

"How can you tell?"

"For one thing, your feet are standing still but the rest of you is swaying like a tree in a typhoon."

"I am drunk with your beauty . . . and a ton and a half of beer."

Diane laughed. "I can believe the second one."

"The toilet's in there, isn't it?"

"You mean you haven't . . . ?"

Kinsman walked past her, carefully. "Nobody owns beer, you know. You merely rent it."

It was a narrow cubicle with an old-fashioned tub that stood on four rusted swans; the toilet was equally ancient. No roaches in sight. No sink. He bent over the tub and splashed cold water on his face, then patted it dry with a limp towel hanging on the back of the door.

He came out and saw Diane still standing in the middle of the room, eyeing him quizzically.

"How do you get a cab around here?" he asked.

"You don't. Not at this hour. No trains or buses, either."

"I'm stuck here?"

Diane nodded.

"A fate worse than death," he muttered.

The room's furnishings consisted of a bookcase crammed with sheet music and a few paperbacks, the water bed, a Formica-topped table with two battered wooden chairs that did not match, the water bed, a pile of books in the corner by the windows, a few colorful pillows strewn across the floor here and there, the water bed, two guitars, a sink and small stove with some cabinets above them, and the water bed.

"We can share the bed," Diane said.

He felt his face turn red. "Are your intentions honorable?"

16

She grinned at him. "The condition you're in, we'll both be safe enough."

"Don't be so sure."

But he fell asleep as soon as he sank into the soft warmth of the bed. His last thought was an inward chuckle that he did not have to spend the night under the same roof as his father.

It was during the misty, dreaming light of earliest dawn that he half awoke and felt her body cupped against his. Still half asleep, they moved together, slowly, gently, unhurried in the pearl-gray fog, touching without the necessity to think, murmuring without the need for words, caressing, making love.

Kinsman lay on his back, smiling peacefully at the cracked ceiling. Diane stroked the flat of his abdomen, saying drowsily, "Go back to sleep. Get some rest and then we can do it again."

It was hours later by the time Kinsman had showered in the cracked tub and climbed back into his wrinkled, sweaty uniform. He was peering into the still-steamed bathroom mirror, wondering what to do about his stubbly chin, when Diane called through the half-open door.

"Tea or coffee?"

"Coffee."

Kinsman came out of the tiny bathroom and saw that Diane had wrapped herself in a thin bathrobe. She had set up toast and a jar of Smuckers grape jelly on the table by the window. The teakettle was on the two-burner stove and a pair of chipped mugs and a jar of instant coffee stood alongside.

They sat facing each other, washing down the crunchy toast with the hot, bitter coffee. Diane watched the people moving along the street below them. Kinsman stared at the bright clean sky.

"How long can you stay?" she asked.

"I've got a funeral to attend . . . in about an hour. Then leave tonight."

"Oh."

"Got to report back to the Academy tomorrow morning."

"You have to?"

17

He nodded.

"But you'll be free this afternoon?"

"After the burial. Yes."

"Come down to the campus with me," Diane said, brightening. "I'm going to try your idea . . . get them to stand just like the Quakers. You can help us."

"Me?"

"Sure! It was your idea, wasn't it?"

"Yeah, but . . ."

She reached across the table and took his free hand in both of hers. "Chet . . . please. Not for me. Do it for yourself. I don't want to think of you being sent out to Central America or someplace like that to fight and kill people. Or to be killed yourself. Don't let them turn you into a killer."

"But I'm going into astronaut training."

"You don't think they'll really give you what you want, do you? They'll use you where *they* want you—Lebanon or Nicaragua or who knows where? They'll put you in a plane and tell you to bomb some helpless village."

He shook his head. "You don't understand . . ."

"No, *you* don't understand," she said earnestly. Kinsman saw the intensity in her eyes, the devotion. Is she really worried that much about me? he wondered. Does she really care so much? And then a truly staggering thought hit him. My father! Is he worried about me? Is he frightened for *my* sake?

"Come with us, Chet," Diane was pleading. "Stand with us against the Power Structure. Just for one hour."

"In my uniform? Your friends would trash me."

"No, they won't. The uniform will be great! It'd make a terrific impact for somebody in uniform to show up with us! We've been trying to get some of the Vietnam vets to show themselves in uniform."

"I can't," Kinsman said. "I've got to go to the funeral, and then catch a ride back to the Academy."

"That's more important than freedom? More important than justice?"

He had no answer.

"Chet . . . please. For me. If you don't want to do it for yourself, or for the people, then do it for me. Please."

He looked away from her and glanced around the

shabby, unkempt room. At the stained sink. The faded wallpaper. The water bed, with its roiled sheet trailing onto the floor.

He thought of the Academy. The cold gray mountains and ranks of uniforms marching mechanically across the frozen parade ground. The starkly functional classrooms, the remorselessly efficient architecture devoid of all individual expression.

And he thought of his father: cold, implacable—was it pride and anger that moved him, or fear?

Then he turned back, looked past the earnest young woman across the table from him, and saw the sky once again. A pale ghost of a Moon was grinning lopsidedly at him.

"I can't go with you," he said quietly, finally. "Somebody's got to make sure that the nation's defended while you're out there demonstrating for your rights."

For a moment Diane said nothing. Then, "You're trying to make a joke out of something that's deadly serious."

"I'm being serious," he said. "You'll have plenty of demonstrators out there. Somebody's got to pay attention to the business of protecting you while you're exercising your freedoms."

"It's our own government that we need protection from!"

"You've got it. You just have to exercise it a little more carefully. I'd rather be flying. There aren't so many of us up there."

Diane shook her head. "You're hopeless."

He shrugged.

"I was going to let you stay here . . . if you wanted to quit the Air Force."

"Quit?"

"If you needed a place to hide . . . or if you just wanted to stay here, with me."

He started to answer, but his mouth was suddenly dry. He swallowed, then in a voice that almost cracked, "Listen, Diane. I wasn't even a teenager when the first men set foot on the Moon. That's where I've wanted to be ever since that moment. There are new worlds to see, and I want to see them."

"But that's turning your back on this world!"

19

"So what?" He pushed his chair from the table and got to his feet. "There's not much in this world worth caring about. Not for me."

He strode to the door, then turned back toward her. She was still at the table. "Sorry I disappointed you, Diane. And, well, thanks . . . for everything."

Diane got up, walked swiftly across the tiny room to him, and kissed Kinsman lightly on the lips.

"It was my pleasure, General."

He laughed. "Hell, I'm not even a lieutenant yet."

"You'll be a general someday."

"I don't think so."

"You could have been a hero today."

"I'm not very heroic."

"Yes, you are." Diane smiled at him. "You just don't know it yet."

Unshaven, in his wrinkled uniform, Kinsman stood at his father's side through the funeral, rode silently in the cortege's limousine to the cemetery, and watched a crowd of strangers file past the casket, one by one, placing on it single red roses. His mother had detested red roses all her life.

As they rode back toward Russian Hill in the velvet-lined, casketlike limousine, Kinsman turned to his darkly silent father.

"I know I've disappointed you," he said in a low swift voice, afraid he would be cut off before he could finish, "and I also realize that you wouldn't be so angry with me if you didn't love me and weren't worried about me."

His father stared straight ahead, unmoving.

"Well . . . I love you, too, Dad."

The old man's eyes blinked. The corners of his mouth twitched. Without moving a millimeter toward his son, he whispered, "You are a disgrace. Staying out all night and then showing up looking like a Bowery derelict. The sooner you leave the better!"

Kinsman leaned back in the limousine's velvet uphol-stery. Thanks, Dad, he said to himself. You've always made it so easy for me.

* * *

Neal McGrath drove him down 101, toward the Navy's Moffet Field, weaving his new Chrysler convertible through knots of traffic and past hulking, hurtling diesel tractor-trailers.

"You're sure you can pick up a flight back to Boulder?" McGrath yelled over the rush of the wind.

"Sure!" Kinsman hollered back. "The guy I rode out with told me he was going back late this afternoon."

McGrath shook his head as he carefully flicked the turn signal and pulled around a station wagon filled with kids. The wind pulled wildly at his long red hair.

"The family's going to be very disappointed that you didn't stay for dinner."

"Not Dad. He threw me out."

McGrath snorted. "You know he didn't mean that."

"Sure."

"Where the hell were you all night, anyway? You look like you got rolled in an alley."

"Just about." Kinsman told him about Diane and her campus activists as the convertible zoomed down the highway.

"Sound like a bunch of Communists," McGrath growled.

Kinsman laughed. "We didn't discuss politics in bed."

"What an easy lay. She sure tried to recruit you, all right."

The Moffet Field turnoff was approaching. McGrath slid into the exit lane.

"Neal . . . I don't even know her last name!"

"So what?"

"So look her up for me, will you? Maybe the family could give her a little help . . . with her singing career."

"A Communist?"

"She's not a Communist, for Chrissakes."

"Worse, then. A liberal." But McGrath was grinning. "See if you can help her."

"I'm a married man, kid," said McGrath.

Kinsman frowned at him. "I'm not asking you to get involved with her. But she's got a marvelous voice, Neal. Maybe somebody in the family can get her a break, some bookings . . ."

21

"Going to reform her, eh? Make her rich and turn her into a capitalist."

"Yeah. Why not?" Kinsman studied McGrath's face. He was smirking. You just don't understand, Neal.

Later that afternoon, thirty thousand feet above the Sacramento Valley with the sun at their backs, Kinsman felt the cares and fears of the Earth below easing out of his tense body.

"How'd you enjoy Frisco?" the pilot asked.

"I didn't see much of it," Kinsman said into his radio microphone.

"Didn't stay very long."

"Neither did you."

The pilot's voice in his earphones broke into a self-satisfied chuckle. "Long enough, pal. Overnight is plenty long enough if you know what you're doing."

Kinsman nodded inside his helmet.

They climbed higher. Kinsman watched the westering sun throw long shadows across the rugged Sierra peaks.

"Sir?" he asked, after a long thoughtful silence. "Do you honestly think that astronaut training would turn a man into a robot?"

He could see the featureless white curve of the pilot's helmet over the back of the seat. There was nothing human about it.

"Listen, son, *all* military training is aimed at turning you into a robot. That's what it's all about. You think a normal human being would rush toward guys who're shooting at him?"

"But . . ."

"Just don't let 'em get inside you," the pilot said, his languid drawl becoming more intense, almost passionate. "Hold on to yourself. The main thing is to get up here, away from 'em. Get flying. Up here they cain't really touch you. Up here you're free."

"They're pretty strict at the Academy," Kinsman said. "They like things done their own way."

"Tell me about it. I'm a West Point man, myself. But you can still hold on to your own soul, boy. You have t'do things

22

their way on the outside, but you be your own man inside. Ain't easy, but it can be done."

Nodding to himself, Kinsman looked up and through the plane's clear canopy. He caught sight of the Moon, hanging just above the rugged horizon. It looked bright and close in the darkening sky.

I can do it, he told himself. I can do it.

Age 25

HE WAS FLYING west again, with the sun at his back. Two years of "peacekeeping" in the volatile Middle East had gone by. He had flown a fighter plane without firing a shot, happy that he was not assigned to the real fighting that flared intermittently in Central America. It had taken almost another two years before he had finally been assigned to astronaut training.

Two years of air patrols along the Gulf Coast, searching for smugglers' planes coming in from Latin America. Two years of watching the United States' economy slide disastrously as the price of foreign oil skyrocketed once again. Even Houston was hit by the new recession; the revitalized OPEC, backed now by Soviet arms, quickly squeezed all American companies out of the nationalized oil industries of the Middle East, Indonesia, and South America.

Diane Lawrence was on her way to stardom. Her haunting voice, singing of simpler, happier times, brought comfort to Americans who faced doubtful futures of unemployment and welfare. Kinsman dated her half a dozen times, flying to cities where she was appearing. He traveled on commercial airliners. New government austerity regulations prevented him from piloting an Air Force plane, except on official duty. He was shocked at the price of airline tickets; the cost of

23

energy was more than money, it was freedom of movement.

But now Kinsman was relaxed and happy as he held the controls of the supersonic twin-engine jet. Months of training in the elaborate mockups of the space shuttle were behind him. Orientation flights on the "Vomit Comet," the lumbering cargo jet that flew endless parabolic arcs to give the astronaut-trainees their first taste of weightlessness, had gone smoothly. Now he was heading for the real thing: spaceflight duty. The cares and problems of the groundlings' world were far below him, for the moment.

Kinsman was sitting in the right-hand seat of the jet's compact cockpit. The plane's ostensible pilot, Major Joseph Tenny, seemed half asleep in the pilot's seat.

Far below them the empty brown desert of New Mexico sprawled. They had left NASA's Johnson Space Center, outside Houston, at sunrise. They would be at Vandenberg Air Force Base in southern California in time for breakfast.

The plane was as beautiful and responsive as a woman. More responsive than most, Kinsman thought. The slightest touch on the crescent-shaped control yoke made the plane move into a bank or a climb with such grace and smooth power that it sent a shudder of delight through Kinsman.

"Sweet little thing, ain't she?" Tenny murmured.

Kinsman shot a surprised glance at the Major. He was not asleep after all. Chunky, short-limbed, barrel-chested, Tenny looked completely out of place in a zippered flight suit and a visored gleaming plastic helmet. His dark-eyed swarthy face peeped out of the helmet like some ape who had gotten into the outfit by mistake.

But he grasped the controls in his thick-fingered hands and said, "Here . . . lemme show ya something, kid."

Kinsman reluctantly let go of the controls and watched Tenny push the yoke sharply forward. The plane's nose dropped and suddenly Kinsman was staring at the mottled gray-brown of the desert rushing up toward him.

"Shouldn't we get an okay from ground control before we . . ."

Tenny shot him a disgusted glance. "By the time those clowns make up their minds," he growled, breathing hard, "we could be having Mai Tais in Waikiki."

24

The altimeter needle wound down. The engines' whine was lost in the shrill of tortured air whistling past their canopy. The plane dived, screaming. The desert filled Kinsman's vision.

And then they zoomed upward. The yoke in front of Kinsman pulled smoothly back as his pressure suit hissed and clamped a pneumatic hold on his guts and legs to keep the blood from draining out of his head, to keep him alive and awake while the plane nosed up smoothly as an arrow, hurtling almost like a rocket, up, up, straight into the even emptier blue desert of the sky.

Kinsman wanted to let loose a wild cowboy's yell, but the weight on his chest made it hard even to breathe. Tenny said nothing, but the gleam in his devilishly dark eyes told Kinsman there was more to come. The afterburners were screeching now as the plane climbed higher, cleaving through the thinning air.

Kinsman grinned to himself as he realized what Tenny was going to do. Sure enough, the Major nosed the plane over again and suddenly Kinsman's arms floated up off his lap. His stomach seemed to be dropping away. He was falling, falling —yet strapped into his seat.

Weightlessness. Kinsman gulped once, twice. Despite everything his inner ear and stomach were telling him, he knew that he was not falling. He was floating. Free! Like a bird, like an angel. Free of gravity.

Tenny leveled the plane off and the feeling of normal weight returned. The Major eyed Kinsman craftily.

"Like the Vomit Comet," Kinsman said, grinning at him.

"You really *like* zero gee, dontcha?"

"It's great."

Tenny shook his head, a ponderous waddling with the bulky helmet. "You're the only guy in the whole group who didn't throw up once. Even Colt tossed his cookies a couple times. But not you. According to the reports."

"The reports weren't faked," Kinsman said.

Tenny grunted. "I didn't think so. But I hadda see for myself."

He gave control of the plane back to Kinsman and they resumed their flight toward Vandenberg.

"Sir?" Kinsman asked. "What's Colonel Murdock like?"

"I never served under him before. Desk jockey, from what I hear."

"I don't see why they didn't put you in command. You're due for promotion to lieutenant colonel, aren't you?"

Tenny made a face that might have been either a smile or a scowl. "Due for promotion and getting promoted are two different things. Besides, there's two other majors who've been running programs for two other squads of trainees, same as me. So we get a light colonel to sit on top of the whole group. That's the Air Force way: solid brass, all the way up the shaft."

Kinsman laughed.

But Tenny grew more serious. "There's something else I wanted to talk to you about. Colt. None of you guys have gotten close to him . . ."

"The black Napoleon? He's not easy to get close to."

"Maybe he needs a friend," said Tenny.

Kinsman thought of Frank Colt, the one night during training when the black man had joined the other guys in the squad for a game of pool. The intensity on Colt's face as he turned a friendly game into a gut-burning competition. How Colt had probed for the weakness in each of the other men; how he had finessed, angered, cajoled, or kidded each one of them into defeat.

"He's a loner," Kinsman said. "He's not looking for a friend."

"He's a black loner in an otherwise white outfit."

"That's got nothing to do with it."

"The hell it hasn't."

Kinsman started to reply, hesitated. There were a dozen arguments he could make, three dozen examples he could show of how Colt had deliberately rebuffed attempts at camaraderie. But one vision in Kinsman's mind kept his tongue silent: he recalled the squad's only black officer eating alone, day after day, night after night. He never tried to join the others at their tables in the mess hall, and no one ever sat down at his.

"If he wasn't the top man in the squad," Tenny said, "he'd have a lot of pals. But he's a better flier than any of you. He's scored higher in the training tests than any of you.

26

Higher than anybody in the other squads, too."

"And he's hell on wheels," Kinsman countered. "I don't think he wants any of us for friends."

Tenny scowled deeply. Then he said, "Yeah, maybe so. But he tossed his cookies. That shows that he's human, at least."

Kinsman said nothing.

Kinsman almost laughed out loud when he first saw Colonel Murdock.

Twenty-four astronaut trainees, all first lieutenants, twenty men, four women, all of them white except one, were sitting nervously in a bare little briefing room at Vandenberg Air Force Base. The air-conditioning was not working well and the room was dank with the smell of anxiety. It was like a classroom, with faded government-green walls and stained acoustical tile ceiling. The chairs in which the lieutenants sat had wooden writing arms on them. There was a podium up front with a microphone goosenecking up, and scrubbed-clean chalkboards and a rolled-up projection screen behind it.

"Ten-HUT!"

All two dozen trainees snapped to their feet as Lieutenant Colonel Robert Murdock came into the room, followed by his three majors.

He looks like Porky Pig, Kinsman said to himself.

Murdock was short, round, balding, with bland pink features and soft, pudgy little hands. He was actually a shade taller than Major Tenny, who stood against the chalkboard behind the Colonel. But where Tenny looked like a compact football linebacker or maybe even a petty Mafioso, Murdock reminded Kinsman of an algebra teacher he had suffered under for a year at William Penn Charter School, back in Philadelphia.

Colonel Murdock scanned his two dozen charges, trying to look strong and commanding. But his bald head was already glistening with nervous perspiration and his voice was an octave too high to be awe-inspiring as he said, "Be seated, gentlemen. And ladies."

Kinsman thought back to the algebra teacher. The man had terrified the entire class for the first few weeks of the semester, warning them of how tough he was and how

27

difficult it would be for any of them to pass his course. Then the students discovered that behind the man's threats and demands there was nothing: he was an empty shell. He could be maneuvered easily. The real trouble was that if he discovered he had been maneuvered by a student, he was merciless.

Kinsman struggled to stay awake during the Colonel's welcoming speech. All the usual buzzwords. Teamwork, orientation, challenge, the honor of the Air Force, pride, duty, the nation's first line of defense . . . they droned sleepily in his ears.

"Two final points," said Colonel Murdock. The lieutenants stirred in their chairs at the promise of release.

"First—we are operating under severe budgetary and equipment restrictions. NASA gets plenty of bucks and plenty of publicity. We get very little. Almost everything we do is kept secret from the American public, and the Congress is constantly cutting back on funds for our operations. We are locked in a deadly battle to prove to Congress, to the people of this nation, and—yes—even to enemies within the Pentagon itself, that the Air Force has a valid and important role to play in manned space flight.

"It's up to you to prove that manned operations in space should not be left to the civilians of NASA. When the Congress one day approves the change of our service's name from just plain Air Force to Aero*space* Force—which it should be—it's going to be your work and your success that gets them to do it."

Kinsman suppressed a grin. He's never studied rhetoric, that's for sure. Or syntax, either.

"Second point," Murdock went on. "Everything you do from now on will be by the buddy system. You're going to fly in the shuttle as two-man teams. You're going to train as two-man teams. You're going to eat, sleep, and think as two-man teams."

Kinsman shot a glance at Jill Meyers, the only woman in his eight-person squad. The expression on her snub-nosed freckled face was marvelous: an Air Force officer's self-control struggling against a feminist's desire to throw a pie in the Colonel's face.

". . . and we're going to be ruthless with you," Murdock

was saying. "You will be judged as teams, not as individuals. If a team fu—eh . . . fouls up, then it's *out!* Period. You'll be reassigned out of the astronaut corps. Doesn't matter who fouled up, which individual is to blame. Both members of the team will be out on their asses. Is that clear?"

A general mumble of understanding rose from two dozen throats.

"Sir?" Jill Meyers was on her feet. "May I ask a question?"

"Go right ahead, Lieutenant." Murdock smiled toothily at her, as if realizing for the first time that there were women under his command.

"How will these training assignments be made, sir? Will we have any choice in the matter, or will it all be done by the Personnel Office?"

Murdock blinked, as if he had never considered the problem before. "Well . . . I don't think . . . that is . . ." He stopped and pursed his lips for a moment, then turned away from the podium to confer with the three majors standing behind him. Instinctively, he held a chubby hand over the microphone. Jill remained standing, a diminutive little sister in Air Force blues.

Finally the Colonel returned to the microphone. "I don't see why you can't express your personal preferences as to teammates, and then we'll have them checked through Personnel's computer to make sure the matchups are satisfactory."

"Thank you, sir." Lieutenant Meyers sat down.

"In fact," Colonel Murdock went on, "I don't see why we shouldn't get a preliminary expression of preferences right now. Each of you, write down the names of three officers you'd like to team with, in order of your preference."

Tenny and the two other majors looked surprised. The briefing room suddenly dissolved into a chattering, muttering, pocket-searching scramble for papers and pens or pencils.

Kinsman took his ballpoint pen from his tunic pocket and borrowed a sheet of tablet paper from the man sitting next to him. Then he found himself staring at the blank paper on the arm of his chair.

Who the hell do I want to team up with?

The magnitude of the decision seemed to hit everyone at

29

once. The room fell deathly quiet.

Kinsman glanced at the tall redhead sitting in the front row. He hadn't met her yet, but she had damned good legs and a pleasant smile. But what if she can't hack it in zero gravity or she's a lousy pilot or something else goes wrong? Then I'm out in the cold.

Jill Meyers was a smoothly competent pilot, Kinsman knew from their weeks of training in Texas. But so is Smitty, and D'Angelo . . . and Colt.

Frank Colt. He was the best man in their eight-officer squad. If what Tenny had told him was true, he was the best man of the whole two dozen trainees. The idea of teaming with the redhead had its charm, but . . .

He gazed across the room to where Frank Colt was sitting, bolt upright, staring straight ahead as if he were trying to burn a hole in the chalkboard at the front of the room with the laserlike intensity of his eyes.

Kinsman looked down at the blank sheet of paper and wrote three names on it:

Franklin Colt
Franklin Colt
Franklin Colt

That evening Major Tenny threw a party.

He had not actually intended to, but right after dinner at the mess hall most of his squad members congregated at Tenny's one-room apartment on the ground level of the new Bachelor Officers' Quarters. Kinsman had stopped off at the Officers' Club; he had heard there was a piano there, and it had been months since he had touched a keyboard. But it had been surrounded already by a dozen ham-fisted amateurs. So he trailed along with his fellow squad members to Tenny's quarters. It was well known that their major was seldom without a bottle of bourbon close to hand. And his quarters opened onto the poolside patio.

As the trainees from the other squads saw Tenny's people spilling out of the glass sliding doors and sitting around the pool, armed with plastic cups and a suspicious-looking bottle, they quickly joined the party. Some brought six-packs of beer from the PX. Others brought soft drinks. The leggy redhead that Kinsman had spotted that morning showed up in tight jeans and T-shirt, toting a half-gallon of Napa Valley rosé wine.

It was time to make new acquaintances.

By the time the sun had gone down and the few skinny palm trees ringing the pool were swaying in the night breeze, the trainees were all comrades in arms.

"So they turn off the damned flight profile computer, tilt the simulator forty degrees, and tell me I've gotta set it straight in twenty seconds—or else."

"Yeah? You know what they pulled on me? Total electrical failure. I told 'em they oughtta hang rosary beads on the dashboard."

"Y'know, these quarters are pretty good. I mean, I been in motels that're worse."

"This was a motel until a coupla months ago. They went outta business and the Air Force bought it up cheap."

Kinsman was sitting on the newly planted grass in a pair of brand-new fatigues. Beside him was the half-gallon of wine, and on the other side of it was the redhead. She had pinned her plastic nametag to her T-shirt. It said O'HARA.

"You do have a first name," Kinsman said to her.

"Yes, of course." Her voice was a cool, controlled contralto.

"I have to guess?"

"It's a game I play. You guess my name and I'll guess yours."

Why are women all crazy? Kinsman asked himself. Why can't they just be straightforward and honest?

"Well, let's see, now." He took a sip of wine. "With that last name and your red hair, I'll bet you get kidded a lot about Scarlett O'Hara. Is that why you're sensitive about your name?"

She smiled at him and nodded. It was a good smile that made her eyes sparkle. "And there was a movie star," she said, "years ago, named Maureen O'Hara. I get that a lot, too."

"But your name isn't that, either. It's something more down to earth."

"Plain as any name can be."

Kinsman laughed. "Well, then, it's either George M. Cohan or Mary."

31

"It's not George M."

Kinsman sang softly, "But it was Mary, Ma-ary . . ." He lifted his plastic cup to her. "Pleased to meet you, Mary O'Hara."

"Pleased to meet you, Chester A. Kinsman."

Now let's see how long it takes you to figure out that I was named after one of the great political disgraces of the Grand Old Party.

But an angry voice cut across everyone's conversation.

"I don't give a shit who they team with me! I left my paper blank."

Frank Colt. Kinsman saw him standing at the pool's edge, silhouetted against the Moon-bright sky. Like most of the others, Colt was wearing off-duty fatigues. But on him they looked like a dress uniform, perfectly fitted, creased to a knife edge.

All other talk stopped. Colt was glaring at one of the trainees from another squad, a stranger to Kinsman, a lanky rawboned kid with light hair, bony face, big fists.

"We already heard about you," the kid was saying in a flat Midwestern twang. "Top scores in the simulator. Best record in the group. Think you're pretty hot stuff, dontcha?"

"I do my job, man. I do the best I can. I'm not here to goof around, like some of you dudes. This isn't a game we're playing. It's life and death."

"Aw, don't be such a pain in the ass! You just think you're better'n anybody else."

"Maybe I do. Maybe I *am*."

Kinsman glanced over at Major Tenny, sitting on a folding chair a few yards away. Tenny was watching the argument, like everybody else. He was frowning, but he made no move to break it up.

"Yeah?" the other lieutenant answered. "Know what think? I think they're givin' you all the high scores b'cause you're black and nobody wants a bunch of civil rights lawyer comin' down here pissin' and cryin' b'cause we flunked ou our token . . ."

Colt's hand flicked out and grabbed the kid by the jaw distorting his face into a ridiculous imitation of a fish: mout pried open, eyes popping.

"Don't say it, man." Colt's voice was murderously controlled. "Call me black, call me dumb, call me anything you want. But if you say 'nigger' to me I'll break your ass."

Tenny was hauling himself out of the chair now. But too late. Colt released the kid's jaw. The lieutenant took a short step forward and swung at Colt, who simply ducked under the wild haymaker and gave a quick push. The lieutenant spun into the pool with a loud splash.

Kinsman found himself on his feet and heading for Colt. Everybody else went to the aid of the kid in the pool. Colt walked away, back toward his quarters. Kinsman followed him and caught up with him in a few seconds.

"Hey, Frank."

Colt turned his head slightly but he did not slow down.

Kinsman pulled up beside him. "Jeez, what a shithead! He got what he deserved."

"At least he said what was on his mind," Colt answered. "Plenty other guys around here feel the same way."

"That's not true."

"No? Suppose I started making time with that redhead the way you were? How many rednecks would come outta the woodwork then?"

"I thought you were married."

"I was. Ain't no more."

"Oh. I'm sorry."

"No big thing. Lots of chicks in the world. Why tie yourself down to just one?"

The grapes sound sour, Kinsman thought.

They had reached the doorway into the section of the BOQ where Colt and Kinsman were quartered. Colt pushed open the fiberboard door and they started up the steps to the second floor. As they headed down the corridor toward their rooms, Kinsman said:

"I hope you're not too tough to live with. I picked you for my partner this morning."

"You *what*?" Colt stopped dead.

Kinsman studied the black lieutenant's face. It was almost totally devoid of expression except for the suspicious, wary eyes. They were probing him, searching for the kicker, the payoff, the flick of the whip.

"This morning," Kinsman said. "Colonel Murdock's buddy system . . . I wrote down your name."

"Why the hell you wanna do that?" Colt started down the corridor again, not waiting for an answer.

Kinsman kept stride with him. "Because you're the best pilot in the group and I don't want to be washed out because my partner fucked up."

"That's it, huh?"

"Yeah."

"Wasn't your good deed for the day? Your contribution to the Air Force's affirmitive action program?"

Kinsman laughed. "Where I come from, we write checks for good causes. We don't *do* anything, especially if it means coming in contact with lower-income types."

Colt saw no humor. He reached his door, unlocked it, and swung it open. "I didn't write any names down. I left my paper blank."

Kinsman leaned against the doorjamb. "We all heard."

"Didn't think anybody'd want to be stuck with me."

"Because you're black."

"Because they're out to *get* me, man! They want to knock me off, pin my balls to their totem pole. And if they get me, they get my buddy, too."

"Nobody's out to get you, Frank. It isn't the Ku Klux Klan out there."

"Sure. Sure. Just wait. You want to be my buddy, man? Then they'll be out to get you, too."

"Listen," Kinsman insisted. "They're down on you because you've been behaving like a paranoid sonofabitch."

Colt smiled coldly. "Maybe you're right. Maybe I ought to act more humble . . . Yassuh, Massa Kinsman, suh. I's shore powerful grateful that y'all took notice of a po' li'l ol' darky lak me."

Grinning, Kinsman said, "Go to hell, Frank."

Immediately Colt replied, "Why this is hell, nor am I out of it."

With a shake of his head, "All I can say, buddy, is that you sure know how to break up a party. And I was just starting to get someplace with Mary O'Hara."

"That's her name, huh?" Colt made an enigmatic little

34

shrug, as if he were carrying on a debate within himself. Then he said, "Guess I owe you for breaking up the evening. Come on in, I've got a bottle of tequila in my flight bag."

"Say no more!"

By the time Major Tenny knocked on Colt's door he and Kinsman were sitting on the floor, passing the half-empty bottle back and forth with elaborate care. Colt climbed slowly to his feet and walked uncertainly to the door. The Major's squat bulk filled the doorway.

"Nice little show you put on down there. The poor bastard damn near drowned."

"Too bad," said Colt.

Tenny walked in and spotted Kinsman sitting on the floor, his back against the bunk. "What the hell are you guys up to?"

Kinsman waved the bottle of tequila at him. "Cultural relations, boss. We're studying the effect of tequila consumption on the gross national product of Mexico."

"Our good neighbor to the south," Colt added.

"Tequila?" Tenny strode swiftly to Kinsman, bent down, and yanked the bottle from his hand. He sniffed at it, then tasted it. "Dammitall, this *is* tequila!"

"What'd you expect?" Kinsman asked. "Hydrazine?"

Tenny shook his head, a frown on his swarthy features. "I can't let you men drink a whole bottle of tequila. You'll be in no shape for duty tomorrow morning."

"I have an idea!" Colt said brightly. "Why'n't you help us finish it up? Might save our lives."

"And our immortal souls," Kinsman muttered.

"To say nothing of our immoral careers," Colt added.

"That's immortal, not immoral."

"You have your career, I'll have my career."

Tenny scowled at them both. "If you think you can manage to shut the door, I'll do my best to help you out."

Within moments Tenny was sitting on the bare wooden floor between the two lieutenants, his back propped against the bunk.

"Did you know," Kinsman was asking him, "that ol' Frank and I were born and raised within a few miles of each other? Right in Philadelphia. Both of us."

"Only my neighborhood wasn't as classy as his," Colt said. "Not as many Quakers where I grew up. Kinsman's a Quaker, y'know . . ."

"Used to be. When I was a child. Not anymore. Now I'm an officer and a gentleman. No more Quaker. No more family ties."

Tenny let them ramble for a while, but he finally said, "Frank—you're gonna get your ass kicked outta here if you can't get along with the others."

"If *I* can't . . ."

"Murdock was puking into a wastebasket when he heard what happened at the pool tonight. He's got a very weak stomach and his first instinct was to transfer you to Greenland. Maybe farther."

"Sonofabitch."

Turning to Kinsman, Major Tenny asked, "You really want to be his partner?"

Kinsman nodded. Gently. His head was already hurting.

"Okay," said Tenny. "Frank, you've got a buddy. You're not alone. And you've got me. I think you're the best damned flier I've ever laid eyes on. Now keep your temper under control and your mouth zipped and you'll be okay. Got it?"

"Sure," Colt said, suddenly dead sober. "The Jackie Robinson bit. Anything else you want me to do, boss? Walk on water? Shine shoes?"

Tenny grabbed him by the shirt. "You stupid bastard! You wanna be an astronaut or not?"

"I want to."

"Then don't fuck yourself over. There's only one man can ruin things for you and that's *you*. Learn some self-control."

Colt said nothing as long as Tenny held his shirt. They merely glared at each other. But when the Major slowly released him, Colt said quietly, "I'll try."

"And stop going around with that goddamned chip on your shoulder."

"I'll try," Colt repeated.

Tenny turned to Kinsman. "And you . . . you help him all you can. He's too good a man to lose."

* * *

"How come you got the window seat?" Colt muttered.

He was lying beside Kinsman in the metal womb of the space shuttle's mid-deck compartment. Zipped into sky-blue coveralls, Kinsman lay on his back in the foam-padded contour seat next to the compartment's side hatch—and its only window.

"Lucky, I guess," he croaked back to Colt. His voice nearly cracked. His throat was dry and scratchy, his palms slippery with nervous perspiration.

Six astronaut-trainees were jammed into the mid-deck area, waiting in tense silence as the shuttle went through the final few minutes of countdown. They had no radio earphones and could hear only muffled, garbled voices from the flight crew on the deck above them.

Kinsman mentally counted the rungs on the ladder that disappeared through the open hatch to the flight deck. By the time I've counted the rungs ten times we'll lift off, he told himself. He counted slowly.

Up on the flight deck, at the other end of the ladder, the shuttle's four-man crew was going through the final stages of the countdown, Kinsman knew. They were watching instruments on their control panel springing into life, listening to the commands flickering across the electronics communications net that spread across the entire globe of the Earth. They could see the automatic sequencer's numbers clicking down toward zero.

Down in the mid-deck compartment, strapped into their seats, the trainees could only wait and sweat.

Kinsman gave up counting and turned his head to look out the small circular window set into the hatch. All he could see was the steel spiderwork of the launch tower, frighteningly close. Could the ship clear those steel beams when it took off? Kinsman knew that it had, hundreds of times. Yet the tower still looked close enough to touch.

He focused his vision on the distant shoreline, where the Pacific curled in to meet the brown California hills. But the nearness of the launch tower still pressed against his awareness.

Hell of a way to go, he said to himself. Lying on your back with your legs sticking up in the air like a woman in heat.

37

"Five seconds!" a voice rang out from the flight deck.

The time stretched to infinity. Then, a vibration, a gushing roar, a banging shock—Christ! Something's gone wrong! Abruptly the whole world seemed to shake as the roar of six million flaming demons burned into every bone of his body. Kinsman caught a brief glimpse of the tower sliding past the corner of his vision, then the brown hills slipped by as he was pressed down into the seat. The force pushing against him was not as bad as the g's he had pulled in fighter planes, but the vibration was worse, an eyeball-rattling shaking that felt as if all the teeth in his head would be wrenched loose.

With an effort he turned to look at Colt and saw that his partner's eyes were squeezed shut, his mouth gaping wide. Kinsman tried to see the other four trainees, but their seats were in front of his and he could not see their faces.

The pressure got worse and there was a jolt when the two strap-on solid rockets were jettisoned.

Going through fifty klicks, Kinsman knew. Maximum pressure ought to be behind us now.

The weight on his chest began to lessen. The bone-conducted rumble of the engines suddenly disappeared.

And he was falling.

Zero gravity, he told himself. We're in orbit. His arms had floated loosely off the seat rests. With a blink of his eyes, Kinsman rearranged his perspective. He was no longer lying on his back; he was sitting upright. They all were.

His stomach was fluttering. He made himself relax the tensed muscles. You're floating, he told himself. Just like at the seashore, when you were a kid. Beyond the breakers. Floating on the swells.

He turned and grinned at Colt. "How do you like it?"

Colt's answering grin was a bit queasy. "I'll get used to it in a couple minutes."

Major Pierce came floating down the ladder from the flight deck. He landed lightly on his booted feet, bobbed up off the metal deck plates. Back on Earth he had been a nondescript little man in his forties, patrician high-bridged nose, darting snake's eyes. Up here he could damned well be a ballet dancer, Kinsman thought.

"Very well, my little chickadees," the Major said, in a sneering nasal tenor. "Anybody feel like upchucking?"

38

The four other trainees had to turn in their seats to see Pierce, who was at the bottom of the ladder. Kinsman stared at the Major's boots, fascinated to see that they were not touching the deck.

"Very well," Major Pierce said when no one replied to his question. "Unstrap and try to stand up. By the numbers. And move *slowly*. Be particularly careful of sudden head movements. That way lies nausea." He pointed at Jill Meyers. "Meyers, you have the honor of being first."

Jill got up from her seat, her face going from brow-knitted concentration to wide-eyed surprise as she just kept rising, completely off her feet, until her mousy-brown hair bumped gently against the metal overhead. While the others laughed, Jill thrashed about and found an anchoring point by grabbing the handle of one of the electronics racks that covered the forward bulkhead.

"No matter how much training we give you Earthside, you still don't understand Newton's First Law of Motion," Pierce said, in a tone of bored disgust. "A body in motion tends to remain in motion unless acted upon by an outside force. In this case," he hiked a thumb upward, "the over-head."

Nobody laughed.

Jill's partner, the lanky, whipcord-lean Lieutenant Smith, got up from his seat next. Smitty was tall enough to raise a long slender arm to the overhead and prevent himself from soaring off his feet.

"That's cheating, Mr. Smith," said the Major.

"Yessir. But it works."

Kinsman smiled at the Mutt and Jeff look of the Meyers-Smith team. Jill was the shortest member of the trainee group; Smitty barely squeezed in under the Air Force's height limit for pilots.

Mary O'Hara and Art Douglas were next. Then Colt got cautiously to his feet, and finally Kinsman. It was like standing in the ocean up to your neck, with the waves trying to pull you this way and that.

"Well, at least you didn't toss any cookies," Pierce sniffed as the six trainees bobbed uneasily in their places.

"Very well then," the Major went on. "We're go for a three-day mission. By the time we touch down at Vandenberg

39

again you will each know every square centimeter of this orbiter more intimately than your mother's"—he hesitated and smiled a fraction—"face. And each of you will get the opportunity to go EVA with Captain Howard, the payload specialist, and perform an actual mission task. In the meantime, stay out of the crew's way and don't get into mischief."

"Sir, will we get a chance to fly the bird?" asked Douglas. He was a shade smaller than Kinsman, prematurely balding, moonfaced, but sharp-eyed and very bright: the group's lawyer.

Pierce closed his eyes momentarily, as if seeking strength from some inner source. "No, Lieutenant, you will *not* touch the controls. You know the mission profile as well as I, or at least you should. We are not going to risk this very expensive piece of aerospace hardware on your very first flight into orbit."

"I know the plan, sir," Douglas replied agreeably, "but I thought maybe the commander would let us sneak in a little maneuver, maybe. Strictly within the mission profile."

"Majors Podolski and Jakes are the commander and pilot, respectively, on this mission. They will handle all the maneuvering. If you are a good little lieutenant, Mr. Douglas, perhaps Major Podolski might allow you to come up on the flight deck and watch him for a few moments."

"Oh, peachy keen!" retorted Lieutenant Douglas.

It was like living in a submarine. Outside, Kinsman knew, was the limitless expanse of emptiness: planets, moons, comets, stars, galaxies stretching out through space to infinity. But inside the Air Force shuttle orbiter, serial number AFASO-002, six young trainees and four middle-aged officers clambered over one another, stuck elbows in one another's food trays, and got in one another's way. Kinsman began to realize that a barrel of monkeys is not much fun for the monkeys.

"If it weren't for zero gee," Kinsman told Colt, "I'd be ready to murder somebody."

"I got my own little list," Colt said.

They were in the lower deck, wedged between canisters of lithium hydroxide and green tanks of oxygen. The metal bulkhead felt cold to the touch, and Kinsman realized that the vacuum of space was on the other side of the floor plates that he hovered a few centimeters above.

"Pierce really meant it when he said we were gonna lay our hands on every stringer and weld in this bucket," Colt grumbled. He was hovering above Kinsman in the hatch, head down, his feet floating above the floor of the mid-deck section.

The rest of the trainees were out in the cargo bay, with the officers, practicing EVAs in their space suits. Colt and Kinsman had been assigned to inspecting the air and water recycling equipment of the life support systems. They had already inspected the zero-gravity toilet, with its foot restraints and seat belt, and the washstand and shower stall. Now they were tracing the plumbing of the water pipes and the scrubbers that filtered impurities out of the air they breathed.

Kinsman consulted the checklist taped to his wrist in the light of the hand lamp that hung weightlessly by his ear. "Okay, that's the lithium hydroxide tank and it's all in one piece."

"Check," said Colt, making a mark on the clipsheet he carried.

"I still don't get it," Kinsman complained as they worked. "Why are we getting all the shit jobs? Jill and Smitty and the others are out there having fun and we're stuck inspecting the toilet."

He could not see Colt's face from where he was wedged in, but the expression came through loud and clear. "We're the special ones, man. You and I got the highest grades, so they're gonna take us down a peg. Keep our heads from getting big."

"You think that's it?"

Colt growled, "Sure. My being black's got nothing to do with it. Neither does your picking me for a partner. Nothing at all."

"It's good to see you're not being overly sensitive about it," Kinsman joked, pushing his way back from between the frigid green tanks.

"Or bitter."

"Well . . . they've got to let us go EVA tomorrow. There's no way they can keep us from going ouside."

For a long moment Colt did not respond. Then he said simply, "Wanna bet?"

The living quarters in the mid-deck were crowded enough when all six trainees were lumped together in the metal shoebox, but when a couple of officers came down from the flight deck the tensions became almost impossible.

The end of the second day, the trainees were bobbing around the galley, which looked to Kinsman like a glorified Coke machine. They were punching buttons, pulling trays of hot food from the storage racks, gliding weightlessly to find an unoccupied corner of the cramped compartment in which to eat their precooked dinners.

Kinsman leaned his back against somebody's sleeping cocoon, legs dangling in the air, and picked at the food. The tray was already showing signs of heavy use; it was slightly bent and it no longer gleamed, new-looking. The food, a combination of precut bite-sized chunks of imitation protein and various moldy-looking pastes, was as appetizing as sawdust.

Jill Meyers drifted past, empty-handed.

"Finished already?" Kinsman asked her.

"This junk was finished before it started," she said.

"It's chock-full of nutrition."

"So's a cockroach."

Major Jakes slid down the ladder and headed for the galley. Automatically the lieutenants made room for him. He had been an overweight, jowly, crew-cut, sullen-looking graying man when Kinsman had first seen him back at Vandenberg. His physical looks had changed in zero gravity: he seemed slimmer, taller, his cheekbones higher. And there was a happy grin on his face.

Jakes brought his tray to the corner where Kinsman was sitting, literally, on air. The Major was humming to himself cheerfully. After setting himself cross-legged beside Kinsman, anchoring his back against the other end of the nylon mesh cocoon, Jakes took a couple of bites of food, then asked, "How's it going, Lieutenant?"

"Okay, sir, I suppose," replied Kinsman. Never complain to officers, he knew from his Academy training. Especially when they're trying to buddy up to you.

42

"I don't see Colt around."

"Frank?" Kinsman realized that Colt was not in sight. "Must be in the pissoir."

Jakes made a small clucking sound. "Your redheaded friend is missing, too."

Kinsman took a sip of lukewarm coffee from the squeeze bulb on his tray while he thought furiously. "Maybe they're in the airlock. You go nuts down here trying to find some elbow room."

Jakes made an agreeable nod. "Yeah, I guess so. Like the fo'c'sle of an old sailing ship, huh?"

Why me? Kinsman wondered. Why is he buddying up to me?

"You're from Pennsylvania, aren't you?"

"Yessir. Philadelphia area . . ."

"Main Line, I know. My people have relatives down there. I'm from the North Shore—Boston. You know, the cradle of liberty."

"Where the Cabots talk only to the Lodges."

"Right." Jakes nibbled at a chunk of thinly disguised soybean meal. "And neither of 'em talk to my folks. We were sort of the black sheep of the clan. My old man could build the yachts for them, all right, but they never let us sail 'em."

"Black sheep," Kinsman muttered. Welcome to the club, buddy. Try to imagine what a black sheep you become when you leave a Quaker family to join the Air Force.

"Did you really pick Colt for a partner?"

"Yes," Kinsman said, warily.

"I hear he's a troublemaker."

"He's a damned fine man."

"Maybe. I hear you're just as good a pilot. Colt's got a reputation, well . . ."

Kinsman could feel his back stiffening. "Sir," he said, "if I were in a tight situation there's no one I'd rather have beside me than Frank Colt. Present company included."

Jakes grinned at him. "Snotty little shavetail, eh? Yeah, that's what I heard. Well, you and Colt are two of a kind, all right. Full of piss and vinegar. I guess that's good, in a way. This isn't a game for marshmallows."

They finished their dinners quickly and stowed the dirty trays in the galley's cleaning unit, which Kinsman knew from

43

his inspection earlier that day was operating properly—after he had tightened a slightly leaky pipe fitting. Jakes swam back up to the flight deck, "officer country," and Kinsman was about to join Jill and Art Douglas in an argument about the Air Force's medical insurance plan for astronauts.

But Major Pierce and Captain Howard eased down the ladder and suddenly the mid-deck compartment was tense again.

"Mission control just sent us a change in schedule," Pierce said. "Meyers and Smith, you've got fifteen minutes before prelaunch inspection of Payload Number Two. Get rid of those trays and start suiting up for EVA. Captain Howard will brief you, starting now."

Howard was a dour, shriveled little man. Kinsman had never seen a crew cut manage to look messy before, but somehow Howard's did. He was gray-haired, old for a captain. Hell, he's old for a major or light colonel, Kinsman thought. But he must know his stuff.

Under Howard's direction, the O'Hara-Douglas team had operated the manipulator arm that had swung the mission's first payload—a small, laser-reflecting navigational satellite—out of the cargo bay and into orbit. And Captain Howard himself had gone EVA twice in the two days of the flight, once to check on a defunct observation satellite that had been orbited years earlier, and once to inspect a newly orbited Russian satellite.

Now Mutt and Jeff are going to go outside again while Frank and I sit around twiddling our thumbs, Kinsman grumbled to himself. They've already been EVA once!

Howard took them up to the flight deck for their briefing, space suits and all. Pierce followed right behind them. Suddenly the mid-deck compartment was empty except for Douglas and Kinsman.

"Where the hell did Colt and Mary get to?" Art asked.

Kinsman peered through the thick glass of the airlock window but they were not inside.

"Maybe they took a walk outside," he said.

Douglas looked annoyed. "I'll bet that sonofabitch has her out in the payload bay."

"If he does, about the only thing they can do out there is hold hands, with gloves on, at that."

44

"Yeah? And what happens when Pierce or Howard look out and see them out there? Unauthorized EVA? They go down the tubes, and we go down with them!"

Kinsman looked at the suit rack. Two space suits missing, all right. He pushed himself over to the airlock hatch.

"What're you doing?" Douglas demanded.

"Maybe they're just outside the airlock, down against the bulkhead where they can't be seen from the flight deck windows."

Douglas's round face was wrinkled with angered worry as Kinsman ducked inside the cold metal womb of the circular airlock. There was a window to the outside, just above the heavy hatch that opened onto the vacuum of space.

Kinsman tapped against the metal wall of the airlock with his Academy ring. Three quick taps, three slower ones, and then three fast ones again. SOS. He did it twice. No response. Feeling a little frantic, he went to the other side and tried again.

A thumping sound. Like a gloved fist knocking against the outer wall.

Kinsman pushed back into the mid-deck compartment and swung the inner airlock hatch shut. Douglas glided over and peered into the window. A pump whined.

"Christ," muttered Douglas, "I hope nobody's watching the indicators on the controls upstairs."

We'll know soon enough, Kinsman said to himself. After long minutes of breath-holding suspense, Colt and Mary O'Hara squeezed through the inner airlock hatch.

"Let's get you out of these suits, pronto," Kinsman urged.

"What's the rush?" Colt asked.

"Howard's going to be down here in another minute. Smitty and Jill are going out with him. Schedule change."

Mary was already unzipping her gloves, her face white with concern.

Colt complained, "Shit! Out there in the payload bay's the only place you can relax."

"You'll relax all four of us into ground assignments," Douglas snapped.

"In South Dakota," added Kinsman. "Come on, Frank. Move it!"

Grousing all the way, Colt allowed Kinsman to help him wriggle out of the space suit. Out of the corner of his eye Kinsman saw Douglas helping Mary. Art's getting a lot more fun out of this than I am, he thought.

They were almost finished when Captain Howard, Major Pierce, Jill Meyers, and Smitty came gliding down the ladder from the flight deck.

"Exactly what is going on here?" Pierce demanded, his voice thin and reedy.

Before Colt or anyone else could reply, Kinsman heard himself say, "I had to go out into the payload bay for a few moments, sir. I was getting a touch of claustrophobia in here."

Pierce glared at him.

"Lieutenant Colt came out with me—in accordance with the regulations that trainees should not attempt EVA without backup. Lieutenant O'Hara stationed herself in the airlock in case we needed further assistance."

Major Pierce looked from Kinsman to Colt to O'Hara and back to Kinsman. His eyes glittered with malice. "That is the dumbest story I've ever heard a shavetail try to pull, Lieutenant!"

"That's the way it happened, sir."

"Claustrophobia?"

"Only a temporary touch of it, sir. We were warned about it in training, if you recall. Since there's no qualified medical officer on board—"

"That's enough!" Pierce snapped. He closed his eyes for a moment. "All right, I'll let it stand. But I'm going to remember this, Kinsman. I'll be watching you—you and your claustrophobia. And the rest of you! Nobody budges out of this compartment without my direct approval. Is that understood?"

"Yessir!" from six relieved throats.

"You all know that you are not—repeat, *not*—authorized for EVA without my okay."

"Unless there's a medical or other type of emergency," said Kinsman.

Glaring, Pierce hissed, "I should put the whole squad of you on report for this."

No one said a word.

46

Pierce looked hard at Colt, who returned his stare evenly. Then he glared at O'Hara; she glanced toward Kinsman.

Shaking his head, the Major muttered, "You're on thin ice, Kinsman. Very thin ice."

"Yessir," Kinsman replied.

Pierce went back up to the flight deck and the tension cracked. Howard took Meyers and Smitty to the airlock. Kinsman puffed out a long, heartfelt breath. He felt as if he had been hanging by his fingernails from a very high cliff.

"Why'd you do that?" Colt asked him.

"Pure instinct, I guess. I figured you'd catch a lot more hell from Pierce than I would."

Frowning, Colt said, "What difference does it make? We're on the same team; he'll kick my ass out the same time he kicks yours."

Kinsman nodded. "Frank, you've memorized the book of regulations but you haven't figured out the people yet. He won't kick us out for something *I've* done. Not unless it's a lot more serious than this."

Colt's reply was a derisive snort.

"You could thank him," Mary suggested to Colt. "He was trying to save both our necks."

"And mine," Douglas chimed in.

"And his own, too," Colt said. "If I go, he goes."

Kinsman laughed. "You're welcome, buddy."

"Think nothing of it," Colt replied.

Kinsman looked at Mary O'Hara. He knew that she would have been in much more trouble, too, if Pierce thought she'd gone outside with Colt. But she doesn't say a word about that part of it. *La belle dame sans merci*. The beautiful lady who never says thank you.

It took an hour before Jill and Smitty came back in from their EVA. Howard, looking smaller and older than ever before, pointed a dirty-nailed finger at Kinsman.

"You and your buddy better get a good night's sleep. You're going to have a big day tomorrow."

But, wrapped in his nylon mesh cocoon after lights-out, floating weightlessly with his arms hanging in front of his eyes, Kinsman could not sleep. He could feel the warmth from Colt's body, bulging the sleeping bag a few centimeters above

47

him, and smell the faint trace of perfume that Mary wore, in the next bunk down. Yet it was not her scent nor Colt's troubled groaning and tossing that kept Kinsman awake. Not even the anticipation of going EVA tomorrow, for the first time.

"To hell with Jakes," he mumbled to himself. "And Pierce. All of them . . . all of them . . ."

He saw in his mind's eye the crystal blue sky of the eastern Mediterranean as he flew his aging F-15 on a "peace-keeping" mission. When the Soviet Union finally admitted that its reserves of fossil fuels were no longer sufficient to meet its needs, and began bidding up the price of Middle Eastern oil, the political repercussions made the oil shocks of the Seventies seem trivial.

The Red Army gobbled up Iran in an eleven-day blitz-krieg while the rest of the world watched, stunned and vacillating. The Russians took over the Iranian oil fields, or what was left of them after the fanatical Iranians gave up their doomed defensc and blew up everything they could. The Arab world split apart, some openly assisting the Iranian resistance, some trying to make an accommodation with the victorious Russian Bear. The industrialized world tottered as oil prices skyrocketed and stayed high.

It took a charismatic leader to bring the Arabs together again, and he focused his leadership on the obvious goal: the destruction of Israel. With relish, the Moslem world forgot its differences and invaded the Jewish homeland for the final time. No ally came to Israel's aid, not with the Soviets threatening nuclear war over the hotline to Washington. The American government, led by a born-again former school-teacher, warned Israel against using its nuclear weapons against its invaders. To their credit, the victorious Arabs did not engage in a bloodbath. Israel simply ceased to exist, although its inhabitants continued to live in the newly consti-tuted nation of Palestine. Only the leaders of the Israeli government and about a third of the Knesset were executed. In America the government that failed to help its ally won re-election on the strength of having avoided a nuclear holocaust.

Rationing and recriminations were the order of the day in every Western capital. Travel curtailments and restrictions

48

on electricity became commonplace, and were used by governments to keep their people under control and make dissent, if not impossible, then at least more difficult than in the earlier days of easy travel and free speech.

The Greeks called for the total dissolution of NATO. The Turks made obvious moves to seize Cyprus. A new series of convulsions racked Lebanon, with Syrian-backed Shi'ites slaughtering Christians by the thousands and Syria itself —long a Soviet client—gaining new power from the Russian victory in Iran and the destruction of Israel but suffering such loss of prestige among its fellow Moslems that the assassination of Syria's president came as no surprise.

Flying out of Cyprus, the handful of Air Force fighter planes was a pitifully weak gesture, more of a public relations ploy than a military move. America was tacitly admitting that the Soviet conquest of Iran and the end of Israel were *faits accomplis*. Flying out of Damascus, a squadron of Soviet MiG-31's symbolized Russian determination to show America and the world that the Middle East was their sphere of influence now, rather than the West's.

In his half-sleep, Kinsman recalled all the feints and mock-dogfights he had gone through. It would have taken only the press of a button to destroy one of the Russian fighters. More than once somebody fired a burst of cannon fire into the empty air. More than once a missile "happened" to *whoosh* out of its underwing rack and trace a smoky arrow of death that came close to one of those beautiful swept-wing planes.

Each time Kinsman waxed the tail of a Russian and lined up the vainly maneuvering MiG in his gunsights he heard his father's stern voice: "Once you put on their uniform, you will do as they order you to do. If they say kill, you will kill."

No, Kinsman said to himself. There are limits. I can hold out against them.

They had not ordered him to kill. The squadron's orders were to defend themselves if attacked, and even then, only after receiving a confirming go-ahead order from ground command. Kinsman had never pressed the firing button on his controls, no matter how many times he centered a MiG in his gunsights.

He was overjoyed when his application for astronaut

training was finally approved. It was as if he had been holding his breath for four years.

Even grimy old Philadelphia looked good to him, after the months in Cyprus. He had dinner with Neal McGrath and his wife, Mary-Ellen, in an Indian restaurant on Chestnut Street, within sight of Independence Hall and the cracked old Liberty Bell. Neal, a Congressman now, informed him that Diane Lawrence had her first million-selling record to her credit and was fast becoming one of the nation's favorite folk-rock singers.

And Kinsman's father—sick, old, his home on the Main Line turned into a private hospital-cum-office—refused to see him as long as he wore an Air Force uniform.

When he finally peeled out of the nylon mesh sleeping bag he felt too keyed up to be tired, despite his wakeful night. Colt seemed also tensed as a coiled spring as they pulled on their space suits.

"So the Golddust Twins finally get their chance to go for a walk around the block," Smitty kidded them as he helped Kinsman with the zippers and seals of his suit.

"I thought they were gonna keep us after school," Colt said, "for being naughty yesterday."

"Pierce'll find a way to take you guys down a notch," Jill said. "He's got that kind of mind."

"Democracy in action," said Kinsman. "Reduce everybody to the same low level."

"Hey!" Art Douglas snapped from across the compartment where he was helping Colt into his suit. "Your scores weren't *that* much higher than ours, you know."

"Tell you what," Colt said. "A couple of you guys black your faces and see how you get treated."

They laughed, but there was a nervous undercurrent to it.

Kinsman raised the helmet over his head and slid it down into place. "Still fits okay," he said through the open visor. "Guess my head hasn't swollen too much."

Captain Howard glided down the ladder already suited up, but with his helmet visor open. The pouches under his eyes looked darker than usual; his face was a gray prison pallor. With six trainees aboard, the officers slept in their seats up on the flight deck, a factor that did not increase officers' love of trainees.

"You both checked out?" Howard asked in a flat, drained voice.

Mr. Personality, thought Kinsman.

Howard was not satisfied with the trainees' check of their suits. He went over them himself. Finally, with a sour nod, he waved Colt to the airlock and went in with him. The lock cycled.

Kinsman slid his visor down and sealed it, turned to wave a halfhearted "so long" to the others, then floated to the airlock and pushed himself through the hatch. The heavy door swung shut and he could hear, faintly through his helmet padding, the clatter of the pump sucking the air out of the phone booth–sized chamber. The red light went on, signaling vacuum. He opened the outer hatch and stepped out into the payload bay.

The orbiter was turned away from the Earth, so that all Kinsman saw as he left the airlock was the endless blackness of space. He blinked as his eyes adjusted to the darkness, and saw tiny points of light staring at him: hard, unwinking stars, not like jewels set in black velvet, as he had expected, not like anything he had ever seen before in his life.

"Glory to God in the highest . . ." Kinsman heard himself whisper the words as he rose, work forgotten, drifting up toward the infinitely beautiful stars.

When I consider thy heavens, the work of thy fingers, the moon and the stars, which thou hast ordained . . .

Howard's grip on his shoulder suddenly brought him back to the here-and-now. The Captain clicked a tether to the clip on Kinsman's waist, then pointed to his own wrist. Kinsman looked down at the keyboard on the wrist of his suit and turned the radio on.

Howard's voice immediately came through his earphones, a much higher fidelity sound quality than Kinsman had expected:

"We're using channel four for suit-to-suit chatter. Ship's frequency is three; don't use it unless you have to talk to the flight deck."

"Yessir," said Kinsman.

"Okay. Let's get to work."

51

Kinsman glanced out at the stars again, then followed Howard and Colt to the padded mound of insulation covering the final satellite in the payload bay. It was a large fat drum, taller than a man and so wide that Kinsman knew he and Colt could not girdle it with their outstretched arms.

"The checkout panels in the flight deck indicate a malfunction in the battery that powers the antenna foldout," Howard's voice grumbled in his earphones.

Under the Captain's direction they peeled the protective covering from the satellite. It was an aluminum cylinder with dead black panels of solar cells circling its middle and four dish-shaped antennas folded across its top.

"Kinsman, you come up here with me to manually unfold the antennas," Howard ordered. "Colt, check out the battery."

Floating up to the top of the satellite with the Captain beside him, Kinsman asked, "What kind of a satellite is this? Looks like communications, but it's going into a polar orbit, isn't it?"

"Seventy-degree inclination," Howard replied curtly. "You know that as well as I do. Or you should."

Kinsman did know. He also knew that the orbit was highly elliptical, so that the satellite hung over the Eurasian land mass for a much longer period of time than it sped past the other side of the globe.

"Start with that one." Howard pointed a gloved hand toward the largest antenna, in the center of the drumhead. "Unlatch the safety retainer first."

Hanging head down over the satellite, Kinsman read the instruction printed on its surface by the light of his helmet lamp, then unlatched and unfolded the antenna arm. His fingers felt clumsy inside the heavy gloves, but the task was simple enough. He remembered von Clausewitz's dictum from his Academy classes:

"Everything is very simple in war, but even the simplest thing is difficult."

That was as good a description of working in zero gravity as any, Kinsman thought as he slowly, deliberately unfolded the antenna arm and carefully opened its fragile, parasollike parabolic dish. No sound, except his own labored breathing and the faint, high-pitched whir of his suit's tiny air-

52

circulating fan. This is hard work, he realized. They had told him it would be, back in the classrooms, but he had not truly believed it until now.

The first man to walk in space, Alexsei Leonov, told his fellow cosmonauts, "Think ten times before moving a finger, and twenty times before moving a hand."

We can do better than *that*, Kinsman told himself. Still, everything takes longer in zero gee than you'd expect.

"Now the waveguide." Howard's laconic voice startled Kinsman. He had floated slightly away from the satellite. The tether clipped to his waist was almost taut.

He returned to his work, voicing his curiosity into his helmet microphone. "No camera windows or sensor ports on this bird. At least, none that I can see."

"Keep your mind on your work," Howard said.

"But what's it for?" Kinsman blurted.

With an exasperated sigh that sounded like a windstorm in Kinsman's earphones, Howard answered, "Space Command didn't take the time to tell me, kid. So I don't know. Except that it's Top Secret and none of our damned business."

"Ohh . . . a ferret."

"What?"

"A ferret," said Kinsman. "We learned about them back at the Academy. Gathers electronic intelligence from Soviet satellites. This bird's going into a high-inclination orbit, right?"

He could sense Howard nodding sourly inside his helmet.

"She'll hang up there over the Soviet Union," Kinsman went on, "and tune in on a wide band of frequencies that the Russians use. Maybe some Chinese and European bands, too. Then when she passes over a command station in the States they send up the right signal and she spits out everything she's recorded on the previous orbit. All data-compressed so they can get the whole wad of poop in a couple of seconds."

"Really." Howard's voice was as flat and as cold as an ice floe.

"Yessir. The Russians have knocked a few of ours out, they told us at the Academy. With their ASAT—their antisatellite weapon."

Howard's response was unintelligible.

"Sir?" Kinsman asked.

"I *said*," the Captain snapped, "that I never went to the Academy, but I still know what an ASAT is. I came up the hard way, Kinsman. I'm not one of you bright boys."

Touchy! thought Kinsman.

"Colt, what the hell's the status of the battery?"

"Dead as an Edsel, sir," Colt's voice came through the earphones. "I just been listening to your conversation."

"All right. Get your backside up here and help unfold the antennas."

Colt glided up alongside Kinsman and together they opened up the satellite's antennas. It was like making a garden of metallic mushrooms bloom. As they worked Kinsman noticed a growing brightening, a flood of light that drowned out the feeble pool from his helmet lamp like the dawning sun overwhelms the stars of night.

He turned, finally, and saw that the payload bay was now facing the gigantic, overpowering splendor of Earth. Huge and bright, incredibly rich with vast sweeps of blue oceans and purest white clouds, the Earth was a spectacle that deluged the senses with beauty. Dumbfounded, speechless, Kinsman forgot what he was doing and drifted like a helpless baby, staring at the world of his birth.

"Fan*ta*stic!" Turning his head slightly, reluctantly, Kinsman saw that Colt was hovering beside him.

"Get your ass back here!" Howard's angry bleat was like ice picks jabbing at his eardrums. "Both of you!"

Kinsman realized his mouth was hanging open. But he did not care. Inside the helmet, with its tinted visor, inside the ultimate privacy of his impervious personal suit, he stared at the Earth, truly seeing it for the first time. He recognized Baja California and the brown wrinkled stretch of Mexico cutting between the blue of the Pacific and the greener blue of the Gulf.

"Kinsman! Colt!"

"I never realized . . ." he heard Colt's voice whispering, awed.

"All right. All right." Howard's voice was suddenly gentler, softer. "Sometimes I forget how it hits you the first time. You've got five minutes to enjoy the show, then we've

54

got to get back to work or we'll miss the orbit injection time." And the Captain's space-suited form drifted up alongside them.

The Earth was *huge*, filling the sky, spreading as far as Kinsman could see: serene blue and sparkling white, warm, alive, glowing, a beckoning, beautiful world, the ancient mother of humankind. She looked untroubled from this distance. No divisions marred her face, not the slightest trace of the frantic works of her children scarred the eternal beauty of the planet. It took a wrenching effort of will for Kinsman to turn his face away from her.

"All right," Howard's voice broke through to him. "Time to get back to work. You'll get plenty chance to see more, soon enough."

Reluctantly, Kinsman turned away from the glowing Earth and back to the rigid metal enclosure of the payload bay. The satellite looked like a toy to him now. But something had softened Howard. He's just as wiped out about all this grandeur as we are, Kinsman realized. Even though he doesn't want to show it.

They finished checking out the satellite, and Howard led them back to the airlock hatch. But instead of going back inside, the Captain had them wait there while Major Jakes operated the manipulator arm from his control station in the flight deck. The arm smoothly, silently, picked up the weightless satellite, swung it out and away from the shuttle, and then released it. It hung in empty space.

Howard told them to switch their suit radios to the flight deck's frequency, and they heard Jakes and Major Podolski's clipped, professional crosstalk as they maneuvered the orbiter away from the free-flying satellite. Kinsman saw the orbital maneuvering jets at the bulging root of the big tail fin flare once, twice—each puff so brief that it was gone almost before it registered on his eyes. When he looked for the satellite again, it was gone from sight.

But Jakes was intoning, ". . . three, two, one, ignition." And Kinsman saw a tiny star wink out in the darkness: the thruster that would push the satellite into its predetermined orbit.

"All systems check. Payload trajectory nominal." Jakes's voice might have been a computer synthesis. But then he added, "Good job, you guys. The antennas are all working right on the money."

Kinsman expected that now they would finally go back inside, but Howard indicated he wanted to talk to them on their suit-to-suit frequency.

"We've got one more chore to do," the Captain said. "It's a big task, and we saved it for you boys."

Kinsman tried to glance at Colt, but his partner was slightly behind him and when he turned his head all he saw was the inside lining of his helmet.

"We haven't detached the booster fuel tank yet," Howard explained. "It's still strapped on to the orbiter's belly."

"Can't re-enter with that egg hanging on to us," said Colt.

"We have no intention to. We're now heading for a rendezvous point where the last six missions have separated their booster tanks and left them in orbit. One of these days, when the Air Force has enough astronauts and enough money, we're going to convert these empty shells into a permanent space station."

"I'll be damned." Kinsman grinned to himself.

"Like the station NASA's building," said Colt.

"Nothing so fancy," Howard countered. "Now, then, your task is to separate the tank from the orbiter manually, and then take it over to the assembly that's already there and attach it to the other tanks."

"Simple enough," Colt said. "We practiced that kind of assembly in the neutral buoyancy tank in Huntsville."

"It sounds easy," Howard said. "But I won't be there to help you. You're going to be on your own with this one."

"We can handle it," Kinsman said.

Howard said nothing for a long moment. Kinsman watched him floating before them, his tinted visor looking like the dead, empty eye of a midget cyclops.

"All right," the Captain said at last. "But listen to me. If something happens out there, don't panic. Do you hear me? Don't panic."

"We're not the panicky kind," said Colt.

What's he worried about? Kinsman wondered. But he pushed the thought aside as Howard helped them to take a pair of Manned Maneuvering Units out of stowage. The

MMUs were one-man jet backs, built like a seat back with arms that held the controls. No seat, no legs. It strapped to their backs over their life-support packs.

Colt and Kinsman spent the next half-hour convincing Howard that they could fly the MMUs. They jetted back and forth along the emptied payload bay, did pirouettes, flew upside down and sideways, even flew in formation, almost touching outstretched fingertips.

"There are no umbilicals or tethers," Howard warned. "You'll be operating independently. On your own. Do you understand?"

"Sure," said Kinsman. "We practiced with these in the simulator a hundred times."

"No funny stuff when you're out there. No sightseeing. You won't have time for stargazing."

"Right," replied Colt.

"Now fill your propellant tanks and oxygen supply."

"Yessir."

Howard busied himself with talking to the flight deck as Kinsman and Colt jetted themselves to the supply tanks down by the tail.

"He's pretty edgy," Kinsman said as he took the propellant supply hose and plugged it into the valve on Colt's MMU.

"Just putting us on, man."

"I don't know. He said this is the most difficult task of the whole mission."

"That's why they saved it for us, huh?"

"Maybe."

He could sense Colt shaking his head, frowning. "Don't take his bullshit seriously. They had other jobs—like inspecting that Russian satellite. That was a lot tougher than what we're gonna be doing."

"That was a one-man task," Kinsman said. "He didn't need a couple of rookies getting in his way. Besides, the Soviets probably have all sorts of alarm and detection systems on their birds."

"Yeah, maybe . . ."

"He's a strange little guy."

Colt said, "You'd think he would've made major by now."

"Or light colonel. He's as old as Murdock."

"Yeah, but he's got no wings. Flunked out of flight training when he was a kid."

"Really?"

"That's what Art told me. Howard's nothing more than a glorified Tech Specialist. No Academy, no wings. Lucky he got as far as captain."

"No wonder he looks pissed most of the time."

"*Most* of the time?"

Kinsman said, "I got the feeling he enjoyed watching the Earth just as much as we did."

"H'mp. Yeah. I forgot about that."

As Kinsman disconnected the hose from Colt's backpack he glanced out at the Earth again. "I wonder if you ever get accustomed to that."

"Sure is some sight," Colt agreed.

"Makes me want to just drift out of here and never come back," murmured Kinsman. "Just go on forever and ever."

"You'll need a damned big air tank."

"Not a bad way to die, if you've got to go. Drifting alone, silent, going to sleep among the stars . . ."

"That's okay for you, maybe. But I intend to be shot by a jealous husband when I'm ninety-nine years old," Colt said firmly. "That's how I wanna go: bareass and humpin'."

"White or black?"

"The husband or the wife? Both of them honkies, man. Screwin' white folks is the best part of life."

Kinsman could hear Colt's happy chuckling.

"Frank," he asked, "have you ever thought that by the time you're ninety-nine there might not be any race problems anymore?"

Colt's laughter deepened. "Sure. Just like we won't have any wars and all God's chillun got shoes."

"All right, there it is," Captain Howard told them.

The three space-suited men hovered just above the open clamshell doors of the payload bay, looking out at what seemed to Kinsman to be a stack of giant beer bottles. Except that they're plastic, not glass.

Six empty propellant tanks, each of them nearly twice the size of the orbiter itself, were hanging in the emptiness in two neat rows. From this angle they could not see the connecting

58

rods holding them together.

"You've got three hours," Howard told them. "The booster tank linkages that hold it to the orbiter are built to come apart and re-attach to the other tanks . . ."

"We know, we know," Colt said impatiently.

Kinsman was thinking, This shouldn't take more than an hour. Two at the outside. Why give us three?

"Pardon me," Howard was saying, acid in his voice. "I should've remembered you guys know everything already." He grabbed at his tether and started pulling himself back inside the payload bay. "All right, you're on your own. Just don't panic if anything goes wrong. Panic kills. Remember that."

Almost an hour later, as they were attaching the empty propellant tank to the other six, Colt asked:

"How many times we practice this stunt in training?"

"This particular business?"

"Naw . . . just taking pieces apart and reassembling them."

Kinsman looked up from the bolt-tightening job he was doing. Colt was floating some forty meters away, up at the nose end of the fat propellant tank. He looked tiny next to the stack of huge eggs, each of them as big as a ten-room house. Sunlight glinted off them and the Earth slid by below, silent and serene.

The hardest part of the job was over: maneuvering the huge mass of the tank to the place where it was to be bolted to the others. Weightless though it may be, the tank still possessed mass, and in the frictionless vacuum of space, once a body starts in motion it keeps on going until something or somebody acts to stop it. The thrusters on their MMUs were pitifully inadequate to the task. The tank had its own thrusters installed at its nose and tail especially for this task.

"Well," Kinsman replied to Colt's question, "we did so much of this monkeywork in Huntsville and Houston that I thought they were training us to work in a garage."

"Yeah. That's what I was thinking. Then why's Howard so shaky about us doing this? You having any troubles?"

Kinsman shrugged inside his suit, and the motion made him drift slightly away from the strut he was working on. He reached out and grabbed it to steady himself.

"I've spun myself around a couple of times," he admitted. "But the tools work well, once you get used to them."

Colt's answer was a soft grunt.

"The suit heats up," Kinsman went on. "I've had to stop work and let it cool down a couple of times."

"Try to keep in the shadows," answered Colt. "Stay out of the direct sun. Makes a big difference."

"Maybe Howard's worried about us being so far from the orbiter without tethers."

"Maybe." But Colt did not sound convinced.

"How's your end going? I'm almost finished here."

"I got maybe another twenty minutes and I'll be through. Three hours! This damned job don't take no three . . . *Holy shit!*"

Kinsman's whole body jerked at the urgency in Colt's voice. "What? What is it?"

"Lookit the orbiter!"

Turning so rapidly that he bounced the upper corner of his MMU against the tank, Kinsman peered out at the ship, some two hundred meters away from them.

"They've closed the payload bay doors. Why the hell would they do that?"

Colt jetted down the length of the tank, stopping himself neatly as an ice skater within arm's reach of Kinsman.

"What on earth are they doing?" Kinsman wondered.

Colt said, "Whatever it is, I don't like it."

Suddenly a puff of white gas jetted from the orbiter's nose. The spacecraft dipped down and away from them. Another soundless gasp from the maneuvering thrusters back near the tail.

"What the fuck are they up to?" Colt shouted.

The orbiter was sliding away from them, scuttling crabwise farther and farther from the tank farm where they were stranded.

"They got trouble! Somethin's gone wrong . . ."

Kinsman punched the stud on his wrist for the flight deck's radio frequency.

"Kinsman to flight deck. What's wrong? Why are you maneuvering?"

No answer. The orbiter was dwindling away from them rapidly.

"Jesus Christ!" Colt yelled. "They're gonna leave us here!"

"Captain Howard!" Kinsman said into his helmet mike, trying to keep the tremble out of his voice. "Major Podolski! Major Pierce! Anybody! Come in. This is Kinsman. Colt and I are still EVA! Answer, please!"

Nothing but the crackling hum of the radio's carrier wave.

"Those sonsofbitches are stranding us!"

Kinsman watched the orbiter getting smaller and smaller. It seemed to be hurtling madly away from them, although the rational part of his mind told him that the spacecraft was only drifting now. It had only fired the vernier thrusters, not the rocket motors that would move it into an altogether different orbital plane. But the difference in relative velocities between the tank farm and the orbiter was enough to make the two fly apart from each other.

Colt was moving. Kinsman saw that he was lining himself up for a dash toward the dwindling orbiter. Grabbing Colt's arm to stop him, Kinsman snapped, "NO!" Then he realized his suit radio was still on the flight deck frequency. Banging the stud on his wrist, he said, "Don't panic. Remember? That's what Howard warned us about."

"We gotta get back to the orbiter! We can't hang here!"

"You'll never reach the orbiter with the MMU," Kinsman said. "They're separating from us too fast."

"But something's gone wrong . . ."

Kinsman looked out toward the dwindling speck that was the orbiter. It was hard to see it now, against the glaring white of the Earth. They were passing over the vast cloud-covered Antarctica. Shuddering, Kinsman felt the cold seeping into him.

"Listen to me," he commanded. "Maybe nothing's gone wrong. Maybe this is their idea of a joke."

"A joke?"

"That's what Howard was trying to tell us." Kinsman silently added, Maybe.

"That's crazy!"

"Is it? They've been sticking it to us all through the mission, haven't they? Pierce is a snotty bastard; this looks like something he might cook up. What would he like better than watching the two of us chasing the damned orbiter until the fuel in our MMUs gives out and they have to come back and rescue us?"

"You don't joke around with lives, man!"

"We're safe enough; got four hours worth of oxygen. As long as we don't panic we'll be okay. That's what Howard was trying to tell us." It was beginning to sound convincing, even to himself.

"But why the hell would they do something like this?" Colt's voice sounded calmer, as if he were trying to believe Kinsman.

Your paranoia's deserted you just when you needed it most, Kinsman thought. He replied, "How many times have they called us hotshots, the Golddust Twins? We're the two top men on the list. They just want to rub our noses in the dirt a little, make us feel foolish . . . just like the upperclassmen do at the Academy."

"You think so?"

It's either that or we're dead. Kinsman glanced at the digital watch set into his wrist keyboard. "They allowed us three hours for our task. They'll be back before that time is up. Less than two hours."

"And if they're not?"

"Then we can panic."

"Lotta good it'll do then."

"It won't do us much good now, either. We're stranded here until they come back for us."

"Bastards." Now Colt was convinced.

With a sudden grin, Kinsman said, "Yeah, but maybe we can turn the tables on them."

"How?"

"Follow me, my man."

Without using his MMU thrusters, Kinsman clambered up the side of "their" propellant tank and then drifted slowly into the nest created by the other huge tanks. Like a pair of skin divers floating in the midst of a pod of whales, Colt and Kinsman hung in emptiness, surrounded by the enormous, curving, hollow tanks.

"Now when they come back they won't be able to see us on radar," Kinsman explained. "And the tanks ought to block our suit-to-suit talk, so they won't hear us, either. We'll throw a scare into *them*."

"They'll think we panicked and jetted away."

"Right."

"Maybe that's what they want."

Kinsman laughed. Colt's paranoia had returned. "No," he said. "They want to scare us, not kill us. That would take too much explaining back at Vandenberg. Losing two cadets would ruin the whole afternoon for Pierce and the rest of them. Wouldn't look good on their files."

Colt laughed back. "Almost worth dying for."

"We'll let them know we're here," Kinsman said, "after they've worked up enough of a sweat. I'm not dying for anyone's joke—not even my own."

They waited while the immense panorama of the Earth flowed beneath them and the distant stern stars watched silently. They waited and they talked.

"I thought she split because we were down in Houston and Huntsville and she couldn't take it," Colt was saying. "White woman with a black husband—the pressure was on her a lot more than on me."

"I didn't think Houston was that prejudiced," said Kinsman. "And Huntsville's pretty cosmopolitan . . ."

"Yeah, sure. Try it with my color, man. You stuck around the base all the time, or you went into town with some of the other guys. Go try to buy some flesh-colored Band-Aids, you wanna see how cosmopolitan this country is."

"Guess I really don't know much about it," Kinsman admitted.

"But now that I think back on it, we were having our troubles in Ohio, too. I'm not an easy man to live with."

"Who the hell is?"

Colt chuckled. "You are, man. You're supercool. Never saw anybody so much in charge of himself. Like a bucket of ice water."

Ice water? Me? "You're mistaking slow reflexes for self-control."

"Yeah, I bet. Is it true you're a Quaker?"

"Used to be," he answered automatically, trying to shut

63

out the image of his father. "When I was a kid." Change the subject! "I was when that damned orbiter started moving away from us. A real Quaker."

With a laugh, Colt asked, "How come you ain't married? Good-looking, rich . . ."

"Too busy having fun. Flying, training for this . . . I've got no time for marriage. Besides, I like women too much to marry one of them."

"You wanna get laid but you don't wanna get screwed."

"Something like that. To quote the Bard, there's lots of chicks in the world."

"Yeah. Can't concentrate on a career and marriage at the same time. Leastwise, I can't."

"Not if you want to be really good at either one," Kinsman agreed. Oh, we are being so wise. And not looking at our watches. Cool, man. Supercool. But out beyond the curving bulk of the looming tanks the sky was empty except for the solemn stars.

"I don't just wanna be good," Colt was saying. "I got to be the best. I got to show these honkies that a black man is better than they are."

"You're not going to win many friends that way."

"Don't give a shit. I'm gonna be a general someday. Then we'll see how many friends I got."

Kinsman shook his head, laughing. "A general. Jeez, you've sure got some long-range plans in your head."

"Damn right! My brother, he's all hot and fired up to be a revolutionary. Goin' around the world looking for wars to fight against oppression and injustice. Regular Lone Ranger. Wanted me to join the underground here in the States and fight for justice against The Man."

"Underground? In the States?"

"Yeah. FBI damn near grabbed him a year or so back."

"What for?"

"Hit a bank to raise money for the People's Liberation Army."

"He's one of those?"

"Not anymore. There ain't no PLA anymore. Most of 'em are dead. The rest scattered. I watched my brother playin' cops and robbers . . . didn't look like much fun to me.

So I decided I ain't gonna fight The Man. I'm gonna *be* The Man."

"If you can't beat 'em . . ."

"Looks like I'm joinin' 'em, yeah," Colt said, with real passion in his voice. "But I'm just workin' my way up the ladder to get to the top. Then *I'll* start giving the orders. And there are others like me, too. We're gonna have a black President one of these days, you know."

"And you'll be his Chief of Staff."

"Could be."

"Where does that leave us . . ."

A small, sharp beeping sound shrilled in Kinsman's earphones. Emergency signal! Automatically, both he and Colt switched to the orbiter's flight deck frequency.

"Kinsman! Colt! Can you hear me? This is Major Jakes. Do you read me?"

The Major's voice sounded distant, distorted by ragged static, and very concerned.

Kinsman held up a hand to keep Colt silent. They were receiving the orbiter's signal scattered off the propellant tanks. No sense allowing Jakes and the others to hear them, even though their suit radios were not as powerful as the transmitter in the flight deck.

"Colt! Kinsman! Do you read me? This is Major Jakes!"

Colt leaned forward and touched his visor against Kinsman's. His muffled voice came through: "Let 'em eat shit for a coupla minutes, huh?"

Kinsman nodded, then realized that Colt could not see through the tinted visor. He made a thumbs-up gesture.

The orbiter pulled into view and seemed to hover about a hundred meters away from the tanks. The flight-deck radio switch was open, and the two lieutenants heard:

"Pierce, goddammit, if those two kids are lost I'll put you up for a murder charge."

"You were in on it, too, Harry!"

Howard's rasping voice cut in. "I'm suited up. Going out the airlock."

"Should we get one of the trainees to help search for them?" Pierce's reedy nasality.

"You've got two of them missing now," Jakes snarled.

65

"Isn't that enough? How about *you* getting your ass outside to help?"

"Me? But I'm . . ."

"That would be a good idea," said a new voice, with such authority that Kinsman knew it had to be the mission commander, Major Podolski. Among the three majors he was the longest in Air Force service, and therefore was as senior as God.

"Eh, yessir," Pierce answered quickly.

"And you, too, Jakes. You were all in on this, and it hasn't turned out to be very funny."

Colt and Kinsman, hanging on to one of the struts that connected the empty tanks, could barely suppress their laughter as they watched the orbiter's payload bay doors swing slowly open and three space-suited figures emerge like reluctant schoolboys from the airlock.

"Maybe we oughtta play dead," Colt said, touching his helmet against Kinsman's again so that he did not need to use the radio.

"No. Enough is too much. Let's go out and greet our rescue party."

They worked their way clear of the tanks and drifted out into the open.

"There they are!" The voice sounded so jubilant in Kinsman's earphones that he could not tell who said it.

"Are you all right?"

"Is everything . . ."

"We're fine, sir," Kinsman said calmly. "But we were beginning to wonder if war had been declared or there was some other emergency."

Dead silence for several moments.

"Uh, no . . ." said Jakes as he jetted closer to Colt and Kinsman. "We . . . uh, well, we sort of played a little prank on you two fellas."

"It's something we always do on first flights," Pierce added. "Nothing personal."

Sure, Kinsman thought. Nothing personal in getting bitten by a snake, either.

They were great buddies now as they jetted back to the orbiter. Kinsman played it straight, keeping himself very formal and correct. Colt fell into line and followed Kinsman's lead.

If we were a couple of hysterical, jibbering, terrified tenderfeet they'd be laughing their heads off at us. But now the shaft has turned.

Once through the airlock and into the mid-deck compartment, the two lieutenants were grabbed by the four other trainees. Chattering, laughing with a mixture of guilt and relief, they helped Colt and Kinsman out of their helmets and suits. Pierce, Jakes, and Howard unsuited without help.

When he was down to his blue coveralls, Kinsman turned to Major Pierce and said, tightly, "Sir, I must make a report to the commanding officer."

"Podolski knows all about . . ."

Looking Pierce straight in his glittering eyes, Kinsman said, "I don't mean Major Podolski, sir. I mean Colonel Murdock. Or, if necessary, the Judge Advocate General."

The blood drained out of Pierce's face. Everything in the crowded mid-deck compartment stopped. Jill Meyers, who had wound up with Kinsman's helmet, let it slip from her hands. It hung in midair as she watched, wide-eyed and open-mouthed. The only sound in the compartment was the hum of electrical equipment.

"The . . . Judge Advocate General?" Pierce looked as white as a bedsheet.

"Yessir. Or I could telephone my uncle, the senior senator from Pennsylvania, once we return to the base."

Now even the trainees looked scared.

"See here, Kinsman . . ." Jakes started.

Turning to face the Major, close enough to smell the fear on him, Kinsman said quietly, "This may have seemed like a joke to you, sir, but it has the look of racial discrimination about it. And it was a very dangerous stunt. *And* a waste of taxpayers' money."

"You can't . . ." Pierce somehow lost his voice as Kinsman turned back toward him. Past the Major's shoulder Kinsman saw Art Douglas grinning at him.

"The first thing I must do is see Major Podolski," Kinsman said firmly. "He's involved in this, too."

With a defeated shrug, Jakes gestured toward the ladder.

Kinsman glanced at Colt, and the two of them glided over to the ladder and swam up to the flight deck, leaving dead silence behind them.

Major Podolski was a big, florid-faced man with a golden old-style RAF Fighter Command mustache. His bulk barely fit into the commander's left-hand seat. He was half turned in it, one heavy arm draped across the seat's back, as Kinsman rose through the hatch.

"I've been listening to what you had to say down there, Lieutenant, and if you think . . ."

Kinsman put a finger to his lips. Podolski frowned.

Sitting lightly on the payload specialist's chair, behind the commander, Kinsman let himself grin.

"Sir," he said, nearly whispering so that Podolski had to lean closer to hear him, "I thought one good joke deserved another. My uncle lost his seat in the Senate years ago."

A struggle of emotions played across Podolski's face. Finally a curious smile won out. "I get it," he whispered back. "You want them to stew in their own juices for a few minutes, eh?"

Glancing at Colt, Kinsman answered, "Not exactly, sir. I want reparations."

"Repa—what're you talking about, Mister?"

"This is the first time Frank and I have been allowed up on the flight deck."

"So?"

"So we want to sit up here while you fly her back through re-entry and landing."

Podolski looked as if he had just swallowed a lemon, whole. "Oh, you do? And maybe you want to take over the controls, too?"

Colt bobbed his head vigorously. "Yes, *sir*!"

"Don't make me laugh."

"Sir . . . I meant it about the Judge Advocate General. And I have another uncle—"

"Never mind!" Podolski snapped. "You can sit up here during re-entry and landing. And that's all! You sit and watch and be quiet and forget this whole stupid incident."

"That's all we want, sir," Kinsman said. He turned toward Colt, who was beaming.

"You guys'll go far in the Air Force," Podolski grumbled.

"A pair of smartasses with the guts of burglars. Just what the fuck this outfit needs." But there was the trace of a grin flitting around his mustache.

"Glad you think so, sir," said Kinsman.

"Okay . . . we're due to begin re-entry checkout in two hours. You guys might as well sit up here through the whole routine and watch how it's done."

"Thank you, sir."

The Major's expression sobered. "Only . . . who's going to tell Pierce and Howard that they've got to sit downstairs with the trainees?"

"Oh, I will," said Colt, with the biggest smile of all. "I'll be glad to!"

Age 27

IN THE COOL shadows of the Astro Motel's bar, Major Joseph Tenny did indeed look like a slightly overage linebacker for the Pittsburgh Steelers. Swarthy, barrel-shaped, his scowling face clamped on a smoldering cigar, Tenny in his casual civilian sports shirt and slacks hardly gave the appearance of that rarest of all birds: a good engineer who is also a good military officer.

"Afternoon, Major."

Tenny turned on his stool to see old Cy Calder, the dean of the press service reporters covering Vandenberg and Edwards Air Force bases, where the fledgling Air Force astronaut corps trained and worked.

"Hi!" said Tenny. "Whatcha drinking?"

"I am working," Calder answered with dignity. But he settled his tall, spare frame on the next stool. He reminded Tenny of the ancient bristlecone pine trees out in the high desert: so old that nobody knew their true age, gnarled and weathered, yet still vital and clinging to life.

"Double scotch," Tenny called to the bartender. "No ice. And refill mine."

"An officer and a gentleman," murmured Calder. His voice was dry and creaking, like an iron gate on rusted hinges, his face seamed with age.

As the bartender slid the drinks down to them, Tenny said, "You wanna know who got the assignment."

"I told you I'm working."

Tenny grinned. "Keep your mouth shut till tomorrow? Murdock's gonna make the official announcement at his weekly press conference."

"If you can save me the tedium of listening to the chubby Colonel recite once more how the peace-loving Air Force is not militarizing space before he gives us the one piece of information we want to hear, I shall buy the next round, shine your shoes for a month, and arrange to lose an occasional poker pot to you."

"The hell you will!"

Calder shrugged. Tenny took a long pull on his beer.

"No leaks ahead of time? Promise?"

Calder sipped at his drink, then said, "On my word as an ex-officer, former gentleman, and fugitive from Social Security."

"Okay. But keep it quiet until Murdock's announcement. It's gonna be Kinsman."

Calder put his glass down on the bar carefully. "Chester A. Kinsman, the pride of the Air Force? That's hard to believe."

"Murdock okayed it."

"I know this mission is strictly for publicity," Calder said, "but Kinsman? In orbit for three days with *Celebrity* magazine's prettiest female? Does Murdock want publicity or a paternity suit?"

"Come on, Kinsman's okay."

"Really? From the stories I hear about him, he's cut a swath right across the Los Angeles basin and has been working his way up toward the Bay Area."

Tenny countered, "He's young and good-looking. The girls haven't had many unattached astronauts to play with. NASA's gang is a bunch of old farts compared to our kids. And Kinsman's one of the best of them, no fooling."

70

"Wasn't he going around with that folksinger . . . what's her name? Diane Lawrence, wasn't it?"

"Yeah, while she was out here. But lemme tell you about what he did over at Edwards. Him and Frank Colt have built a biplane, an honest-to-god replica of an old Spad fighter. From the wheels up. He's a solid citizen."

"And I hear he's been playing the Red Baron with it. Is it true he buzzed Colonel Murdock's helicopter?"

They were cut off by a burst of noise and laughter. Half a dozen lean, lithe young men in Air Force blues—shining new captain's double bars on their shoulders—trotted down the carpeted stairs that led into the bar.

"There they are," said Tenny. "You can ask Kinsman about it yourself."

Kinsman was grinning happily at the moment as he and five other astronauts grabbed chairs and circled them around one little table in the corner, while calling their orders to the bartender.

Calder took his drink and headed for the table, followed by Major Tenny.

"Hold it," Frank Colt warned the other astronauts. "Here comes the media."

"Tight security."

"Why, boys," Calder tried to make his gravelly voice sound hurt, "don't you trust me?"

Tenny pushed a chair toward the old reporter and took another one for himself. Turning it backward and straddling it, so that his chunky arms rested on the chair back, the Major told his young captains, "It's okay. I spilled it to him."

"How much he pay you, boss?"

"That's between him and me."

As the bartender brought a tray of drinks, Calder said, "Let the Fourth Estate pay for this round, gentlemen. I want to pump some information out of you."

"That might take a lot of rounds."

To Kinsman, Calder said, "Congratulations, my boy. Colonel Murdock must think very highly of you."

They all burst out laughing.

"Murdock?" said Kinsman. "You should've seen his face when he told me I was it!"

"Looked like he was sucking on lemons."

Tenny explained. "The selection for the mission was made by the personnel computer. Murdock wanted to be absolutely unprejudiced, so he went strictly by the performance ratings in the computer—and out came Kinsman's name."

"It was a fix," muttered Colt, mainly for effect.

"If Murdock hadn't made so much noise about being so damned impartial," Tenny went on, "he could've reshuffled the program and tried again. But I was right there when the personnel officer came in with the name, so he couldn't back out of it."

"We was robbed," said Smitty.

Calder's ancient, weathered face creased into a grin. "Well, at least the computer thinks highly of you, Captain Kinsman, even if Colonel Murdock doesn't. I suppose that's still some kind of honor."

"More like a privilege. I've been watching that *Celebrity* chick through her training. Ripe."

"She'll look even better up in orbit."

"Once she takes off her space suit . . . et cetera."

"Hey, y'know, nobody's ever done it in orbit."

"Yeah . . . weightlessness, zero gravity."

Kinsman looked thoughtful. "Adds a new dimension to the problem, doesn't it?"

"Three-dimensional." Tenny took the cigar butt from his mouth and laughed.

Calder rose slowly from his chair and spread his arms to silence the others. Looking fondly down on Kinsman, he said:

"My boy—more years ago than I care to think about, I became a charter member of the Mile High Club. It was in 1915, during the height of the Great War, when, at an altitude of precisely 5,280 feet—as near as my altimeter could tell me—while circling over St. Paul's Cathedral, I successfully penetrated an Army nurse. This was in an open cockpit, mind you. I achieved success despite fogged goggles, cramped working quarters, and a severe case of windburn."

"Nineteen-fifteen?"

"How the hell old are you, Cy?"

"You sure it wasn't your father you're talking about?"

"Or your grandfather?"

Ignoring them, Calder continued, "Since then, there has

72

been precious little to look forward to. The skin divers claimed a new frontier, of course, but in fact they were retrogressing. Any silly-ass dolphin can do it in the water."

He beamed at Kinsman. "But you have something new going for you: weightlessness. Floating around in zero gravity, chasing tail in three dimensions. It beggars the imagination!"

Even Tenny looked impressed.

"Captain Kinsman, I pass the torch to you. To the founder of the Zero Gee Club!"

As one man, they all rose and silently toasted Kinsman.

Once they sat down again, Tenny burst their balloon. "You guys don't give Murdock credit for any brains at all. You don't think he's gonna let Kinsman go up with that broad all alone, do you? The Manta isn't as big as a shuttle, but it still holds three people."

Kinsman's face fell, but the others' lit up.

"It's gonna be a three-man mission!"

"Two men and the blonde."

Tenny warned, "Don't start drooling. Murdock wants a chaperon, not a gang bang."

It was Kinsman who understood first. Slouching back in his chair, chin sinking to his chest, he muttered, "Goddammitall, he's sending Jill along."

A collective groan.

"Murdock made up his mind an hour ago," Tenny said. "He was stuck with you, Chet, so he hit on the chaperon idea. He's giving you some real chores to do, too. Keep you busy. Like mating the power pod."

"Jill Meyers," said Art Douglas, with real disappointment on his face. "At least he could've picked Mary O'Hara. She's fun."

"Jill's as qualified as you guys are, and she's been taking this *Celebrity* gal through her training. I'll bet she knows more about this mission than any of you guys do."

"She would."

"In fact," Tenny added, with a malicious grin, "she *is* the senior captain among you rocket jocks. So show some respect."

Kinsman had only one comment. "Shit."

* * *

73

The key to the Air Force astronaut's role in space was summed up in two words: *quick reaction*. The massive space shuttle that NASA had developed was fine for missions that could be planned months in advance, but the Air Force needed a spacecraft that could be sent off on a mission without such preparation. The smaller, delta-shaped Manta was the answer. Launched by throwaway solid rocket boosters, carrying no more than three astronauts, the Manta could put Air Force personnel into orbit within a few hours of the decision to go.

The bone-rattling roar and vibration of lift-off suddenly died away. Strapped into the contour seat, scanning the banks of controls and instruments a few centimeters before his eyes, Kinsman could feel the pressure and tension slacken to zero. He was no longer flattened against his seat, but touching it only lightly, almost floating, restrained only by his safety harness.

He had stopped counting how many times he had felt weightlessness after his tenth orbital mission. Yet he still smiled inside his helmet.

Without thinking about it he touched a control stud in his seat's armrest. A maneuvering thruster fired briefly and the ponderous, dazzling bulk of Earth slid into view through the narrow windshield before him. It curved huge and awesome, brilliantly blue, streaked with white clouds, beautiful, serene, shining.

Kinsman could have watched it forever, but he heard the sounds of motion through his helmet earphones. The two women were stirring behind him. The Manta's cabin made the shuttle orbiter seem like a spacious hotel: their three seats were shoehorned in among racks of instruments and equipment. And they rode into orbit wearing full space suits and helmets, thanks to some Air Force functionary who wrote the requirement into the flight regulations.

Jill was officially second pilot and biomedical officer for this mission. The photographer, Linda Symmes, was simply a passenger, a public relations project, occupying the third seat, beside Jill.

Kinsman's earphones crackled with a disembodied link from Earth. "AF-9, you are confirmed in orbit. Trajectory nominal. All systems green."

"Roger, ground," Kinsman said into his helmet mike.

The voice, already starting to fade, switched to ordinary conversational speech. "Looks like you're right on the money, Chet. We'll get the rendezvous parameters and feed 'em to you when you pass over Woomera. Rendezvous is set for your second orbit."

"Roger, big V. Everything here on the board is in the green."

"Rog. Vandenberg out." Faintly. "And hey . . . good luck, Founding Father."

Kinsman grinned at that. He slid his visor up, loosened his harness, and turned in his seat. "Okay, ladies, we're safely in orbit."

Jill snapped her visor open.

"Need any help?" Kinsman asked Linda Symmes.

"I'll take care of her," Jill said firmly. "You handle the controls."

So that's how it's going to be, Kinsman thought.

Jill's face was round and plain and bright as a new penny. Snub nose sprinkled with freckles, wide mouth, short hair of undistinguished brown. Kinsman knew that under her pressure suit was a figure that could most charitably be described as ordinary.

Linda Symmes was another matter entirely. She had lifted her visor and was staring out at him with wide blue eyes that combined feminine curiosity with a hint of helplessness. She was tall, nearly Kinsman's own five-eleven height, with thick honey-colored hair and a body that he had already memorized down to the last curve.

In her sweet, high voice she said, "I think I'm going to be sick."

"Oh, for . . ."

Jill reached into the compartment between their two seats. "I'll take care of this," she said to Kinsman as she whipped a white plastic bag open and stuck it over Linda's face.

Shuddering at the realization of what could happen in zero gravity, Kinsman turned back to the control panel. He snapped his visor shut and turned up the air blower in his suit, trying to cut off the obscene sounds of Linda's wretching.

"For Chrissake," he yelled to Jill, "turn off your mikes,

will you! You want me upchucking all over the place too?"

"AF-9, this is Woomera."

Trying to blank his mind to what was going on behind him, Kinsman thumbed the switch on his communications panel. "Go ahead, Woomera."

For the next hour Kinsman thanked the gods that he had plenty of work to do. He matched the orbit of the Manta with that of the Air Force orbiting station, which had been up for nearly a year, occupied intermittently by two- or three-astronaut teams.

Kinsman had thought that the Air Force would make use of the emptied propellant tanks from shuttle flights that were left in orbit to be clustered together in the "tank farm" where he and Colt had been initiated to orbital tomfoolery a couple of years earlier. But the tanks remained unused, and the Air Force sent aloft a completely separate little spacecraft that they were developing into a permanent station in orbit.

It was a fat cylinder, silhouetted against the brilliant white of the cloud-decked Earth. As he pulled the Manta close enough for a visual inspection, Kinsman could see the antennas and airlock and other odd pieces of gear that had accumulated on the station. Looks more like an orbital junk heap every trip, he thought. Riding behind it, unconnected in any way, was the squat cone of the new power pod.

Kinsman circled the unoccupied station once, using judicious squeezes of the maneuvering thrusters. He touched a command signal switch and the station's radar beacon came to life, announced by a blinking green light on his control panel.

"All systems green," he said to ground control. "Everything looks okay."

"Roger, Niner. You are cleared for docking."

This was more complicated. Be helpful if Jill could read off . . .

"Distance, eighty-eight meters," Jill's voice pronounced clearly in his earphones. "Rate of approach . . ."

Kinsman instinctively turned his head, but the helmet cut off any possible sight of her. "Hey, how's your patient?"

"Empty. I gave her a sedative. She's out."

"Okay," said Kinsman. "Let's get ourselves docked."

He inched the spacecraft into the docking collar on one

76

end of the station, locked on and saw the panel lights confirm that the docking was secure.

"Better get Sleeping Beauty zipped up," he told Jill.

Jill said, "I'm supposed to check the hatch."

"Stay put. I'll do it." Kinsman unbuckled and rose effortlessly out of his seat to bump his helmet lightly against the overhead hatch.

"You two both sealed tight?"

"Yes."

"Keep an eye on the air gauge." He cracked the hatch open a scant centimeter.

"Pressure's steady. No red lights."

Nodding, Kinsman pushed the hatch open all the way. He pulled himself up and through the shoulder-wide hatch.

Light and easy, he reminded himself. No big motions. No sudden moves.

Sliding through the station hatch he slowly rotated, like an underwater swimmer doing a lazy rollover, and inspected every millimeter of the docking collar in the light of his helmet lamp. Satisfied that it was locked in place, he pushed himself fully inside the station. Carefully he pressed his cleated boots into the gridwork flooring and stood upright. His arms tended to float out, but they bumped the equipment racks on either side of the narrow central passageway. Kinsman turned on the station's interior lights, checked the air supply, pressure and temperature gauges, then shuffled back to the hatch and pushed himself through again.

He re-entered the Manta upside-down and had to contort himself around the pilot's seat to regain a "normal" attitude.

"Station's okay," he said at last. "Now how in hell do we get her through the hatch?"

Jill had already unbuckled the harness over Linda's shoulders. "You pull, I'll push. She'll bend around the corners easily enough."

And she did.

The station interior was about the size and shape of a small transport plane's cabin. On one side nearly its entire length was taken up by instrument racks, control equipment, and electronics humming almost inaudibly behind lightweight plastic panels. Across the narrow separating aisle were the

77

crew stations: control desk, two observation ports, lab benches. At the far end, behind a discreet curtain, were the head and the sleeping bags.

Kinsman stood at the control desk, in his blue fatigues now, his cleated shoes gripping the holes in the gridwork flooring to keep him from floating off. The desk was almost shoulder height, a convenient level in zero gee. His space suit had been stored in the locker beneath the floor panels. He was running a detailed checkout of the station's life-support systems: air, water, heat, electrical power. All operating within permissible limits, although the water supply would need replenishment at the rate it was being depleted. Recycling was never a hundred percent effective. He stepped leftward carefully to the communications console; everything operating normally. The radar screen showed a single large blip close by: the power pod.

He looked up as Jill came through the curtain from the bunkroom. She was still in her space suit, with only the helmet removed.

"How is she?"

Looking tired, Jill answered, "Okay. Still sleeping. I think she'll be all right when she wakes up."

"She'd better be. We can't have a wilting flower around here. I'll abort the mission."

"Give her a chance, Chet. She just lost her cookies when free-fall hit her. All the training in the world can't prepare you for those first few minutes."

Kinsman shook his head. But it's fun! he thought. Like skiing. Or skydiving. Only better.

Jill floated toward him, pushing along the handgrips set into the equipment racks and desk fronts. Kinsman pulled his feet free of the restraints and met her halfway.

"Here, let me help you out of that suit."

"I can do it myself."

"Sure. But it's easier with help."

After several minutes Jill was free of the bulky suit and standing in front of the miniaturized biomed lab. Ducking slightly because of the curving overhead, Kinsman glided to the galley. It was about half as wide as a phone booth, not as deep nor as tall.

"Coffee, tea, or milk?"

Jill grinned at him. "Orange juice."

He reached for a concentrate bag. "You're a tough woman to satisfy."

"No, I'm not. I'm easy to get along with. Just one of the guys."

That's a dig, Kinsman recognized. But who's it aimed at? And why?

For the next couple of hours they checked out the station's equipment in detail. Kinsman was re-assembling one of the high-resolution cameras after cleaning it, parts hanging in midair all around him as he worked intently. Jill was nursing a straggly-looking philodendron that had been smuggled aboard months earlier and was now inching from the biomed bench toward the ceiling light panels.

"How's the green monster?" Kinsman asked.

"It survived without us," said Jill, "but just barely. Maybe we could keep the temperature up a little higher in between missions once we get the power pack operating."

Linda pushed back the curtain from the sleeping area and stepped uncertainly into the main compartment.

Jill noticed her first. "Hi. How're you feeling?"

Kinsman looked up. She was in tight-fitting coveralls, coral red. He turned abruptly, scattering camera parts in every direction.

"Are you all right?" he asked.

Smiling sheepishly, "I think so. I'm kind of embarrassed . . ." Her voice was high and soft.

"Oh, that's all right," Kinsman said eagerly. "It happens to practically everybody. I got sick myself my first time in orbit."

"That," said Jill, dodging a slowly tumbling lens that had ricocheted gently off the ceiling, "is a little white lie, meant to make you feel at ease."

Kinsman forced himself not to frown.

Jill added, "Chet, you'd better pick up those camera parts before they get so scattered you won't be able to find them all."

He wanted to snap an answer, thought better of it, and replied merely, "Right."

As he finished the job on the camera he studied Linda carefully. The color was back in her face. She seemed steady, clear-eyed, not frightened or upset. Maybe she'll be okay, after all. Jill made her a cup of tea, which she sucked from the lid's plastic spout.

Kinsman went to the control desk and punched up the mission schedule on the computer screen.

"Jill, it's past your bedtime."

"I'm not sleepy," she said.

"Yeah, I know. But you've had a busy day, little girl, and tomorrow's going to be even busier. Now get your four hours and then I'll get mine. Got to be fresh for the mating."

"Mating?" Linda asked from the far end of the cabin, a good five strides from Kinsman. Then she remembered. "Oh . . . you mean linking the power module to the station."

Suppressing half a dozen possible retorts, Kinsman spelled out soberly, "Extravehicular activity."

Jill reluctantly drifted toward the bunkroom. "Okay, I'll sack in. I am tired, I guess, but I never seem to get really sleepy up here."

Wonder what kind of a briefing Murdock gave her? She's sure acting like a goddamned chaperon.

Jill glided into the shadows of the sleeping area and pulled the curtain firmly shut. After a few minutes of silence Kinsman turned to Linda.

"Alone at last."

She smiled back at him.

"Um . . . you just happen to be standing where I've got to install this camera." He nudged the assembled hardware so that it floated gently toward her.

She moved away slowly, carefully, holding the handgrip on the nearest equipment rack with both hands as if she were afraid of falling. Kinsman slid to the observation port and stopped the camera's slow-motion flight with one out-stretched hand. He started mounting the camera into the fixture set into the observation port.

"You really feel okay?"

"Yes, honestly."

"Think you'll be up to EVA tomorrow?"

"I hope so," Linda said. "I want to go outside with you."

I'd rather go inside with you, Kinsman said to himself as he worked.

An hour later they were hovering side by side at the

80

observation port, looking out at the curving bulk of Earth, the blue and white splendor of the cloud-mottled Pacific. Kinsman was trying to remember the mission flight plan, comparing the times when Jill would be sleeping against the long stretches when the station would be orbiting between ground stations, with no possibility of interruptions.

"Is that land?" Linda asked, pointing to a thick band of clouds wrapping the horizon.

Glancing at the computer display of their orbital track, down by the control desk, Kinsman replied, "The coast of Chile, South America."

"There's another tracking station down there, isn't there?"

"NASA station, not part of our network. We only use Air Force stations."

"Why is that?"

"This is strictly a military operation. We have to be able to operate entirely separately from the civilian space agency."

"Doesn't that cost more money?"

Kinsman thought of Murdock, and the reason why the Pentagon had agreed to let *Celebrity* magazine send a photo-journalist to the Air Force space station. "Maybe. But it lets the civilians do their thing without getting involved in military operations. And vice versa. Like the separation of church and state."

"So everything you do here," Linda said, "is strictly military."

He made himself grin at that. "Yep. But it's not very warlike. We don't have any weapons aboard. We couldn't hurt a flea."

"I thought you tested giant laser weapons up here. You know, for the Star Wars program."

"No," he replied, shaking his head. "No death rays. No killer satellites. We have reflectors mounted outside, to test laser beams fired at us from the ground. And someday we *will* test antimissile lasers and other SDI stuff, I guess. But for now, all we do is observe the Earth and check out hardware that's supposed to run in zero gravity. And people," he added. "We test people up here. Jill's specialty is biomedicine. She's studying how well people perform in zero gee."

Linda repeated, "But this station will become a testing

81

center for Star Wars weapons."

"When and if the Pentagon and the Congress can agree on the matter," Kinsman admitted. "Then we'll get a lot more secrecy, a lot more of the hup-two-three crap."

She smiled. "You don't like that?"

"There's only one thing the Air Force has done lately that I'm in complete agreement with."

"What's that?"

"Bringing you up here."

The smile stayed on her face but her eyes moved away from him. "Now you sound like a guy on the make."

"Not like an officer and a gentleman?"

She looked straight at him again. "Let's change the subject."

It's already been changed, he thought. We're off the weapons-in-space kick, and we're going to stay off it. "Sure. Okay," he said aloud. "You're here to get a story. Murdock wants as much publicity for us as NASA gets. And the Pentagon wants to show the world that we're not testing death rays in orbit. We may be military, but we're *nice* military."

"And you?" Linda asked, seriously. "What do you want? How does an Air Force captain get into the space cadets?"

"By dint of personal valor. I thought it would be fun—until my first orbital flight. Now it's a way of life."

"Really? You like it that much? Why?"

With an honest grin he answered, "Wait until we go outside. Then you'll see."

Jill came back into the cabin precisely on schedule, and it was Kinsman's turn to sleep. He seldom had difficulty sleeping on Earth, never in orbit. But he wondered about Linda's reaction to going EVA as he zippered himself into his mesh sleeping bag and adjusted the band across his forehead that kept his head from bobbing weightlessly under the pressure of the blood pumping through his carotid arteries.

Worming his arms inside the nylon mesh, snug and secure, he closed his eyes and sank into sleep. His last conscious thought was a nagging worry that Linda would be terrified of EVA.

When he awoke and Linda took her sleep shift, he talked it over with Jill.

"I think she'll be all right, Chet. Don't hold those first few minutes against her."

"I don't know. There's only two kinds of people up here: you either love it or you're scared shitless. And you can't fake it. If she goes ape out there . . ."

"She won't," Jill said. "Anyway, you'll be out there to help her. She won't be going outside until you're finished with the mating task. She wanted to get pictures of you actually at work, but I told her she'll have to settle for some posed shots."

Kinsman nodded. But the worry persisted. I wonder if Cy Calder's nurse was scared of flying?

He was pulling on his boots, wedging his free foot against an equipment rack to keep from floating off, when Linda returned from her sleep.

"Ready for a walk around the block?" he asked her.

She smiled and nodded without the slightest hesitation. "I'm looking forward to it. Can I get a few shots of you getting into your suit?"

Maybe she'll be okay, he hoped.

Finally he was sealed into the space suit. Linda and Jill stood back as Kinsman floated to the EVA airlock hatch. It was set into the floor, directly beneath the hatch that the Manta was linked to. Kinsman opened the massive hatch, slid himself down into the airlock, and closed the hatch securely. He always felt a little like a blimp in the bulky, pressurized space suit. The metal airlock chamber was roughly the size of a coffin; he had to worm his arm up to reach the control panel. He leaned against the stud and heard the whine and clatter of the pump sucking the air out of the cramped chamber.

The red light came on, indicating vacuum. He touched the stud that opened the outer hatch. It was beneath his feet, but as it slid open to reveal blackness flecked with stars, Kinsman's weightless orientation flip-flopped and he suddenly felt that he was standing on his head.

"Going out now," he said into his helmet mike.

"Roger," Jill's professional voice responded.

Carefully he eased himself through the open hatch, gripping its rim with one gloved hand as he slid fully outside, the way a swimmer holds the rail for a moment before kicking free into the deep water. Outside. Swinging his body around slowly he took in the immense beauty of Earth, overwhelmingly bright even through his tinted visor. Beyond its curving limb was the darkness of infinity, with the beckoning stars watching gravely.

Alone now. He worked his way along the handgrips to where the MMUs were stored and backed himself into the nearest one, then fastened the harness across his chest. He pushed away from the station, eyes still on the endless panorama of Earth. Inside his own tight, self-contained universe. Independent of everything and everybody. How easy it would be to jet away from the station and float away by himself forever. And be dead in six hours. Ay, there's the rub.

Instead, he used the thrusters to nudge him over to the power pod. It was riding silently behind the station, a squat truncated cone, one edge brilliantly lit by the sun, the rest bathed in the softer light reflected from the dayside of Earth.

Kinsman's job was to inspect the power pod, check the status of its systems, and then mate it to the electrical system of the station. It was a nuclear power generator, capable of providing the electricity to run a multimegawatt laser. Everything necessary for the task of mating it to the station —checkout instruments, connectors, tools—had been built into the pod, waiting for an astronaut to use them.

It would have been simple work on Earth. In zero gee it was complicated. The slightest motion of any part of your body started you drifting. You had to fight against all the built-in instincts of a lifetime; had to work hard constantly to remain in one place. It was easy to become exhausted in zero gee, especially when your suit began to overheat.

Kinsman accepted all this with hardly a conscious thought. He worked slowly, methodically, like a sleepwalker, using as little motion as possible, letting himself drift slightly until a more-or-less natural motion counteracted and pulled him back in the opposite direction. Ride the waves, he told himself, slow and easy. There was rhythm to his work, the natural dreamlike rhythm of weightlessness.

His earphones were silent. He said nothing. All he heard was the purring of the suit's air blowers and his own steady breathing. All he saw was his work.

Finally he inserted the last thick power cable to the receptacle waiting on the sidewall of the station. I pronounce you station and power source, he said silently. Inspecting the checkout lights alongside the connectors, he saw that they were all green. May you produce many kilowatts.

"Okay, it's finished," he announced, pushing slightly away from the station. "How's Linda doing?"

Jill answered at once, "She's all set."

"Send her out."

She came out of the hatch slowly, uncertainly, wavering feet sliding out first from the bulbous airlock. It reminded Kinsman of a film he had seen of a whale giving birth.

"Welcome to the real world," he said once her helmet cleared the airlock hatch.

She turned to answer him and he heard her gasp and he knew that now he liked her.

"It's . . . it's . . . ."

"Staggering," Kinsman suggested. "And look at you—no hands!"

She was floating freely, space suit laden with camera gear, tether flexing easily behind her. Kinsman could not see her face through the tinted visor, but he could hear the awe in her voice, even in her breathing.

"I've never seen anything so absolutely overpowering . . ."

And then suddenly she was all business, reaching for a camera, snapping away at the Earth and the station and even the distant Moon, rapid-fire. She moved too fast and started to tumble. Kinsman jetted over and steadied her, holding her by the shoulders.

"Hey, take it easy. They're not going away. You've got lots of time."

"I want to get some shots of you, and the station. Can you go over by the power pod and go through some of the motions of your work on it?"

Kinsman posed for her, answered her questions, rescued a camera when she fumbled it out of her gloved hands and missed several grabs at it.

"Judging distances out here is a little wacky," he said as he handed the camera back to her.

Jill called them twice and ordered them back inside.

"Chet, you're already fifteen minutes over the schedule limit!"

"There's plenty slop in the schedule; we can stay out a while longer."

"You're going to get her exhausted."

"I really feel fine," Linda said, her voice lyrical.

"How much more film do you have?" Kinsman asked her.

Without needing to look at the camera she answered, "Six more shots."

"Okay. We'll come in when the film runs out, Jill."

"You're going to be in darkness in another five minutes."

Turning to Linda, floating upside-down with the cloud-decked Earth behind her, he said, "Save your film for the sunset, and then shoot like hell when it comes."

"The sunset? What'll I focus on?"

"You'll know when it happens. Just watch."

It came fast but she was equal to it. As the station swung in its orbit toward the Earth's night shadow, the Sun dropped to the horizon and shot off a spectacular few moments of the purest reds and oranges and finally a heart-catching blue. Kinsman watched in silence, hearing Linda's breath going faster and faster as she worked the camera.

Then they were in darkness. Kinsman flicked on his helmet lamp. Linda was just hanging there, camera in hand.

"It's . . . impossible to describe." Her voice sounded empty, drained. "If I hadn't seen it . . . if I didn't get it on film, I don't think I'd be able to convince myself that I wasn't dreaming."

Jill's voice rasped in his earphones. "Chet, get inside! This is against every safety reg, keeping her outside in the dark."

He looked toward the station. Lights were visible from the ports along its side. Otherwise he could barely make out its shape, even though it was only a few meters away.

"Okay, okay. Turn on the airlock lights so we can see the hatch."

Linda was still bubbling about the view outside long after they had pulled off their space suits and eaten sandwiches and cookies.

"Have you ever been out there?" she asked Jill.

Perched on the biomed lab's desk edge, near the mouse colony, Jill nodded curtly. "Eight times."

"Isn't it spectacular? I hope the pictures come out; some of my exposure settings . . ."

"They'll be fine," Jill said. "And if they're not we have a backlog of photos you can use."

"Oh, but they wouldn't have the shots of Chet working on the power pod."

Jill shrugged. "Aren't you going to take more pictures in here? If you want to get some photos of real space veterans, you ought to take the mice here. They've been up here for six months now, living and raising families. And they don't make a fuss about it, either."

"Well, some of us do exciting things," Kinsman said lightly, "and some of us tend mice."

Jill glowered at him.

Glancing at his wristwatch, Kinsman said, "Ladies, it's my sack time. I've had a very trying day: mechanic, tour guide, photographer's model. Work, work, work."

He glided past Linda with a smile, kept it for Jill as he went by her. She was still glaring.

When he woke up again and went back into the main cabin, Jill was talking pleasantly with Linda as the two of them hovered over the microscope and a specimen rack at the biomed lab.

Linda saw him first. "Oh, hi. Jill's been showing me the spores she's studying. And I photographed the mice. Maybe they'll go on the cover instead of you."

Kinsman grinned. "She's been poisoning your mind against me." But to himself he wondered, Just what in hell has Jill been telling her?

Jill drifted over to the control desk and examined the mission log on the computer display screen.

"Ground control says the power pod checks out all okay," she said. "You did a good job."

"Thanks." He hesitated a moment. Then, "Whose turn in the sack is it?"

"Mine," Jill answered.

"Okay. Anything special?"

"No. Everything's on schedule. Next data transmission comes up in twelve minutes. Kodiak station."

Kinsman nodded. "Sleep tight."

Once Jill shut the curtain to the bunkroom, Kinsman went to the control desk and reviewed the mission schedule. Linda stayed at the biology bench, three gliding paces away.

After a glance across the control board to check all the systems status indicators, Kinsman turned to Linda.

"Well, now do you know what I meant about this being a way of life?"

"I think so. It's so different . . ."

"It's the real thing. Complete freedom. Brave new world. After ten minutes of EVA everything else is just toothpaste."

"It certainly was exciting."

"More than that. It's *living*. Being on the ground is a drag. Even flying a plane is dull now. This is where the fun is . . . this is where you can feel alive. Better than booze. Better than drugs. It's the highest kick there is, as close to heaven as anyone can get."

"You're really serious?"

"Damned right I am. I've been thinking of asking Murdock for a transfer to NASA duty. Air Force missions don't include the Moon, and I'd like to walk around on the new world, see the sights."

She smiled at him. "I'm afraid I'm not that enthusiastic. And besides, not even NASA's been on the Moon for years."

"They will be," he replied. "Sooner or later."

"You really think so?"

"Sure. But what's really important is that up here you're free, really free. All the laws and rules and prejudices that they've been dumping on us all our lives—they're all *down there*. Up here it's a new start. You can be yourself and do your own thing, and nobody can tell you differently."

"As long as your air holds out."

"That's the physical end of it, sure. We live in a microcosm, courtesy of the aerospace industry and the scientists. But there're no strings on us. The brass can't make us follow their rules. We're writing the rulebooks ourselves. For the first time since 1776 we're writing new social rules."

Linda looked thoughtful. Kinsman could not tell if she was genuinely impressed by his line or if she knew what he was trying to lead up to. He turned back to the control desk and busied himself with the mission flight plan again.

He had carefully considered all the possible opportunities and narrowed them down to two. Both of them tomorrow, over the Indian Ocean. Forty-five minutes between ground stations and Jill asleep both times.

"AF-9, this is Kodiak."

He reached up for the radio switch. "AF-9, Kodiak. Go ahead."

"We are receiving your automatic data transmission loud and clear."

"Roger, Kodiak. Everything normal here. Mission profile unchanged."

"Okay, Niner. We have nothing new for you. Oh, wait . . . Chet, Lew Regneson is here and he says he's put twenty bucks on your butt to uphold the Air Force's honor. Keep 'em flying."

Keeping his face as straight as possible, Kinsman answered, "Roger, Kodiak. Mission profile unchanged."

"Good luck!"

Linda's thoughtful expression had deepened. "What was that all about?"

He looked straight into those cool blue eyes and lied, "Damned if I know. Regneson's one of the astronaut corps. Been assigned to Kodiak for the past six weeks. He must be going ice-happy. Thought it'd be best just to humor him."

"I see." But she looked unconvinced.

"Have you checked any of your pictures through the film processor yet?"

Shaking her head, Linda replied, "No. I don't want to risk them on Air Force equipment. I'll process them in New York when we get back."

"Damned good equipment," Kinsman said, "even if it was built by the lowest bidder."

"I'm fussy."

He shrugged and let it go. At least the subject of the conversation had been changed.

"Chet?"

"What?"

"The power pod . . . what's it for? Colonel Murdock got awfully coy when I asked him."

"It's classified," he said. "I don't know myself."

"It's a nuclear reactor, isn't it?"

"A little one."

"Isn't it dangerous?"

He laughed. "You're getting more cosmic rays through your pretty bod right now than any radiation that might come from the reactor."

"Cosmic rays?" She looked alarmed.

"Nothing to worry about."

"They're not dangerous?"

"Not as dangerous as living in Manhattan."

Linda spent a moment thinking that over. Then, "The reactor's going to power Star Wars stuff, isn't it?"

"We call it SDI: Strategic Defense Initiative."

"But that's what it's for, isn't it?"

His shrug would have lifted him off the floor if his cleated shoes hadn't been wedged into the grillwork. "Could be."

"So your brave new world is involved in war."

"Defensive systems like SDI won't kill anybody," he said. "Their purpose is to prevent nuclear war from happening."

"But this *is* a military station."

"Unarmed. Two things this brave new world doesn't have yet: death and love."

"People have died in space."

"Never in orbit. Three Russian cosmonauts died during re-entry. People have been killed in ground or flying accidents. But no one's ever died up here. And no one's made love, either."

Despite herself, it seemed to Kinsman, she smiled. "Have there been any chances for it?"

"Not among NASA's astronauts, not in the shuttle. And the Russians have had a couple of women cosmonauts, but you know how puritanical they are."

Linda thought it over for a swift moment. "This isn't exactly the bridal suite at the Waldorf. I've seen better motel rooms along the Jersey Turnpike."

"Pioneers have to rough it."

"I'm a photographer, Chet, not a pioneer."

Kinsman spread his hands helplessly. "Strike three; I'm out."

"Better luck next time."

"Thanks." He returned his attention to the mission flight plan. *Next time will be in exactly sixteen hours, sweetface.*

When Jill came out of the sack it was Linda's turn to sleep. Kinsman moved to the camera monitor screen, sucking on a container of lukewarm coffee. They were passing over Plesetsk, the Soviet military launching center. Clouds covered the area, so he switched the monitor to display the radar imagery. A space shuttle sat at one end of the ten-thousand-foot runway down there. And, as usual, at least six of the dozens of launch pads had boosters on them.

They launch their antisatellite stuff from there, he thought. *Does one of those boosters have an ASAT on it, primed to take us out?*

No, he told himself. *That would mean war. Nuclear war.* The rumors that unmanned reconnaissance satellites had been destroyed by ASATs were just the usual scuttlebutt that military people liked to scare each other with.

He pulled his eyes away from the screen and looked at Jill. She was taking a blood sample from one of the mice.

"How're they doing?"

Without looking up she answered, "Fine. They've adapted to weightlessness beautifully. Calcium levels have evened off, muscle tone is good. They're even living longer than they would on Earth."

"Then there's hope for us two-legged types?"

Jill returned the mouse to the colony entrance and snapped the plastic lid shut. It scampered to rejoin its clan in the transparent maze of tunnels.

"I can't see any physical reason why humans couldn't live in orbit indefinitely," she answered. "It might even be beneficial."

"You mean we'd live longer?"

Jill nodded. "Maybe. I'd certainly be better off up here. No allergies."

"That's right," he said. "No pollen or dust."

"I never sneeze up here. I never get headaches." Jill smiled, a trifle ruefully. "Living up here eliminates a lot of physical problems."

Kinsman caught a slight but definite stress on the word

physical. "You think there might be emotional problems, in the long run?"

"Chet, I can see emotional problems on a three-day mission." Jill forced the blood specimen into a stoppered test tube.

"What do you mean?"

"Come on," she said, her face showing disappointment and distaste. "It's obvious what you're trying to do. Your tail's been wagging like a puppy dog whenever she's in sight."

"You haven't been sleeping much, have you?"

"I haven't been eavesdropping, if that's what you mean. I've simply been watching you watching her. And some of those messages from groundside . . . is the whole Air Force in on this? How much money's being bet?"

"I'm not involved in any betting. I'm just . . ."

"You're just taking a risk on fouling up this mission and maybe killing the three of us just to prove that you're Tarzan and she's Jane."

"Goddammitall, Jill, now you sound like Murdock."

The sour look on her face deepened. "Do I? Okay, you're a big boy. If you want to play Tarzan while you're on duty, that's your business. I won't get in your way. I'll take a sleeping pill and stay in the bunk."

"You will?"

"That's right. You can have your blond Barbie Doll, and good luck to you. But I'll tell you this . . . she's a phony. I've talked to her long enough to dig that. You're trying to use her, but she's trying to use us, too. She was pumping me about the power pod while you were sleeping. She's here for her own reasons, Chet, and if she plays along with you it won't be for the romance and adventure of it all."

My God Almighty, thought Kinsman. Jill's jealous!

It was tense and quiet when Linda returned from the bunkroom. The three of them worked separately: Jill fussing over the algae colony on the shelf above the biomed desk; Kinsman methodically taking film from the surveillance cameras for return to Earth and reloading them; Linda clicking away efficiently at both of them.

Ground control called up to ask how things were going. Both Jill and Linda threw sharp glances at Kinsman.

He replied merely, "Following mission profile. All systems green."

They shared a meal of precooked boneless chicken and bland vegetables together, still mostly in silence, and then it was Kinsman's turn in the sack again. But not before he rechecked the flight plan. *Jill goes in next, and we'll have four hours alone, including a stretch over the Indian Ocean.*

He found himself whistling a romantic theme from *Scheherazade* as he zippered himself into his sleeping bag.

Once Jill retired, Kinsman immediately called Linda over to the radar display on the pretext of showing her the image of a Soviet satellite.

"We're coming close now." They hunched side by side in front of the orange-glowing radar screen, close enough for Kinsman to scent her delicate but very feminine perfume. "Only a couple hundred kilometers away."

"Should we blink our lights at them or something?"

"It's unmanned."

"Oh."

"It *is* a little like flying in World War I up here," Kinsman realized, straightening up. "Just being up here is more important than which nation you're from."

"Do the Russians feel that way, too?"

He nodded. "I think so."

Linda stood in front of him so close that they were almost touching.

"You know," Kinsman said, "when I first saw you on the base I thought you were the photographer's model, not the photographer."

Gliding slightly away from him, she answered, "I started out as a model . . ." Her voice trailed off.

"Don't stop. What were you going to say?"

Something about her had changed, Kinsman realized. She was still coolly friendly, but now she was alert, as wary as a deer in hunting season, and . . . sad?

She sighed. "Modeling is a dead end. I finally figured out that there's more of a future on the other side of the camera."

"You had too much brains for modeling."

"Don't flatter me."

"Why on Earth should I flatter you?"

"We're not on Earth."

"Touché."

She drifted, dreamlike, self-absorbed, toward the galley. Kinsman followed her.

"How long have you been on the other side of the camera?" he asked.

Turning back toward him, "I'm supposed to be getting the story of your life, not vice versa."

"Okay . . . ask me some questions."

"How many people know that you're supposed to lay me up here?"

Kinsman felt his face make a smile, an automatic delaying tactic. What the hell, he thought. Aloud he replied, "I don't know. It started out as a little joke among a few of the guys . . . apparently the word has spread."

"And how much money do you stand to win or lose?" She was not smiling.

"Money?" Kinsman was genuinely surprised. "Money doesn't enter into it."

"Oh, no?"

"No. Not with me."

The tenseness in her body seemed to relax a little. "Then why . . . I mean . . . what's it all about?"

Kinsman ran a hand across his jaw. It felt stubbly. "It's about making love. That's all. I mean, you're damned pretty, neither one of us has any strings, nobody's tried it in zero gee before . . . why the hell not?"

"But why should I?"

"That's the big question. That's what makes an adventure out of it."

She looked at him thoughtfully, leaning her tall frame against the galley paneling. "An adventure. There's nothing more to it in your mind than that?"

"Depends," Kinsman answered. "Hard to tell ahead of time."

"You live in a very simple world, Chet."

"I try to. Don't you?"

She shook her head. "No, my world's very complicated."

"But it includes sex."

Now she smiled, but there was no pleasure in it. "Does it?"

94

"You mean never?" Kinsman's voice sounded incredulous, even to himself.

She did not answer.

"Never at all? I can't believe that . . ."

"No," she said, nearly whispering. "Not never at all. But never for . . . for an adventure. For job security, yes. For getting the good assignments. For teaching me how to use a camera in the first place. But never for fun . . . at least, not for a long, long time has it been for fun."

Kinsman looked into those cold blue eyes and saw that they were completely dry and aimed straight back at him. His insides felt strange. He put out a hand toward her but she did not move a muscle.

"That's . . . that's a damned lonely way to live," he said.

"Yes, it is." Her voice was a steel ice pick, without a trace of self-pity in it.

"But how did it happen? Why . . . ?"

She leaned her head back against the galley paneling, her eyes looking away, into the past. "I had a baby. He didn't want it. I had to give her up for adoption—or have it aborted. The kid should be five years old now. I don't know where she is." She straightened up, looked back at Kinsman. "But I learned that sex is for making babies or making careers. Not for fun."

Kinsman hung there in midair, feeling as if he had just taken a low blow. The only sound in the cabin was the faint hum of electrical machinery, the whisper of air fans.

Linda broke into bitter laughter. "I wish you could see your own face: Tarzan the Ape Man, trying to figure out a nuclear reactor."

"The only trouble with zero gee," he grumbled, "is that you can't hang yourself."

Jill sensed something was wrong, it seemed to Kinsman. The moment she came out of the bunkroom she started sniffing around, giving quizzical looks. When Linda retired for her final rest period before re-entry, Jill asked him:

"How're you two getting along?"

"Okay."

"Really?"

95

"Really. We're going to open a disco in here. Wanna boogie?"

Her nose wrinkled. "You're hopeless."

For more than an hour they worked at their separate tasks. Kinsman was concentrating on recalibrating the radar mapper when Jill handed him a bulb of hot coffee.

He turned toward her. Even floating several inches off the floor, Jill was shorter than he.

"Thanks."

Her round face was very serious. "Something's bothering you, Chet. What did she do to you?"

"Nothing."

"Really?"

"For Chrissake, don't start that again! Nothing, absolutely nothing happened. Maybe that's what's bothering me."

Shaking her head, "No, you're worried about something and it's not yourself."

"Don't be so damned dramatic, Jill."

She put a hand on his shoulder. "Chet . . . I know this is all a game to you, but people can get hurt at this kind of game and . . . well . . . nothing in life is ever as good as you expect it will be."

Looking into her intent brown eyes, Kinsman felt his irritation vanish. "Okay, little sister. Thanks for the philosophy. I'm a big boy, though, and I know what it's all about."

"You just think you know."

Shrugging, "Okay, I think I know. Maybe nothing is as good as it ought to be, but a man's innocent until proven guilty, and everything new is as good as gold until you find some tarnish on it. That's my philosophy."

"All right, slugger." Jill smiled ruefully. "Be the ape man. Fight it out for yourself. I just don't want to see her hurt you."

"I won't get hurt."

"You hope. Okay, if there's anything I can do . . ."

"Yeah, there is something."

"What?"

"When you sack in again, make sure Linda sees you take a sleeping pill, will you?"

Jill's face went expressionless. "Sure," she answered flatly. "Anything for a fellow officer. And gentleman."

She made a great show, several hours later, of taking a sleeping pill so that she could rest well on her final nap before re-entry. It seemed to Kinsman that Jill deliberately laid it on with a trowel.

"Do you always take sleeping pills on the final time around?" Linda asked Kinsman after Jill had gone into the bunkroom and yanked the curtain shut.

"Got to be fully rested and alert for the re-entry," Kinsman said. "Trickiest part of the mission."

"I see."

"Nothing to worry about, though."

He went to the control desk and busied himself with the tasks that the mission plan called for. Linda hovered beside him, within arm's reach. Kinsman chatted briefly with Kodiak station, on schedule, and made an entry in the log.

Three more ground stations and we're over the Indian Ocean, with world enough and time.

But he did not look up from the control panel. He tested each system aboard the station, fingers flicking over the keyboard pads, eyes focused on the screen readouts that told him exactly how each system was performing.

"Chet?"

"Yes?" Without looking up.

"Are you sore at me?"

Still not looking at her, "No. Why should I be sore at you?"

"Well, maybe not angry, but . . ."

"Feeling put down?"

"Yes. Hurt. Something like that."

He punched in the final commands for the computer, then turned to face her. "Linda, I haven't had the time to figure out what I feel. You're a complicated woman, maybe too complicated for me. Life's got enough twists to it."

Her mouth drooped a little.

"On the other hand," he grinned, "we WASPs ought to stick together. Not many of us left."

That brought a faint smile. "But I'm not a WASP. My real name's Szymanski. I changed it when I started modeling."

"Another complication."

She was about to reply when the radio speaker crackled,

97

"AF-9, this is Cheyenne. Cheyenne to AF-9."

Kinsman leaned over and thumbed the transmitter switch. "AF-9 to Cheyenne. You're coming through faint but clear."

"Roger Nine. We're receiving your telemetry. All systems look good from here."

"On-board systems check also green," Kinsman said. "Mission profile nominal. No excursions. Tasks about ninety-five percent complete."

"Roger. Vandenberg suggests you begin checking out your spacecraft on the next orbit. You are scheduled for re-entry in ten hours."

"Right. Will do."

"Okay, Chet. Everything looks cool from here. Anything else to report, ol' Founding Father?"

"Mind your own business." He snapped the transmitter off.

Linda was grinning at him.

"What's so funny?"

"You are. You're getting very touchy about this whole thing."

"I'm going to stay touchy for a long time to come. Those guys'll hound me about this for years."

"You could always tell lies."

"About you? No, I don't think I could do that. If the girl were anonymous, that's one thing. But they all know you, where you work . . ."

"You're a gallant officer. I suppose that kind of story *would* get back to New York."

He grimaced. "You'd be on the cover of *Penthouse*, like that Miss America was."

She laughed at that. "They'd have a hard time finding nude pictures of me."

"Careful now." Kinsman put up a warning hand. "Don't stir up my imagination any more than it already is. It's tough enough being gallant, under these circumstances."

They remained apart, silent, Kinsman cleated firmly at the control desk, Linda drifting back toward the galley, nearly touching the curtain that screened off the sleeping area.

Patrick Air Force Base called in and Kinsman gave a terse report. When he looked at Linda again she was hovering by the observation window across the aisle from the galley. Looking back at him, her face was troubled, her eyes—he was not sure what he saw in her eyes. They looked different: no longer ice-cool, no longer calculating. They looked aware, concerned, almost frightened.

Still Kinsman stayed silent. He checked and double-checked the control board, making absolutely certain that every valve and transistor aboard the station was functioning perfectly. He glanced at the digital clock blinking below the main display screen. Five more minutes before Ascension calls. He started checking the board again.

Ascension called precisely on schedule. Feeling his innards tightening, Kinsman gave his standard report in a deliberately calm and detached way. Ascension signed off.

With a last long look at the controls, Kinsman pushed himself away from the desk and drifted, hands faintly touching the grips along the aisle, toward Linda.

"You've been awfully quiet," he said, standing next to her.

"I've been thinking about what you said a while ago." What was it in her eyes? Anticipation? Fear? "It . . . it *is* a damned lonely life, Chet."

He took her arm and gently pulled her toward him. He kissed her.

"But . . ."

"It's all right," he whispered. "No one will bother us. No one will know."

She shook her head. "It's not that easy, Chet. It's not that simple."

"Why not? We're here together . . . what's so complicated?"

"But life is complicated, Chet. And love—there's more to life than having fun."

"Sure there is. But it's meant to be enjoyed, too. What's wrong with taking a chance when it comes along? What's so damned complicated or important? We're above the cares and worries of the Earth. Maybe it's only for a few more hours, but it's here and it's now. It's us. Alone. They can't touch us, they can't force us to do anything or stop us from doing what we want to. We're on our own. Understand? Completely on our own."

99

She nodded, her eyes still wide with the look of a frightened doe. But her hands slid around him and together they drifted back toward the control desk. Wordlessly, Kinsman turned off all the lights so that all they saw was the glow from the control board and the flickering of the computer as it murmured to itself. They were in their own world now, their private universe, floating freely and softly in the darkness. Touching, drifting, caressing, searching the new seas and continents, they explored their world.

Jill stayed in her bedroll until Linda entered the sleeping area, quietly, to see if she had awakened yet. Kinsman went to the control desk feeling, not tired, yet strangely numb.

The rest of the flight was strictly routine. Jill and Kinsman did their jobs, speaking to each other only when they had to. Linda took a brief nap, then returned to snap a few last pictures. Finally they crawled back into the Manta, disengaged from the station, and started the long curving flight back to Earth.

Kinsman took a last look at the majestic beauty of the planet, serene and unique among the stars. Then they felt the surge of the rocket's retrofire and dipped into the atmosphere. Air heated beyond endurance blazed around them in a fiery grip as they buffeted through re-entry, their tiny craft a flaming falling star. Pressed down into his seat, his radio useless while the incandescent sheath of re-entry gases swathed them, Kinsman let the automatic controls bring them through the heat and pummeling turbulence, down to an altitude where the bat-winged craft smoothed out and began behaving like an airplane.

He took control and steered the Manta across the Pacific, checking the computer's programmed flight path against his actual position. Right on the money. The coast of California rose to meet him, brown and gray and white where the beaches met the ceaseless cadence of the surf. Gliding like a bird now, Kinsman brought the Manta back toward the dry lake at Edwards Air Force Base, back to the world of men, of weather, of cities and hierarchies and official regulations. He did this alone, silently, without the help of Jill or anyone else. He flew the craft with featherlight touches on the controls, from inside his buttoned-tight space suit, frowning at the instrument panel displays through his helmet visor. But even in the heavy gloves, man and machine acted together like a single creature.

The voices from ground control rasped in his earphones. He saw the long concrete scar of the all-weather runway laid across the Mojave's rocky waste. The voices crackled with information about wind conditions, altitude checks, speed estimates. He knew, without looking, that a pair of jet fighters were trailing behind him, armed with cameras in place of guns. In case I crash, he knew.

They dipped through a thin layer of stratus clouds. Kinsman's eyes flickered to the radar screen slightly to his right. The Manta shuddered briefly as he lined it up with the long gray slash of the runway. He eased back slightly on the controls, hands and feet and mind working instinctively, flashed over scrubby brush and bare cracked lake bed, flared the craft onto the runway. The wheels touched down once, bounced them up momentarily, then touched again with a shrill screech. They rolled for almost a mile before stopping.

He leaned back in the seat and let out a deep breath. No matter how many flights, he still ended oozing sweat after the landing.

"Nice landing," Jill said.

"Thanks."

He turned off all the spacecraft's systems, hands moving automatically in response to long training. Then he slid the visor up, reached overhead, and popped the hatch open.

"End of the line," he said, feeling suddenly exhausted. "Everybody out."

He clambered up through the hatch, his own weight a sullen resentment to him, then helped Linda and finally Jill out of the Manta's cramped cockpit. They hopped down onto the concrete runway. Two vans, an ambulance, and two fire trucks were rolling from their standby stations at the end of the runway, nearly half a mile ahead.

Kinsman watched their blocky dark forms wavering in the heat haze. He slowly pulled off his helmet as he sat on the lip of the hatch. A helicopter thundered overhead, cutting across the clear blue sky, but when Kinsman looked up at it the glaring desert sunlight annoyed him, made him squint, started a headache back behind his eyes.

Jill began trudging away from the Manta, toward the approaching trucks. Kinsman clambered down to the concrete and walked up to Linda. Her helmet was off, her sun-drenched hair shaking free. She carried a plastic bag of film rolls.

"I've been thinking," Kinsman said to her. "That business about having a lonely life. . . . You're not the only one. And it doesn't have to be that way. I can get to the East Coast, or . . ."

Her eyes widened with surprise. "Hey, who's taking things seriously now?" She looked calm again, cool, despite the baking heat.

"But I mean . . ."

"Chet, come on. We had our kicks. Now you can tell your pals about it and I can tell mine. We'll both get a lot of mileage out of it, won't we?"

"I never intended to tell anybody . . ."

But she was already moving away from him, striding toward the men who were running up from the vans. One of them, a civilian, had a camera. He dropped to one knee and snapped a half-dozen pictures of Linda as she walked toward him, holding the plastic bag of film up in one hand and smiling broadly, like a fisherman who had just bagged a big one.

Kinsman stood there with his mouth open.

Jill came back to him. "Well? Did you get what you were after?"

"No," he said slowly. "I guess I didn't."

She started to put her hand out to him. "We never do, do we?"

Age 30

KINSMAN SNAPPED AWAKE when the phone went off. Before it could start a second ring he had the receiver off the cradle.

"Captain Kinsman?" The motel's night clerk.

"Yes," he whispered back, squinting at the luminous digits of his wristwatch. Two twenty-three.

"I'm awfully sorry to disturb you, Captain, but Colonel Murdock himself called . . ."

"How the hell did he know I was here?"

"He doesn't. He said he was phoning all the motels around the base. I didn't admit that you were here. He said when he found you he needed you to report to him in person at once. Those were his words, Captain: in person, at once. Something about a General Hatch."

Kinsman frowned in the darkness. "Okay. Thanks for playing dumb."

"Not at all, Captain. Hope it isn't trouble."

"Yeah." Kinsman hung up. For a half-minute he sat on the edge of the king-size bed. Murdock's making the rounds of the motels at two in the morning, Hatch is coming to the base, and the clerk hopes it isn't trouble. Funny.

He stood up, stretched his lanky frame, and glanced at the blonde wrapped obliviously in the bed's tangled sheets. With a wistful shake of his head Kinsman padded to the bathroom.

He shut the door softly and flipped the light switch, wincing. He turned on the coffee machine that hung on the wall above the light switch. It's lousy but it's coffee. Almost. As the machine started gurgling he rummaged in his travel kit for his electric razor. The face that met him in the mirror was lean and long-jawed and just the slightest bit bloodshot. He kept his hair at a length that made Murdock uncomfortable:

103

slightly longer than regulations allowed, not long enough to call for a reprimand.

Within a few minutes he was shaved, showered, and back in Air Force uniform. He left a scribbled note on motel stationery propped against the dresser mirror, took a final long look at the blonde, wishing he could remember her name, then went out to his car.

The new fuel regulations had put an end to fast driving. The synfuels were too expensive to waste, and when you tried to get some speed out of them they began to eat out the engine's guts. There were even those who insisted that the synfuels were specially doctored to tear up an engine's innards at anything over fifty: Washington's way of enforcing energy conservation.

His hand-built convertible was ready to burn hydrogen fuel, if and when the government made the stuff available. For now, he had to go with a captain's monthly allotment of synfuel. It was enough to keep him moving—cautiously —through the predawn darkness.

Some instinct made him turn on the car radio. Diane's haunting voice filled the starry night:

". . . and in her right hand
There's a silver dagger,
That says I can never be your bride."

Kinsman listened in dark solitude as the night wind whistled past. Diane Lawrence was a major entertainment star, with scant time for an Air Force captain who spent half his life in space. How long has it been since I've seen her? he asked himself. Could it be more than a year?

A limousine and an official Air Force car with a general's flag fluttering from its antenna zoomed past him, doing at least eighty, heading for the base. No fuel scarcity for them. Their engines whined and faded into the distance like wailing ghosts. There was no other traffic at this hour. Kinsman held to the legal limit all the way to the base's main gate, but he could feel the excitement building up inside him.

Half a dozen Air Policemen were manning the gate, looking brisk and polished, instead of the usual sleepy pair.

"What's the stew, Sergeant?" Kinsman asked as he

pulled his car up to the gate.

The guard flashed his hand light on the badge Kinsman held in his outstretched hand.

"Dunno, sir. We got the word to look sharp."

He flashed the light full in Kinsman's face, checking the picture on the badge. Painfully sharp, Kinsman groused to himself.

The guard waved him on.

There was that special crackle in the air as Kinsman drove to the administration building. The kind that only comes when a manned launch is imminent. As if in answer to his unspoken hunch, the floodlights of Complex 204 bloomed into life, etching the tall silver booster standing there embraced by the dark spiderwork of the gantry tower.

People were scurrying in and out of the administration building. Some were sleepy-eyed and disheveled, but their feet were doing double time. Colonel Murdock's secretary was coming down the hallway as Kinsman signed in at the security desk.

"What's up, Annie?"

"I just got here myself," she said. There were hairclips still in her sandy-colored curls. "The boss told me to flag you down the instant you arrived."

Even from completely across the Colonel's spacious office, Kinsman could see that Murdock was a round little kettle of nerves. He was standing by the window behind his desk, watching the activity on Pad 204, clenching and unclenching his fists behind his back. His bald head was glistening with perspiration despite the room's frigid air-conditioning. Kinsman stopped at the door with the secretary.

"Colonel?" she said softly.

Murdock whirled around. "Kinsman. So you're here."

"What's going on? I thought the next manned shot wasn't until . . ."

The Colonel waved a pudgy hand. "The next manned shot is as fast as we can damned well make it." He walked around the desk and eyed Kinsman. "Christ, you look a mess."

"It's three in the morning!"

"No excuses. Get over to the medical section for a
105

preflight checkout. They're waiting for you."

"I'd still like to know—"

"Tell them to check your blood for alcohol content," Murdock grumbled.

"I've been celebrating my liberation. I'm not supposed to be on duty, remember? My leave starts at 0900 hours."

"Your leave is canceled. General Hatch just flew in from Norton and he wants you."

"Hatch?"

"That's right. He wants the most experienced man available."

"Twenty astronauts on the base and you have to make me available."

Murdock fumed. "Listen, dammit. This is a military operation. I may not insist on much discipline from you glamour boys, but you're still in the Air Force and you will follow orders. Hatch says he wants the best man we've got. Personally, I'd rather have Colt, but he's back East attending a family funeral or something. That means you're *it*. Like it or not."

With a grin, Kinsman said, "If you saw what I had to leave behind me to report for duty here you'd put me up for the Medal of Honor."

Murdock frowned in exasperation. Anne tried unsuccessfully to suppress a smile.

"All right, lover-boy. Get your ass down to the medical section on the double. Annie, you stick with him and bring him to the briefing room the instant he's finished. General Hatch is already there."

Kinsman stood at the doorway, not moving. "Will you just tell me what this is all about?"

"Ask the General," Murdock growled, walking back toward his desk. "All I know is that Hatch wants the best man we have and wants him *fast*."

"Emergency shots are volunteer missions," Kinsman pointed out.

"So?"

"I'm on leave. There are eighteen other astronauts here who—"

"Dammit, Kinsman, if you—" Murdock's face began to turn red.

106

"Relax, Colonel, relax. I won't let you down. Not when there's a chance to put a few hundred miles between me and all the brass on Earth."

Murdock stood there fuming as Kinsman left with Anne. They paced hurriedly out to his car and sped off to the medical building.

"You shouldn't bait him like that," Anne said over the rush of the dark wind. "He feels the pressure a lot more than you do."

"He's insecure," Kinsman replied, grinning. "There are only twenty people on base qualified for orbital missions and he's not one of them."

"And you are."

"Damned right, sugar. It's the only thing in the world worth doing. You ought to try it."

She put a hand up to her wind-whipped hair. "Me? Fly in orbit? I don't even like airplanes!"

"It's a clean world up there, Annie. Brand-new every time. Your life is completely your own. Once you've done it there's nothing left on Earth except to wait for the next time."

"My God, you sound as if you really mean it."

"I'm serious," he insisted. "Why don't you wangle a ride on one of the shuttle missions? They usually have room for an extra person."

"And get locked inside a spacecraft with you?"

Kinsman shrugged. "There are worse things."

"Some other time, Captain. I've heard all about you guys and your Zero Gee Club. Right now we have to get you through preflight and then off to see the General."

General Lesmore D. ("Hatchet") Hatch sat in dour silence in the small briefing room. The oblong conference table was packed with colonels and a single civilian. They all look so damned serious, Kinsman thought as he took the only empty chair, at the foot of the table. The General, naturally, sat at the head.

"Captain Kinsman." It was a statement of fact.

"Good morning, sir."

Hatch turned to a moonfaced aide. "Borgeson, let's not waste time."

Kinsman only half-listened to the hurried introductions

around the table. He felt uncomfortable already, and it was only partly due to the stickiness of the crowded little room. Through the only window he could see the first faint glow of dawn.

"Now then," Borgeson said, introductions finished. "Very briefly, your mission will involve orbiting and making rendezvous with an unidentified satellite."

"Unidentified?"

Borgeson went on: "It was launched from Plesetsk in the Soviet Union. It's a new type, something we haven't seen before. We don't know what it contains or what its mission is. We don't even know if it's manned or not."

"And it is big," Hatch rumbled.

"Intelligence," Colonel Borgeson nodded at the colonel sitting on Kinsman's left, "had no prior word about the launch. We must assume that the satellite is potentially hostile in intent. Colonel McKeever will give you the tracking data."

They went around the table, each colonel adding his bit of information. Kinsman began to build up the picture in his mind.

The satellite had been launched nine hours earlier. It was in a low-altitude, high-inclination orbit that allowed it to cover every square mile of territory between the Arctic and Antarctic Circles. Since it had first gone up not a single radio transmission had been detected going to or from it. And it was big, twice the size of the *Soyuz* spacecraft the Soviets used for their manned flights.

"A satellite of that size," said the colonel from the Special Weapons Center, "could easily contain a beam weapon . . . the kind of laser or particle beam device that would be used to knock down missiles or destroy satellites."

"If it does," said Borgeson, "it could threaten every satellite we have in orbit; even the commsats up at geosynchronous orbit."

"Or it could be the first step in an effective antimissile defense," the Special Weapons man added. "You know, their version of Star Wars."

"Or it could be," said General Hatch, "a twenty-megaton nuclear weapon." His face was etched with deep lines of worry. Or is it hate? Kinsman asked himself. "A bomb that size, exploded at that altitude, could cause an electromagnetic pulse that would knock out every computer, every telephone, every auto ignition, every power station across the North American continent."

Borgeson nodded. "The chaos factor. It could be the precursor to a full-scale nuclear attack."

"And in a little more than two hours," Hatch went on, gloomy as death, "that satellite will be passing over the Middle West, the heartland of America."

"Why don't we just knock it down, sir?" Kinsman asked. "We can hit it with an ASAT, can't we?"

"We could try," the General answered. "But suppose the damned thing just zaps our missile? Then what? Can you imagine the panic in Washington? It'd make *Sputnik* look like a schoolyard scuffle. And suppose it *is* a nuke. Salvage fusing could set it off and the whole damned country will be blacked out. The Russians could even accuse us of starting hostilities by attacking their goddamned satellite."

Kinsman watched the General shake his head morosely. He puffed out a deep sigh. "Besides, we have been ordered by the Chief of Staff himself to inspect the satellite and determine whether or not its intent is hostile."

"In two hours?" Kinsman blurted.

"Perhaps I can explain," said the civilian. He had been introduced as a State Department man. Kinsman had already forgotten his name. He had a soft, sheltered look to him.

"We are officially in a position of cooperation, *vis-à-vis* the Soviets, in our outer space programs. Our NASA civilians and the Soviet civil space program people are working cooperatively on exploring the Moon and sending probes to the planet Mars. Officially, we are sharing information on our strategic defense programs, as called for in SALT III."

The State Department representative seemed unmindful of the hostility that Kinsman could feel rising from the others around the table. He went on in his low, Ivy League voice, "So if we simply try to destroy this new satellite it would violate our agreements with the Soviet government and set back our cooperative programs—perhaps ruin them altogether."

"On the other hand," Hatch cut in, his voice like a rusty

109

saw, "if we do nothing, the Russians will know that they can get away with bending those agreements whenever they feel like it."

"But . . ."

Hatch silenced the State Department with a baleful glance. Then he turned back to Kinsman. "This is a test, Captain. The Russians are testing our ability to react. They are testing our *will* to react. We have got to show them that we can detect, inspect, and verify that satellite's nature and mission."

"We ought to blow it out of the sky," snapped one of the colonels.

"And if it's a peaceful research station?" asked the civilian, with some steel in his voice. "If there are cosmonauts aboard? What if we kill Russian nationals?"

"Serve 'em right," somebody muttered.

"And then the Soviets will feel justified in launching a nuclear attack." The civilian shook his head. "No. I agree with General Hatch. This is a test of our abilities and our will. We must prove to the Soviets that we can inspect their satellites and see for ourselves whether or not they contain weaponry."

Colonel Borgeson said calmly, "If they've gone to the trouble of launching this massive vehicle, then military logic dictates that it's a weapon carrier. There's no point to placing a dummy in orbit, just to bother us."

"No matter whether it's a weapon or not, the satellite could be rigged with booby traps to prevent us from inspecting it."

Thanks a lot, Kinsman said to himself.

Hatch focused his gunmetal eyes on Kinsman. "Captain, I want to impress one thought on you. The Air Force has been working for more than ten years to achieve the capability of placing a military officer in space on an instant's notice, despite the opposition of NASA and other parts of the government."

He never so much as flicked a glance in the civilian's direction as he continued, "This incident proves the absolute necessity for such a capability. Your flight will be the first practical demonstration of all that we've battled to achieve

110

over the past decade. You can see, then, the importance of your mission."

"Yessir."

"This is strictly a volunteer mission. Exactly because it is so important to the future of the Air Force, I don't want you to try it unless you are absolutely certain about it."

"I understand, sir. I'm your man."

Hatch's weathered face unfolded into a grim smile. "Well spoken, Captain. Good luck."

The General rose and everyone scrambled to their feet and snapped to attention, even the civilian. As the others filed out of the briefing room, Murdock drew Kinsman aside.

"You had your chance to beg off."

"And the General would've drawn a big red circle around my name. My days in the Air Force would be numbered."

"That's not the way he—"

"Relax, Colonel," Kinsman said. "I wouldn't miss this for the world. A chance to play cops and robbers in orbit."

"We're not in this for laughs! This is damned important. If it really is a weapon up there, a nuclear bomb . . ."

"I'll be the first to know, won't I?"

The countdown of the solid rocket booster went smoothly, swiftly, as Kinsman sat alone in the Manta spacecraft perched atop the rocket's nose. There was always the chance that a man or machine would fail at a crucial point and turn the intricate, delicately poised booster into a very large and powerful bomb.

Kinsman sat tautly in the contoured seat, listening to them tick off the seconds. He hated countdowns, hated being helpless, completely dependent on faceless voices that flickered through his earphones, waiting childlike in a mechanical womb, not truly alive, doubled up and crowded by the unfeeling impersonal machinery that automatically gave him warmth and breath and life.

Waiting.

He could feel the tiny vibrations along his spine that told him the ship was awakening. Green lights blossomed across the control panel, telling him that everything was functioning

111

and ready. Still the voices droned through his earphones in carefully measured cadence:

". . . three . . . two . . . one . . ."

And she bellowed to life. Acceleration flattened Kinsman into the seat. Vibration rattled his eyes in their sockets. Time became a meaningless roar. The surging, engulfing, overpowering bellow of the rocket engines made his head ring even after they had burned out into silence.

Within minutes he was in orbit, the long slender rocket stages falling away behind, together with all sensation of weight. Kinsman sat alone in the squat, delta-shaped spacecraft: weightless, free of Earth.

Still he was the helpless unstirring one. Computers sent guidance corrections from the ground to the Manta's controls. Tiny vectoring thrusters squirted on and off, microscopic puffs that maneuvered the craft into the precise orbit needed for catching the Soviet satellite.

What if she zaps me as I approach her? Kinsman wondered.

Completely around the world he spun, southward over the Pacific and then up over the wrinkled cloud-shrouded mass of Eurasia. They must have picked me up on their radars, he thought. They must know that I'm chasing their bird. As he swung across Alaska the voices from the ground began talking to him again. He answered them as automatically as the machines did, reading numbers off the control panels, proving to them that he was alive and functioning properly.

Then Smitty's voice cut in. He was serving as communicator from Vandenberg. "There's been another launch, fifteen minutes ago. From the cosmonaut base at Tyuratam. High-energy boost. Looks like you're going to have company."

Kinsman acknowledged the information, but still sat unmoving.

Finally he saw it hurtling toward him. He came to life. To meet and board the satellite he had to match its orbit and velocity exactly. He was approaching too fast. Radar and computer data flashed in amber flickers across the screens on Kinsman's control panel. His eyes and fingers moved constantly, a well-trained pianist performing a new and tricky

112

sonata. He worked the thruster controls and finally eased his Manta into a rendezvous orbit a few dozen meters from the massive Russian satellite.

The big satellite seemed to hang motionless in space just ahead of him, a huge inert chunk of metal, dazzlingly brilliant where the sun lit its curving flank, totally invisible where it was in shadow. It looked ridiculously like a crescent moon made of flush-welded aluminum. A smaller crescent puzzled Kinsman until he realized it was a rocket nozzle hanging from the satellite's tailcan.

"I'm parked off her stern about fifty meters," he reported into his helmet microphone. "She looks like the complete upper stage of a Proton-class booster. I'm going outside."

"Better make it fast." Smitty's voice was taut, high-pitched with nervousness. "That second spacecraft is closing in fast."

"E.T.A.?"

A pause while voices mumbled in the background. Then, "About twenty minutes . . . maybe less."

"Great."

"Colonel Murdock says you can abort the mission if you feel you have to."

Same to you, pal. Aloud, he replied, "I'm going to take a close look at her. Get inside if I can. Call you back in fifteen minutes, max."

No response. Kinsman smiled to himself at the realization that Colonel Murdock did not see fit to remind him that the Russian satellite might be booby-trapped. Old Mother Murdock hardly forgot about such items. He simply had decided not to make the choice of aborting the mission too attractive.

Gimmicked or not, the satellite was too near and too enticing to turn back now. Kinsman quickly checked out his space suit, pumped the air from his cockpit into the storage tanks, and then popped the hatch over his head.

Out of the womb and into the world.

He climbed out and teetered on the lip of the hatch, coiling the umbilical cord attached to his suit. Murdock and his staff had decided on using an umbilical instead of a bulky backpack and MMU because he was alone in orbit, without

113

backup, and because they wanted Kinsman to be able to slide through the hatch of the Soviet satellite and inspect its interior. They had been confident that Kinsman could bring the Manta close enough to the Russian craft so that an umbilical could keep him supplied with air and electrical power, and provide a safety tether back to his own cockpit.

Kinsman pushed off from the hatch and floated like a coasting underwater swimmer toward the Russian satellite. He glanced down at the night side of Earth. City lights glittered through the clouds; he could make out the shape of the Great Lakes and a distant glow that had to be the Boston-to-Washington corridor.

They're right, he realized. A bomb set off here will black out the whole damned country.

As he approached the satellite the sun rose over the curve of its hull and nearly blinded him, despite the automatic darkening of his visor. He kicked downward and ducked behind the satellite's protective shadow. Still half-blinded by the glare, he bumped into its massive body and rebounded gently. With an effort he reached out and grabbed one of the handgrips studding its surface.

I claim this island for Isabella of Spain. Now where the hell's the hatch?

It was over on the sunlit side, he found after spending several precious minutes searching. It was not difficult to figure out how to open it, even though the instructions were in Cyrillic letters. Kinsman floated head-down and turned the locking mechanism. He felt it click.

For an instant he hesitated. *It might be booby-trapped,* he heard the Colonel warn.

The hell with it.

Kinsman pulled the hatch open. No explosion, no sound at all. A dim light came from within the satellite. Carefully he slid down inside, trailing the umbilical cord. A trio of faint emergency lights glowed weakly.

"Saving battery power," he muttered to himself.

It took a moment for his eyes to adjust to the dimness. Then he began to appreciate what he saw. The satellite was packed with equipment. He could not make out most of it, but it looked like high-powered scientific gear to him. He opened a few panels and saw capacitor banks, heavy-looking magnetic field coils, neatly stacked electronic replacement parts. A particle accelerator device? he wondered. It was not a laser, of that he was certain.

Up forward was living quarters, room enough for three cosmonauts, maybe four. Compact cabinets holding cans of food. Microwave oven. Freezer stocked with more food. Cameras and recording equipment.

"Very cozy."

He stepped back into the main compartment, where the enigmatic scientific gear was. Take home some souvenirs, he thought, opening cabinets, searching. No documents, no instruction books or paperwork of any kind. He found a small set of hand wrenches and unfastened them from their fixture.

Glancing at his watch, he saw that he had five or ten minutes before the estimated arrival of the second Soviet spacecraft. Holding the wrenches in one hand, Kinsman went forward again and looked through the living compartment for some paperwork he could take back to General Hatch and his intelligence aides. Nothing. A blank computer screen and a keyboard marked with Cyrillic letters and Arabic numerals.

Made in CCCP. He let the wrenches hang in midair and reached for the tiny camera in his leg pouch. Snapping away like a manic vacationer, he took pictures of the entire interior of the spacecraft.

As he tucked the camera back and reached for the wrenches once more, something flickered in the corner of his eye. He turned to the observation port and stared out. Nothing but stars: beautiful, cold.

Then another flash. This time his eye caught and held the slim crescent of another spacecraft gliding toward him. Most of the ship was in deep shadow. He would never have found it without the telltale burst from its thrusters.

She's damned close!

Kinsman gripped his tiny horde of stolen wrenches and headed for the hatch. In his haste he got his foot wrapped in the trailing umbilical cord and nearly went tumbling. He wasted a few seconds righting himself, then reached the satellite's hatch and pushed through it.

He saw the approaching Russian spacecraft make its final

115

rendezvous maneuver. A flare of its thrusters and it seemed to come to a stop alongside the satellite.

Kinsman ducked across the satellite's hull, swinging hand over hand along the grips until he was crouched in the shadow of its dark side. Waiting there, trying to figure out what to do next, he coiled his umbilical so that it would be less obvious to whoever was inside the new arrival.

The new spacecraft was considerably smaller than the satellite, built along the lines of Kinsman's own delta-winged Manta. Abruptly a hatch popped open. A space-suited figure emerged and hovered dreamlike for a long moment. Kinsman saw the cosmonaut had no umbilical. Instead, he wore bulging packs on his back: life support and maneuvering units.

How many of them are there? he wondered.

A wispy plume of gas jetted from the cosmonaut's backpack as he sailed purposefully over to the satellite's hatch.

Unconsciously Kinsman hunched deeper in the shadows as the Russian approached. Only one of them; no one else had appeared from the spacecraft. The newcomer reached the still-open hatch of the satellite. For several moments he did not move. Kinsman tried every frequency on his suit radio, to no avail. The Russians used different frequencies; they could not talk to one another, could not listen in on each other's chatter.

The cosmonaut edged away from the satellite and, hovering, turned toward Kinsman's Manta, still hanging a scant fifty meters away.

Kinsman felt himself start to sweat, even in the cold darkness. The cosmonaut jetted away from the satellite, toward the Manta.

Dammitall! Kinsman raged at himself. First rule of warfare, you stupid ass: keep your line of retreat open!

He pushed off the satellite and started floating back toward the Manta. It was nightmarish, drifting through space with agonizing slowness while the cosmonaut sped on ahead. The cosmonaut spotted Kinsman as he cleared the shadow of the satellite and emerged into the sunlight.

For a moment they simply stared at each other, separated

116

by some forty meters of nothingness.

"Get away from that spacecraft!" Kinsman shouted, knowing that their radios were not on the same frequency.

As if to disprove the point, the cosmonaut put a hand on the lip of the Manta's hatch and peered inside. Kinsman flailed his arms and legs trying to raise some speed. Still he moved with hellish slowness. Then he remembered the wrenches he was carrying.

Almost without thinking he tossed the entire handful of them at the cosmonaut. The effort swung him wildly off balance. The Earth slid across his field of vision, then the stars swam by dizzyingly and the Russian satellite. He caught a glimpse of the cosmonaut as the wrenches rained around him. Most of them missed and bounced noiselessly off the Manta's hull. But one banged into the intruder's helmet hard enough to jar him, then rebounded crazily out of sight.

Kinsman lost sight of the Manta as he spun around. Grimly he struggled to straighten himself, using his arms and legs as counterbalances. Finally the stars stopped whirling. He turned and faced the Manta again, but it was upside-down. It did not matter.

The intruder still had one hand on the spacecraft hatch. His free hand was rubbing the spot where the wrench had hit his helmet. He looked ludicrously like a little boy rubbing a bump on his head.

"That means back off, stranger," Kinsman muttered. "No trespassing. U.S. property. Beware of the eagle. Next time I'll crack your helmet in half."

The cosmonaut turned slightly and reached for one of the equipment packs attached to his belt. A weird-looking tool appeared in his hand. Kinsman drifted helplessly and watched the cosmonaut take up a section of his umbilical line. Then he applied the tool to it. Sparks flashed.

Electron torch! He's trying to cut my line! He'll kill me!

Frantically Kinsman began clawing along the long umbilical line hand over hand. All he could see, all he could think of, was that flashing torch eating into his lifeline.

Desperately he grabbed the line in both hands and snapped it hard. Again he tumbled wildly, but he saw the wave created by his snap race down the line. The piece of the

117

cord that the cosmonaut held suddenly bucked out of his hand. The torch spun away and winked off.

Both of them moved at once.

The cosmonaut jetted away from the Manta, going after the torch. Kinsman hurled himself directly toward the hatch. He grasped its rim with both hands, chest heaving, visor fogging slightly from the heat of his exertion and fear.

Duck inside, slam shut, and get the hell out of here.

But he did not move. Instead he watched the cosmonaut, a strange, sun-etched figure now, drifting some twenty meters away, quietly sizing up the situation.

That sonofabitch tried to kill me.

Kinsman coiled catlike on the edge of the hatch and sprang at his enemy. The cosmonaut reached for the jet controls at his belt but Kinsman slammed into him and they both went hurtling through space, tumbling and clawing at each other. It was an unearthly struggle, human fury in the infinite calm of star-studded blackness. No sound except your own harsh breath and the bone-conducted shock of colliding bodies.

They wheeled out of the spacecraft's shadow and into the painful glare of the sun. The glorious beauty of Earth spread out below them. In a cold rage, Kinsman grabbed the airhose that connected the cosmonaut's oxygen tank with his helmet. He hesitated a moment and glanced into the bulbous plastic helmet. All he could see was the back of the cosmonaut's head, covered with a dark skintight flying hood. With a vicious yank Kinsman snapped the airhose out of its mounting. A white spray of gas burst from the backpack. The cosmonaut jerked twice, spasmodically, then went inert.

With a conscious effort Kinsman unclenched his teeth. His jaw ached. He was trembling and soaked in a cold sweat.

He saw his father's face. They'll make a killer out of you! The military exists to kill.

He released his death grip on his enemy. The two human forms drifted slightly apart. The dead cosmonaut turned gently as Kinsman floated alongside. The sun glinted brightly on the white space suit and shone full into the enemy's lifeless, terror-stricken face.

Kinsman looked into that face for an eternally long

118

moment and felt the life drain out of him. He dragged himself back to the Manta, sealed the hatch, and cracked open the air tanks with automatic, unthinking motions. He flicked on the radio and ignored the flood of interrogating voices that streamed up from the ground.

"Bring me in. Program the AGS to bring me in, full automatic. Just bring me in."

It was six weeks before Kinsman saw Colonel Murdock again. He sat tensely before the wide mahogany desk while Murdock beamed at him, almost as brightly as the sunshine outside the Colonel's office.

"You look thinner in civvies," the Colonel said.

"I've lost weight."

Murdock made a meaningless gesture. "I'm sorry I haven't had a chance to see you sooner. What with the intelligence and State Department people crawling around here the past few weeks, and all the paperwork on your citation and your medical disability leave . . . I haven't had a chance to, eh, congratulate you on your mission. It was a fine piece of work."

Kinsman said nothing.

"General Hatch was very pleased. He recommended you for the Silver Star himself."

"I know."

"You're a hero, Kinsman." There was wonder in the Colonel's girlish voice. "A real honest-to-God hero."

Again Kinsman remained silent.

Murdock suppressed a frown. "The Russians won't make a squawk about it, from what the State Department boys tell me. They're keeping the whole thing hushed up. We made a deal with them. We don't complain about them testing a beam weapon in orbit and they don't complain about losing a cosmonaut."

"We both lose," Kinsman said.

"But you've proved that the Air Force has an important mission to perform in space, by God! The only way we could tell they were cheating on the treaty was to look into their damned satellite. Bet the Congress will change our name to the Aerospace Force now!"

119

"I committed a murder."

For a long moment Murdock was silent. He drummed his fingers on his desktop. "It's one of those things," he said finally. "It had to be done."

"No, it didn't," Kinsman insisted quietly. "I could have gone back inside the Manta and de-orbited."

"You killed an enemy soldier. You protected your nation's frontier. Sure, you feel rotten now, but you'll get over it."

"You didn't see the face I saw inside that helmet."

Murdock shuffled papers on his desk. "Well . . . okay, it was rough. You're getting a medical furlough out of it when there's really nothing wrong with you. For Chrissakes, what more do you want?"

"I don't know. I've got to take some time to think it over."

"What?" Murdock stared hard at him. "What are you talking about?"

"Read the debriefing report," Kinsman said tiredly.

"It . . . eh, hasn't come down to my level. Too sensitive. But I don't understand what's got you so spooked. You killed an enemy soldier. You ought to be proud . . ."

"Enemy," Kinsman echoed bleakly. "She couldn't have been more than twenty years old."

Murdock's face went slack. "She?"

"That's right," said Kinsman. "She. Your honest-to-God hero murdered a terrified girl. That's something to be proud of, isn't it?"

Age 31

LIEUTENANT COLONEL MARIAN CAMPBELL drummed her fingers lightly on her desktop. The psychological record of Captain Kinsman lay open before her. Across the desk sat the Captain himself.

She appraised him with a professional eye. Kinsman was lean, dark, rather good-looking in a brooding way. His gray-blue eyes were steady. His hands rested calmly in his lap; long, slim pianist's fingers. No tics, no twitches. He looked almost indifferent to his surroundings. Withdrawn, Colonel Campbell concluded.

"Do you know why you're here?" she asked him.

"I think so," he replied with no hesitation.

Marian leaned back in her chair. She was a big-boned woman who had to remind herself constantly to keep her voice down. She had a natural tendency to talk at people in a parade-ground shout. Not a good attribute for a psychiatrist.

"Tell me," she said, "what you think you're here for."

When she tried to keep her voice soft it came out gravelly, rough. The voice had the power for an opera stage or an ancient amphitheater, despite the fact that its owner was tone-deaf.

Kinsman took a deep breath, like an athlete about to exert himself to the utmost. Or like a man who is bored.

"I've been under psychiatric observation for five months now. Suspended from active duty. Your people have been trying to figure out the effect on me of killing that Russian girl."

Colonel Campbell nodded. "Go on."

"You're the chief of the psychiatric section. I guess my case is in your hands for a final decision."

"That's quite true," she said. "It's up to me to decide

121

whether you return to active duty or not."

Kinsman regarded her steadily for a moment, then shifted his attention to the window. The blinds were half closed against the burning afternoon sun. For a moment he seemed like a little boy in a stuffy classroom, yearning for the bell that would free him to go outside and play.

"Colonel Murdock wants you permanently removed from duty. He'd like you honorably discharged from the Air Force, except that it might look bad in Washington."

"I'm not surprised," Kinsman said.

"Why not?"

He made a small motion of his shoulders that might have been a shrug. "Murdock would be happy to get rid of me. I'm not his type of marionette." He considered that for a moment, then added, "That's not paranoia. You can check it out with any of the other astronauts."

Marian chuckled. "We already have. You're not paranoid."

"I didn't think so."

"But you do seem to have some problems. I've got to determine if your problems are too big to allow you to fly again."

"That's what I thought."

She did not respond and he did not add anything. They sat looking at each other across the cluttered desk for several moments. Colonel Campbell's office bore the privilege of her rank and station. It was just another one of the starkly functional offices at the Air Force hospital, but a lieutenant colonel who is chief psychiatrist has more latitude in decorating her office than most others. The square little room was festooned with hanging plants. A young rubber tree sprouted in the corner near the window. Instead of a couch, there was a long metal stand bearing exotic tropical flowers.

He's outstaring me, thought Marian Campbell.

"Well," she said at last, "how do you feel about all this? What do you want to do?"

This time his answer was slow in coming. "I don't honestly know. Sometimes I think I ought to get out of the Air Force, accept a medical discharge. But that would take me out of the space program, and that's all I really want."

"To be out of the space program."

"No!" he snapped. "To be *in* it. NASA's sending astronauts to the Moon again. I want to be part of that."

"You want to go to the Moon?"

"Yes."

"To get away from here?"

"As far away as I can," he answered fervently.

She shook her head. "You can't run away from your problems."

Kinsman gave her a look of pitying superiority. "You've never been in orbit, have you?"

"No, of course not."

"Then you don't know. That business about not running away from your problems—it's a slogan. Pure crap. Like telling poor people that money can't buy happiness. You get your feet off the ground, get out of this office and up into a plane where you can be on your own—you'll get away from your problems easily enough."

"I've done my share of flying," she replied. "But you have to come down sometime. You have to return and face things."

"I suppose so." He looked toward the window and the hot Texas afternoon on the other side of the blinds. "You know, I sometimes wonder if some airplane crashes . . . some of the unexplained ones . . . aren't caused by the pilot's unconscious desire to get away from his problems for good."

"Suicide?" She suppressed an impulse to make a note in his file. Do it after he leaves; don't do anything now to break his train of thought.

"Not suicide exactly. Not the desire to die. But . . . well, every now and then a really good pilot wracks up his plane for no apparent reason. Maybe he just didn't want to put his feet back on the ground."

"How do you think you'd feel if you were allowed to fly again?"

His grin was immediate. "Terrific!"

"You wouldn't try to . . . avoid your problems?"

"No." The grin turned into a knowing smile. "I've got a better way to get rid of my problems. That's what the Moon is for."

Colonel Campbell thought, Never-never land.

"That's the one thing I want," Kinsman said. "The one

thing I need. To return to active astronaut status. To get in on the lunar program."

"But that's not an Air Force program," Colonel Campbell said. "The civilians are doing it—NASA and the Russians, isn't it? It's a cooperative program."

Nodding, he answered, "But they're looking for experienced astronauts. The Air Force is letting some of our people work for NASA on detached duty. Friends of mine have already been to the Moon."

He was set up for the tough questions now.

"What do you think your real problem is?" Colonel Campbell asked, letting her voice grow to its normal powerful volume.

Kinsman looked startled for a moment. "I killed that Russian girl . . ." His facial expression went from surprise to pain.

"She tried to kill you, didn't she?"

"Yes."

"You're a military officer. You were on a military mission. The satellite you were inspecting might have had weaponry on it that could have killed millions of people."

"I know that."

"Then why did you become . . ." She reached for the glasses on her desk and perched them on the tip of her nose. Reading from the file, ". . . despondent, withdrawn, hostile to your fellow officers." She looked up at him. "It also says you lost weight and complained of insomnia."

Kinsman hunched forward in his chair, clasped his long-fingered hands together. Looking up at her, he asked, "Have you ever killed someone?"

Marian Campbell moved her head the barest centimeter to indicate *no*.

"Lots of Air Force officers have," Kinsman said. "But at remote distances. You press a button and a machine falls out of the air or a building on the ground explodes. I killed her in hand-to-hand combat. I saw her face."

"You were doing your duty . . ."

"I could have done my duty without killing her!"

"In hindsight."

He ran a hand through his hair. "You ever hear of Richard Bong?"

124

"Who?"

"I've had the chance to read up on Air Force history quite a lot over the past few months," Kinsman said. "Dick Bong was a fighter pilot in World War Two. In the Pacific. Our top ace. Shot down forty Japanese planes in the first couple of years of the war. All in aerial combat, man-to-man victories, not strafing planes on the ground."

Colonel Campbell regretted that she had not turned on the tape recorder in the bottom drawer of her desk. Too late now, she chided herself.

"His commanding general came over to the island where he was stationed to pin a medal on him. The Japanese pulled an air raid on the base in the middle of the ceremonies. Bong and the general dived into the same slit trench. One of the Jap planes was hit by antiaircraft fire and started to burn. The Japanese pilot didn't have a parachute. Or maybe it just didn't open. Anyway, he jumped out of his burning plane and fell to the airstrip like a rock. He hit the ground just a few feet in front of Bong and the general."

"But what does—"

"Bong never shot down another plane for the rest of the war. He flew combat missions, but he couldn't hit anything with his guns."

"I see," Colonel Campbell said softly. "I understand."

"It makes a difference," said Kinsman. "It's one thing to kill by remote control. It's something else when you see who you've killed, face-to-face."

"And you think that's what's bothering you?"

Kinsman nodded.

"But you can handle it now?" she prompted him.

"As long as I'm not put into combat missions," he answered.

"And the fact that the person you killed was a woman has nothing to do with it?"

Kinsman's jaw dropped open and suddenly he was glaring at her. "How the hell should I know?" he shouted. "How high is up?"

"I don't know, Captain. You tell me."

He turned angrily away from her. There was perspiration beading his brow, Colonel Campbell noticed.

"That's enough for today, Captain. You may go."

She watched him stand up slowly, looking slightly puzzled. He went to the door, hesitated, then opened it and left
the office without looking back.

Colonel Campbell opened the bottom drawer of her desk
and pulled out the book-sized tape recorder. She turned it on
and began speaking into the built-in microphone. After more
than fifteen minutes she concluded:

"He's definitely looking for help. That's good. But we're
nowhere near his problem yet. We've only scratched the
surface. He's built a shell around himself and now not only
can no one break through it to get to him, he can't crack it
himself to get out. It could be something from his childhood;
we'll have to check out the family."

She clicked the recorder's STOP button and turned to look
out the window. The hot Texas sky was turning to molten
copper as the sun went down. A helicopter droned overhead
somewhere, like a lazy summertime dragonfly. The screeching whine of a jet fighter shrilled past.

She turned the tape recorder on again. "One thing is
certain," she said. "Killing the cosmonaut was only the
triggering trauma. There's more, buried underneath. If it's
buried too far down, if we can't get to it quickly, he's finished
as an Air Force officer. And as an astronaut."

The breeze whipping across the flight line did little to
alleviate the heat. It felt like the breath from a hot oven. The
sun beat down like a palpable force, broiling the life juices out
of you.

Marian Campbell walked slowly around the plane,
checking the control surfaces, the propeller, sweating in her
zippered coveralls and waiting for Kinsman to show up. It was
a single-engine plane with broad, stubby wings and a high
bulbous canopy that made it look like a one-eyed insect. It
was painted bright red and yellow except for the engine
cowling, where permanent black streaks of oil stains marred
the decor.

She saw a tall lithe figure approaching through the
shimmering heat haze along the flight line. The sun baked the
concrete ramp so that it felt like standing on a griddle. Come
on, she groused to herself, before I melt into a puddle. Then

126

she grinned sheepishly. It would be a damned big puddle, she knew.

Kinsman was in civilian clothes, an open-necked short-sleeved shirt and light blue slacks. He looked wary as he came up to the plane.

"No need to salute," Marian called to him. "We're off duty, okay?"

He nodded and put out a hand to touch the plane's wing. The metal must have been scorchingly hot but Kinsman ran his fingers along it lightly and almost smiled.

"Piper Cherokee. She's an old bird, but she still looks good," he said.

"Are you talking about the plane or about me?" Marian asked.

He looked startled more than amused. "The plane, of course, Colonel."

"My name's Marian . . . as in Robin Hood. And yes, I know the joke: 'Who's Maid Marian? Everybody!'"

Kinsman still did not smile.

With an inner sigh, Marian asked, "Do I call you Chet, Chester, or what?"

"Chet."

"Okay, Chet. Let's get upstairs where the air is cooler."

She climbed heavily up onto the wing and squeezed through the cabin hatch. Kinsman followed her and sat in the copilot's seat, on the right. He stuck his foot out to keep the hatch open as Marian gunned the engine to life.

He stayed silent, watching, as she taxied to the very end of the two-mile-long runway. It had been built to accommodate heavy bombers. This puddle-jumper could take off and land along the runway seven times and still have concrete to spare ahead of it.

They got the control tower's clearance, Kinsman dogged the hatch shut, and the little engine buzzed its hardest as they rolled down the runway and lifted into the air.

Marian banked the plane and made a right turn as ordered by the tower controller. They headed away from the Air Force base, across the Texas scrubland.

"Want to see the Alamo?" she asked.

"Sure," said Kinsman.

She asked the controllers for a route to San Antonio.

"Whose plane is this?" Kinsman asked as they climbed to cruising altitude.

"Mine," said Marian.

"Yours? You own it?"

"Sure. You think you jet jocks are the only guys who like to fly? Why do you think I joined the Air Force in the first place?"

He grinned at her. "You like to fly."

"Doesn't everybody?"

She could see him visibly relaxing. They were barely five thousand feet above the ground but already he felt safe and insulated from the pressures below.

"Want to take over for a while?" she asked.

"Sure."

She let go of the controls and Kinsman took the wheel in his hands.

"No aerobatics unless you warn me first," she offered.

"I'm not a stunt flier."

"It's a good thing you're slim," Marian said. "It's usually a pretty tight squeeze in here with most men. I take up more than my fair share of space."

He did not take his eyes off the horizon, but he asked, "Is this supposed to be some form of therapy? I mean, why'd you invite me for this?"

"Because I know you like to fly and I thought you could use some relaxation. We're not just brain-pickers, you know. We're doctors. We're concerned about your overall health."

Kinsman made a small sound that might have been a grunt. "One of your doctors liked to talk to me whenever I tried playing the piano down in the rec hall. Every time I'd sit down to play he'd pop up and start asking me questions. Then he said I was hostile and suspicious."

Marian laughed. "That was Jeffers. He's the idiot on my staff."

They flew for a while and chatted easily enough, but he never got close to anything about his emotional problems. Finally Marian had to dredge the subject up to the surface.

"We had to check back into your family history," she said.

"I know. I got a phone call from a friend."

"Senator McGrath?"

"Yes. He wanted to know if it was okay to talk to you. I told him it was."

"We had a good chat on the telephone."

"What did you find out about me?"

Marian pursed her lips for a moment and considered what she would do if he suddenly decided to dive the plane into the ground.

"He told me about your parents. The conflict with your father. He died while you were stationed in California, didn't he?"

Kinsman nodded. "While I was in orbit, as a matter of fact. I had gone to see him while he was in the hospital, like a dutiful son. He didn't recognize me. Or at least, he didn't admit to recognizing me."

"That's a pity," Marian said.

Very coolly, Kinsman replied, "We didn't see each other very clearly when he was alive and well, you know."

He talked easily enough, seemingly holding nothing back. But it was like a blank wall. All he wanted was to be reassigned to astronaut duty for the lunar missions. Nothing else seemed to matter to him. And yet there was something choking him. Something inside his brain that had put a wall around him, an invisible barrier that cut him off from any real human contact.

"I've been waiting for the zinger," he said, after nearly an hour of talk.

Marian's hands were resting in her lap. "The zinger? What's that?"

He glanced at her. "Aren't you going to ask me if I'm impotent? Jeffers and all your other shrinks did."

Is he asking for help? "I've read your file," Marian answered. "You told them you're not."

"I told them I don't think I am."

"Explain?"

"I've been more or less restricted to quarters for the past five months. Not much of a chance to find out."

"Go on . . ."

"I can get an erection easily enough," Kinsman went on, as clinically cool as if he were reading from a textbook. "I've awoken from my nightmares with a hard-on."

"Nocturnal emissions?" Marian asked.

"Wet dreams? Yeah, a few times."

"Then you're functional."

"The equipment works," he said, still as distant as the horizon. "What bothers me is I haven't felt much like trying. I mean, it's been five *months* and I haven't even felt horny. I haven't even made a pass at any of the nurses."

We know, Colonel Campbell said to herself.

"You're closer to me right now than any woman's been since . . . since . . ."

Suddenly his hands were shaking. The plane, built for amateur pilots, flew onward as steadily as a plow horse.

Marian took over the controls as Kinsman sagged back in his seat.

"Since when?" she prompted.

"You know."

"Tell me."

"Since I murdered that girl in orbit. Since I killed her. I ripped the air line out of her helmet and killed her. Deliberately. I could've backed off. I could've gotten back into my own craft and de-orbited. But I killed her. I murdered her."

"Good," said Marian.

"Good?" He glared at her with pain-filled eyes.

"It's good that you're showing some emotion. You've kept it frozen beneath the surface for too long. You've been acting more like a robot than a human being for the past five months."

Kinsman looked down at his hands. They were still trembling.

"It's all right, Chet. It's all over and done with. There's nothing you can do to bring her back. What you have to decide now is . . . where do you want to go from here?"

He pressed his hands palms-down on his thighs. "What did Richard the Third say? 'Let's to it, pell-mell. If not to heaven, then hand in hand to hell.'"

Marian gave an unladylike snort. "Neither one," she said, pointing off to her left. "It's only San Antonio."

The Alamo is the heart of San Antonio, but the four corners of the city are held by military bases. Colonel Campbell landed her plane at Kelly Air Force Base and they commandeered a synfueled gray sedan from the motor pool to go to town.

GENTLEMEN WILL TAKE OFF THEIR HATS, read the sign above the Alamo's front entrance. Marian saw that most of the visitors crowding the old shrine this muggy late afternoon were either Mexicans or Mexican-Americans. The signs on the displays spoke of the great American triumph that won Texas its independence. But it was only a temporary triumph, Marian saw. The erstwhile losers of the Mexican-American battle were winning the war over the long haul, simply outbreeding the gringos and reclaiming the territory they had temporarily lost.

Outside, in the shade cast by the graceful trees beyond the old mission's battered walls, Kinsman suddenly asked, "May I take you to dinner?"

Marian felt pleased. "It's been some time since a young man has invited me to dinner."

He grinned at her. "Maybe you can help me with my problem."

Her cheeks went hot and she cursed herself for an idiot. He's joking with you, she told herself sternly. You're old enough to be his . . . well, his big sister, anyway.

"You are qualified for I.F.R., aren't you?" Kinsman asked, suddenly serious again. "No problem if we stay out after dark."

Marian nodded. "I'd feel a lot safer, though, if you made the instrument landing. I don't like landing at night."

"Okay," he said. "So let's find some dinner. My treat."

They found a dinner theater in one of the hotels along the scenic riverway park. The ballroom floor was covered with small round tables jammed so close together that chair-backs touched each other whenever someone wanted to get up. Marian wrinkled her nose. This was too much like New York or Chicago. Where was the Old West, where cattle barons dined in the regal splendor of ornately paneled restaurants with high ceilings and crystal chandeliers?

The tiny stage set up at one end of the ballroom was for a revival of a show featuring songs written by a Parisian café entertainer named Jacques Brel. Only two men and two women, in street clothes. The management did not spend lavishly on the entertainment, Marian thought. But the

131

singers were excellent and the songs highly charged, emotional, theatrical, pointed.

Marian began watching Kinsman in the darkened ballroom as the singers hit antiwar themes again and again. He sat calmly, laughed at the right places, applauded along with everyone else. Until a song titled "Next."

He sat straighter in his chair as the theme of the song became clear: a young European soldier being marched along with his comrades into a mobile army whorehouse, "gift of the army, free of course." Marian felt her eyes burning brighter than the stage lights as she watched Kinsman's face freeze in something very close to horror.

His hand slowly reached out toward her and she grasped it tightly. He hung on as the lead male sang:

"All the naked and the dead
Should hold each other's hands
As they watch me scream at night
In a dream no one understands."

The song ended and Kinsman released her hand. When the show finally finished and the ceiling lights came on once more, he avoided looking directly at Marian. He seemed embarrassed, more than a little.

They drove back to Kelly through the muggy hot night in silence. Marian was content to wait until they were airborne again before trying to open him up. He talked better off the ground; he seemed more relaxed up there. They checked the car back into the motor pool and allowed a sleepy-eyed corporal to drive them in a jeep to the flight line.

Kinsman hopped up on the Cherokee's wing and pulled the hatch open, ducked inside, and took the pilot's seat. Then he helped Marian settle her bulk in the right-hand seat. He checked the control panel's gauges carefully, got his clearance from the tower controller, and taxied out to the runway. The edge lights stretched like glowing pearls, seemingly off to the horizon.

As he waited for final takeoff clearance he revved the engine. The whole plane shuddered and strained like an excited terrier being held in check by a leash. Somehow the engine roar seemed louder in the darkness to Marian. And then they were racing down the runway and up into the air. Kinsman handled the plane smoothly, his hands sure and steady. As they climbed to cruising altitude Marian saw a sky full of stars above them and the even more numerous lights of San Antonio below.

"One of the best Mexican restaurants this side of the Rio Grande is down there," she said, over the drone of the engine.

"Really?" Kinsman replied.

Marian nodded vigorously. "Too bad we missed it."

"Yeah. The food we had wasn't all that good, was it?"

"But I enjoyed the show."

Kinsman might have nodded in the darkness. She could not tell.

"How did you like it?" she asked.

"The show?"

"Yes."

Suddenly he started laughing, a soft, happy, satisfied chuckle.

Puzzled, Marian asked, "What's funny?"

"You are."

"I'm *funny*?" She did not know whether to be glad or angry.

"No, not you yourself," Kinsman corrected. "It's the situation that's funny. The relationship between us."

He turned to their homeward course, changed the frequency on the radio for the mid-route controller, then turned in his seat toward her.

"Look," he said, "you know damned well that something clicked in my head during the show, when I grabbed for your hand. And I know you know. But you're trying to lead up to the subject subtly, to see if you can get me to talk about it."

"What clicked?" Marian felt eager, as if she were a hunter close to her quarry.

"During that song I finally realized what the hell has been bothering me."

"Yes?"

"They got to me," he said flatly.

Marian felt her eyebrows rise. "They got to you? Who . . . ?"

Kinsman said, "All these years I've been telling myself

133

that I'm my own man. I joined the Air Force to get into space, to get away from all the ugliness of Earth. But I didn't escape it. I couldn't."

"You brought the ugliness along with you."

"Yeah." He was silent for a long moment. "I murdered that cosmonaut. Maybe if she had been a man I wouldn't feel so badly about it. But the thing is—they got to me."

"Who?" Marian demanded.

"The Air Force," he said. "The training. The military mind-set."

"I don't understand."

Gesturing with one hand in the cramped cabin, Kinsman said, "Look, when I joined the Air Force it was strictly to be an astronaut. Sure, they put me through the same training everybody gets and even made me fly combat in Cyprus. But I never fired a gun or a missile. Never."

"So?"

"So once I got into the astronaut program I thought I had it made. I had what I wanted. The Air Force hadn't gotten to me. Their training hadn't turned me into a military machine. I was my own man."

Marian began to feel the inner tingle she always got when a puzzle became clear to her.

"But I was wrong," Kinsman went on. His voice was serious now, but not somber. Not morose or wooden. "When I got into a combat situation—hand-to-hand fight, yet—all that military training took over. I wasn't an astronaut any-more. I was a fighting machine. A trained killer. A military automaton. I killed her just the way an infantryman becomes conditioned to sticking a bayonet into another human being's belly."

"And you think that's what's been bothering you?" Marian asked, as softly as she knew how.

"For the past five months I've been trying to figure it out. How could I have done it? How in the hell could I have deliberately ripped out a human being's air line? How could I willingly kill somebody?"

"And now you have the answer."

"Yes." It was an unshakably firm response. "I'm not as smart as I thought I was. The military training got to me. God knows, put me in the same situation and I might even do the same thing all over again."

"Chet, listen to me very carefully," Marian said slowly. "You *think* you have the answer and you're feeling pretty good about it . . ."

"Damned right!"

"But what you have is only the beginning of the answer. There's still a lot more, buried down inside you. A lot that you haven't brought up into the light yet."

He shook his head. "I don't think so."

"Listen to me!" Marian urged. "You've kept a shell around yourself all your life. Your Quaker upbringing. Your conflict with your father. Your Air Force duties. The one time you let go, the one time you let your emotions override your self-control, you kill a person. A woman. A girl. Now you've clamped that self-control down again and made your shell thicker than ever. You've isolated yourself from any real human contact . . ."

As if none of her words had penetrated his awareness, Kinsman said, "If you keep me off-duty, under observation, for much longer, Murdock's going to drum me out. You know that."

"I can protect you."

"You can't keep me proficient. He can drop me from the astronaut corps—for good."

"Yes," she admitted. "That's true."

"What I need now is to get back to active duty. But not with the Air Force. I want to get into NASA's lunar exploration program."

"You want to run off to the Moon?"

"It's not running away. I know better now. I know myself better."

"Well enough to risk your life, and the lives of others?"

He grinned at her. She could see his teeth in the faint light from the instrument panel. "You're trusting me with your life right now, aren't you?"

Almost ruefully she admitted, "I suppose I am."

"Just tell it to Murdock."

The next morning Lieutenant Colonel Marian Campbell was back in uniform, back in her office, sitting behind her desk. Colonel Murdock's round, bald face looked distinctly

135

unhappy, even in the small screen of the telephone display.

"Just what are you trying to tell me, Colonel Campbell?" he asked testily.

She took a deep breath, then replied, "In my opinion, Colonel, Captain Kinsman is now fit to resume his duties."

"Resume . . . ? But I thought he was psychologically, er, well . . . unbalanced."

"He was troubled by what happened to him on his last mission, of course. Anyone would be. But in my opinion, he's worked through those troubles and he's ready to go back to active duty."

Murdock's face wrinkled with suspicion. "I don't get it. For five months you shrinks have been working him over without a word of progress. Now all of a sudden you say he's okay?"

Feeling almost as if she should cross her fingers, Marian Campbell answered, "It happens that way sometimes. He's gained the insight he needed to understand what happened to him. He's adjusted to it. He's fit for duty."

"Not under me," Murdock said fervently. "I'm going to transfer him out of here just as soon as he comes marching through my door."

"You can't do that!"

Murdock looked startled. Her voice had boomed.

"I mean," Marian said, trying to tone it down, "that I would recommend he be allowed to continue in the astronaut program. It's what he's trained for and what he enjoys doing."

"That doesn't mean—"

She overrode him. "I understand there's a shortage of trained personnel with his qualifications. It would be against Air Force policy to waste a man of his training and experience in a different slot."

"If he's psychologically fit for such duty," Murdock retorted.

"He is," Marian said.

The Colonel gave her a shrewd stare. It seemed almost ludicrous, his face was so tiny on the phone screen. But still it sent a shiver of apprehension along Marian's spine.

"You are guaranteeing that he's mentally sound?" Murdock asked.

Marian Campbell stiffened her back. "There are no guarantees in the medical profession, Colonel. But I will personally draft the report on Captain Kinsman, recommending that he be returned to the duties for which he has been trained."

"That ties my hands if I want to transfer him."

"Unless you transfer him to the NASA program," Marian blurted.

Murdock's face took on a knowing leer. "So that's how he worked out his emotional problem. Twisted you around his little finger, didn't he?"

Just to wipe the smirk off his face, Marian made herself smile and say, "It wasn't his *little* finger, Colonel."

Murdock's face flamed red. He snapped, "Well, then write your report and make your recommendation! I'll handle my own problems my own way." He cut the connection and the phone screen went blank.

Marian leaned back in her chair. Well, old gal, now you've got a reputation for screwing around with your patients. She almost wished it were true.

She hauled the tape recorder out of its drawer and started to dictate her final report on Kinsman. But in the back of her mind she was thinking, What else can you do? Keep him here? That will kill him just as surely as cutting off his oxygen. You've got to let him go.

Over the faint hum of the air-conditioning she thought she heard distant piano music. From the recreation hall. A light, happy piece of Mozart. She listened for several minutes. No one interrupted the pianist.

So now he can go to the Moon. Maybe he'll find what he needs there. But he won't. He's locked up inside himself. If you let him go, he'll never break free. He'll carry that shell around him forever. You know that. You know it and you're letting him go. He's going to kill himself, one way or the other. Himself, and maybe others besides. And you're letting him go out and do it because you're too weak to keep him here and watch him die one day at a time.

She turned on the tape recorder and watched the cassette slowly turning as she fought back an urge to cry.

Age 32

"ANY WORD FROM him yet?"

"Huh? No, nothing."

Kinsman swore to himself as he stood on the open platform of the little lunar rocket jumper. It was his second trip to the Moon and it was not going well.

"Say, where are you now?" Bok's voice sounded gritty with static in Kinsman's helmet earphones.

"Up on the rim. He must've gone inside the damned crater."

"The rim? How'd you get . . ."

"Found a flat spot for the jumper. Don't think I walked this far, do you? I'm not as nutty as the priest."

"But you're supposed to stay down here on the plain! The crater's off-limits."

"Tell that to our holy friar. He's the one who marched up here. I'm just following the seismic rigs he's been planting every three, four klicks."

He could sense Bok shaking his head. "Kinsman, if there are twenty officially approved ways to do a job, I swear you'll pick the twenty-second."

"If the first twenty-one are lousy."

"Mission control is going to be damned upset with you. You won't get off with just a reprimand this time."

"I suppose mission control would prefer that we just let the priest stay lost."

"You're not going inside the crater, are you?" Bok's voice edged up half an octave. "It's too risky."

Kinsman almost laughed. "You think sitting inside that aluminum casket you're in is *safe*?"

The earphones went silent. With a sigh, Kinsman wished for the tenth time that hour that he could scratch his

138

twelve-day-old beard. Get zipped into the suit and the itches start. He did not need a mirror to know that his face was haggard, sleepless, his black beard mean-looking.

He stepped down from the jumper—a rocket motor with a railed platform and some equipment on it, nothing more —and planted his boots on the solid rock of the ringwall's crest. With a twist of his shoulders to settle the weight of his bulky backpack he shambled over to the packet of seismic instruments and the fluorescent marker that the priest had left there.

"He came right up to the top and now he's off on the yellow brick road, playing Moon explorer. Stupid bastard."

Did you really think you'd leave human stupidity behind you? a voice in his head asked. Or human guilt?

Reluctantly he looked into the crater. The brutally short horizon cut across the middle of its floor, but the central peak stuck its worn head up among the solemn stars. Beyond it there was nothing but dizzying blackness, an abrupt end to the solid world and the beginning of infinity.

Damn the priest! God's gift to geology. And I've got to play guardian angel for him.

Kinsman turned back and looked outward from the crater rim. He could see the lighted radio mast and squat return rocket, far below on the plain. He even convinced himself that he saw the mound of rubble marking their buried base shelter, where Bok lay curled safely in his bunk. The Russian base was far over the horizon, almost on the other side of the Mare Nubium. He could talk to the Russians by bouncing a signal off one of the commsats orbiting the Moon. But what good would that do? They were much farther away from the wandering priest than he was.

"Any sign of him?" Bok's voice asked.

"Sure," Kinsman retorted. "He left me a big map with an X to mark the treasure."

"Don't get sore at me!"

"Why not? You're sitting inside. I've got to find our fearless geologist."

"Regulations say one man's got to remain in the base at all times."

But not the *same* one man, Kinsman replied silently.

"Anyway," Bok went on, "he's still got a few hours'

oxygen left. Let him putter around inside the crater for a while. He'll come back under his own power."

"Not before his air runs out. Besides, he's officially missing. Missed his last two check-in calls. Houston knows it, by now. My assignment is to scout his last known position. Another of those sweet regs."

Silence again. Bok did not like being alone in the Base, Kinsman knew.

"Why don't you come on back in," the astronomer's voice said at last, "until he calls in. Then you can go out again and get him with the jumper. You'll be running out of air yourself before you can find him in the crater."

"I've got to try."

"You can't make up the rules as you go along, Kinsman! This isn't the Air Force; you're not a hotshot jet jockey anymore. NASA has rules, regulations. They'll ground you if you don't follow their game plan."

"Maybe."

"You don't even like the priest!" Bok was almost shouting now, the fear-induced anger making his voice shrill, ugly. "You've been tripping all over yourself to stay clear of him whenever you're both inside the base."

Kinsman felt his jaw clench. So it shows. If you're not careful you'll tip them both off.

Aloud, he replied, "I'm going to look around. Give me an hour. Call Houston and give them a complete report; all they've got so far is a gap in the automatic record where the priest's last two check-ins ought to be. And stay inside the shelter until I come back." Or until a relief crew arrives, he added silently.

"You're wasting your time. And taking unnecessary risks. They'll ground you for sure."

"Wish me luck," Kinsman said.

A delay. Then, "Luck. I'll sit tight here."

Despite himself, Kinsman grinned. I know damned well you'll sit tight there. Some survey team. One goes over the hill and the other stays in his bunk for two weeks straight.

He gazed out at the bleak landscape surrounded by starry emptiness. Something caught in his memory.

"They can't scare me with their empty spaces," he

muttered to himself. There was more to the verse but he could not recall it.

"Can't scare me," he repeated softly, shuffling to the inner rim of the crater's ringwall. He walked very deliberately, like a tired old man, and tried to see from inside his bulbous helmet exactly where he was placing his feet.

The barren slopes fell away in gently terraced steps until, many kilometers below, they melted into the cracked and pockmarked crater floor. Looks easy . . . too easy. Like the steps to hell. With a shrug that was weighted down by the lunar suit's backpack, Kinsman started to descend into the crater.

He picked his way across the gravelly terraces and crawled feet-first down the breaks between them. The bare rocks were slippery and sometimes sharp. Kinsman went slowly, step by careful step, trying to make certain that he did not tear the metallic fabric of his suit. His world was cut off now and circled by the dark rocks. Inside the vast crater he was cut off from the direct radio link with Bok; in the shadow of these terraced rock walls, he could not even make contact with the communications satellites orbiting over the Moon's equator. The only sounds were the creaking of the suit's joints, the electrical hum of the pump that circulated water through its inner lining, the faint wheeze of the helmet air blower. And his own heavy breathing. Alone, all alone. A solitary microcosm. One living creature in the universe.

They cannot scare me with their empty spaces.

Between stars—on stars where no human race is. There was still more to it: the tag line that he could not remember.

Finally he had to stop. The suit was heating up too much from his exertion. He took a marker beacon from the backpack and planted it on the broken ground. The Moon's gray rocks, churned by eons of infalling micrometeors and whipped into a frozen froth, had an unfinished look about them, as if somebody had been blacktopping the place but stopped before he could apply the final smoothing touches.

From a pouch on his belt Kinsman took a small spool of wire. Plugging one end into the radio outlet on his helmet, he held the spool at arm's length and released its catch. He could not see it in this dim light, but he felt the spool's spring fire the antenna wire high and out into the crater.

"Father Lemoyne," he called as the antenna drifted slowly in the Moon's gentle gravity. "Father Lemoyne, can you hear me?"

No answer.

Down another flight, Kinsman told himself.

After two more stops and nearly an hour of sweaty descent, Kinsman got his answer.

"Here . . ." a weak voice responded. "I'm here . . ."

"Where?" Kinsman snapped, every sense alert, all fatigue forgotten. "Do something. Make a light."

". . . can't . . ." The voice faded out.

Kinsman reeled in the antenna and fired it out again. "Where in hell are you?"

A cough, with pain behind it. "Shouldn't have done it. Disobeyed. And no water, nothing . . ."

Great! Kinsman raged. He's either hysterical or delirious. Or both.

After firing the spool antenna a third time, Kinsman flicked on the lamp atop his helmet and looked at the radio direction-finder dial on his forearm. The priest had his suit radio open and the carrier beam was coming through even though he was no longer talking. The gauges alongside the radio-finder reminded Kinsman that he was about halfway down on his oxygen. More than an hour had elapsed since he had last spoken to Bok.

"I'm trying to zero in on you," Kinsman called. "Are you hurt? Can you—"

"Don't, don't, don't. I disobeyed and now I've got to pay for it. Don't trap yourself, too . . ." The heavy reproachful voice lapsed into a mumble that Kinsman could not understand.

Trapped. Kinsman could picture it. The priest was using a canister suit, a one-man walking cabin, a big, plexidomed, rigid metal can with flexible arms and legs sticking out of it. A man could live for days inside it, but it was too clumsy for climbing. Which is why the crater was off-limits.

He must've fallen and now he's stuck, like a goddamned turtle on its back.

"The sin of pride," he heard the priest babbling. "God forgive us our pride. I wanted to find water; the greatest

142

discovery a man can make on the Moon. . . . Pride, nothing but pride . . ."

Kinsman walked slowly, shifting his eyes from the direction-finder to the roiled, pockmarked ground underfoot. He jumped across a two-meter drop between terraces. The finder's needle snapped to zero.

"Your radio still on?"

"No use . . . go back . . ."

The needle stayed fixed. *Either I broke it or I'm right on top of him.*

He turned a full circle, slowly scanning the rough ground as far as his light could reach. No sign of the canister. Kinsman stepped to the terrace edge. Kneeling with deliberate care, so that his backpack would not unbalance him and send him sprawling down the tumbled rocks, he peered over.

In a zigzag fissure a few meters below him was the priest, a giant armored insect gleaming white in the glare of the lamp, feebly waving with one free arm.

"Can you get up?" Kinsman saw that all the weight of the cumbersome suit was on the pinned arm. *Banged up his backpack, too.*

"Trying to find the secrets of God's creation . . . storming heaven with rockets. . . . We say we're seeking knowledge but we're really after our own glory . . ."

Kinsman frowned. He could not see the older man's face behind the canister's heavily tinted visor. Just as he could not see the face of the cosmonaut, years ago.

"I'll have to bring the jumper down here."

The priest rambled on, coughing spasmodically. Kinsman got to his feet.

"Pride leads to death," he heard in his earphones. "You know that, Kinsman. It's pride that makes us murderers."

The shock boggled Kinsman's knees. He turned, shaking. "What . . . did you say?"

"I know you, Kinsman. Anger and pride. Destroy not my soul with men of blood . . . whose right hands are . . . are . . ."

Kinsman ran. He fought back toward the crater rim, storming the terraces blindly, scrabbling up the inclines with four-meter-high jumps. Twice he had to turn up the air blower in his helmet to clear the sweaty fog from his

143

faceplate. He did not dare to stop. He raced on, breath racking his lungs, heart pounding until he could hear nothing else.

Finally he reached the crest. Collapsing on the deck of the jumper, he forced himself to breathe normally again, forced himself to sound normal as he called Bok.

The astronomer listened and then said guardedly, "It sounds like he's dying."

"I think his regenerator's shot. His air must be pretty foul by now."

"No sense going back for him."

Kinsman hesitated. "Maybe I can get the jumper close enough to him." But his mind was screaming at him, *The priest found out about me!*

"You'll never get him back here in time," Bok was saying. "And you're not supposed to take the jumper near the crater, let alone inside it. It's too risky."

"You want to just let him die?" *He's hysterical. If he babbles about me where Bok can hear it . . . Christ, it'll be piped straight back to Houston, automatically!*

"Listen," the astronomer said, his voice rising again. "You can't leave me stuck here with both of you gone! I know the regulations, Kinsman. You're not allowed to risk yourself or the third man in the team in an effort to help a man in trouble. Those are the rules!"

"I know. I know." *You've already killed one human being. Are you going to let another one die because of it? Where does it end, Kinsman? Where does it end?*

"You don't have enough oxygen in your suit to get down there and back again," Bok insisted. "I've been calculating—"

"I can tap the jumper's propellant tank."

"But that's crazy! You'll get yourself stranded!"

"Maybe." *If NASA finds out about it they'll bounce me straight back to the Air Force. Back to Murdock.*

"You're going to kill yourself over that priest! And you'll be killing me, too!"

"He's probably dead by now," Kinsman said, as much to himself as to Bok. "I'll just place a marker down there so another crew can get him out when the time comes. I won't be long."

"I'm calling Houston," said the astronomer. "You can't make a move until mission control okays it."

"By then he'll be dead for sure."

"But the regulations . . ."

"Were written Earthside," Kinsman snapped. "The brass never planned on anything like this. I've got to go back, just to make sure."

"Kinsman, if you go . . ."

"I'm gone," he said. Then he turned off his suit radio.

He flew the jumper back down the crater's inner slope, leaning over the platform railing to see his marker beacons while listening to their radio peeps. In a few minutes he eased the spraddle-legged platform down on the last terrace before the helpless priest, kicking up a small spray of dust with the rockets.

"Father Lemoyne."

Kinsman stepped off the jumper and made it to the edge of the fissure in two lunar strides. The white shell was inert, the lone arm unmoving.

"Father Lemoyne!"

Kinsman held his breath, listening. Nothing . . . wait . . . the faintest, faintest breathing. More like gasping. Quick, shallow, desperate.

"You're dead," Kinsman heard himself mutter. "Give it up. You're finished. Even if I got you out of here you'd be dead before I could get you back to the base."

The priest's faceplate was opaque to him. He saw only the reflected spot of his own helmet lamp. But his mind filled with the shocked face he had seen in that other visor, the horrified expression when she realized that she was dead.

Kinsman looked away, out at the too-close horizon and the uncompromising stars beyond. Then he remembered the rest of it.

They cannot scare me with their empty spaces
Between stars—on stars where no human race is.
I have it in me so much nearer home
To scare myself with my own desert places.

Like an automaton he turned back to the jumper. His mind was a blank now. Without thought, without even

145

feeling, he rigged a line from the jumper's tiny winch to the metal lugs in the canister suit's chest. Then he took apart the platform railing and wedged three rejoined sections into the fissure above the fallen man, to form a hoisting lever arm. Looping the line over the spindly metal arm, he started the winch.

He climbed down into the fissure as the winch silently took up the slack in the line, and set himself as solidly as he could on the bare, scoured-smooth rock. Grabbing the priest's armored shoulders, he guided the oversized canister up from the crevice while the winch strained steadily.

The railing arm gave way when the priest was only partway up and Kinsman felt the full weight of the monstrous suit crush down on him. He sank to his knees, gritting his teeth to keep from crying out.

Then the winch took up the slack. Grunting, fumbling, pushing, Kinsman scrabbled up the rocky slope with his arms wrapped halfway around the big canister's middle. He let the winch drag them both to the jumper's edge, then reached out and shut off the motor.

With only a hard breath's pause Kinsman snapped down the suit's supporting legs so the priest could stand upright even though unconscious. Then he clambered onto the jumper's platform and took the oxygen line from the rocket tankage. Kneeling at the bulbous suit's shoulders, he plugged the line into its emergency air tank.

The older man coughed once. That was all.

Kinsman leaned back on his heels. His faceplate was fogging over again, or was it fatigue blurring his vision? The regenerator was hopelessly smashed, he saw. The old bird must've been breathing his own juices. Once the emergency tank registered full, he disconnected the oxygen line and plugged it into a special fitting below the regenerator.

"If you're already dead, this is probably going to kill me, too," Kinsman said. He purged the entire suit, forcing the contaminated fumes out and replacing them with oxygen that the jumper's rocket motor needed to get them back to the base.

He was close enough now to see through the canister's tinted visor. The priest's face was grizzled, eyes closed. His

146

usual maddening little smile was gone; his mouth hung open slackly.

Kinsman hauled him up onto the railless platform and strapped him down to the deck. He saw himself, for an absurd moment, as Frankenstein's assistant, strapping the giant monster to the operating table. Then he turned to the control podium and inched the throttle forward just enough to give them the barest minimum of lift. Steady, Igor, he said to himself. We can't use full power now.

The jumper almost made it to the crest before its rocket motor died and bumped them gently onto one of the terraces. There was a small emergency tank of oxygen that could have carried them a little farther, but Kinsman knew that he and the priest would need it for breathing.

"Wonder how many Jesuits have been carried home on their shields?" he asked himself as he unbolted the section of decking that the priest was lying on. By threading the winch line through the bolt holes he made an improvised sled, which he carefully lowered to the ground. Then he took the emergency oxygen tank and strapped it to the deck section also.

Kinsman wrapped the line around his fists, put his shoulder under it, and leaned against the burden. Even in the Moon's light gravity it was like trying to haul a truck.

"Down to less than one horsepower," he grunted, straining forward.

For once he was glad that the scoured rocks had been smoothed by micrometeors. He would climb a few steps, wedge himself as firmly as he could, then drag the sled to him. It took a painful half-hour to reach the ringwall crest.

He could see the base again, tiny and remote as a dream. "All downhill from here," he mumbled.

He thought he heard a groan.

"That's it," he said, pushing the sled over the crest, down the gentle outward slope. "That's it. Stay with it. Don't you die on me. Don't you put me through all of this for nothing!"

"Kinsman!" Bok's voice. "Are you all right?"

The sled skidded against a meter-high rock. Scrambling after it, Kinsman answered, "I'm bringing him in. Just shut up and leave us alone. I think he's alive."

147

"Houston says no," Bok answered, his voice strangely calm. "They've calculated that his air went bad on him. He can't possibly be alive. You are ordered to leave him and return to base shelter. Ordered, Kinsman."

"Tell Houston they're wrong. He's still alive. Now stop wasting my breath."

Pull the sled free. Push it to get it started downhill again. Strain to hold it back. Don't let it get away from you. Haul it out of the damned craterlets. Watch your step, don't fall.

"Too damned much uphill . . . in this downhill."

Once he sprawled flat and knocked his helmet against the edge of the sled. He must have blacked out for a moment. Weakly, he dragged himself to the oxygen tank and refilled his suit's supply. Then he checked the priest's suit and topped off its tank.

"Can't do that again," he said to the silent priest. "Don't know if we'll make it. Maybe we can. If neither one of us has sprung a leak. Maybe . . ."

Time slid away from him. The past and future disappeared into an endless now, a forever of pain and struggle, with the heat of his toil welling up to drench him in his suit.

"Why don't you say something?" Kinsman panted at the priest. "You can't die. Understand me? You can't die! I've got to explain it to you. I didn't mean to kill her. I didn't even know she was a girl. You can't tell, can't see a face until you're too close. She must've been just as scared as I was. She tried to kill me. How'd I know their cosmonaut was just a scared kid? When I saw her face it was too late. But I didn't know. I didn't know . . ."

They reached the foot of the ringwall and Kinsman dropped to his knees. "Couple more klicks now. Straightaway. Only a couple more . . . kilometers."

His vision blurred and something in his head was buzzing angrily. Staggering to his feet, he lifted the line over his shoulder and slogged ahead. He could just make out the lighted top of the base's radio mast.

"Leave him, Kinsman!" Bok's voice pleaded from somewhere. "You can't make it unless you leave him!"

"Shut . . . up."

One step after another. Don't think, don't count. Blank your mind. Be a mindless plow horse. Plod along. One step at

148

a time. Steer for the radio mast. Just a few . . . more . . . klicks.

"Don't die on me, priest! Don't you . . . die on me! You're my penance, priest. My ticket back. Don't die on me . . . don't die . . ."

It all went dark. First in spots, then totally. Kinsman caught a glimpse of the barren landscape tilting weirdly, then the grave stars slid across his view, then darkness.

"I tried," he heard himself say in a far, far distant voice. "I tried."

For a moment or two he felt himself falling, dropping effortlessly into blackness. Then even that sensation died and he felt nothing at all.

A faint vibration buzzed at him.

The darkness started to shift, turn gray at the edges. Kinsman opened his eyes and saw the low curved ceiling of the underground base. The hum was the electrical generator that lit and warmed and brought good air into their tight little shelter.

"You okay?" Bok leaned over him. His chubby face was frowning worriedly.

Kinsman nodded weakly.

"Father Lemoyne's going to pull through," Bok said, stepping out of the cramped space between the two bunks. The priest was awake but unmoving, his eyes staring blankly upward. His canister suit had been removed and one arm was covered with a plastic cast.

Bok explained, "I've been getting instructions from the medics in Houston. They contacted the Russians. A paramedic's coming over from their base. Should be here in an hour. Lemoyne's in shock and his right arm's broken, but otherwise he seems pretty good. Exhausted, but no permanent damage."

Kinsman pulled himself up to a sitting position on the bunk and leaned his back against the curving wall. His helmets and boots were off, but he was still wearing the rest of his lunar suit.

"You went out and got us," he realized.

Bok nodded. "You were less than a kilometer away. I could hear you on the radio, babbling away. Then you

149

stopped talking. I had to go out."

"You saved my life."

"And you saved the priest's."

Kinsman stopped for a moment, remembering. "I did a lot of raving out there, didn't I?"

Bok wormed his shoulders uncomfortably. "Sort of. It's, uh . . . well, at least the Russians didn't pick up any of it."

"But Houston did."

"It was relayed automatically. Emergency procedure. You know . . . it's the rules."

That's it, Kinsman said to himself. Now they know.

"They, uh . . ." Bok looked away. "They're sending a relief crew to fly us back."

"They don't trust me to pilot the return rocket."

"After what you've been through?"

That's the end of it. NASA won't want any neurotic Air Force killers on their payroll. It would ruin their cooperative programs with the Russians.

"You haven't heard the best of it, though," Bok said, eager to change the subject. He went over to the shelf at the end of the priest's bunk and took a small plastic bottle. "Look at this."

Kinsman took the stoppered bottle in his hands. Inside it, a small sliver of ice floated on water.

"It was stuck in the cleats of his boots."

"Father Lemoyne's?"

"Right. It's really water! Tests out okay and I even snuck a taste of it. It's real water, all right."

"It must have been down in that fissure, after all," Kinsman said. "He found it without knowing it. He'll get into all the history books now." And he'll have to watch his pride even more.

Bok sat on the shelter's only chair. "Chet . . . about what you were saying out there . . ."

Kinsman expected tension, but instead he felt only numb. "I know. They heard it in Houston."

"I'm sure they'll try to keep it quiet."

Kinsman heard himself replying calmly, "They can't keep the lid on something that big. Somebody will leak it. At the very least it means I'm finished with NASA."

"We'd all heard rumors about an Air Force astronaut

150

killing a Russian during a military mission. But I never thought . . . I mean . . ."

"The priest figured it out. Or he guessed it."

"It must've been rough on you," Bok said.

Kinsman shrugged. "Not as rough as what happened to her."

"I'm . . . sorry." Bok's voice trailed off helplessly.

"It doesn't matter."

Surprised, Kinsman realized that he meant it. He sat upright. "It doesn't matter anymore. They can do whatever they want to. I can handle it. Even if they ground me and throw me to the media wolves, I think I can take it. I did it and it's over with and I can take whatever I have to take."

Father Lemoyne's free arm moved slightly. "It's all right," he whispered hoarsely. "It's all right."

The priest turned his face toward Kinsman. His gaze moved from the astronaut's eyes to the plastic bottle in Kinsman's hands. "It's all right," he repeated, smiling weakly. "It's not hell we're in. It's purgatory. We'll get through. We'll make it all right."

Then he closed his eyes and relaxed into sleep. But his smile remained, strangely gentle in that bearded, haggard face; ready to meet the world or eternity.

Age 33

It LOOKED LIKE a perfectly reasonable bar to Kinsman. No, he corrected himself. A perfectly reasonable pub.

The booths along the back wall were empty. A couple of middle-aged men were conversing quietly as they stood at the bar itself with pints of light Australian lager in their hands. The bartender was a beefy, red-faced Aussie. Only the ceiling of raw rock broke the illusion that they were up on the surface in an ordinary Australian city.

Kinsman ordered a scotch and walked slowly with it to the last booth, where his back would be to the rock wall and he could see the entire pub. Tiredly he wondered when the British Commonwealth was going to discover the joys of ice cubes. Half a tumbler of good whisky and just two thumbnail-sized dollops of ice that immediately melted away and left the scotch lukewarm.

Like the Wicked Witch of the West, he thought. Melting, melting. Like me.

Kinsman glanced at his wristwatch. The dedication ceremonies should soon be over. The pub would start to fill up then. Better finish your drink and find someplace to hide before they start pouring in here.

He gulped at the whisky, but as he put the glass down on the bare wood of the booth's table, Fred Durban walked into the pub. Durban looked damned good for a man pushing seventy. Tall and spare as one of the old rocket boosters he had engineered, back in the days when you pressed the firing button and ducked behind sandbags because you had no idea of what the rocket might decide to do.

Kinsman felt trapped. He could not get up and leave because he would have to walk past Durban and the old man would recognize him. If he stayed, Durban would spot him. Even in a civilian's slacks and sports jacket, Kinsman could not hide his identity.

The old man walked slowly toward the bar, looking almost British in his tweed jacket and the pipe that he almost always had clamped in his teeth. He looked down the bar, then toward the booths. His face lit up as he spotted Kinsman. Briskly he strode to the booth and slid into the bench on the other side of the narrow table.

"You couldn't take all the speechifying either, eh?"

Wishing he were somewhere else, Kinsman nodded.

"Can't blame you. I've been in this game for a thousand years now and the *only* part of it I don't like is when those stuffed shirts start congratulating themselves over the things you and I did."

"Uh, sir, I was just leaving . . ."

"Hey, come on! You wouldn't leave me here to drink all alone, would you?"

Before Kinsman could answer or maneuver himself out

152

of the booth, Durban turned toward the barkeep and called, "Can I have a mug of lager, please, and another of whatever my friend here is drinking?"

The bartender nodded. "Ryte awhy, mate."

"Now then, the logistics are taken care of." Durban put his unlit pipe in the battered ashtray, then fished in his jacket pockets to produce a pouch of aromatic tobacco, lighter, and all the surgical instruments that pipe smokers carry.

"I really should be going," Kinsman said, starting to feel desperate.

"Where to?"

"Well . . ."

"There's nothing going on except that damned dedication ceremony. Everybody else is there, except for thee and me. And except the miners." He started reaming out the pipe and dumping the black soot into the ashtray. The barkeep brought their drinks and put them down on the table.

"How much?" Durban asked.

"I'll keep a tab runnin'. Got a bloody computer t' keep track of you blokes. Prints up your bill neat an' clean when you're ready t' go. Even keeps track o' the ice!" He laughed his way back to the bar.

"I haven't seen much of the mines yet," Kinsman said, still trying to get away.

"Nothing much to see," Durban muttered, putting his pipe back together. "Take the tour tomorrow morning. Just some tunnels with automated machinery chipping away at the rock. The real work's done by a half-dozen engineers in the control center. Looks just like mission control at Kennedy or Vandenberg."

"I haven't even seen the surface. We landed last night . . ."

"Desert. They won't let you up there by yourself. Fifty degrees Celsius. That's why the miners live down here."

"I know." The sun will broil you in minutes. And it's empty up there. Clean and empty. No one to see you. No one to watch you. They wouldn't find your body for days.

Durban took a long swallow of beer. "Fifty degrees," he murmured. "Sounds hotter if you say 120 Fahrenheit."

"Like the Moon."

Durban nodded. "That's why we're opening this training

153

center here. People will have to live underground on the Moon, so we'll train them here at Coober Pedy."

"It was your idea, wasn't it?"

Another nod. "Not mine exclusively. Several other people thought of it, too. Years ago. But when you live long enough to be an old fart like me in this game, they give you credit for enormous wisdom." He laughed and reached for his beer again.

Kinsman sat quietly, wondering how he could break away, while Durban alternately sipped his beer and packed his pipe. The old man still had a tinge of red in his silvery hair. His face was thin, with a light, almost delicate bone structure showing through skin like ancient parchment. But the cobalt-blue eyes were alive, alert, inquisitive, framed by bushy reddish brows. Durban had seen it all, from the struggling beginnings of rocketry when people scoffed at the idea of exploring space to the multinational industry that was now on the verge of colonizing the Moon.

"You look damned uncomfortable, son. What's wrong?"

Kinsman felt himself wince. "Nothing," he lied.

Those bushy eyebrows went up. "Am I bothering you? Did I say something I shouldn't? Am I keeping you from a date or something?"

"Nosir. None of the above. I'm just . . . well, I guess I feel out of place here."

Durban studied him. "You were on the plane with me, the L.A. to Sydney flight last night, weren't you?"

"Yessir."

"I thought I recognized you. Saw your picture in the papers or something a few years back. But you were in uniform then."

He can't know, Kinsman told himself. There's no way he could possibly know.

"I'm still in the Air Force," he said to Durban. "I'm on . . . inactive duty."

"Astronaut?"

"I was."

Durban said, "Do I have to buy you another drink to get you to tell me your name?"

"Kinsman," he blurted. "Chet Kinsman." He grabbed the whisky in front of him and took a long pull from it.

154

"Chester A. Kinsman," Durban murmured. "Now where did I . . . of, of course!" He grinned broadly. "The Zero Gee Club! Now I remember. Old Cy Calder told me about you."

Kinsman put his drink down with a trembling hand. "The Zero Gee Club. I had forgotten about that."

"Forgotten about it?" Durban looked impressed. "You mean you've gone on to even greater things?"

"No." Kinsman shook his head. "Different. But not greater."

"Calder died a couple of years ago," Durban said. "Ninety-three."

"I didn't know."

His voice lower, "Just about all my old friends are dead. That's the curse of a long life. You get to feel that you're the last of the Mohicans."

"You think dying young is better?"

Instead of answering, Durban picked up his lighter and started puffing his pipe to life. Clouds of bluish smoke rose slowly, swirled around his head, then were pulled ceilingward toward the vents in the solid rock.

"You said," he asked between puffs, "you're on . . . inactive duty. . . . What brought that about?"

"Accident," Kinsman said automatically, feeling his insides congealing.

"Where? In orbit?"

"Yes."

"You got hurt? Funny, I didn't hear anything—"

"It happened a long time ago," Kinsman said, seeing the face of the cosmonaut screaming as she died. "It's just . . . one thing led to another. You know how it is."

Durban blew out another cloud of smoke. "Still, I've got a pretty good network of spies in all parts of this business. Odd I never heard about it."

Stop pumping me, Kinsman snarled silently. "Maybe it wasn't important enough to make the scuttlebutt rounds," he lied. "Except to me."

Durban looked skeptical. "An able-bodied astronaut sitting on his backside? For how long now?"

"A while."

"H'm. And what are you doing here?"

155

Kinsman shrugged. "Looking for a job, I guess."

"A job?"

"I can get an honorable discharge from the Air Force. I thought I might get a civilian job."

Durban's bushy brows knit together. "The Air Force is willing to let an experienced astronaut go? Who's your boss out there at Vandenberg?"

"Colonel Murdock."

"Bob Murdock?" Durban broke into a grin. "I've known Bobby since we used to fill out requisition forms over his forged signature. Don't tell me he's still a light colonel!"

"No, he's got his eagles."

"And he's willing to let you quit the Air Force? Why?"

Kinsman shook his head. Because I make him uncomfortable. Because I don't follow the rules. Because I'm a nervous wreck and a murderer. Or is it the other way around?

"Personal, eh?"

"Very."

"I can introduce you to some NASA people who . . ."

"I've done a tour of duty with NASA. They shipped me back to the Air Force. The big aerospace corporations are where the jobs are now. Or so they tell me."

"And that's why you're here. To talk to the corporation people. Any luck?"

"All negative. They won't touch me without seeing my Air Force record, and my record shows a big blank space where it counts most."

Durban stared at him. "What the hell happened?"

Kinsman did not reply.

"Okay, okay . . . it's very personal. I'm just plain curious, though. Not much happens in this game without me hearing about it, you know."

Kinsman picked up his drink again, thinking, You've heard about this one. You've heard the rumors. You just haven't connected me with the story. He drained the thick-walled glass and put it back on the table again.

"I hope you won't go probing into this, Mr. Durban. It's very sensitive . . . to me personally, as well as to the Air Force."

"I can see that," Durban said.

"I wouldn't have mentioned anything at all about it,"

Kinsman went on, "except that you . . . well, you seem like someone I can trust."

"But only so far."

"Believe me, I've told you more than anyone else. But please don't push it any father . . . I mean, farther."

"All right."

"I'd like your word on that."

The eyebrows shot up again. "My word? You mean there's a gentleman left in this world who'll take a man's word and a handshake on something bigger than a five-dollar bet?"

Smiling despite himself, Kinsman answered, "I don't even need the handshake. Your word is good enough for me."

"Well, I'll be . . ." Durban turned slightly on the bench and looked toward the front of the pub. "Looks like a couple more fugitives from the ceremonies just slinked in."

Kinsman glanced toward the pub's front entrance and saw Frank Colt, in his sharply creased Air Force blues, looking slightly uncomfortable next to a lanky, sandy-haired Russian in the tan and red uniform of the Soviet Cosmonaut Corps.

Durban stuck his head out from the booth and called, "Piotr . . . over here."

"Ahah! An underground meeting," the Russian boomed out in a voice three times his size.

The two men came over and slid into the booth: the Russian next to Durban and Colt beside Kinsman.

Durban said, "Chet, may I introduce Major Piotr Leonov, Cosmonaut First Class. And a fine basso, if you ever want to get up an operatic quartet."

"We have already met," the Russian said, taking Kinsman's extended hand in a friendly but not overly strong grip.

"We have?"

"At your base near Aristarchus. I piloted the craft that brought medical aid for your renegade Jesuit."

Comprehension began to light in Kinsman's mind.

"You were quite asleep at the time," Leonov went on, in English that had a slight British accent. "Apparently, you had gone through a strenuous time, rescuing the priest."

Kinsman nodded. "Well, it's good to meet you when my eyes are open."

Leonov laughed.

"This is Captain Frank Colt," Kinsman said to Durban. "Top flier in the Vandenberg crew. I don't know how well he sings but he's a damned good man to work with in orbit."

"I've got a natural sense of rhythm," Colt said, straight-faced, testing Durban.

"I've heard about you," Durban said. "Aren't you the one who saved that cee-cubed satellite when its final stage misfired and it looked like the whole damned thing was going to splash in the Pacific?"

With a nod, "I got a replacement thruster mated to the bird, yeah."

"And damned near fried his ass off," Kinsman added.

"You should have asked us for assistance," Leonov said, grinning. "We would have been happy to help you save your command-and-control satellite."

"You sure would," Colt snapped. "You'd tote it back to Moscow with you."

Leonov shrugged elaborately. "Wouldn't you, with one of ours?"

A waitress appeared at their table: very young, miniskirt showing smooth strong thighs, low-cut blouse showing plenty of bosom, long blond hair, and a pretty face with placid cow eyes.

"Service is improving," said Durban.

"The ceremonies are breaking up," Colt told him. "This place'll be jammed in a few minutes."

The waitress took their order and flounced off to the bar.

"Nothing like that in Cosmograd, eh, Piotr?" Durban nudged the Russian.

"My dear Frederick," Leonov countered, an enigmatic smile on his bony face, "just because you did not see any of the beautiful women of our city does not mean that they do not exist. Being good Soviet women, naturally they hid themselves from the prying eyes of capitalist spies."

"Hid themselves? Or were hidden by others?"

Leonov shrugged. "What difference? The important fact is that I know where they are and you do not."

As the girl came back with their drinks, Colt asked Kinsman quietly, "How's it going?"

Kinsman jabbed his thumb toward the floor. "Lousy."

"I still wish you'd let me help. We can go over Murdock's head. The other astronauts will—"

"You don't want to get involved in this, Frank. It won't do you any good."

Colt made a disgusted face.

"A toast!" Leonov called, raising his glass. It looked like a tumbler of water. Kinsman guessed that it was at least four ounces of straight vodka. "To international cooperation in space. An end to all military secrets. Peace and total disarmament. Brotherhood throughout the cosmos. Friendship among all . . ."

"Is this a toast or a speech?" Colt grumbled.

"*Nazdrovia!*" Leonov snapped back and tossed down half his drink in one gulp.

"I've got a toast," Durban said. "May the work that is done here, underground, result in the four of us meeting underground again . . . on the Moon."

They drank again. And again. The waitress brought fresh drinks. Through it all Kinsman kept wishing he could get away, escape. The whisky was not making him drunk. It couldn't. He would not let it.

"Frank, my friend," Leonov said over their glasses, "why are you scowling? It is no crime to be drinking with a Russian."

Colt hunched his shoulders and leaned forward over the table. "Pete, I'm just drunk enough to tell you to go to hell. You know I don't believe a word of this peace and friendship bullshit."

"And I am drunk enough to know capitalist brainwashing when I hear it."

"Come on now," Durban said, relighting his pipe for the *n*th time. "Let's not get into a political squabble."

"Easy enough for you," Colt growled. "Mr. International Astronautical Federation. You can go around the world being friendly and setting up programs where we gotta cooperate with the Reds. But we"—Colt's gesture included Kinsman—"we gotta figure out how to cooperate with 'em without letting 'em steal the whole fucking store! We gotta defend the nation against 'em and cooperate with 'em at the same time. How d'you do that?"

159

"By giving up all weapons in space," Leonov answered. "Put an end to this Star Wars program of yours and dismantle your antisatellite weapons and we will do the same."

"Uh-huh. And you'll let me come over and inspect your boosters and satellites to make sure you're not cheating?"

"Allow you to spy on our space bases? Never!"

Kinsman leaned back in the booth, utterly sober, staring at his emptied glass and wishing he could disappear from the face of the Earth. Colt's superpatriotism always surprised and embarrassed him. Childhood prejudice, he knew. Blacks were anti-Establishment when you were a kid and you expected them all to be anti-Establishment forever.

But America was truly multiracial now. There were black generals, Hispanic bank presidents, Oriental board chairmen. The talk was that there would be a black President before much longer.

What will they call the White House then? Kinsman wondered. Will they repaint it? More likely they'll repaint the new President.

Leonov was chuckling. "Frank, my hotheaded friend, I refuse to get angry with you. We are both alike! You want to fly in space; so do I. Your government has ordered you to be an intelligence-gatherer for the duration of this international conference and ferret out as many of our secrets as you can. My government has ordered me to be an intelligence officer for the duration of this meeting and ferret out as many of your secrets as I can. How do you think I can roam around this underground rabbits' nest without a KGB 'guide' at my elbow?"

Intelligence officer? Kinsman snapped his attention to Leonov's eyes. The Russian met his gaze, smiling pleasantly, a bit drunkenly. There was no hatred there, not even suspicion. *He doesn't know about me.* Still, Kinsman's knees felt suddenly weak.

"You already know all our goddamned secrets," Colt groused.

"Just as you know ours," countered Leonov.

"Then let's get off the subject," Durban suggested, his voice a bit edgy, "and talk about something more congenial."

"Such as what?"

Durban sucked on his pipe for a moment. It was out

again. He took it from his mouth and jabbed the stem in Kinsman's direction.

"Chet here is looking for a job. What can we do for him?"

Jesus Christ, he's going to spill it all over the place! Kinsman heard himself stammering, "No, really . . . there's no need . . . I'd rather . . ."

"Defect!" Leonov suggested jovially. "We will treat you handsomely in the Soviet Union."

Colt glowered. "Yeah. In the basement of some psychiatric prison."

The Russian pretended not to hear.

"I'm serious," Durban insisted. "There are too few experienced astronauts—and cosmonauts—to let one walk away from the game."

For God's sake leave me alone! Kinsman screamed silently. But he could say nothing to them. He was frozen there, pinned into the booth. Trapped.

"They don't want experience anymore," Colt said. "They want youth. Murdock's even got *me* slated to train the little bastards instead of doing the flying myself."

"The private corporations . . ." Durban began.

"Are all talk and not much else," Colt said. "Chet and I are executive timber, as far as they're concerned. But they're not hiring fliers. They'd rather let Uncle Sam take the risks while they sit back and wait till everything's set up for them at the taxpayers' expense. *Then* they'll move in and make their profits."

"In all honesty," Durban said, "the military space program has gotten so big that it's swamping the civilian program. The corporations can make assured profits working for the Air Force. That makes it damned hard for them to justify the risks of private operations in orbit."

Suddenly serious, Leonov said, "I know how you must feel. If I thought that I would have to spend the rest of my life at a desk, or training others to do what I most want for myself, I would go mad."

"We need a new program," Durban said. "A priority program that's got to get going *now*, before they have time to train the next generation of kids."

"Such as what?" Colt asked.

161

"Not a military program," Leonov said. "Both our nations are putting enough military hardware into space. Too much."

"I agree," said Durban. "It ought to be an international program . . . something we can all participate in."

"Something that needs a corps of experienced astronauts," Kinsman heard himself chime in. "Something that will get us out there to stay. Away from here permanently."

"I've been mulling over an idea for a while now," Durban said. "Maybe the time is ripe for it."

"What is it?"

"A hospital."

"Huh?"

"On the Moon. A lunar hospital, for old gaffers like me, with bad hearts. For people with muscular diseases who are cripples here in this one-gravity field but could lead normal lives again on the Moon, in one-sixth gee."

Leonov smiled approvingly.

"Nobody's gonna put up the funding for an old soldiers' home on the Moon," Colt said.

"Want to bet?" Kinsman was suddenly surging with hope. "What's the average age of the U.S. Senate? Or the Presidium of the USSR?"

"My father . . ." Leonov realized. "He is confined to bed because of his heart's weakness. But in zero gravity, or even on the Moon . . ."

"And Jill Meyers," Kinsman added, "with all those damned allergies of hers." *I can stay in the Air Force! If they go into a medical base on the Moon I can stay and work on that. I can stay on the Moon, away from it all!*

They drank and made plans. Kinsman's head started to spin. The pub filled up with dignitaries from the conference that had officially inaugurated the underground training facility. The four men stayed in their booth, drinking and talking, ignoring everyone else. The international businessmen and government officials drifted away after a while and the pub began to fill up with its regular customers—the hard-drinking, hard-handed miners who dug for opal and copper, who lived underground to escape the searing heat of the desert above, the miners who were being crowded out of half their living area to make room for the space training facility.

The noise level went up in quantum leaps. Laughing, rowdy men. Blaring music from the stereo. Higher-pitched laughter from the extra barmaids and waitresses who came on duty when the regulars came off shift.

Durban was yelling over the noise of the crowd, "Why don't we adjourn to my room? It's quieter there and I've got a couple of bottles of liquor in my luggage."

"Gotta make a pit stop first," Colt said, nodding toward the door marked GENTS near their booth.

"Me too," said Kinsman.

Inside the washroom the noise level was much lower. Colt and Kinsman stood side by side at the only two urinals.

"Y'know, I think the old guy's really got a workable idea," Colt said happily. "We can lay this hospital project on top of everything else that the Air Force is doing . . . and with Durban pushing it, with his connections . . ."

"I still won't get off the ground," Kinsman suddenly realized.

"Huh? Sure you will. Murdock can't . . ."

Kinsman shook his head. "It doesn't matter, Frank. My psychological profile will shoot me down. They won't let me back into space again."

Zipping up and heading for the only sink, Colt said, "You can't let it beat you, man. You can't let it take the life outta you."

Wonderful play on words.

Gesturing Kinsman to the sink ahead of himself, Colt said, "What happened is over and done with. You gotta stop acting . . . well, you know."

Kinsman looked into the mirror above the sink, into the haunted eyes that always stared back at him. "I act sick? Mentally unwell? Disturbed?"

"You act like a goddamned dope," Colt grumbled.

Wiping his hands on the cloth toweling that hung from a wall-mounted fixture, Kinsman said, "Frank, for a minute back there I got excited. I thought maybe Durban was right and this hospital project would make enough new slots for astronauts that I'd get another chance. But we both know better. They won't let me fly again. You, sure. But not me. I'm grounded."

Colt went to the sink as a couple of miners banged

163

through the door and headed for the urinals. A gust of noise and raucous laughter bounced off the tile walls as the door swung shut.

"Listen, man, one thing I've learned about the Air Force—and everything else," Colt said over the splashing water of the sink. "If you take just what they want to give you, you'll get shit every time. You gotta fight for what you want."

Kinsman shook his head. "My family were Quakers, remember?"

Colt was moving to the towel machine when one of the miners jostled him.

"D'ya mind, mate?"

Wordlessly Colt stepped away from him, turned, and started wiping his hands on the toweling.

"Bloody foreigners all over th' plyce, ain't they?" said the miner's companion.

Kinsman looked at them for the first time. They were no taller than he or Colt, but they were heavy-boned, big-knuckled, and half drunk.

Colt was wiping his hands very deliberately now, looking at Kinsman with his back to the two miners.

"Bad enough they're tykin' up half th' bloody pits to put their bloody spyce cadets in," said the one at the sink, "but now they're goin' t' stink up th' bloody pub."

"An' myke goo-goo eyes at th' girls."

"We oughtta bring in a few bloody chimpanzees t' serve 'em their drinks."

"Foreigners," said the second miner, loudly, even though the washroom was small enough to hear a whisper. "You remember what we did t' those Eye-Tyes back in Melbourne, Bert?"

"They weren't Eye-Tyes; they were bloody Hungarians."

"Wops, Hunkies, whatever. Treated 'em ryte, din't we?"

"Gave 'em what they deserved."

Kinsman was between Colt and the door. He wanted to tell his friend to leave, to ignore the drunken Aussies and walk out. But he couldn't.

Colt was slowly, methodically, wiping his black hands on the white toweling. The first miner stepped from the sink to stand a few inches away from him.

164

"Least we never had t' deal with bloody Fiji Islanders before."

Colt said nothing. He surrendered the towel. The miner grinned at him with crooked teeth.

"Or Yank niggers," he added.

Colt grinned back. His right fist traveled six inches and buried itself in the man's solar plexus. The miner gave a silent gasp and collapsed, legs folding as he sank to the tiled floor. The other miner stared but said nothing.

Kinsman opened the door and Colt followed him out into the noisy, crowded pub. They saw Durban and Leonov already standing at the end of the bar, near the door that led to the corridor.

"See what I mean?" Colt said as they elbowed their way through the press of bodies. "Gotta fight for respect, every inch of the way."

Out in the corridor Leonov said, "I was about to call your embassy to send a searching party for you."

"We got into a small discussion with a couple of the friendly natives," Colt replied.

"Say, if you youngsters will slow down a little," Durban pleaded, "I'll show you where my room is."

"And the liquor!" Leonov beamed, immediately slowing his pace to walk beside the elderly Durban.

They labored up the rising slope of the corridor. It had originally been a tunnel hewn out of solid rock. Only the floor had been smoothed and covered with spongy plastic tiles. The walls and ceiling were still bare grayish-brown unfinished rock. Fluorescent lights hung every ten meters, connected by drooping wires.

The others were busily chatting among themselves about the new hospital project. Kinsman stayed silent, thinking, Could I talk Murdock into it? Would they let me fly again? I'd have to work it out so that I was assigned to the hospital project permanently. They'd never let me get away with that. They could reassign me whenever . . .

"HEY, YOU THERE! THE YANKS!"

Turning, Kinsman saw a dozen or so miners advancing up the tunnel corridor toward them. In the lead were the two from the washroom. They all looked drunk. And violently angry.

"That's the black barstard that beat me up!" the miner yelled. "Him an' his friend there."

Colt moved to stand beside Kinsman. And suddenly Leonov was on his other side.

The miners halted a few feet in front of them. They wanted to fight. They were spoiling for blood. Kinsman stood rooted there, his mind blazing with the memory of the moment when he had felt bloodlust. He was sweating again, panting with exertion, reaching for the cosmonaut's fragile airhose . . .

Not again, he told himself, trying to control his trembling so that the others could not see it. Not again!

"What is this?" Leonov demanded. "Why are we accosted by a mob?"

"Back off, Russkie," said one of the miners. "This is none of your fight."

"These are my friends," Leonov said. "What concerns them concerns me."

"He beat me up," said the miner Colt had hit.

"An' him." His companion pointed at Kinsman. "He helped th' black bugger."

"Beat you up?" Leonov asked mildly. "Where are your scars? Where is the blood? I see no bruises. Are you certain you did not merely faint?"

The miner turned red as the men around him grinned.

"I was there with 'im," the other miner said. "They jumped Bert and pummeled 'im till he dropped. In the midsection."

"While you watched?" Leonov asked.

"We ain't tykin' that from no foreigners!"

The mob surged forward.

"Now that's enough!"

Frederick Durban stepped between Kinsman and Leonov to face the angry miners. "We are the guests of the Australian government," he said firmly, "and if any harm comes to us you'll all go to jail."

"What about 'im?" one of the miners yelled. "They can't go beatin' up our blokes and get awhy with it!"

"Nobody beat anybody up," Colt shouted back. "The guy called me a nigger and I punched him in the gut. He folded like a pretzel. One punch."

166

"That's a bloody lie! The other one held me and the black barstard kicked me, too!"

Very calmly, Durban took the pipe from his mouth and said, "All right, let's settle this here and now. But not with a riot."

"How then?"

"There's an old custom where I come from . . . mining country, back in Colorado." He turned slightly back toward Kinsman and winked. "When two men have a difference of opinion, they settle it fairly between themselves. Do you two want to fight it out right here . . . Marquess of Queensberry rules?"

Colt shrugged, then nodded.

"Oh, no, you don't!" screeched the miner. "He's a bloody tryned killer. A soldier. Probably a karate expert . . . chops bricks with 'is bare hands an' all that."

Durban scowled from under his shaggy brows. "Very well then. Suppose *I* represent the American side of this argument. Would you be afraid to fight me?"

"You? You're an old man!"

"I may be almost seventy," Durban said, stuffing his pipe into a jacket pocket, "but I can still take on the likes of you."

The miner looked bewildered. "I . . . you can't . . ."

"Come on," Durban said, very seriously. He raised his fragile-looking fists.

One of the other miners put a hand on the first one's shoulder. "Forget it, Bert. He's crazy."

Bert wavered, uncertain. Durban was ramrod straight, looking like a slim rod of knobby bamboo next to a snorting red-eyed bull. Kinsman watched, unable to move. That guy'll kill Durban with one punch. Then what can we do? What can I do?

The miner finally stepped back, muttering and shaking his head. They all turned and began walking slowly back down the tunnel corridor, toward the pub.

Durban let his hands drop to his sides.

Colt puffed out a breath of relief. "Thanks, man."

"Very courageous of you," Leonov said thoughtfully.

But Kinsman said nothing. What would I have done if it had come to a brawl? What would I have done?

The four men walked slowly back to Durban's room, two

167

levels up closer to the surface.

"The whisky's in the brown carryall," Durban said as they entered the windowless room. "Help yourselves." He went straight to the bed and stretched out on it.

Colt and Leonov went to the whisky. Kinsman took a close look at the old man. His face was ashen, his thin chest heaving.

"Are you all right?"

"I've got some pills here . . ." He fished in his jacket pocket. The pipe fell out and dropped to the floor, spilling black ashes across the cheap carpeting.

"I'll get you a glass of water."

Kinsman went to the sink across from the bed and took a plastic cup from the dispenser on the wall above it. Durban propped himself on one elbow to drink down the pill, then dropped back onto the mattress and stared at the ceiling.

Leonov had taken the small room's only chair. Colt was sitting on the dresser top next to the open whisky bottle. They both had plastic cups in their hands.

"Hey, you need a doctor?" Colt asked.

"No . . ." Durban closed his eyes and took a deep breath. "Just a little too much excitement for my heart. That, and the climb upstairs."

Leonov said, "We have a cardiac specialist with the Soviet delegation."

Pushing himself up to a sitting position, Durban waved a hand at the Russian. "No, it's all right. I'll be okay in a minute."

Kinsman sat on the edge of the bed and helped the old man out of his jacket, then pulled off his shoes.

"You see," Durban said, sinking back against the pillows, "I really do need a low-gravity home. Damned heart's not fit to live on Earth anymore. It wants to be on the Moon."

"We'll get you there," Colt said.

"Yes," Leonov agreed, raising his cup to the proposition.

Kinsman shook his head. "If that miner had punched you, it probably would have killed you. You were taking your life in your hands."

Durban smiled at him. "Oh, I knew he wouldn't hit me. He couldn't."

"He came damned close."

"Not a bit of it. I'm obviously a frail old man. It would ruin his self-image if he hit me. He knew that I'd go down with one punch. I could see it in his eyes. Where's the *machismo* in beating up an old man?"

"Then why . . ."

"I got in front of you fellows so that he would be forced to hit me before anybody else started fighting. That was the best way to prevent a fight from starting."

"You still could've gotten hurt. Killed."

Durban's shaggy eyebrows rose a bit. "Well, sometimes you have to put yourself on the line. You guys know that, you've all done it yourselves, one time or another."

"More than once," Leonov murmured.

"We could've taken on the bunch of them," Colt said. "They were brawlers, not trained fighters."

Leonov took a swallow of whisky and said, "I, for one, am glad that the fight did not come about. My training is not in hand-to-hand combat."

You have to put yourself on the line, Kinsman was repeating to himself.

"Maybe you could have taken them all single-handedly, Frank," Durban said. "But I doubt it. Besides, there are better ways of winning what you want than punching people. Much better ways."

"The tongue is mightier than the fist?" Colt jabbed.

"The brain is mightier than the biceps," Durban replied.

Kinsman got to his feet. "I've got to phone Colonel Murdock."

"Bobby? Why?"

"To tell him that I'm not quitting the Air Force. I'm not going to take an honorable discharge or any kind of discharge. I'm not quitting."

Colt broke into a wide grin. "Great! And tell him for me what I think of being assigned to training."

Leonov said, "You realize, of course, that if you start a high-priority program to build a hospital complex on the Moon, my superiors will become very suspicious of you."

"That's fine, Piotr," Durban said. "I'll put the idea before the International Astronautical Federation and get them to make this an international cooperative project. Then you can come in on it, too."

169

"We shall all meet on the Moon," said Leonov.

"The sooner the better," Durban agreed.

"To the Moon." Colt raised his cup.

"I'll be there," said Kinsman.

Age 35

As SOON AS he stepped through the acoustical screen inside the house's front doorway the noise hit Kinsman like a physical blow. He stood there a moment and watched the tribal rites of a Washington cocktail party.

My battlefield, he thought.

The room was jammed with guests and they all seemed to be talking at once. It was an old Georgetown parlor, big, with a high ceiling that sagged slightly and showed one hairline crack along its length. The streets outside had been quiet and deserted except for the police monitors in their armored suits standing at each intersection. They looked like a bitter parody of astronauts in space suits.

But here there was life, chatter, laughter. The people who made Washington go, the people who ran the nation, were here drinking and talking and ignoring the enforced peace of the streets outside. America was on a wartime footing, almost. The oil shock of ten years ago had inexorably pushed the United States toward military measures. The Star Wars strategic defense satellites that could protect the nation against Soviet missiles were being deployed in orbit, despite treaties, despite opposition at home, despite—or because of—the Soviet deployment of a nearly identical system. Unemployment at home was countered by a new public-service draft that placed millions of eighteen-year-olds in police forces, hospitals, public works projects, and the armed services. Dissidence was smothered by fear: fear of dangers real and imagined, fear of government retaliation, fear of

ruinous unemployment and economic collapse, and the ultimate fear of the nuclear war that hovered remorselessly on
the horizon waiting for the moment of Armageddon.

In the midst of these tightening tensions Kinsman was
devoting every ounce of his energies to creating a permanent
medical facility on the Moon.

As he stood at the doorway looking over the crowd, he
recognized fewer than one in ten of the partygoers. Then he
saw his host, Neal McGrath, now the junior Senator from
Pennsylvania. Neal was standing over at the far end of the
room by the empty fireplace, tall drink in hand, head bent
slightly to catch what some wrinkled matron was saying to
him. The target for tonight. McGrath was the swing vote on
the Senate's Appropriations Committee.

"Chet, you did come after all!"

He turned to see Mary-Ellen McGrath approaching him,
hands outstretched in greeting.

"I hardly recognized you without your uniform," she
said.

He smiled back at her. "I thought Aerospace Force blues
might be a little conspicuous around here."

"Nonsense. And I wanted to see your new oak leaves. A
major now."

Promoted for accepting hazardous duty: lobbying on
Capitol Hill.

"Come on, Chet. I'll show you where the bar is." She
took his arm and led him through the jabbering crowd.
Mary-Ellen was small, slender, almost frail-looking. But she
had the strength of a tigress and the open, honest face of a
woman who could stand beside her husband in the face of
anything from Washington cocktail parties to the tight infight-
ing of rural Pennsylvania politics.

The bar dispenser hummed impersonally to itself as it
produced a heavy scotch and water. Kinsman took a stinging
sip of it.

"I was worried you wouldn't come," Mary-Ellen said
over the noise of the crowd. "You've been a hermit ever since
you arrived in Washington."

"Pentagon keeps me pretty busy."

"And no date? No woman on your arm? That isn't the
Chet Kinsman I used to know back when."

"I'm preparing for the priesthood."

"I'd almost believe it," she said, straight-faced. "There's something different about you since the old days. You're quieter . . . more subdued."

I've been grounded. Aloud, he said, "Creeping maturity. I'm a late achiever."

But she was serious, and as stubborn as her husband. "Don't try to kid around it. You've changed. You're not playing the dashing young astronaut anymore."

"Who the hell is?"

A burly, balding man jarred into Kinsman from behind, sloshing half the drink out of his glass.

"Whoops, didn't get it on ya, did . . . oh, hi, Mrs. McGrath. Looks like I'm waterin' your rug."

"That won't hurt it," Mary-Ellen said. "Do you two know each other? Tug Wynne . . ."

"I've seen the Major on the Hill."

Kinsman said, "You're with Satellite News, aren't you?"

Nodding, Wynne replied, "Surprised to see you here, Major, after this morning's committee session."

Kinsman forced a grin. "I'm an old family friend. I've known the Senator since we were kids."

"You think he's gonna vote against the Moonbase program?"

"I hope not," Kinsman said.

Mary-Ellen kept silent.

"He sure gave your Colonel Murdock a going-over this morning." Wynne chuckled wheezily. "Mrs. McGrath, you shoulda seen your husband in action."

Kinsman changed the subject. "Say, did you know old Cy Calder? Used to work for Allied News Syndicate out on the West Coast."

"Only by legend," Wynne answered. "He died four, five years ago, I heard."

"Yes, I know."

"Musta been past eighty. Friend of yours?"

"Sort of. And he was past ninety."

"Ninety!"

"I knew him . . . lord, it was almost ten years ago. Back when we were just starting the first Air Force manned space missions. Helluva guy."

172

Mary-Ellen said, "I'd better pay some attention to the other guests. There are several old friends of yours here tonight, Chet. Mix around, you'll find them."

With another rasping chuckle, Wynne said, "Guess we *could* give somebody else a chance to get to the bar."

Kinsman started to drift away but Wynne followed behind him.

"Murdock send you over here to soften up McGrath?"

Pushing past a pair of arguing, arm-waving cigar smokers, Kinsman frowned. "I was invited to this party weeks ago. I told you, the Senator and I are old friends."

"And how friendly are you with Mrs. McGrath?"

"What's that supposed to mean?"

Wynne let his teeth show. "Handsome astronaut, good-looking wife, busy Senator . . ."

"That's pretty foul-minded, even for a newsman."

"Just doin' my job," Wynne said, still smiling. "Nothing personal. Besides, you got nothing to complain about, as far as news people are concerned. The rumor is that you're the astronaut who killed that Russian cosmonaut several years ago."

It was the hundredth time since Kinsman had arrived in Washington that a reporter had faced him with the accusation. The Aerospace Force public relations people had worked assiduously to keep the story "unofficial," citing the slender thread of cooperation that still remained between the Soviet and American civilian space programs. The media had backed off, spurred more than a little by the government's tough new regulations on licenses for broadcasting stations and mail permits for newspapers and magazines. But individual newsmen still braced Kinsman with the story, trying to get an admission from him.

Freezing his emotions within himself, Kinsman answered merely, "I've heard that rumor myself."

"You deny that it's true?"

"I'm not a public relations officer. I don't go around denying rumors. Or confirming them."

"Look," Wynne insisted, "the Air Force can't cover up this story forever."

"Aerospace Force," Kinsman said. "The name's been changed to Aerospace Force."

Wynne shrugged and raised his glass in a mock salute. "I stand corrected, Major."

Kinsman turned and started working his way toward the other end of the room. A grandfather clock chimed in a corner, barely audible over the human noises and clacking of ice in glassware. Eighteen hundred. Royce and Smitty ought to be halfway to Copernicus by now.

And then he heard her. He did not have to see her, he knew it was Diane. The same pure, haunting soprano; a voice straight out of a fairy tale:

"Once I had a sweetheart, and now I have none.
Once I had a sweetheart, and now I have none.
He's gone and leave me, he's gone and leave me,
He's gone and leave me to sorrow and mourn."

Her voice stroked his memory and he felt all the old joy, all the old pain, as he pushed his way through the crowd.

Finally he saw her, sitting cross-legged on a sofa, guitar propped on one knee. The same ancient guitar; no amplifiers, no boosters. Her hair was still straight and long and black as space. Her eyes were even darker and deeper. The people were ringed around her, standing, sitting on the floor. They gave her the entire sofa to herself, an altar that only she could use. They watched her and listened, entranced by her voice. But she was somewhere else, living the song, seeing what it told of, until she strummed the final chord.

Then she looked up and looked straight at Kinsman. Not surprised. Not even smiling. Just a look that linked them as if all the years since their brief time together had dissolved into a single yesterday. Before either of them could say or do anything the others broke into applause. Diane smiled and mouthed, "Thank you."

"More, more!"

"Come on, another one."

"'Greensleeves.'"

Diane put the guitar down carefully beside her, uncoiled her slim legs, and stood up. "Later, okay?"

Kinsman grinned to himself. He knew it would be later or nothing.

The crowd muttered reluctant acquiescence and broke

174

the circle around her. Kinsman stepped the final few paces and stood before Diane.

"Good to see you again." He felt suddenly awkward, not knowing what to do. He held his drink with both hands.

"Hello, Chet." She was not quite smiling.

"I'm surprised you remember. It's been so long . . ."

Now she did smile. "How could I ever forget you? And I've seen your name in the news every once in a while."

"I've listened to your records everywhere I've gone," he said.

"Even on the Moon?" Her look was almost shy, almost mocking.

"Sure," he lied. "Even on the Moon."

"Here, Diane, I brought you some punch." Kinsman turned to see a fleshy-faced young man with a droopy mustache and tousled brown hair, carrying two plastic cups of punch. He wore a sharply tailored white suit with a vest and a wide floral scarf.

"Thank you, Larry. This is Chet Kinsman. Chet, meet Larry Davis."

"Kinsman?"

Diane explained, "I met Chet in San Francisco a thousand years ago, when I was just getting started. Chet's an astronaut."

"Oh, really?"

Somehow the man antagonized Kinsman. "Affirmative," he snapped in his best military manner.

"He's been on the Moon," Diane went on.

"That's where I heard the name," Davis said. "You're one of those Air Force people who want to build a permanent base up there. Weren't you involved in some sort of rescue a couple of years back? One of your people got stranded or something . . ."

"Yes," Kinsman cut him short. "It was all blown up out of proportion by the news media."

They stood there for a moment, none of them able to think of a thing to say, as the party pulsated around them.

Finally Diane said, "Mary-Ellen told me you might be here tonight. You and Neal are both working on something about the space program?"

"Something like that," Kinsman said. "Organized any
175

more protest demonstrations?"

She forced a laugh. "There's nothing left to protest about. Everything's so well organized in the Land of the Free that nobody can raise a crowd anymore. Public safety laws and all that."

"It does seem quieter. Nobody's complaining."

"They can't," Diane said. "You ought to see what we have to go through before every concert. They want to check the lyrics of every song I do. Even the encores. Nothing's allowed to be spontaneous."

"You manage to get in some damned tough lyrics," Kinsman said. "I've listened to you."

"The censors aren't always very bright."

"Or incorruptible," Davis added, smirking.

"So everybody's happy," Kinsman said. "You get to sing your songs about freedom and love. The crowd gets its little thrill of excitement. And the government people get paid off. Everybody gets what they want."

Diane looked at him quizzically. "Do you have what you want, Chet?"

"Me?" Surprised. "Hell no."

"Then not everybody's satisfied."

"Are you?"

"Hell no," she mimicked.

"But everything *looks* so rosy," Davis said, with acid in his voice. "The government keeps telling us that unemployment is down and the stock market is up. And our President promises he won't send troops into Brazil. Not until after the elections, I bet."

Diane nodded. Then, brightening, "Larry, did I ever tell you about the time we tried to get Chet to come out and join one of our demonstrations? In uniform?"

"I'm agog."

She turned to Kinsman. "Do you remember what you told me, Chet?"

"No . . ." It was a perfect day for flying, for getting away from funerals and families and all the ties of Earth. Flying so high above the clouds that even the rugged Sierras looked like nothing more than wrinkles. Then out over the desert at Mach 2, the only sounds in your earphones from your own breathing and the faint distant crackle of earthbound men

176

giving orders to other earthbound men.

"You told me"—Diane was laughing with the memory of it—"that you'd rather be flying and defending us so that nobody bombed us while we were demonstrating for peace!"

It was funny now; it had not been then.

"Yeah, that sounds like something I might have said."

"How amusing," Davis smirked. "And what are you protecting us from now? The Brazilians? Or the Martians?"

You overstuffed fruit, you wouldn't even fit into a cockpit. But Kinsman replied merely, "From the politicians. My job is Congressional liaison."

"Twisting Senators' arms is what he means," came Neal McGrath's husky voice from behind him.

Kinsman turned.

"Hello, Chet, Diane . . . em, Larry Davis, isn't it?"

"You have a good memory for names!"

"Goes with the job."

Kinsman studied McGrath. It was the first time they had been physically close in many years. Neal's hair was still reddish; the rugged outdoors look had not been completely erased from his features. He looked like a down-home farmer; Kinsman knew he had been a Rhodes scholar. McGrath's voice was even softer, throatier than it had been years ago. The natural expression of his face, in repose, was still an introspective scowl. But he was smiling now.

His cocktail party smile, thought Kinsman. Then he realized, Neal's starting to get gray. Like me.

"Tug Wynne tells me I was pretty rough on your boss this morning, Chet." The smile on McGrath's face turned just a shade self-satisfied.

"Colonel Murdock lost a few pounds, and it wasn't all from the TV lights," Kinsman replied.

"I was only trying to get him to give me a good reason for funneling money into a permanent lunar base."

Kinsman said, "The House Appropriations Committee approved the funding. They're satisfied with the reasons we gave them."

"Not good enough," McGrath said firmly. "Not when we've got to find money to reclaim every major city in the nation, plus new energy exploration, *and* crime control, *and*—"

177

"And holding down the Pentagon before they go jumping into Brazil," Diane added.

"Thanks, pal," Kinsman said to her. Turning back to McGrath, "Look, Neal, I'm not going to argue with you. The facts are damned clear. There's energy in space, lots of it. And raw materials. To utilize them we need a permanent base on the Moon."

"Then let the corporations build it. They're the ones who want to put up solar power satellites. They want to mine the Moon. Why should the taxpayers foot the bill for a big, expensive base on the Moon?"

"Because the heart of that base will be a low-gravity hospital that will—"

"Come on, Chet! You know it'll be easier and cheaper to build your hospital in orbit. Why go all the way to the Moon when you can build it a hundred miles overhead? And why should the Air Force do it? It's NASA's job."

Kinsman could see that McGrath looked faintly amused. *He enjoys arguing. He's not fighting for his life.*

Glancing at Diane, then back at McGrath, Kinsman answered, "NASA's fully committed to building the space stations and helping the corporations to start industrial operations in orbit. Besides, we've got an Air Force team of trained astronauts with practically nothing to do."

"So build your hospital in orbit. Or cooperate with NASA, for a change, and put your hospital into one of their space stations."

"And running the hospital will cost twenty times more than a lunar base will," Kinsman said. "Every time you want a Band-Aid you'll have to boost it up from Earth. That takes energy, Neal. And money. A permanent base on the Moon can be entirely self-sufficient."

"In a hundred years," McGrath said.

"Ten. Maybe five."

"Come on, Chet. You guys are already spending billions on the strategic defense system. You can't have the Moon, too. Let it go and stop pushing this pipe dream of Fred Durban's."

"A lunar base makes sense, dammitall, on a straight cost-effectiveness basis. You've seen the numbers, Neal. The base will pay for itself in ten years. It'll *save* the taxpayers billions of dollars in the long run."

A crowd was gathering around them. McGrath automatically raised his voice a notch. "That's just like Mary-Ellen saves me money at department store sales. I can't afford to save that kind of money. Not this year. Or next. The capital outlay is too high. To say nothing of the overruns."

"Now wait . . ."

"There's never been a military program that's lived within its budget. No, Chet. Moonbase is going to have to wait."

"We've already waited twenty years."

The rest of the party had stopped. Everyone was watching the debate.

"Our first priority," McGrath said, more to the crowd than to Kinsman, "has got to be for the cities. They've become jungles, unfit for human life. We've got to reclaim them and save the people who're trapped in them before they all turn into savages."

"But what about energy?" Kinsman demanded. "What about jobs? What about natural resources? You can't save the cities without them, and space operations can give us all those things."

"Let the corporations develop those programs. Let them take the risks and make the profits. We're putting enough money into space and too much into the Pentagon—including plans for a manned antisatellite spaceplane that your brass won't even tell us lowly Senators about."

The spaceplane, Kinsman realized. Neal's pissed because nobody's briefed him on the new spaceplane interceptor concept.

Aloud he was still arguing, "The corporations aren't going to develop anything, Neal, unless the government backs them. You know how they work: let Uncle Sam take the risks and when it's safe they'll come in and take the profits."

McGrath nodded. "Sure. Fine. But NASA's the agency that's running with that particular ball. The Aerospace Force has no business extending its gold-plated tentacles all the way to the Moon."

It's like he's running for re-election, Kinsman said to himself. Then he realized, Of course he is! They always are.

"Sure, Neal, play kick the Pentagon," he said. "That's an

179

awfully convenient excuse for ducking the issue."

With the confident grin of a hunter who had finally cornered his quarry, McGrath asked, "So you want to build a permanent base on the Moon, despite the fact that we've signed treaties with the Russians to keep the Moon demilitarized . . ."

"This base isn't going to be a fortress, for god's sake. You know that. It's a hospital. We're just using military astronauts to get the job done because we have a trained corps of people who aren't being utilized. The Russians *want* to work with us on this."

"All right, all right." McGrath waved his hand, still grinning. "Even so. You put up this hospital of Durban's, this super geriatrics ward on the Moon, at a cost of billions. How's that going to help the welfare class in the cities? How's that going to rebuild New York or Detroit?"

"Or Washington," someone murmured.

Kinsman said, "It will create jobs . . ."

"For white engineers who live in the suburbs."

"It will save lives, for Chrissake!"

"For rich people who can afford to go to the Moon to live."

"It'll give people hope for the future."

"Ghetto people? Don't be silly."

"Neal," Kinsman said, exasperation in his voice, "maybe space operations won't solve any of those problems. But neither will anything else you do. Without a strong space effort you won't have the energy, the raw materials, the new wealth you need to rebuild the cities. Space gives us a chance, a hope—space factories and space power satellites will create new jobs here on Earth, increase the Gross National Product, bring new wealth into the economy. Nothing that you're promising to do can accomplish that, and nothing short of that can solve the problems you're so damned worked up about."

His smile a bit tighter, McGrath said, "Perhaps so. But your Moonbase won't do that. Industrial operations in orbit might do it. The corporations could do it, if they wanted to take the risks."

"But the corporations aren't moving fast enough. They're waiting for us to pave the way for them."

"That's why NASA's building the space stations," Mc-Grath said. "To encourage the corporations to push harder on industrial operations in orbit."

"But that's not enough! The most economical way to supply those space stations and orbital factories is with raw materials from the Moon."

Diane touched his arm, a curious gleam in her dark eyes. "Chet, why do you want a Moonbase so much?"

"Why? Because . . . I was just telling you . . ."

She shook her head. "No, I don't mean the official reasons. Why do *you* dig the idea? Why does it turn you on?"

"We need it. The whole human race needs it."

"No," she repeated patiently. "*You*. Why are you for it? What's in it for you?"

"What do you mean?"

"What makes you tick, man? What turns you on? Is it a Moonbase? Power? Glory? What moves you, Chet?"

They were all watching him, the whole crowd, their faces eager or smirking or inquisitive. Kinsman looked past them, through them, remembering. Floating weightless, standing on nothing, alone, free, away from them all. Staring back at the overwhelming beauty of Earth, rich, brilliant, full and shining against the black emptiness. Knowing that people down there are killing themselves, killing each other, killing their world and teaching their children how to kill. Knowing that you are part of it, too. Your eyes filling with tears at the beauty and the horror. To get away from it, far away, where they can't reach you, where you can start over, fresh, clean, new. How could they see it? How could any of them understand?

"What moves you, Chet?" Diane asked again.

He made himself grin. "Well, for one thing, since they started using synthetic coffee in the Pentagon . . ."

A few people laughed, a nervous titter. But Diane would not let him off the hook. "Get serious, Chet. This is important. What turns you on?"

They don't really want to know, he told himself. They would never understand. How could they?

"You mean, aside from the obvious things, like women?"

Diane nodded gravely.

"I never really thought about it. Hard to say. Flying, I guess. Getting out on your own responsibility, away from all the committees and chains of command."

"There's got to be more to it than that," Diane insisted.

"Well . . . have you ever been out on the desert, at an Israeli outpost, dancing all night by firelight because you know that at dawn there's going to be an attack and you don't want to waste a minute of living?"

There was a heartbeat's span of dead silence. Then one of the women asked in a near-whisper, "When were you . . . ?"

Kinsman said, "Oh, I've never been there. But isn't it a romantic picture?"

They all broke into laughter. That burst the bubble, Kinsman knew. The crowd began to dissolve, fragmenting into smaller groups. Dozens of conversations began to fill the silence that had briefly held them.

"You cheated," Diane said, frowning.

"Maybe I did."

"Don't you have anything but ice water in your veins?"

He shrugged. "If you prick us, do we not bleed?"

"Don't talk dirty."

He took her by the arm and headed for the big glass doors at the far end of the room. "Come on, we've got a lot of catching up to do."

He pushed the door open and they stepped out onto the balcony. Shatterproof plastic enclosed it and shielded them from the humid, hazy Washington evening—and from the occasional sniper who might be on the roofs across the street.

"Being a senator hath its privileges," Kinsman said. "My apartment over in Alexandria is about the size of this balcony. And no air-conditioning allowed."

Diane was not listening. She stretched catlike and pressed against the plastic shielding. To Kinsman she looked like a sleek black leopard: supple, fascinating, dangerous.

"Sunset," she said, looking toward the slice of red sky visible down the street. "Loveliest time of the day."

"Loneliest time, too."

She turned to him, her eyes showing genuine surprise. "Lonely? You? I never thought of you as being lonely. I always pictured you surrounded by friends."

"Or enemies," Kinsman heard himself say.

"You never did marry, did you?"

"You did."

"That was a long time ago. It's even been over for a long time."

"I orbited right over your wedding," he said. "I waved, but you didn't wave back."

Her eyebrows went up. "You walked out on me, remember? More than once. It wasn't my idea for you to go. You chose a goddamned airplane over me."

"I was young and foolish."

"You'd still make the same choice today, and we both know it. Only now you want to go to the Moon."

Kinsman looked into her deep, dark eyes. She was not angry with him. Curious, perhaps. Puzzled. Hurt?

He said, "That doesn't mean I *like* making the choices that way, Diane. We all have our problems, you know."

"You? You have problems? Weaknesses?"

"I've got a few, tucked away here and there."

"Why do you hide them?"

"Because nobody else gives a damn about them." Before Diane could reply, he said, "I sound sorry for myself, don't I?"

"Well . . ."

"Who's this Larry character?"

"He's a very nice guy," she said firmly. "A good agent and a good business manager. He doesn't go whizzing off into the wild blue yonder . . . or, space is black, isn't it?"

"As black as the devil's heart," Kinsman answered. "I don't go whizzing off anymore, either. I've been grounded."

She blinked at him. "Grounded? What does that mean?"

"Clipped my wings," he said. "Deballed me. No longer qualified for flight duty. No orbital missions. No lunar missions. They won't even let me fly a plane anymore. Got some shavetail to jockey me around. I work at a desk."

"But . . . why?"

"It's a long, dirty story. Officially, I'm too valuable to risk. Some shit like that."

"Chet, I'm so sorry. Flying means so much to you, I know." She took a step toward him.

"Let's get out of here, Diane. Let's go someplace safe and watch the Moon come up and I'll tell you all the legends about your namesake."

He could hear her breath catch. "That's . . . that's some line."

He wanted to reach out and hold her. Instead he said lamely, "Yeah, I suppose it is."

She came no closer. "I can't leave the party, Chet. They're expecting me to sing."

"Screw them."

"All of them?"

"Don't talk dirty."

She laughed, but shook her head. "Really, Chet, I can't leave."

"Then let me take you home afterward."

"I'm staying here tonight."

There were things he wanted to tell her, but he checked himself.

"Chet, please . . . it's been a long time."

"Yeah. Hasn't it, though."

The party ended at midnight when the sirens sounded the curfew warning. Within fifteen minutes Kinsman and everyone else had left the stately red-brick Georgetown house and taken taxis or buses or limousines homeward. Precisely at twelve-thirty electrical power along every street in the District of Columbia was cut off.

Kinsman fumbled his way in darkness up the narrow stairs to his one-room apartment. It was still unfamiliar enough for him to bark his shins on the leg of the table alongside the sofabed. The long, elaborately detailed string of profanity he muttered started and ended with his own stupidity.

In less than an hour of staring into the darkness he drifted to sleep. If he had any dreams he did not recall them the next morning. For which he was grateful.

The Pentagon looked gray and shabby in the rain. It bulked like an ancient fortress over the greenery of Virginia. The old parking lots, converted into athletic fields for the Defense Department personnel, were bare and empty except for the growing puddles pockmarked by the raindrops. Off in the mists, like enchanted castles in the clouds, the glass-walled office buildings of Crystal City lent a touch of contrast to the brooding old concrete face of the Pentagon.

184

Feeling as cold and gray within himself as the weather outside, Kinsman watched the Pentagon approach through the rain-streaked windows of the morning bus. As always, the bus was jammed with office workers, many of them in uniform. They were silent, morose, wrapped in their own private miseries at 7:48 in the morning.

The Pentagon corridors had once been painted in cheerful pastels, but now they were faded and grim. Kinsman checked into his own bilious green cubbyhole, noted the single appointment glowing on his desktop computer screen, and immediately headed for Colonel Murdock's office.

Frank Colt was already there, slouched in a fake leather chair in the Colonel's outer office. Otherwise the area was unpopulated. Even the secretaries' desks were empty. Frank always arrives on the scene ahead of everybody else, creases sharp and buttons polished, Kinsman thought. Wonder how he does it?

"Morning," said Colt, barely glancing up at Kinsman.

"I'm glad you didn't say *good* morning," Kinsman replied.

"Sure as shit ain't that."

Kinsman nodded. "Murdock's not in yet?"

Colt gave him a surly look. "Hey, man, it's only eight o'clock. He told us to be here at eight sharp, right? That means he won't waltz in here for another half-hour. You know that."

The Colonel's got his own car, he doesn't have to hit the bus on schedule.

"How'd the party go last night?" Colt asked.

"Lousy. Neal's getting more stubborn every year."

"We're gonna hafta lower the boom on him."

"That might not be so easy."

"I know, but what else is there?"

"Maybe if we got somebody to brief him on the space-plane interceptor . . . he's pissed about not being in on that."

"Murdock don't have the guts to suggest that upstairs."

"I know."

The secretaries began drifting in, chatting over their plastic cups of synthetic coffee. True luxury now consisted of obtaining real coffee, smuggled in through the embargo that extended from Mexico's borders southward.

185

Sniffing at the aroma, Colt said, "How can they make it smell so good and taste so lousy?"

Kinsman shook his head.

"Damned Commies won't stop at nothing," Colt complained to the world in general. "First they cut off our oil, and now our coffee."

The Colonel's private secretary, an iron-gray woman with a hawklike unsmiling face, arrived last—as befitted her rank.

"Colonel Murdock is upstairs," she informed Kinsman and Colt. How she knew this was a mystery they did not question. "He's briefing the General on yesterday's testimony."

Yesterday's fiasco, thought Kinsman.

The two majors sat in front of the chief secretary's desk. Kinsman felt like a traveling salesman kept waiting before being allowed to make his pitch to the prospective customer.

"You catch the late news last night?" Colt asked.

Kinsman shook his head.

"Shoulda seen our beloved leader," Colt said solemnly.

The secretary glared at him, but quickly returned her attention to the morning mail on her desk.

"Murdock was on the news last night?"

"Sure was. Big floppy handkerchief and all."

"Terrific."

"They showed the part where he got mixed up between miles and kilometers and wound up saying the Moon's bigger'n the Earth."

They both laughed. The secretary glowered at them.

Colonel Murdock burst into the anteroom, his usual worried frown etched into near panic, his uniform jacket unbuttoned, his tie pulled loose.

The secretary rose with a handful of papers.

"Not now!" Murdock's voice was high and shrill.

Christ, Kinsman thought, he's already four o'clock nervous and it isn't even eight-thirty yet!

"Get in here, both of you!" the Colonel snapped as he opened the door to his private office.

By Pentagon standards, Murdock's room was almost sumptuous: a real wood desk, several cushioned chairs, even a synthetic leather couch along the far wall, beneath the National Space Society map of the Moon. The Colonel had a standard-issue desktop computer, but no less than four television sets bunched side by side against the wall opposite the desk. Most impressive of all, it was an outside office with a real window that looked out on the gray river and the fog-shrouded National Airport.

That's the only thing he's really good at, Kinsman said to himself: feathering his own nest. He doesn't believe in Moonbase any more than McGrath does, but he'll use it to worm his way farther up the ladder.

"We've got troubles," the Colonel said. He sat at his desk hard enough to make his jowls quiver.

Colt and Kinsman took the chairs closest to the desk.

"What kind of troubles, sir?" Colt always addressed the Colonel in the formally correct manner. But he always looked to Kinsman as if he were on the edge of laughing at the man. Something about Murdock amused Colt; probably the same flustered incompetence that infuriated Kinsman.

"The General is apeshit over the way the Appropriations Committee hearings are going. He's getting pressure from the Deputy Secretary and the Deputy Secretary's getting it from the Secretary himself. Which means that the White House is putting on the squeeze. The White House!"

Kinsman smiled inwardly. Newton was right. For every force there is a reaction. If the Senate weren't putting up resistance to Moonbase, the White House wouldn't even know it was in the budget request.

Colt was saying, "Sir, if the White House is interested why don't they put the squeeze on the Committee directly? If they leaned on Senator McGrath, for example . . ."

"Can't, can't, can't!" Murdock panted. "McGrath is aiming at Minority Leader next time around. He'd use the pressure from the White House to show his people how good he is—fighting against the Pentagon and even against the President to save the taxpayers' precious dollars."

"Politics," Colt said, making it sound disgusting.

"We've got to come up with something, and *fast*," Murdock said, his pudgy little hands fluttering around the desktop. "The General wants us to go with him to the Deputy

187

Secretary's office at three this afternoon."

No wonder he's terrified, Kinsman realized. It's guillotine time.

Colt seemed completely unawed. "It seems to me, sir, that there's only one thing we can do."

Murdock's hands clenched into childlike little fists. "What? What is it?"

"Well, sir, of course I'm not in on all the details of the upper echelon's big picture . . ."

He's deliberately drawing it out. Kinsman suppressed a grin as he watched Murdock's wide-eyed, open-mouthed anticipation.

". . . but it seems to me, sir, that Senator McGrath would be much more sympathetic to the entire Aerospace Force program if he were fully briefed on the spaceplane interceptor program."

Sonofabitch! Kinsman almost laughed aloud. You stole that right out of my pocket, Frank.

"No!" Murdock shrieked. "Can't do that! He'd run right to the media with it! We can't let them know we're designing a manned interceptor to knock out the Russians' satellites! McGrath would *love* to leak that one!"

"But the Senate Appropriations Committee already knows about the program," Colt said. "Sir."

"Only the chairman," Murdock snapped. "Nobody else has been briefed. Nobody!"

"But they all know that the program exists," Kinsman pointed out. "McGrath knows about it, and he's steamed because he hasn't been formally briefed. He *is* the ranking minority member of the committee."

Murdock shook his head. "There's no connection between our Moonbase program and SDI's interceptor."

"There could be," Colt answered. "There *will* be, sooner or later."

"The Moon is not a militarized area," Kinsman said.

"Then why the fuck are we tryin' to set up a base there?" Colt's profanity, like his cool, was carefully planned and judiciously used, Kinsman knew. But Murdock's reaction was a startled gasp.

"We're *military* men," Colt went on. "We can talk about hospitals and peaceful applications of space technology and even cooperate with the Russians here and there, but we're in this for military reasons. Anything else is just bullshit."

"We are bound by the Space Treaty of 1967," Kinsman said, keeping his voice low, calm. "Military weaponry cannot be put on the Moon."

"You think the Soviets won't put weapons there?"

"No, they won't, because we'll be right alongside them on the Moon. We'll watch each other."

Colt edged forward in his chair. "Listen, man. Both sides are starting to deploy their Star Wars stuff, right? We're developing the spaceplane so we can knock out their ABM satellites as fast as they put 'em in orbit, right? They're gonna be doing the same to us, you can bet on it. There's gonna be a war in orbit, man. Maybe it'll be only the machines that get hurt, but it's gonna be a war, all the same."

"We can't tell people like McGrath that we'll be fighting in space!" Murdock's voice was quaking. "He'd have it all over the media in a hot second. We'd go down in flames."

Kinsman glanced at his wristwatch. "Sir . . . I've got to get over to the Capitol. The committee hearings resume at ten."

He left the Colonel's office like a suburban businessman fleeing a downtown pornography shop, hoping that nobody had seen him there. Once in his own office he squeezed behind his battered metal desk and punched out a phone number.

Mary-Ellen's face filled the tiny display screen on his desk. "Hello, Chet! How are you feeling this morning?"

"Okay, I guess. It was a good party. Aspirin helps."

She smiled ruefully. "I've got to get this place into some semblance of order for a dinner party tonight."

"Uh, Mary—I've got to bug out of here and get to the hearings. Is Diane there?"

Her face clouded briefly. "I don't think she's awake yet."

Dammitall! "Look . . . when she gets up, would you ask her to meet me at the hearings at noon? I've got to talk with her. It's important."

Mary-Ellen nodded as if she understood. "Certainly, Chet. I don't know if she'll be free, but I'll tell her."

"Thanks."

The District Metro connected the Pentagon with the

189

Capitol, so Kinsman did not have to go out into the bleak morning again. The subway train was bleak enough: crowded, noisy, dirty with graffiti and shreds of refuse. It was hot and rancid in the jam-packed train. Smells of human sweat, a hundred different breakfasts, cigarettes, and the special steamy reek of rain-soaked clothing.

The morning's hearing was given over to an antimilitary lobby consisting of, it seemed to Kinsman, housewives, clergymen, and public relations flaks. The old rococo hearing chamber was buzzing with witnesses and their friends, photographers, reporters, senators and their scurrying aides. TV cameras were jammed into one side of the chamber, their glaring hot lights bathing the long green-topped table where the committee members sat facing the smaller table for witnesses.

Who signs the TV stations' energy permits? Kinsman wondered idly as a middle-aged woman with too much makeup on her face read from a prepared statement in a penetrating voice that jangled with New York nasality:

"We are not against the development of useful programs that will benefit the American taxpayer. We support and endorse the efforts of American industry to develop Solar Power Satellites and thereby provide new energy for our nation. But we cannot support, nor do we endorse, spending additional billions of tax dollars on military programs in space. Outer space should be a peaceful domain, not a place in which to escalate the arms race."

Kinsman slouched on a bench in the rear of the crowded hearing chamber, watching the TV monitors because they gave him a better view of the witness. He wished that he did not agree with her.

The woman looked up from her prepared text and said, "Let us never forget the words that we left on the Moon, engraved on the *Apollo 11* landing craft: 'We came in peace for all humankind.'"

The crowd she had brought with her applauded, as did several of the senators. Kinsman snorted at the misquotation. Feminist revisionism. He saw that McGrath was smiling at the woman as she got up from the witness's chair, but not applauding her.

An aide came to McGrath's side, appearing magically

190

from behind the Senator's high-backed chair and whispering into McGrath's ear. He looked up, shading his eyes against the TV lights, and scanned the room. Then he spoke briefly to the aide, who disappeared as magically as he had arrived.

The next witness was a minister and former Army chaplain who now headed his own church in Louisiana. As he was being introduced McGrath's aide suddenly popped up beside Kinsman.

"Major Kinsman?"

Kinsman jumped as if a cop had suddenly clapped him on the shoulder.

"Yes," he whispered.

Wordlessly the young man handed him a note which read: *See you in the corridor when the session ends. Diane.*

It was neatly typed, even the signature. She must have phoned Neal's office, Kinsman realized. By the time he looked up from the yellow paper the aide was gone.

Kinsman sat through two more witnesses, both university professors. The first one, when he was not toying with his mustache, was an economist who showed charts which he claimed proved that *private* investment in space industries would help the national economy greatly, but *government* investment in space would only increase the inflation rate. The other, an aging, grossly overweight biophysicist, insisted that space development of any kind was unsound ecologically.

"It will cost more in energy and environmental degradation," he intoned in a deep, shaking, doomsday voice, "to place large numbers of workers into space than those workers will ever be able to return to the people of this Earth in the form of energy or usable goods. Space is only good for the very rich, and it will be the poor peoples of the Earth who will pay the price for the privileged few."

As soon as Kinsman saw that the committee chairman was going to gavel the session into adjournment he ducked out the big gleaming oak double doors and into the quiet, marble-walled corridor. Diane was walking up the hall toward him.

"Perfect timing," Kinsman said, taking her by the arm.

Her smile was good to see. "I can't make it a long lunch, Chet," she warned. "I've got to meet Larry and fly up to New York for a contract negotiation."

191

"Oh."

"I'll only be gone overnight. I've got a concert up there Friday night, then the whole weekend's taken up with briefings and medical checkups . . ."

"With what?"

The click of their footsteps on the marble floor was lost as the rest of the crowd poured out of the hearing chamber and into the corridor.

Raising her voice, Diane said, "I've been invited to fly up to the opening of Space Station Alpha. Didn't Neal tell you?"

"No, he didn't."

"I thought he had. We're going up on the special VIP shuttle Monday. Just for the day."

Kinsman felt stunned.

Diane was grinning at him. "I thought it'd be fun to see what it's like up there. Maybe I'll find out what fascinates you about it so much."

Nodding absently, he led Diane to the elevators that went down to the basement cafeteria. "You've been invited to Alpha," he muttered. "That's more than anybody's done for me."

Diane said nothing.

An elevator opened and he ushered her into it, then slapped the DOOR CLOSE button before any of the crowd coming down the corridor could reach them.

"You'll be tied up all weekend?" Kinsman asked.

"That's what they told me."

"I thought maybe we could get together for dinner or something."

Diane gave a little shake of her head. "I don't think so, Chet. I'm sorry."

The elevator door slid open and they were faced with another crowd, the clerks and secretaries who were lined up for their cafeteria lunch. Silently, numbly, Kinsman got into the line behind Diane. They picked up their trays and selected their food: Diane a fruit salad, Kinsman a bowl of bean soup. Both passed the steam tables with their pathetic-looking "specials." Both took iced fruit drinks.

Kinsman led Diane through the crowd to the farthest corner of the busy, clattering cafeteria and found a table that was big enough only for the two of them.

"It's not the fanciest restaurant in town," he said as they sat down. "But it's the toughest to bug."

"What did you say?" Diane's eyes went wide.

He gestured at the crowded cafeteria. "Nobody knows who's going to sit where. And the background noise is high enough to defeat mikes hidden in the ceiling."

"You're serious?"

Kinsman nodded. "You remember last night, you were asking me why I want Moonbase so much?"

She nodded.

"It's not just a lunar base, Diane." He hesitated, wondering how much he could tell her, how far he could trust her. "It's a new world. I want to build a new world."

"On the Moon."

"That's the best place for it."

"You *are* serious, aren't you?"

"I sure as hell am."

She tried to laugh; it came out as an unsure giggle. "But the Moon . . . it's so desolate, so foresaken . . ."

"Have you been there?" he countered. "Have you watched the Earth rise? Or planted footprints where no human being has ever walked before? Have you been anywhere in your whole life where you really were on your own? Where you had the time and the room and the peace to think?"

"That's what you want?"

"Being here is like being in jail. It's a madhouse. I'm locked into Pentagon level three, ring D, corridor F, room number—"

"But we're all in that same jail, Chet. One way or another, we're all locked up in the same madhouse."

"It doesn't have to be that way." He reached out to grasp her hand. "We can build a new world, a new society, all those things you sing about in your songs—love, freedom, hope. We can have them."

"You can have them," Diane said. "What about all the billions of others who can't get to your new world, no matter what?"

"We've got to start someplace. And we've got to start now, right *now*, before we sink so far back into the mud that we won't have the energy or the materials or the people to do

193

the job. Civilization's cracking apart, Diane."

"And you want to run away from the catastrophe."

"No! I want to prevent it." Realizing the truth of it as he spoke the words, Kinsman listened to himself, as surprised as Diane at his revelation. "We can build a new society on the Moon. We can set an example, just the way the new colonies of America set an example for the old world of Europe. We can send energy back to the Earth, raw materials—but most of all, we can send hope."

"That's not your real reason," she said. "Nobody ever did anything for the sake of philosophy. That's not what's really driving you."

"It's a part of it. A big part."

Diane studied his face. "But only part. What's the rest of it, Chet? Why is this so important to you?"

"It's the freedom, Diane. There are no rulebooks up there. No chains of command. You can work with people on the basis of their abilities, not their rank or their connections. It's—it's so completely different that I don't know if I can describe it to you. There's nothing like it on Earth."

"Freedom," Diane echoed.

"In space. On the Moon. A new society. A new world. A world that you could be part of, Diane."

She shook her head. "Not me. I can see how important it is to you, Chet, but it's not for me." Her hand slid away from his. "If I'm going to help build a new world, it'll be right here on *terra firma*. That's where we need it."

He leaned back in his chair. "By singing folk songs."

"They give people hope, too, you know."

Kinsman clenched his empty hand. "You'll never make a new society on Earth, kid. Too many self-interests. Too much history to undo. Society's locked in place here. The only way to unlock it is to build a showplace . . ."

"A Utopia?" She grinned at the thought.

"It won't be Utopia. But it'll be better than anything here on Earth."

She started to shake her head again, but Kinsman leaned forward intently. "Listen to me," he said urgently. "Whether you agree with me or not doesn't matter. But you've got to tell Neal that the longer he fights against the Moonbase appropriation the closer he's pushing us into a major confron-

194

tation in space, a full-scale conflict with the Russians that can only end in nuclear war."

Diane stared at him. "I should tell Neal . . . why do you think that I—"

"You've got to!" Kinsman insisted. "I can't talk to him directly. Not even through Mary-Ellen. They'll know what I'm doing: the brass, the people who are pushing us toward war. But you can warn him. He'd listen to you."

Her face was a frantic mixture of fear and disbelief. "But I won't see him until—"

"See him! Tell him! It's important. Vital."

"But why can't you—"

"He'd want specifics from me that I can't give him. And any conversations I have with him are probably monitored."

"How did you—"

"You can talk to him," Kinsman went on, ignoring her objections. "Tell him it's either a peaceful Moonbase or the spaceplane interceptor. He'll understand."

Kinsman walked Diane to the front entrance of the Capitol and down the long granite steps that gave the building its impressive facade. Larry Davis was waiting for her in a real limousine, long and luxurious, pearl gray, with a liveried black driver.

"Come on!" he yelled out the car window. "We'll miss the flight and there's not another one till six!"

Kinsman deliberately held Diane for a moment and kissed her. She seemed surprised.

"Call me when you get back to town," he said.

"Okay," she answered shakily.

"And talk to Neal."

"Yes . . . yes." She ran down the last few steps and into the waiting limousine.

The car pulled away with a screech of tires on the wet paving, a rare sound in conservation-conscious Washington. Kinsman watched the limousine thread its way through the sparse traffic. Not a bad way to travel, he mused, for somebody who sings about the hungry poor.

The weather had cleared enough for Kinsman to take the bus back to the Pentagon. The sky was still gray as he waited for the bus in the L-shaped enclosure at the curb, but the rain had ended. The enclosure was filthy with litter, its plastic walls scribbled with graffiti. It stank of urine. Finally the steamer came chugging into sight. Just as its doors opened for Kinsman, another man came running down the sidewalk hollering for the driver to wait for him.

Kinsman saw that it was Tug Wynne puffing toward the bus, and silently wished the driver would close the doors and hurry on. But the sallow-faced Hispanic was in no hurry. He waited patiently for the burly newsman.

Kinsman took a back seat in the nearly empty bus. Sure enough, Wynne came over to him.

"Mind if I sit with ya?"

"Not at all," Kinsman lied. "Go right ahead."

Wynne slid into the seat, wedging Kinsman solidly between the window and his own bulk. From the smell of it, Wynne's lunch had been mostly bourbon.

"Not much fireworks in this morning's hearings, eh?"

"Not much," Kinsman agreed. The bus lurched around a corner and headed down Delaware Avenue, chuffing.

"You see the look on the chairman's face when that perfessor started talkin' about the dangers of beaming microwaves through the atmosphere?"

"That's when he closed the session, wasn't it?"

"Sure was. He's not gonna give any eco-nut a chance to scare people about power satellites. Not with GE back in his home state!" Wynne chuckled to himself.

"It was time to break for lunch anyway," said Kinsman.

"Yeah. Say, wasn't that Diane Lawrence in the cafeteria with you?"

"Yes. She was singing at the party last night. Didn't you hear her?"

Wynne looked impressed. "And now she's breaking bread with you. Fast work. Or is she an old family friend, too?"

"I've known Diane for years," Kinsman said, staring out of the bus window at the passing buildings. This part of Washington was drab and rundown. Not much money between the Capitol and the Navy Yard. Just people's homes. Kids playing on the sidewalks. They'll grow up to stand in unemployment lines.

Wynne jarred him out of it. "Haven't seen you with any women since you arrived in Washington."

"My private life," Kinsman said, still staring out the window, "is my private life."

"Sure. I know. And I guess it must make some kinda mental block . . . killing that girl like that."

Kinsman whirled on him. "Stop fishing, dammit! I've got nothing to say to you on that subject."

"Sure. I understand. But you know, reporters hear things . . . rumors float around. Like, I heard you got hurt pretty bad yourself up there." He waggled a forefinger skyward.

"Bullshit," Kinsman snapped.

"I know you gotta deny it, and all. But what I heard was that you got hurt . . . radiation damage, they say. And now you're impotent. Or sterile."

Thinking of the thousands of nights he had spent alone since returning from that mission and the agonies of the few times he had tried to make love to a woman, Kinsman laughed bitterly.

"That's what they say, do they?" he asked Wynne.

The older man nodded, his expression blank.

"Well, you can tell them for me that they're all crazy."

Wynne nodded gravely. "Glad to hear it. But how come nobody's ever seen you go out with a woman? In all the time since you've been in the District . . ."

The sonofabitch thinks I'm gay! "Listen. I am heterosexual and I'm not sterile. I've never been involved in any accidents in space or anywhere else that would impair my ability to make a woman pregnant. Is that clear?"

"Major, you have a way of making your points."

"Good." And it's not a lie, either. Not completely. I'm not impotent—except when I'm with a woman.

The office of the Deputy Secretary made Colonel Murdock's painfully acquired luxuries seem petty and vain. The office was huge, and in a corner of the Pentagon so that it had *two* windows. Rich dark wood paneling covered the walls. Deep carpeting. Plush chairs. Flags flanking the broad, polished mahogany desk.

General Sherwood was a picturebook Aerospace Force officer: handsome chiseled profile, silver-gray hair, the piercing eyes of an eagle. He sat before the Deputy Secretary's desk looking perfectly at ease in his blue, beribboned uniform, yet so alert and intelligent that one got the impression he could instantly take command of an airplane, a spacecraft, or an entire war.

He carries those two stars on his shoulders, thought Kinsman, with plenty of room to add more.

The Deputy Secretary, Ellery Marcot, was a sloppy civilian. Tall, high-domed, flabby in the middle, and narrow in the chest, he peered at the world suspiciously through thick old-fashioned bifocals. His suit was gray, his thinning hair and mustache grayer, his skin as faded as an old manila file folder. Kinsman had never seen the man without a cigarette. His desk was a chaotic sea of papers marked by islands of ashtrays brimming with cigarette butts.

"Gentlemen," he said after the polite handshakes were finished and the four uniformed officers seated according to rank before his desk, "we have reached a critical decision point."

General Sherwood nodded crisply but said nothing. It would have been easy to assume that his Academy-perfect exterior was nothing but an empty shell. His eyes were *too* sky-blue, his hair just the right shade of experienced yet virile silver. But Kinsman knew better. He'll get those other two stars. And soon.

Marcot blinked myopically at them. "For the past four years the Aerospace Force has struggled to maintain some semblance of an effective program for manned spaceflight. We have had to battle against NASA, the Congress, and the White House."

"And our own SDI Office," Colt added.

Murdock turned sharply toward Colt. But then he saw General Sherwood smiling and nodding.

"Yes, the Strategic Defense group," Marcot agreed, "and their ideas of doing everything with automation."

"But we have made significant progress," the General said.

"Along the wrong road," Marcot snapped.

"It was the only road available at the time," General Sherwood replied, his voice just a trifle harder than it had been a moment earlier. "We had no way of knowing that the SDI Office would try to outflank us with this manned interceptor program."

198

Kinsman spoke up. "Sir, if it hadn't been for our Moonbase program, and the cooperative Soviet program that's linked to it, the Aerospace Force would have had to surrender its entire manned spaceflight capability to NASA several years ago."

"I understand that, Major," said Marcot. "But the Appropriations Committee is not impressed."

"Their attitude is disastrous," General Sherwood agreed. "If they have their way, they'll shoot down Moonbase *and* the spaceplane. They'll leave us entirely defenseless in space. What good are the ABM satellites if we can't protect them against Soviet interceptors?"

Marcot lit another cigarette, then rummaged through his messy papers. "State Department doesn't agree. Sent a memo . . . it's here someplace . . ."

"The State Department," Sherwood muttered, real loathing in his voice.

Colt said, "It's like our military presence in Antarctica. We've got to show the Soviets that we're able and willing to defend our interests, wherever they are."

"The Russians are going ahead with their share of the lunar base," Colonel Murdock said, his voice sounding almost hopeful.

"All the more reason for us to be up there alongside them," Sherwood said. "We must not allow them to have the Moon for themselves."

Feeling like a tightrope walker, Kinsman said, "With all due respect, sir, the Appropriations Committee won't be impressed by that argument. Senators like McGrath are dead-set against anything that looks like the old Space Race of the Sixties."

Marcot peered at him through a haze of smoke. "McGrath," he murmured.

"That's why we initiated the hospital program." Kinsman went on. "The old Air Force pioneered in flight medicine and it would be in keeping with Aerospace Force traditions and missions to build a hospital on the Moon. That would give us a presence on the Moon *plus* a role that has real meaning."

"And whose idea was it," Marcot asked, "to make the base a joint Soviet-American project? Durban's, wasn't it? Him and his internationalist pipe dreams!"

199

"That was done for funding purposes," Kinsman said. "It was easier to get the program started by showing that the Russians were going to share its costs."

"Well, the funding is about to run out," Marcot grumbled. "Our munificent Congress is backing out of the program now that the preliminary explorations are finished and it's time to commit major money for the permanent base."

"And we can't expect the SDI guys to divert funds from their program," General Sherwood said.

"Maybe we should forget about the Moon and concentrate on the antimissile defense. If we can prevent the Soviets from putting up their own version of Star Wars . . ." Marcot let his voice trail off.

"Leave the Moon to the Russians?" General Sherwood sounded almost alarmed.

"What good is the Moon?" Marcot asked. "It has no real military value."

Colt pointed out, "It will when it starts supplying fuels and expendables like oxygen for the SDI satellites. And for the factories the corporations claim they want to build."

"That's ten years away," Marcot said. "Twenty."

Kinsman said nothing, but thought to himself, So the Russians will win control of the Moon after all, in spite of everything we've done over all these years. He shrugged inwardly. Maybe they deserve it. Maybe men like Leonov will do better with it than we would.

"I still don't want Reds on the Moon alone," General Sherwood said. "Bad enough we have to share it with them. Ten, twenty, even fifty years from now—if and when the Moon has any military significance, then we must not allow the Soviets to have it totally to themselves. Especially by default!"

Marcot sank back in his chair, cowed temporarily by the General's fire. "Well, then," he said at last, sucking hard on his cigarette, "how do we get around this man McGrath —without compromising the spaceplane program?"

"We could brief him on the interceptor," Kinsman heard himself saying, "in exchange for a written oath of secrecy. I think a large part of his resistance to the Moonbase idea is that he feels out in the cold on the spaceplane."

Shaking his head, Marcot replied, "The White House has forbidden us to tell McGrath anything about it. He's a rabble-rouser—a secrecy oath won't mean a thing to him."

"I disagree, sir," Kinsman said. "I've known Neal since we were kids. He has a very strong sense of responsibility. If he signed a secrecy oath, he would keep his word."

But Marcot's head was still waggling negatively. "And he's nosing after the Minority Leader's job. From there he can aim for the White House. We can't give him anything that would help him along *that* route."

"But—"

"No," Marcot went on, tapping the ash from his cigarette, "I don't see any way around it. Either you convince McGrath that Moonbase is necessary or we have to forget about the Moon and concentrate all our resources on the spaceplane and strategic defense."

General Sherwood turned to Kinsman. "It's up to you, then, Major. Do you think you can handle it?"

"If he can't, sir, no one can," Colt said before Kinsman could open his mouth.

Colonel Murdock's expression could have turned sweet cream into paint remover, but he remained silent.

"The first thing I'll need," Kinsman heard himself say, "is a seat on that VIP flight Monday to Alpha. McGrath's going up for the dedication ceremonies. It might be a good chance to work on him."

"Or flush him out of an airlock," Marcot muttered.

Sherwood gestured to Colonel Murdock. "See to it, will you?"

"Yessir. But we'll have to bump—"

"Then bump," the General snapped. "Whoever."

Marcot blew a big, relieved cloud of smoke toward the ceiling. "That's it, then. We push ahead with the interceptor program and handle the Moonbase problem separately."

"And let McGrath determine whether we build Moonbase or not," General Sherwood muttered. He was not pleased.

"He's going to make that determination anyway," Marcot said. "We might as well face up to the obvious."

Kinsman said nothing.

201

Returning to his office, Kinsman slumped behind his desk and stared at the old photograph of a lunar landscape he had taped to the wall. The picture showed an astronaut —himself—kneeling in his lunar suit, working over a gadgety-looking piece of scientific gear. He had forgotten what the equipment was, what it was supposed to do. The photograph was faded, its edges browned and curling.

Getting old, he said to himself. And useless.

Beyond the machine and the man in the picture, the broad plain of a lunar *mare* stretched out to the abrupt horizon, where a rounded worn mountain showed its tired-looking peak. Above, riding in the black sky, was the half-sphere of Earth. Years earlier, when the photo had been new, the Earth had been a brilliant blue and white. Now it looked faded and gray, along with everything else in the office.

Suddenly Kinsman got up from his desk and went out into the corridor, heading for Colonel Murdock's office.

What are you going to tell him? he asked himself.

The answer was a mental shrug. Damned if I know. But I've got to tell him *something*.

You can quit, you know. Walk away from it. Murdock would be happy to see you go.

The voice in his head became sardonic. And do what? Wait till I'm Durban's age and have them carry me to the Moon on a stretcher?

There's more to life than getting to the Moon.

He answered immediately, No there's not. Not for me. That's where I've got to be, away from all this crap.

They're going to bring all this crap with them! You know that.

He shook his head doggedly. Not if I can help it.

The Colonel's outer office was empty again. Not even the secretary was there. Kinsman went straight to Murdock's door and rapped sharply on it.

"What? Who is it?"

Kinsman smiled at the thought of how the Colonel must have jumped at the unexpected knocking. He tried the door, but it was locked.

"It's Kinsman," he called. Then, thinking there might be

202

a superior officer locked inside with Murdock, he added, "Sir."

Footsteps. Muffled voices. Then the door opened. Murdock looked flustered.

"What is it?" the Colonel demanded, holding the door open just a few centimeters.

Kinsman heard the other door, the one that opened directly onto the corridor outside, snap shut softly. Whoever had been in the office with Murdock had left.

"I've got to talk to you," Kinsman said, "about this McGrath business."

Colonel Murdock was one of the few men Kinsman knew who could look furious and terrified at the same time. Now he also looked sheepish, with a little boy's caught-in-the-act expression on his chubby face.

He yanked the door open all the way. "All right, come on in."

"If I'm interrupting anything . . ."

Murdock glared at him. "Just a White House liaison man, a representative from the National Security Agency who briefs the President every morning. That's all!"

"I spooked him?" Kinsman punned.

Murdock ignored it. He went behind his desk and plopped into his swivel chair. "Make it fast, Kinsman. I've got a golf date that I can't afford to miss."

Taking the chair directly in front of the Colonel's desk, Kinsman realized he did not know quite where to begin.

"I . . . it's this McGrath thing," he said. "I've been put squarely on the spot. If I can't turn Neal around, Moonbase goes down the tubes."

Murdock nodded. "That's right."

"I don't like it."

"You don't like it? You don't like what?"

"The whole setup," Kinsman said. "Making the whole Moonbase program hinge on my ability to pressure McGrath."

"You can apply all the pressure to him that you can lay your hands on. We'll back you."

With a shake of his head, Kinsman replied, "That's what I don't like."

"So what?" Murdock snapped. "You still have to follow orders, just like the rest of us."

"But Neal's been a friend of mine since—"

"Which is why you got picked for this job. You ought to be able to find a few things in his background that could help to persuade him. Everybody's got bones in their closet."

"Yeah," Kinsman murmured. "Everybody."

"It's either a success with McGrath," the Colonel pointed out needlessly, "or the whole Moonbase program goes into mothballs."

"And the Russians get the Moon to themselves."

"And all of us—including you, Kinsman—get transferred to the Strategic Defense Initiative Office. Since you're grounded, you won't even get to play with the spaceplane. You'll sit at a desk here in the Pentagon for the rest of your life." Murdock smiled slyly.

"It's wrong."

"It's *decided*. You heard the Deputy Secretary. Your job is to convince McGrath. Otherwise, forget about Moonbase."

"We shouldn't be throwing the Moon away," Kinsman insisted.

"Then get McGrath to vote in favor of the base. Get him to swing the minority vote on the committee. Put Durban to work on him. Do whatever you like."

"Durban's in the hospital."

Murdock shrugged.

"Dammitall!" Kinsman exploded. "I don't want this! I don't want any part of it. I want to be flying, not crawling around these goddamned corridors like some roach!"

"Listen to me, hotshot," Murdock snapped back, his face reddening. "You're grounded. Understand? You'll never fly another Air Force plane or spacecraft again. Never! We should never have let you back on flying duty after you killed that Russian."

Kinsman could not answer. His voice choked in his throat.

"You want the Moon so goddamned much," Murdock was yelling now, "you better get your friend McGrath to vote the right way! Because the only way you're ever going to get off the ground, mister, is as a passenger!"

Kinsman's pulse was thundering in his ears the way it had

so long ago, when he had let his temper run away and lead him to murder.

But Murdock was smiling triumphantly at him now. "I know you, Kinsman. I know what makes you tick. You want to get to the Moon and leave us all behind you. Fine! I'm all for it. But you'd better make sure there's a base up there for you to go to; otherwise, you'll be flying a desk for the rest of your life."

"McGrath," Kinsman croaked, "will never go for it. Never."

"I've sweated blood over you," Murdock went on, ignoring Kinsman's words. "You always thought you were so goddamned superior. Hotshot flier. You and Colt, a couple of smartasses. Well, you just goddamned better do the job you're assigned to do or you'll be shuffling papers at a desk until you drop dead!"

For a moment Kinsman said nothing. It took every effort he could muster not to get up from the chair and punch the fat leering face gloating at him.

Finally he said, "I could resign my commission. I could quit the Aerospace Force."

"And do what?" Murdock asked smugly. "Get a job with NASA? Or one of the aerospace corporations?"

"You don't think I could?"

The Colonel's stubby-fingered hands were rubbing together as if by their own volition. "I don't know who would hire a man with a disturbed mental background like yours, Kinsman. After all, if they ask us for your background, we'd have to tell them how . . . unbalanced you can be."

Kinsman was on his feet and grabbing the Colonel's lapels before he realized what he was doing. Murdock was white-faced, half out of his chair, hanging by Kinsman's fists.

Closing his eyes, Kinsman released the Colonel.

"Okay," he said, forcing his breath back to normal. "You win. I'll work on McGrath."

Murdock dropped back into his chair. He smoothed his tunic and looked up at Kinsman furiously. But there was still fear in his eyes.

"You'd better work on McGrath," the Colonel said, his voice trembling. "And the next time—"

"No!" Kinsman leveled a pointed finger at him. "The

205

next time you try holding that over my head, the next time you say anything about it to me or anyone else, there'll be another murder."

"You . . . you just get to McGrath."

"Sure. I'll get to him." Kinsman headed for the door, thinking, I'll take him just like Lee took Washington.

He was staring at the ceiling, waiting for the sleep that was taking longer each night to reach him, when the buzzer sounded. In the darkness he groped for the switch over his sofabed. "Yes?"

"Chet, it's me. Diane."

Wordlessly he groped for the button that opened the lobby door of the apartment building. Only after he let go of it did he think to ask if she was alone.

He rolled out of the sofabed and turned on the battery-powered lamp on his end table. The main electrical service was shut down for the night, of course. Only battery-operated devices, like the building's security locks, could be used after twelve-thirty. Kinsman often wondered if his refrigerator was really insulated well enough to keep everything fresh overnight. He never kept enough food in it to worry over.

By the time Diane knocked on his thin apartment door he was wrapped in a shapeless gray robe and had lit a couple of candles. His wristwatch said 1:23 A.M.

He opened the door. Diane stood there alone, wearing a light sleeveless blouse and dark form-fitting slacks.

"I thought you were in New York," Kinsman said.

"I took the bus back after dinner," Diane replied, stepping into the room.

Even in candlelight the apartment looked shabby. The open sofabed was a tangled mess of sweaty sheets. The desk was littered with paperwork. The room's only chair looked stiff and uninviting.

"It's been an exhausting day," Diane said. "Those bastards in the Public Safety Office damned near canceled Friday's concert. Said my songs were too inflammatory. Thank God for Larry."

"Would you like a drink?" Kinsman asked as he locked the door. "I've got some scotch and there's a bottle of vodka around here someplace."

"Any beer?"

"Might not be very cold."

Diane unslung the heavy leather bag from her shoulder and let it clunk to the floor. She sat on the edge of the bed, kicked her boots off, and leaned back tiredly.

"Beer's fine . . . even warm beer."

"Why the hell did you come back tonight? And how'd you get from the bus terminal this time of night?"

"Phoned for a cab and waited at the terminal until they scared one up for me."

Kinsman took the four steps to his kitchenette and bent down to open the refrigerator. The beer bottles seemed fairly cold to his touch.

"That terminal's not a good place to hang around," he said, peering into the shadowy shelves above the sink for a clean glass. "Especially at night."

"There were a couple of cops. I talked with them while I waited. They recognized me from my videos. They even encouraged the taxi company to find a cab for me."

Handing her the bottle and a glass, Kinsman said, "It pays to be beautiful."

"And famous," she added immediately.

"But . . . why?" he asked, sitting on the floor beside the bed. "What was so important about getting back here?"

She took a swallow of beer from the bottle. "That was a pretty heavy message you laid on me this afternoon."

"Yeah, I guess it was. Have you had a chance to see Neal?"

"Not yet."

"When?"

"Tomorrow. I mean, later today—right after his committee hearings."

"Good."

"But I've got to know something, Chet. That's why I'm here."

"I can't go into the details, Diane. They're classified. But it's damned important that Neal realizes what's at stake."

"What the hell *is* at stake?" she asked.

"I can't tell you all of it . . ."

"Is this room bugged?"

He shook his head in the shadows. "No, I go over the

place pretty thoroughly every few days. And I've got a couple of friends in the Pentagon who keep track of who's listening to whom. My conversations with Neal are monitored, but I'm not important enough to have my apartment wired."

He could not see her face too well in the flickering candlelight, but Diane's voice was high with concern. "Is Neal always watched? Is his office wired, or . . ."

"His office must be. And his home was during the party. They spot-check his phones, I'm sure. That's pretty standard procedure for a senator. He knows about it; they all do. And they know how to protect themselves from it. But it means that I can't tell him everything that he needs to know."

"Just what is it he needs to know?"

Instead of answering, Kinsman got up and padded to the kitchenette for the scotch.

Almost an hour later, after two more beers for Diane and several long pulls of scotch for himself, he was saying, ". . . and that's the politics of it. I can't tell you what the other program is all about, but Marcot and the White House will clobber Neal if they get the chance. Unless, of course, he goes along with the Moonbase program."

Diane asked, "But what about you, Chet? Where do you stand in all this?"

"Right in the middle. I want Moonbase because I want to be there. I want to live on the Moon. I want to set up that new world I was telling you about."

"But if it's a military base . . ."

"Yeah, I know. Even if we start out as a hospital, even if we work jointly with the Russians, there's always the chance that the brass will start turning it into a supply center for a *real* military effort."

"They could do that?"

"Sure. Mine the lunar ores and build military satellites out of them, then place them in orbit around the Earth. Just like the corporations want to build their solar power satellites."

"But the Russians will be there too, won't they?"

Kinsman nodded. "And they'll do the same thing, once they see us do it."

"And you're caught in the middle of all this."

"Yeah, they've got me surrounded." He leaned his head

back against the wall and heard himself go on, "But that doesn't matter. It's where I've got to be if I'm ever going to make it back there."

"There?"

"To the Moon."

"It's like an obsession with you," Diane said.

He smiled at her. "Leonardo da Vinci."

"What?"

"He built gliders and tried them out himself. They never worked too well, but it was enough to make him write, 'Once you have tasted flight, you will walk the Earth with your eyes turned skyward. For there you have been, and there you long to return.' "

Diane smiled at him. "I see . . ."

"Do you?" Kinsman asked. "Do you know what it's like to have everybody around you call you a nut? You were nice about it, you called it an obsession. At the Pentagon they calls us *Luniks*."

"Us?"

"Yeah, there's a few of us, here and there. A couple in NASA, too. Guys like me. Guys willing to fight with everything we've got to get the hell off this lousy dungheap and out into the new world. Hell, I'll bet I could build a mountain just out of the paperwork in the Pentagon that'd reach the Moon. We could *walk* there!"

Diane laughed.

"Murdock and Sherwood and Marcot think we're crazy. Maybe we are. But they use us. They use us to get what they want."

"And you?"

"Sure, I'm using them to get what I want, too. But now the game's getting rough and I don't think we can all stay happy. The big boys are starting to use their muscle on us, and we *Luniks* don't have much muscle to fight back with."

"So what are you going to do now?"

"You know, once I said I'd sell my soul for the chance to get back to the Moon. Now I might have to make that choice."

"You need Neal's help, don't you?"

"He's got to vote for the Moonbase program. If he doesn't there'll be nobody left in space except the warbirds."

209

"Chet . . . do they know about us? Can they use our relationship to hurt Neal? To threaten him?"

Suddenly confused, Kinsman asked, "Us? What relationship?"

"Neal and me . . ."

Kinsman felt as if he were in free-fall, everything dropping away.

Diane pulled herself bolt upright on the bed. "You didn't know about us?"

"Mary-Ellen," Kinsman heard himself mutter.

"She knows," Diane said. "We've tried to keep it as quiet as possible, of course. Nobody in Washington would really care, but they would use it against Neal back in Pennsylvania. A divorce case and an affair with a pop singer—they'd crucify him back home."

"You and Neal," Kinsman said, still stunned by it. "And Mary-Ellen knows."

"We love each other, Chet. Neither of us wanted it to happen, but it has."

"Then when you stayed at their place after the party . . . Jesus Christ, I talked him into going out and finding you, way back in San Francisco!"

"Yes, that's when I first met him. But it wasn't until the Presidential campaign, when I was doing benefits for the New Youth Alliance . . ."

"And Mary-Ellen's just sitting back and letting the two of you have your fun. Or does she have a lover, too?"

"She's being awfully good about it. Says she doesn't want to hurt Neal's career. It makes me feel like hell."

But you sleep with him anyway, Kinsman growled silently. In her home. Aloud, he asked, "Are they going to get a divorce?"

Diane pushed her hair back away from her face with an automatic gesture. "I don't know. We'll see what happens after his re-election campaign next year."

Kinsman pictured Neal campaigning through the state, the solid family man with his wife and two children by his side and Diane waiting for him in motel rooms.

"I think I'm pregnant," she said in a small, almost frightened voice.

"Jesus Christ."

"I can't let anyone know it's Neal's baby. He doesn't know it himself yet."

"What'll you do?"

She shook her head. "I don't know. Have an abortion, I guess."

"And he invited you up to the space station. It wasn't just public relations." He put a slight emphasis on the word *public*. "It's a chance to be with you."

"Your people in the Pentagon don't know about this, do they?" Diane asked. "I mean, if they did they could use it to pressure Neal to vote their way . . ."

He looked up at her. "Diane—I'm one of those Pentagon people."

"But you're his friend. You wouldn't . . ."

"I'm Mary-Ellen's friend, too."

"She doesn't want him hurt."

"Yeah."

Diane swung off the bed and sat on her heels beside Kinsman, on the floor. "Chet . . . you're *my* friend, too. You wouldn't hurt the three of us, would you?"

"And what about me? What do I get?"

Diane reached out and put a hand on his shoulder.

He wanted to laugh. "When you came tapping at my chamber door, I had the crazy notion that you had come all the way down from New York to see me, to be with me."

"That was part of it," she said.

"I wanted you, Diane. I really did. I needed you."

"I'm here."

He brushed her hand away. "No. Not as a bribe. Not because Neal's home with his wife and you're lonely. Not to make me think there's a chance you might leave him for me."

"Chet . . . what can I do? What can I say?"

"Nothing. Not a damned thing."

She got to her feet. "I'd better go, then."

"Where to? There are no taxis this time of the morning. Bus service won't start again until six. You can't walk the streets after curfew."

"But there's no room here."

Kinsman stood up beside her. "Stretch out on the bed. Get some sleep. Just don't take your clothes off."

He padded around to the other side of the bed, blew out

211

the candles and lay down in the darkness. He could feel the warmth of her body next to his, hear her breathing slowly relax into sleep.

For a moment he thought of his interrogation by Tug Wynne. If he could see me now! Kinsman grinned at the irony of it. Sleeping next to a pregnant woman. He did not have to reach down to his crotch to know what was happening. I'm not impotent. Stupid, maybe. But not really impotent.

Several times his eyes closed and he drifted toward sleep. But each time he saw the cosmonaut drifting in silent space, her dead arms reaching out toward him.

McGrath took Mary-Ellen and their two children back to Pennsylvania, where they would stay while he flew to Florida and the new space shuttle that would take the VIPs to the dedication ceremonies aboard Space Station Alpha.

Kinsman spent the weekend doing Murdock's work for the Colonel. He pulled a fistful of Pentagon strings and became a VIP, much to the disappointment of a one-star general at Wright-Patterson Aerospace Force Base, who received a sudden phone call informing him that he had been bumped from the Alpha dedication junket.

Before flying down to Kennedy Space Center, Kinsman visited Walter Reed Hospital, where Fred Durban was. The old man was a permanent invalid now, in the cardiac ward. Kinsman sat beside his bed, the smell of antiseptics and quiet death everywhere; the clean, efficient, coldly impersonal feel of the hospital setting his nerves on edge. Durban's room was bright with flowers. The window looked out on leafy trees and a bright lovely blue sky. But the bed next to his held a retired admiral engulfed by life-support equipment that snaked wires and tubes into every part of his body. He was more machine than man.

It did not bother Durban, though. "I know it looks awful," he said cheerfully, "but that's just what I want them to do for me when I'm sinking below the red line. None of this 'death with dignity' for me! I intend to fight for every minute I can get."

He was painfully emaciated. His once-reddish hair was now nothing more than a wisp of white. His arms were bone-thin, his skin translucent. He belongs in a china shop,

212

not a hospital, Kinsman thought. But those shaggy eyebrows were still formidable, and Durban's voice was doggedly optimistic.

"I'm just trying to hang on long enough so that you youngsters can build my lunar hospital. Up there I'll be a whole lot better. I've warned the staff here that they better keep me alive until they can transfer me to Moonbase."

Kinsman nodded and tried to smile for him. "We're working on it. Working hard."

"Damned right. Wish they had room to set up a hospital section aboard the new space station, though. I'd settle for that, right now."

"I'm going up there tomorrow."

"To Alpha? Good! Tell me about it when you get back."

"I will."

"But how's our Moonbase program working out?"

Kinsman shrugged. "The usual snags with Congress. Committees . . . you know."

Durban closed his eyes. "I've spent my entire damned life arguing with those shortsighted bastards. Anything farther downstream than the next election—forget it, as far as they're concerned."

"They don't have much foresight, that's true."

Durban lay quiet for a moment. The conversation stalled. Then he asked, "But the survey work . . . the site selection and the preliminary planning . . . that's all been done, hasn't it?"

"Yessir. I can bring you the reports, if you like. Once we get the appropriation for the coming fiscal year we can begin actual construction."

"Good." Durban smiled. "In a couple of years I'll be on the Moon, getting my second wind."

Kinsman said nothing.

Still smiling, the old man lifted a frail hand. "I know what you're thinking. In a couple of years I'll be six feet under."

"No . . ."

"Don't try to kid me, son. I can read your face like a blueprint. Von Braun never made it into space at all. Neither did Clarke or Sagan. At least I've been in orbit."

"We'll get you to the Moon, don't worry."

"I don't have a worry in the world. I know they'll never let me ride the shuttle in the shape I'm in now. If I can build my strength back up, then fine. If not, I'll die here . . . probably in this room."

Kinsman had nothing to say.

Durban went on, "But I'll *still* be with you on the Moon. I've left instructions in my will that I want to be buried there. At Moonbase. And I've got enough money stashed away to pay for it, too, by damn!"

"You're a stubborn *Lunik.*" Kinsman smiled.

"Damned right, sonny. One thing I learned early in this game. It takes more than talent, more than brains, more than connections, even. Takes stubbornness. Look at von Braun. Not the world's most brilliant engineer, but a hard-driving man who knew what he wanted and went after it, hell or high water. By God, World War Two was an *opportunity,* as far as he was concerned! The Cold War, the Space Race, he turned them all to his advantage. Other people sneered at him, called him a Nazi, an opportunist, an amoral monster. But he never wavered from his goal. He wanted the Moon and he went out and got it. We *all* got it, thanks to him."

Not all of us, Kinsman answered silently.

"You go get Moonbase started," Durban said. "Don't let them sidetrack you."

"We're trying."

"Going to the new space station, eh? Rubbing shoulders with the politicians and their sycophants. Good. But don't let them stop there. Keep driving for the Moon."

"Yessir."

Durban lifted his head slightly from the pillow. "I'll watch the ceremonies on TV. At least I can turn them off when they get too boring."

Kinsman laughed. The old man was still as feisty as ever.

"All right, son, you run along now. No fun watching an old man trying to stay alive." Durban winked at him. "Besides, I'm due for a bath . . . got a cute young nurse who thinks I'm too feeble to do her any harm."

Getting up from the bedside chair, Kinsman said, "I'll come back when I return from the ceremonies."

"Fine. I'll be waiting right here. I'm not going anyplace."

* * *

214

Even in the earliest morning the Florida sun was blindingly hot. Merritt Island was flat and scrubby, not at all like the hilly California coast at Vandenberg.

Kinsman had flown to Patrick Aerospace Force Base the previous night on a government charter jet filled with Congressional aides and their families. He had slept at the base's Bachelor Officers' Quarters. Now, just after dawn, he had driven a motor pool car to the space center to see the place before the newshounds and tourists cluttered it up.

In the old days of the Apollo moon shots and the original space shuttle launches, the roads and beaches would be covered with upward of half a million onlookers, as thick as ants on sugar. Official guests would have to arise at two in the morning to get to the VIP viewing stands before the roads became totally blocked with tourist cars and campers. But now, with government restrictions on travel and synfuels astronomically expensive, the roads leading to Kennedy Space Center were nearly empty. People watched launches on television, if they watched at all.

Most of the old buildings were still there, including the mammoth Vehicle Assembly Building, the largest enclosed structure on Earth, which was still used by the NASA people. The ancient launch towers, tall stately spiderworks of steel standing against the brazen sky, were strictly tourist attractions now. History had been made there, blasting out flames and mountainous billows of steam as the Saturns and Deltas and shuttles had launched men and automated probes into space. Now they stood empty and quiet, gawked at by a trickle of visitors from all around the world, lectured over by National Park Service guards surrounded by eager, curious youngsters and their sweating, sunburned, slightly bored parents.

The real action now was at the airstrip, where the new shuttles took off and landed. Unlike the older vehicles that Kinsman had flown in, the new designs were truly reusable spacecraft that took off and landed like airplanes.

The shuttle was a double-decker craft, two vehicles one atop the other, joined together like a pair of technological Siamese twins. The bottom one was the jet-powered Lifter. It was all fuel and engines, with a tiny cockpit perched high up on its massive blunt nose. It flew to the topmost reaches of the atmosphere, more than a hundred thousand feet above the ground, and then released its piggyback partner. The Orbiter, smaller of the two mates, carried the passengers and payload on into space on the thrust of its rocket engines. Both planes landed at the airstrip, separately, to be reunited for another flight.

Standing at the airstrip's edge, Kinsman stared at the ungainly-looking pair, one atop the other. She'll never fly, Orville. Gimme a good old rocket booster and a lifting body re-entry vehicle like the Manta, the way God meant men to go into space. But he knew that this new shuttle was making space operations practical. Military men could rocket into orbit atop bellowing boosters, but businessmen and their cargoes rode the new shuttle and saved money. It was cheaper, more efficient, and the gee loads on the passengers were negligible.

Fred Durban could ride into orbit on that bird, Kinsman knew, if he was healthy enough to get out of bed.

The shuttle would carry fifty passengers on this trip. NASA was making three flights with the same bird to the completed space station, all on this one day. The entire world would watch the station's official dedication ceremonies via satellite-relayed television.

"Hey, you! What the hell are you . . ."

Kinsman turned to see an Air Policeman yelling at him from a jeep parked a dozen meters away. The AP was in crisp uniform, with gleaming helmet and dead-black sidearm buckled to his hip. Kinsman was in his summer-weight blues. He walked slowly toward the jeep.

"Oh, sorry, Major. I couldn't see your rank with your back turned." The kid sprang out of the jeep and saluted. He dwarfed Kinsman.

"You expecting trouble, Sergeant?" Kinsman asked, returning the salute.

"Hard to say, sir. We were told some kook groups might try to stage an antigovernment demonstration. Or maybe something more violent by terrorists, like a bomb attempt."

"Well, I'm on your side. I just wanted to see the bird before everybody else got here."

"Sorry I hollered, sir."

"It's okay. Can you give me a lift back to the administration building parking area?"

"Yessir, sure." He waited for Kinsman to seat himself in the jeep, then sprinted around and slid under the steering wheel. As he switched on the nearly silent electric motor, the big sergeant asked incredulously, "You *walked* out here from the admin building, sir?"

Kinsman nodded as the salty breeze blew into his face. All the way back to the administration building he wondered at the insanity of anyone who would even think of bombing a beautiful piece of hardware like this shuttle.

The rest of the morning was a hateful blur to Kinsman. *Now I know what it's like to be invaded and conquered. Crowds of strangers. Solicitous young Air Police—men and women—pointing you in the right direction. Smiling unctuous public relations people from NASA and the big corporations taking you by the elbow and telling you how proud and happy you should be that you're here to help make this day a success.*

Not one of them knew Kinsman. No one recognized his name. No one commented on the astronaut's emblem on his tunic. He was a six-foot chunk of meat to them, a statistic. *I was working in orbit when you were in high school*, he fumed at them silently. But they just smiled and pointed and moved him along: an anonymous visitor, a VIP, a nonperson.

Kinsman was locked into a group of forty-nine strangers and walked through all the preflight ceremonies. A brief physical exam, little more than blood pressure, heartbeat, and breathing rate. The medic giving the blood-pressure tests muttered something about everybody being so excited about flying into orbit that all the pressures were reading high. Kinsman shook his head. *The equipment's miscalibrated*, he thought. *I'm not excited enough to raise my blood pressure.*

The safety lecture was designed to soothe the nerves of jittery civilians who had never gone into orbit before. Then came a five-minute video about how to handle the brief spell of weightlessness until the shuttle docked with the space station—mainly how to use the retch bag under zero-gee conditions. And every minute of the preflight rites took place under the staring eyes of the news cameras.

Kinsman resented it all: these newcomers, these strangers, these moneygrubbers who had fought against *any* pro-

217

grams in space until their boards of directors finally became convinced that there were profits to be made Up There.

His forty-nine "shipmates" included sixteen news reporters (eight female), three freelance writers (one a scenarist from Hollywood), eleven board members of thirteen interlocked corporations (none of them less than fifty years old), nine NASA executives who had never been out of downtown Washington before, and ten men and women (five each) who had been chosen by national lottery to represent "average taxpayers."

They all looked excited and chattered nervously as they were marched from the briefing room, past a double column of news cameras, and out into the muggy morning sunlight. A couple of the business executives seemed to be having some qualms about the thought of actually taking off in a vehicle that was built entirely by the lowest bidders, and several of the NASA desk jockeys looked a bit green. Maybe the space-sickness video got to them, Kinsman thought.

"I thought there were going to be entertainment stars," said one of the women taxpayers.

"They're on the other flight," someone answered.

The PR guide hovering nearest them said, "Two dozen stars from various fields of entertainment will be aboard the second flight, together with an equal number of senators and Congresspersons. There will also be religious leaders from all the major denominations coming up, as well."

Feeling thoroughly out of place and resentful, like an architect who is forced to serve as a clown, Kinsman climbed aboard the big glass-topped, air-conditioned bus that would take them out to the shuttle waiting on the airstrip. He took the seat that a young PR woman with a frozen smile directed him to.

"Have a pleasant flight, Colonel," she said.

"Thanks for the promotion," Kinsman replied to her departing back.

The bus chugged into motion and the speakers set into each chairback came alive with the news report of the momentous day:

"And there goes the first busload of visitors to Space Station Alpha. They're on their way!" gabbled a voice that had spent most of its life hawking consumer products. "This

218

marks the beginning of a new era in space! Fifty ordinary people, just like you and me, will be riding to the space station just as easily and comfortably as we ride the daily bus to our homes and offices and shopping malls. Ordinary people, going into orbit, to a great man-made island in the sky . . ."

Ordinary people, thought Kinsman. Am I ordinary? Is anybody?

One of the "average taxpayers" was seated beside him, on the aisle. She stared at him for several minutes as the bus huffed slowly toward the airstrip and the radio voice prattled on.

"They didn't tell us there'd be any soldiers on this flight," she said at last.

Kinsman turned from the window to look at her. A youngish housewife: softly curled light brown hair, oval face. Dressed in a brand-new flowered pantsuit.

"I'm not a soldier," he answered, almost in a whisper. "I'm in the Aerospace Force."

"Well, why are they letting *you* up? This isn't a military satellite." She looked almost resentful.

An educated taxpayer. Glancing around and keeping his voice low, Kinsman replied, "Confidentially, I . . . well, I used to be an astronaut. They're letting me see what this new stuff is all about. Sort of like a homecoming for me."

Her minifrown softened. "Oh, I get it. Like inviting the old graduates to the school reunion."

Nodding, "More or less."

"I was wondering why you looked so cool and relaxed. You've been through all this before."

"Well, not exactly anything like this."

"Gosh . . . I've never met an astronaut before. I'm Jinny Woods. I'm from New Paltz, New York."

"Chet Kinsman." He shook her hand lightly. "And if you don't mind, I'd just as soon stay in the background here. I'm just a guest. You're the stars of today's show."

She wriggled with pleasure at his flattery. "You mean I shouldn't tell anybody you're an astronaut?"

"I'd rather you didn't. I don't want a fuss made about it."

"Okay . . . It'll be our secret."

Kinsman smiled at her while his mind recalled a line that

a friend of his had once uttered: Hell is, I'm booked into Grossinger's for a week and every girl's mother in the place knows I'm an unmarried medical student.

The bus ride was mercifully brief, but Kinsman wound up being placed beside the same woman inside the shuttle. The interior of the orbiter was much like the interior of a standard commercial jet airliner, except that the seats were plusher, the decor plainer, and there were no windows. Each seatback had a small TV screen built into it. The seats themselves were large, roomy, comfortable, and equipped with a double safety harness that crisscrossed over the shoulders and across the chest.

Jinny Woods fumbled with her harness until Kinsman leaned across and helped her with it. She told him about her two children and her husband back in New Paltz, who was a salesman. He nodded and admired the way she breathed.

And then they waited.

"What's wrong? Why aren't we moving?" Jinny whispered to Kinsman. She looked as if she were afraid of making a fuss, yet genuinely frightened at the same time.

"It'll take several minutes," Kinsman answered. In his mind he pictured what was going on in the cockpit of the orbiter, and in the massive lifter beneath them.

Range safety?

Clear.

Main engine fuel pressure?

Green.

Life support systems?

All green.

Full internal power.

On.

Shuttle One, you are cleared for taxi.

Roger, Tower. One taxiing.

One-quarter throttle. And steer clear of the bumps on the ramp. Let's not shake up the passengers.

The muffled whine of the lifter's hydrogen turbine engines vibrated through the cabin's thick acoustical insulation. Kinsman felt the shuttle surge forward. Sitting in the heavily padded seat with nothing to look at but the gray curving walls of the cabin or the dead eye of the TV screen in front of him, Kinsman imagined himself sitting in the Command Pilot's seat, nudging the throttles forward and handling the controls. The huge, cumbersome double-plane rolled out along the approach ramp and swung onto the five-kilometer-long runway: a broad black road that reached to the horizon and the sky beyond.

Shuttle One, hold for final clearance.

One holding.

Range tracking Go.

Range safety Go.

Meteorology Go.

Mission control Go.

All systems green.

Shuttle One, you are cleared for takeoff.

Roger.

Give 'em a nice easy ride, Jeff.

Only way to fly!

Full takeoff flaps. Full throttle.

Rolling.

Kinsman felt the acceleration pressing him back slightly in his seat. But it was gentle, gentle, nothing like a rocket boost. Hardly any vibration at all.

Two hundred.

Rotate.

The nose came up. Kinsman's hands clutched on his lap, thumb pressing an imaginary controller, and the giant rocket-plane lifted off the ground.

He turned to the woman beside him. "We're up."

She was staring at the TV screen in front of her, still looking scared. Kinsman glanced at his own screen. It showed a view from the camera in the nose of the orbiter as it rode piggyback on the lifter. He could see the bulbous nose and cockpit of the lifter below them, and scudding clouds that they had already climbed past.

"When did they turn the screens on?" he wondered.

"Just as we started down the runway. Didn't you notice?"

"No."

Within fifteen minutes they were high over the Atlantic, a cloud-flecked sheet of hammered gray metal far below them.

The intercom speakers hummed to life. "This is Captain

Burke speaking. I'm the Command Pilot of your orbiter aerospace craft. Our big brother down underneath us will be releasing us in approximately five minutes. They'll fly back to the Cape while we light our rocket engines and head onward into orbit and rendezvous with Space Station Alpha. You will hear some noise and feel a few bumps when we separate. Don't be alarmed."

The separation, when it came, was barely discernible. Kinsman felt a slight sinking sensation as the TV screen showed the lifter swing away and out of sight. Then a dull throbbing pulsed through the cabin, felt in the bones more than heard. The cabin vibrated slightly as the orbiter nosed up.

"Look!" Jinny Woods exclaimed. "I can see the curve of the Earth!"

I know. I've been there. But Kinsman felt the thrill of it all over again. Swiftly their weight diminished until they were in zero gravity, hanging loosely against their restraining harnesses.

Jinny swallowed hard several times but managed to keep herself together. Kinsman watched her closely.

"It feels like falling, at first," he said. "But once you get used to it, it's more like floating. Just don't make any sudden head motions."

She smiled weakly at him.

He relaxed and luxuriated in the freedom of zero gee. How many times has it been? Lost count. Someplace back there I stopped counting. He wondered what would happen if he unbuckled and got up from his seat and glided freely along the aisle separating the double rows of seats. Probably the PR guides would get hysterical. He pictured himself drifting up to the cockpit, going inside to join the crew and their smoothly functioning equipment. He laughed to himself at the thought of commandeering the spacecraft, bypassing the space station and heading on to the Moon. The first space hijack, he mused. Oh, for ten toes!

Soon enough the flight ended as the orbiter lined up with the loading dock at the center of Alpha's set of concentric rings. This was a piece of piloting that Kinsman had never done, and he watched the TV screen, fascinated, as the ship approached the space station like a dart seeking the bull's-eye. Alpha looked like a set of different-sized bicycle wheels nested within one another. Kinsman knew that the biggest one, the outermost wheel, was turning at a rate that would induce a full Earth gravity for the people who lived and worked inside it. The smaller wheels—most of them still under construction—had lighter gravity pulls. The loading dock at the center of the assembly was at zero gee, effectively.

The rendezvous and docking maneuvers were flawless, and soon Kinsman and the other passengers were shuffling, still weightless, along the narrow ladder that led through the orbiter's hatch into the station loading bay.

The loading bay was even more tightly organized than the groundside takeoff had been. There was a NASA or corporate representative for each of the fifty visitors to personally guide each of the individual visitors to the stairs that led "down" to the main living quarters in the outermost wheel.

Kinsman was relieved to be separated from Jinny Woods, although his guide—a sparkling bright young industrial engineer—treated him like a fragile grandfather.

"Just this way, sir. Now you don't actually need the stairs up here in the low-gravity area, but I'd recommend that you use them anyway."

"I've been in zero gee before," Kinsman said.

Ignoring him pleasantly, the young man went on, "We'll be going down—that is, outward toward Level One—where the gravity is at normal Earth value. Your weight will feel like it's increasing as we go down the stairs."

He led Kinsman to a circular hatch set into the "floor" of the loading bay. A metal stairway spiraled down to the other levels of the station.

"Easy does it now!" he said cheerfully, holding Kinsman by the elbow as they took the first steps down.

Kinsman wanted to break free of his grip and glide down the tube until the gravity built up enough for him to walk normally. Instead, grumbling inwardly, he patiently allowed the young engineer to guide him along.

"It's easy to get disoriented in low gee," the kid said.

Feeling like an invalid, Kinsman let himself be led down the stairs. The metal tube they were in was one of the "spokes" that connected the hub of the station with its various wheel-shaped levels. The tube was softly lit by patches of fluorescent paints glowing palely along the circular walls. No power drain, Kinsman realized.

Once safely down to Level One, the fifty first comers were organized into a guided tour. Kinsman endured it, together with the sullen weight of a full Earth gravity that tugged at him like a prisoner's chains.

The station's first level included some laboratory areas, individual living compartments that made submarines look roomy, a galley, and a mess hall. It all looked efficient and compact, although the decor was depressingly familiar to anyone who worked in a government office: bare pastel walls and spongy plastic floor tiles. But the floor curved upward no matter which direction you looked in, and the occasional windows showed stars turning over and over in lazy spirals against the blackness of infinity.

The tour started at one end of the mess hall and finished at the opposite end, where a bar had been set up. Kinsman took a plastic cup of punch from the automatic dispenser just as the second batch of arrivals appeared, exactly at the spot where his own tour had started.

Looking across the bolted-down tables and swiveling chairs along the sloping floor, Kinsman spotted Neal McGrath's tall, dour form among the newcomers. McGrath stared straight at Kinsman and scowled. Kinsman lifted his cup to the Senator, wondering, Is that his normal scowl or is he really sore at me?

Diane was in McGrath's group, surrounded by station personnel and public relations flaks. They all want to be in show biz, thought Kinsman. He did not recognize any of the other personalities.

Gradually the mess hall filled with visitors. Kinsman chatted quietly with several people and tried to avoid being pinned down by several others—including Jinny Woods, who had that "I've got a secret" gleam in her eye whenever she looked Kinsman's way.

Some of the station people hoisted Diane atop one of the bigger tables. As she began tuning her guitar the chattering voices of the crowd diminished into expectant silence.

"I've never been in orbit before," she said. "At least, not this way." They all laughed. "So I'd like to sing a song that's

224

dedicated to the people who made all this possible, the farsighted people who pioneered the way here. It's called 'The Green Hills of Earth.' "

Kinsman ignored the words of her song and bathed in the magic of Diane's voice. Everyone was silent, turned toward her as flowers face the sun, listening and watching her sad, serious face as she sang.

He felt Neal McGrath's presence beside him. Kinsman turned slightly and McGrath said in a throaty whisper, "We've got to talk."

Kinsman nodded.

McGrath put a hand on his shoulder. "Come on."

"Shh. Wait a minute."

"Now!"

A surge of anger welled up in him and Kinsman brushed McGrath's hand off his shoulder. But then it ebbed away and he whispered back, "All right . . . where to?"

McGrath led him back through the corridor that ran the length of Level One, to the area where the living quarters were. He found an empty cubbyhole, no name on the door, and gestured Kinsman inside it.

The two of them filled the tiny compartment. There was nothing much in it: just a bunk built into the curving wall, a sliver of a desk with a bolted-down swivel chair in front of it, and some cabinets along the other wall. Kinsman tried the bunk. It was springy, comfortable, but narrow. He knew that if he stretched out on it, it would be barely long enough for him.

"You'd have a hard time sleeping on one of these," he said to McGrath.

"What's that supposed to mean?" McGrath growled. Neal had taken the chair. It looked pitifully small for him. Kinsman thought of an underfed burro bearing an overfed American tourist.

Shrugging, he replied, "Not a damned thing, Neal, except that these are pretty damned small bunks."

McGrath's scowl did not ease. "Diane told you about her and me."

"That's right."

"Who've you told about it?"

"Nobody."

225

"Nobody yet," McGrath said, emphasizing the second word.

"Yeah," Kinsman agreed. "Nobody yet."

"Mary-Ellen knows all about it."

"So Diane said."

Hunching forward in his chair, spreading his hands in a gesture that would have indicated helplessness in a smaller man, McGrath asked, "What are you going to do with the information, Chet?"

"I don't know."

He could see the pain on McGrath's face. It was not easy for the man to beg. "Most of the people around me know about it."

"But your constituents back on the farm don't."

"We . . . I was planning to get the divorce after I'm re-elected."

"After you become the Minority Leader."

McGrath nodded.

"Mary-Ellen's going to help you campaign, and you'll troop your kids all across the state, and after the voters send you back to Washington for another six years you'll get your divorce. Pretty sweet."

"What else can I do?" McGrath asked, real misery in his voice. "It's not the divorce so much as the timing. Should I throw away my chance for Minority Leader over a matter of a few months?"

"Those farmers and coal miners and churchgoers wouldn't like knowing that you're going around with a singer, an entertainment star, a left-wing ex-radical from show business. They'd think you're pretty lousy, cheating on your wife. Wouldn't they?"

"Yes," he admitted. "They would."

"They'd be right."

McGrath's eyes flashed. "Don't be too righteous about this, Chet. I never would have met her if it weren't for you."

"I know." Kinsman felt his own temper rising. "And she never would have gotten her chance for stardom if it weren't for me. And you wouldn't be in the Senate if it weren't for my family's money and connections."

McGrath took it like a body blow, the breath gushing out of him. But he dropped his chin only for a moment before

226

plunging ahead. "I fell in love with her right off the bat, the first time I laid eyes on her. I just didn't do anything about it . . . until . . ."

"Will Diane marry you after the divorce?"

"I don't know. We've talked about it. The baby complicates things. I want to marry her, but she's not sure."

"She'd make a lousy senator's wife."

Exploding out of the flimsy chair, McGrath raised his hands wildly. They banged into the compartment's low plastic-sheeted ceiling. "Christ Almighty! I didn't want any of this! I didn't go out looking for it. I never intended to break up my marriage. It wasn't all that good anymore, between Mary-Ellen and me, but . . . Chet, when I'm with Diane I feel like a kid again! Just being in the same room with her! And then when she told me she felt the same way about me . . ."

Kinsman leaned back on the bunk and watched his old friend pace the tiny compartment. Middle-age change of life, he told himself. Neal always was precocious. He found himself envying the fact that McGrath could let go of himself so completely.

McGrath stopped in front of Kinsman. Looming over him he asked, "So what are you going to do about it?"

"I told you, Neal. I haven't decided what to do. Probably nothing."

"If you're thinking of using this to pressure me on the Moonbase deal, forget it! I won't knuckle under."

Kinsman looked up at him. Is Neal stubborn enough to throw his career into the flames?

"The trouble is," Kinsman said evenly, "if I've found out about it, it's only a matter of time until guys like Marcot and the rest find out . . ."

"They won't. Congress takes care of its own."

"Neal, some crap artist like Tug Wynne will nudge it out of somebody sooner or later."

"Wynne's bureau chief is a friend of mine. He'll keep it quiet or he'll lose a helluva good inside source. More than one. Other senators will clam up if he breaks silence. And their aides."

Shaking his head, Kinsman countered, "Look, Neal, I haven't been around Washington as long as you have, but I know this much: the White House is out to get you. Some-body in the Administration sees you as a threat. And they've got their own channels into the media, you know. You're playing in the big leagues now."

McGrath slowly sank down on the bunk beside Kinsman.

"Do you think for one second," Kinsman went on, "that Wynne or his bureau chief will sit on your story when it comes out of the Pentagon? Or the White House? For God's sake, somebody like Marcot could break it to the fucking *National Enquirer* or plant rumors in any of sixty daily columns. They could give it to the Hollywood gossip-mongers. Diane's a video personality, you know."

"I know."

"And when the Pentagon does find out about you," Kinsman said, "you're going to think I told them."

"What you're saying is that you might as well tell them yourself and collect the credit for it because they're going to find out about it sooner or later anyway."

Kinsman snapped, "No, that's *not* what I'm saying! Goddammitall, Neal, I'm warning you that you're going to have to face this pressure one way or the other."

"And if I vote for your Moonbase program the pressure will be off."

"That's right."

"For the time being. Until they want something else."

"I won't be involved in anything else," Kinsman said. "All I want is Moonbase."

"A military base on the Moon."

"It's not a military base, Neal. Not in the sense that it has anything to do with weapons."

For a long moment McGrath said nothing. Then, "This spaceplane thing . . . it's being built so we can knock out Soviet satellites, isn't it?"

"I'm not supposed to say anything about that."

"But you don't deny it?"

"No," Kinsman said. "I don't deny it."

"It's not a very well-kept secret. They've already spent nearly a billion on the design phase."

"So?"

"I'm still against your Moonbase," McGrath said quietly, but with the implacability of a glacier. "No matter what you

228

say, Chet, they'll turn it into an armed military camp."

"No. They can't."

"Of course they can. They've already escalated the arms race into orbital space. First the antimissile satellites with their lasers and particle beam weapons. Now a manned interceptor to knock out the satellites. Next they'll start the interceptors shooting at each other. They're going to fight a war out there, and your Moonbase will become part of it whether you want it to or not."

Wearily, Kinsman pulled himself up from the bunk. "Maybe you're right. Maybe."

"But you want to go to the Moon anyway."

Turning back to face him, "I sure as hell do."

"At any cost."

"At *almost* any cost."

"So what should I do about it?" McGrath muttered, more to himself than to Kinsman.

"I wish I knew," Kinsman said, feeling trapped and helpless. "I sure as hell wish I knew."

When they got back to the bar at the galley Diane was nowhere in sight. McGrath went off to look for her. Kinsman took another cup of punch. It was weak stuff, but his mouth felt dry, his soul arid.

People were drifting through the mess hall, drinks in hand, conversing in small groups. Kinsman wandered over to one of the hall's small oval windows and stared out at the slowly revolving stars. Most of the PR flaks had disappeared, leaving the visitors to themselves for the time being.

"Well, Major, what do you think of it?"

Kinsman turned to see a cheerful-looking man of about fifty standing before him, two beer bottles clenched in each hand.

"Very efficient." Kinsman grinned at him.

"Oh, the beer! Beats going back to the bar every five minutes. But I was referring to the station." He tucked two bottles under his arm and extended his right hand. "I'm T. D. Dreyer. My outfit did the main structural work on this flying doughnut."

"Your outfit?"

"General Technologies, Inc."

"General Tech. You're *that* Dreyer!"

T. D. Dreyer grinned boyishly, happy to be recognized. He was slightly shorter than Kinsman, barrel-chested and burly of build. His blue-gray leisure suit had been carefully tailored to make him look as slim as possible, but his face betrayed him: a heavyset, happy ex-footballer who constantly battled overweight. It was a deeply tanned face. He either has a sunlamp at his desk, Kinsman concluded, or he spends most of his time in the field.

"And I know who you are," Dreyer said. "You're Major Chester Arthur Kinsman, former astronaut, now part of the Aerospace Force's team for Moonbase."

A faint chill of panic raced through Kinsman. "You've got a good intelligence network."

Dreyer's eyes lit up. "You bumped a Wright-Patterson general who's been giving one of my divisions a hard time over a contract we have with him. I was going to try a little friendly persuasion on him while we were both here and away from our desks. When I heard my pigeon had been bumped I made it my business to find out who had bumped him—and at the last minute, too. That takes some clout."

"Hell, if I had known . . ."

"Naah, don't worry about it. I'll catch up with him next week." Dreyer moved half a step closer to Kinsman and lowered his voice slightly. "Frankly, I have a feeling the guy's scared to fly. I was kinda looking forward to watching him shit his pants when I dragged him over to the observation window."

They laughed together.

"You've been up here before," said Kinsman.

"Sure. Big job like this, I come up and look as often as I can get away from that damned desk in Dallas. Gives my insurance people fits, but I like it up here. It's a relief to be away from all those damned numbers crunchers and ribbon clerks."

"I'll drink to that!" Kinsman lifted his cup.

After a long pull of beer, Dreyer said, "Y'know, the trouble with being chairman of the board is that you're supposed to be dignified and conservative. My board members don't believe me when I tell 'em we should be pouring every dollar we can into space operations."

"They think it's too risky?"

"It's not that so much as the fact that it's so easy to take government contracts instead. The profit is low but it's guaranteed. No risk at all, as long as you do a halfway decent job."

"What about the talk I hear about private companies building their own facilities up here? Factories and research labs and solar power satellites?"

Dreyer made a sour face. "Yeah, maybe. But not anybody who's got a board of directors to satisfy. Not as long as there are government contracts to be had."

"Dreyer! I thought that was you." A tall, lithe, hollow-cheeked man with a small pointed beard joined them. He seemed to Kinsman to be in his thirties. He wore a white one-piece jumpsuit. His face was lean and bony, ascetic; his reddish-brown hair was shaved so close to the scalp that he almost looked bald. His hands were empty.

"Well," the newcomer asked, gesturing out toward the view of space, "what do you think of it?"

"Very nice," Dreyer answered. "I think there's a future in it."

"You're being facetious."

"No, but I'm not being polite. Major Kinsman, allow me to introduce Professor Howard Alexander of Redlands University. Howard, this is Chet Kinsman."

Alexander's hands stayed at his sides. "I didn't know that any Air Force people were on the invitations list. You're on duty with NASA, I take it."

"No," Kinsman said.

"Chet's a former astronaut. Now he's on the Moonbase team."

"Oh, *that*." The temperature of the conversation dropped fifty degrees.

Dreyer seemed amused. "Professor Alexander is the apostle of the True Faith. He wants the military out of space so he can build colonies and make them into heavenly paradises."

"And you want to build them and make profit out of them," Alexander shot back testily.

"Sure, why not?"

"Because space should be free for all humankind, that's why. Because we shouldn't bring our selfish, petty greeds out

231

into this beautiful new world."

"Right on," said Kinsman.

Alexander turned to him. "Nor should we be trying to build weapons and fortifications in space. This is a domain for peaceful existence, not for war."

"I couldn't agree more."

The professor blinked at him.

Kinsman said, "I think it would be wonderful if we could leave all the greed and anger and suspicion of our fellow men back on Earth and come out here fresh and clean and newborn."

"I got news for you, fellas," Dreyer said, with a rueful grin. "It ain't gonna happen that way."

"I'm afraid not," Kinsman agreed.

Alexander shook his head, as if dismissing such unpleasant thoughts from his mind. "It *will* happen that way if we make it happen that way."

"How'm I gonna do that?" Dreyer asked, suddenly very serious. "You think my board of directors will risk the company's capital on dreams? They want profits and they want 'em *now*."

"They'll get their profits, from the solar power satellites."

"Sure. Twenty years downstream. We could be in receivership by then. We can't tie up billions of dollars for twenty years at a time. Nobody can. So where are you going to get the capital to build those big-assed colonies of yours? Plus the lunar mining facilities, the processing plants, the factories . . ."

"It would only take five or six billion."

"Per year!"

"Surely the major corporations could invest that much in their own future," Alexander said. "And in the future of the human race."

Dreyer shook his head. "Like I said, we're not in the investment business. We work for profits. This year. Nobody in his right mind is going to risk the kind of money your space colonies require."

Alexander countered, "Think of the profits you'll eventually make from selling energy back to Earth once you've built a few solar power satellites."

"I know," Dreyer said, gesturing with a beer bottle in his hand. "But you don't need your supercolossal colonies to build solar power satellites. All you need is a tough crew of workmen on the Moon, where the raw materials are, and another crew in orbit, where the construction will take place."

"But there's more to it than just building the satellites," Alexander insisted. "The space colonies will also be involved in building more colonies, more self-sufficient islands in space."

"What for?" Kinsman asked.

"So that more people can leave the Earth and live in space!" Alexander's exasperated tone reminded Kinsman of a Sunday school teacher he and Neal had once suffered through.

But how do we know that God loves us?

Because the Scriptures tell us so!

But how do we know the Scriptures are right?

Because they were inspired by God!

But how do we know they were inspired by God?

Because it says so, right in the Scriptures!

Repressing a grim smile, Kinsman told himself, At least the Quakers never fell into that dogmatic tailspin. I'll bet Alexander was schooled by Jesuits.

"And who's gonna pay for these additional colonies?" Dreyer was asking.

"They'll be paid for out of the profits from the solar power satellites!" Alexander was getting edgy.

"Let's sit down," Kinsman suggested, pointing to an empty table. Most of the visitors were still clustered around the bar.

"Lemme get a refill," said Dreyer, hefting his emptied beer bottles.

The three of them pushed their way to the bar. Dreyer got another pair of beers, Kinsman another cup of the weak punch. Alexander abstained. Then they sat at one of the long mess tables, Dreyer at its head, Alexander and Kinsman flanking him on either side.

Kinsman took a sip of the punch. It felt cold and sticky-sweet.

"Now look," Dreyer said to the professor, "don't get me

233

wrong. I like the colony idea. I've liked it since O'Neill first proposed it, back in the Seventies. And I agree that solar power satellites could make a considerable profit—in time. *If* the government doesn't nationalize them, once they're built. But how do you raise the initial capital? You're talking about a hundred billion bucks or more."

"Over a ten-year period," Alexander said.

Dreyer shrugged. "That's still ten billion a year, minimum. That's a helluva lot of bread. With no payoff until way downstream, and maybe not even then. Who in hell is going to buy into this? My board of directors would toss me into the loony bin if I tried to put that past them."

"If the corporations would all work together and pool their resources . . ."

"They won't. They can't! The antitrust guys would be all over us in ten minutes."

Kinsman said, "I thought NASA was involved in this."

"Only on the transportation end of it," Dreyer said. "NASA's not going to build any colonies. Congress won't appropriate that kind of money."

"Not for solar power satellites?" Kinsman wondered.

Dreyer explained, "See, the power satellites and the colonies are two different things. The power satellites are gonna get built, probably by the government, at least the first one. But nobody's going to put up the money for a colony that'll house ten thousand university professors in a big suburbia in the sky."

Alexander frowned.

They talked around and around the subject, Alexander waxing poetic and pathetic by turns, Dreyer shaking his bulldog head and insisting on the economic facts of life. Kinsman looked over his shoulder at the star-filled window and saw their reflections in the glass: Alexander in profile, earnest and ascetic as a saint; Dreyer massive and solid as reality; his own face lean, dark, bored with their arguments that circled as repetitiously as the stars outside the window. But there was something nagging at Kinsman's mind, something that the two of them were overlooking. What?

Finally it hit Kinsman. He broke into their argument. "How are you going to defend this colony?"

"Huh?"

234

Alexander looked aghast. "Defend it? Against what? The Martians?"

"Against other Earthlings," said Kinsman. "Maybe the Soviets won't want a capitalist colony in space. Or terrorists. Your colony would be wide open to a small nuclear bomb. Look what they did in Cape Town."

"That's ridiculous," Alexander snapped. "Why would the Russians attack a space colony? And terrorists could never get up to a space colony. We wouldn't allow any weapons aboard it."

"You're not afraid of the Russians?" Dreyer asked.

"No. Why should I be? They're cooperating with us in our civilian space program, aren't they?"

"And competing with us to put their Star Wars system in orbit."

Alexander dismissed the idea with a wave of his hand. "The space colonies will be far beyond the militarists and their weapons."

"I hope you're right," said Kinsman.

Turning to Dreyer, Alexander asked, "I want to know how much your corporation is willing to invest in the space colony project."

"Nothing."

"Nothing?"

"Zero."

The professor's mouth went slack, but only for a moment. "Nothing at all? Are you serious?"

"Nothing at all," Dreyer said, with a good-natured grin. "Nothing for the colony. The lunar mining operation . . . now that's a different story. I think maybe we could go in on that. But not as part of your colony scheme. Find another pigeon for your flying Garden of Eden."

"That's *extremely* shortsighted!"

"Yeah, maybe. But if I was as visionary as you I would've gone bust years ago."

Abruptly Alexander pushed his chair back as far as it would go on the little track welded to the floor. Standing, he looked down on Kinsman and Dreyer.

"Someday we will have our space colonies and we will start a new era for the human race—without soldiers and without capitalists!"

"Good luck," Kinsman said. Dreyer grinned and took a pull of beer.

Alexander stalked off.

Dreyer watched him. "That's why he isn't afraid of the Russians. He's a goddamned socialist himself." He shook his head and laughed bitterly. "When he finds a place that doesn't have soldiers or capitalists he's going to be in heaven."

"Guess he'll snub Saint Michael," Kinsman said, "unless Mike puts away his armor and sword."

"Yeah. And there's a few capitalist saints he won't get along with, either."

Kinsman chuckled.

"He reminds me," Dreyer went on, "of what a kid in the office said about the head of the Office of Technology Assessment: 'He's no prophet; he's a loss.'"

They laughed together and got up and went to the bar for another drink. As they walked slowly back toward the window that looked out on the stars, Kinsman said:

"I've been thinking . . . let me ask you a hypothetical question."

"Shoot."

Kinsman put out his free hand and touched the plasti-glass. It was cold. Space cold. Death cold. He could feel it drawing the heat out of him, pulling his soul into space.

He yanked his hand away and said to Dreyer, "Suppose the government was willing to sink a few billion dollars into building a mining facility on the Moon. Would your board of directors be interested in putting some of your own money into the operation?"

"Sure!" Dreyer answered immediately. "If Uncle Sugar is taking most of the risk, why the hell not?"

"That's what I thought," Kinsman said.

"You talking about a space colony now or something else?"

"Not a colony. Just the lunar mining facilities. And factories, either on the Moon or in orbit."

"To build solar power satellites?"

"No. Something else."

Dreyer said nothing for a long moment. Then, "Just what do you have in mind?"

Kinsman shook his head.

With a knowing grin, Dreyer said, "There used to be talk about building the Star Wars satellites in space, out of lunar raw materials."

Kinsman answered, "So I've heard."

Dreyer's grin spread. "We'd be happy to work on that kind of project. With the government providing the investment capital and the Aerospace Force behind it, it would be a project we could depend on. We'd be willing to sink a helluva lot of our own discretionary funds into it, too."

"Do you think the other industrial contractors would feel the same way?"

"Why the hell wouldn't they?" Dreyer said. Then he started laughing again. "I'd like to see the look on Alexander's face when he finds out that his precious idea for building colonies in space has been bumped by factories for turning out military hardware!"

Kinsman nodded and tried to smile back at the man, but he could not.

He sat once again next to Jinny Woods on the shuttle's return flight to Florida, but Kinsman's mind was a quarter-million miles away.

"I didn't see you hardly at all," the woman was saying, "once we got up there. You were always in *deep* dark conversations with somebody or other. Who were all those people anyway? Wasn't one of them Senator McGrath? I saw him on television, one of those late-night talk shows. He's so handsome!"

Kinsman made noncommittal noises at her while his mind raced:

Is this the way history gets made? Somebody wants to find a retreat, a place to hide, and we get a lunar base out of it? Somebody wants to make a buck, open a new trade route, get the tax collectors off his back. That's what makes the world go 'round?

". . . and the way she sang! I'll bet you didn't even hear her, did you? I looked for you but you weren't anywhere in sight. You missed the dancers, too. They took us down to the low-gravity section . . ."

I'll have to spring it on Murdock first. No, first I'll tell

237

Frank about it. If there are any flaws in the picture he'll spot them. Pick out the weak points and fix them. Then Murdock. Then we'll work up a presentation for General Sherwood. Probably for Marcot, too. It all ties together so neatly. Why haven't the others seen it?

"You haven't been listening to a word I've said," Jinny Woods complained.

"I'm sorry," Kinsman said. "I was thinking about some of the problems I've got ahead of me, back at the office."

"You sound just like my husband. I guess I talk too much. That's what he tells me."

"No . . . it's my fault."

She brushed a curl away from her eyes. "I'm just so excited by all this! It's all old stuff for you, I know. But nothing like this has ever happened to me before. It's all so new . . . so thrilling!"

She's kind of pretty, Kinsman noticed. Nice eyes. Happy as a kid.

"It's exciting for me, too," he told her. "Don't let this calm exterior fool you. No matter how many times you go into orbit, it's always a ball."

She seemed pleased. "Really? It's not just me? I guess I just never learned to control my feelings very well. I get awfully gushy, don't I? Do you think we'll ever get up there again?"

Do I think about anything else?

She went on, "They said they're going to bring us to Washington next week for a press conference. You live in Washington, don't you? I've never been there before and Ralph says he can't take any days off to come with me. I'll be alone in the city."

"Where will you be staying?"

"Some government hotel, I guess. They haven't told us where."

Kinsman nodded. "Well, I'll find out and phone you when you're in town."

"Oh, that'd be wonderful! Do you have a card or something, so I can call you? That'd be easier . . ."

"I'm afraid I can't give out my phone number," Kinsman said, taking on a man-of-mystery disguise.

She fell for it. "Really? Why?"

He put a finger to his lips. "I'll find out where you're going to be staying and give you a call when you get into town. Trust me."

She nodded slowly, her eyes filled with something approaching awe.

And that was the last time he thought about her.

As soon as he arrived back in his one-room apartment Kinsman phoned Fred Durban. But the old man had slipped into a coma and the hospital would allow no visitors except family.

Then he called Colt and invited himself to Frank's apartment for a drink.

Colt's pad was lush compared to Kinsman's spartan little cell: richly carpeted living room with a balcony that overlooked Arlington National Cemetery; big bedroom with a fake zebra hide thrown over the water bed.

Scotch in hand, Kinsman explained his idea to Colt. The black officer listened silently, stretched out on his synthetic leather recliner.

". . . and that's it," Kinsman finished. "We mine the ores on the Moon, process them there, ship them to orbital factories, where they're manufactured into the antimissile satellites. Instead of working against the SDI Office, we make Moonbase a partner of theirs."

For a long moment Colt said nothing. Then, "People talked about building the satellites in orbit when the SDI idea was first proposed."

"I know. But we can do it now. All the pieces are in place—almost."

"You got all the pieces tied together," Colt said. "One big program that's got something for everybody. Moonbase becomes an important mining center instead of a geriatrics hospital. The big corporations get Uncle Sam to finance factories in orbit for them. And the Star Wars guys get their ABM satellites deployed for half the cost of building them on Earth and launching 'em from the ground."

"Not really half the cost," Kinsman said. "It won't be that cheap, I don't think. They'll want to continue to build the first-generation satellites on the ground. The space-manufactured stuff is for the next generation, the satellites that'll be carrying the high-power lasers."

Colt kicked his recliner upright and bounced to his feet. "Shee-it, man, you've got it made! You've pulled the two projects together into one big beeyootiful program that makes sense! Nobody could vote against it! It'd be like spittin' on the motherlovin' flag!" Colt laughed and stuck his hand out to Kinsman, palm up. "Man, it's the best piece of strategical thinking since Moses led the Children of Israel out of Egypt!"

Kinsman slapped at his hand, then grabbed it. "You really think so?"

"Hell yes! The brass'll love it. And you get your god-damned Moonbase out of it. Shrewd, man. Shrewd."

A sigh of relief eased out of Kinsman. "Okay, great. Now the first thing we've got to do is tell Murdock about it."

"First thing tomorrow we'll corner him."

"Could you do me a favor, Frank?" Kinsman asked. "You tell him. Leave me out of it. As soon as I try to tell him anything he shuts me off. If I bounce this plan off him he'll find a million reasons to junk it without bucking it further up the chain of command. It'll die right there in his office."

Colt eyed his friend. "Yeah, maybe. But you're the guy who knows all the shit about this. I don't. I couldn't put it across to Murdock as well as you could."

Glancing at the purpling sky and the dark shadow of the Pentagon on the horizon, Kinsman said slowly, "Well . . . we've got all night to rehearse it. Unless you have something else to do."

Colt frowned. "Lemme make a phone call. This is gonna break the heart of the best-looking piece of ass the Secretary of Agriculture ever had working for him."

"Aw, hell, Frank, I didn't want . . ."

With a wink, Colt said, "Forget it, buddy. She'll keep. And you're right, I *do* impress Murdock with my keen military bearing."

Kinsman would have paced his office if it had been big enough. Instead he sat at his desk, the chair tilted back against the faded pastel wall, and had nothing to do but think.

You're selling out, you know that. You're giving them what they want: a military base on the Moon. Neal was right; you're spreading the arms race all the way to the Moon.

240

You're willing to start a war up there.

But another part of his mind answered, They're putting up the ABM satellites anyway. And the manned interceptor comes next. This way, at least we get a Moonbase out of it. At least I'll be there, away from all this madness.

And what are you going to do, he asked himself, when you're on the Moon and they order you into battle? What are you going to do when they start blowing up the cities of Earth?

He had no answer for that.

Colt burst into his cubbyhole office, his grin dazzling. "He bought it! He was on the horn to Sherwood before I even finished. Man, did he go for it! Whammo!" Colt smacked a fist into his open palm.

Suddenly Kinsman felt too weak to get to his feet. "And General Sherwood?"

"He wants to see us this afternoon."

"Us?"

"Yeah. I told him this was all your idea. After he finished talkin' to Sherwood. You shoulda seen his face! Like he crapped in his pants!" Colt roared with laughter.

General Sherwood tried to contain his enthusiasm, but as he sat behind his big, aerodynamically clean desk listening to Kinsman, he began nodding. At first his head moved only slightly, unconsciously, as Kinsman unfolded the logic of his plan. But by the time Kinsman was summing up, the General's head was bobbing vigorously and he was smiling broadly.

Colonel Murdock was sitting on the edge of his chair, alternately watching the General intently and eyeing Kinsman suspiciously, waiting for a misstep or an outright goof. Soon, though, his own bald head was going up and down in exact rhythm with the General's. Colt sat farther from the desk, back far enough so that Kinsman could not see him.

Standing in front of the General's desk, too wrapped up in presenting the ideas to feel nervous, Kinsman ignored Murdock, ignored Colt, ignored the self-doubts that gnawed at his innards. This is the only way, he kept telling himself. We'll never get to the Moon any other way. It's this or nothing.

Finally he finished. Kinsman stood in front of the General's desk, arms limp at his sides, sweat trickling down his ribs. My uniform must be soaked, he thought.

General Sherwood stopped nodding, but his smile remained. "Fascinating," he said, in a voice so low that he might have been talking to himself. "We can bring the Moonbase program up to full partnership with the Strategic Defense program, and bring the aerospace industry along with us."

Colonel Murdock objected slightly, "But the idea of building the satellites in orbit out of lunar materials—that's not really new."

"True enough," said the General. "But I think it's an idea whose time has arrived."

"Oh, well, of course . . ."

Sherwood turned back toward Kinsman. "Good work, Major. Very good work. Get the presentations staff and the numbers crunchers into this immediately. I want a detailed presentation of this plan before the end of the week."

All his exhaustion blew away. "Yes, *sir*," Kinsman responded crisply.

The rest of the week was a madhouse of meetings, rehearsals, discussions, arguments. Kinsman raced along the Pentagon corridors from cost-computing analysts to technical artists drawing the block diagrams, from long scrambled phone conversations with industrial leaders such as Dreyer to longer face-to-face meetings with their local marketing representatives and engineers. Days, nights blurred together. Meals were sandwiches gobbled at desks, crumbs spilling onto printout sheets of numbers, coffee staining artists' sketches of lunar installations. Sleep was something you grabbed in snatches, on couches, in a chair: once Kinsman dozed off in the shower of the officers' gym.

The full-scale presentation took two hours. Deputy Secretary Marcot chain-smoked through it. Kinsman stood at the head of the darkened conference room, squinting at the solitary light of the viewgraph projector, half-hypnotized by the clouds of blue smoke gliding through the light beam as he explained picture after picture, graph after graph, list after list. He could not see his audience but he could tell their interest from the rapt silence and, after the lights went on

242

again, from their eager questions.

"What was the basis for the cost estimates on the lasers?"

"Latest industrial information, sir."

"And the comparison between the costs of lunar raw materials and raw materials on Earth?"

"The comparison, sir, is between finished products manufactured in space from lunar materials and finished products manufactured on the ground and boosted into low Earth orbit. The space-manufactured items average five to eight times cheaper, including the capital costs of the lunar facility."

"That's based on what, Major?"

Kinsman grinned. "Mainly, sir, on the fact that the Moon is an airless body of natural resources that has only one-sixth the gravitational pull of the Earth. It's twenty times cheaper to launch a pound of payload from the Moon to low Earth orbit than it is to boost a pound from the Earth's surface."

Marcot's sarcastic voice offered, "And those figures are based on Isaac Newton, not some industrial contractor who wants to buy into the program. You can trust Newton. He's dead."

Everyone around the table chuckled.

They questioned Kinsman for another hour after the final slide had been shown and the overhead lights turned on. Colt fielded some of the questions, as did some of the other men and women who had worked on the presentation. But Kinsman remained at the head of the room and took most of the questions himself.

Finally Marcot got to his feet. Waving his inevitable cigarette in Kinsman's general direction, he said, "Okay. Hone it down to half an hour and be prepared to show it to the Secretary first thing next week."

Back in his own office, Colt grabbed Kinsman by the shoulders. "We're on our way, man! The Secretary of Defense! The big brass boss his own self. Marcot bought it!"

Kinsman was too tired and numb to feel exultant.

"C'mon, I'm gonna buy you a drink."

"I just want some sleep, Frank. Thanks, anyway."

Colt shrugged. "Yeah. We got a weekend's worth of work figurin' out how to squeeze all this gorgeous stuff down to half an hour."

Kinsman said, "Let me lock up all this gorgeous stuff in the vault." The pile of viewgraph slides was scattered across Colt's desk, each stamped along its border in bold red letters: TOP SECRET.

It took both of them to carry the pile of slides over to Kinsman's cubbyhole. As he wearily tapped out the combination on the electronic lock to his file cabinet, Colt beamed happily at him.

"Man, you were a ball of fire in there. You coulda sold General Motors stock to the Kremlin. You've really changed, man. You've really come out of your shell."

Over his shoulder Kinsman said, "I want to go to the Moon, Frank. Even if I have to bring the whole goddamned Aerospace Force with me."

Colt grinned. "You figured it out, huh? You wear The Man's uniform, you gotta do The Man's work. That's the law of life, my friend. But it's good to see you thinking like an Aerospace Force officer. Always thought you had a good head on your shoulders. No more of this peaceful hospital crap."

Kinsman piled the slides into the file drawer, then shut it and clicked the lock. He took the card atop the cabinet and turned it from the white OPEN side to the red LOCKED side.

"Frank," he said, turning back to Colt, "don't get the wrong idea. The Moon is still legally restricted, as far as military weaponry goes. The mining operation, okay. What they do with the ores after they leave the Moon is somebody else's business. But Moonbase will never be used as a place for war. Understand that. Never."

Colt's grin faded. "And how are you gonna get the Russians to go along with that? They're gonna be up there with you, remember? You start mining operations, they'll start mining operations."

"We'll work it out some way."

"Without fighting."

"That's right."

"Damn! You're just as dumb as you always were."

Late Monday afternoon Kinsman stood at the head of the long polished mahogany table in the private conference room of the Secretary of Defense. No need to turn out the lights here; his slides were presented on a wall-sized rear projection screen. Kinsman spoke directly to the Secretary himself, despite the fact that the table was occupied by Marcot and two Under Secretaries of the Aerospace Force, four generals, including Sherwood, and a half-dozen civilian advisers to the Secretary. Colt was in the next room, feeding the slides into the projector.

Every man at the table watched Kinsman intently. The same thoughts were going through each of their heads, he knew: How does this affect my programs, my organization, my position in the Defense Department?

"To summarize," Kinsman said to the Secretary, "we can bring down the costs of strategic defense by a factor of five or more if we build the ABM satellites in orbital facilities, using raw materials mined from the Moon. The major industrial contractors are eager to begin space manufacturing operations, but have hesitated to risk the resources necessary for the task. This program will, therefore, have significant spinoff value in the civilian economy. More than significant: the eventual payoff to the civilian economy could more than pay for the investment made on this program. Thank you, gentlemen."

The men around the table stirred, glanced at one another, then all settled their gazes on the Secretary. He sat at the far end of the table, looking relaxed and thoughtful. He was the tweedy gray university type. An unlit pipe was clamped in his teeth.

"We are deploying the ABM satellites under any circumstances," General Sherwood said, filling the silence. "This plan allows us to build them more cheaply—and replace them more easily, in case of attrition."

The Defense Secretary nodded and started lighting his pipe.

"And by building the satellites in orbit," Kinsman added, still standing in front of the now-blank screen, "out of lunar materials, we not only get the SDI network, we get a powerful industrial capacity in space and a full-scale, permanent base on the Moon."

"A base," General Sherwood pointed out, "that will be under the administrative control of the Department of Defense."

The Secretary slowly took the pipe from his mouth. "You mean you blue-suiters get your Moonbase, eh, Jim?"

General Sherwood broke into a boyish smile. "Yes, sir, that is exactly what I mean."

Smiling back at him, the Secretary said, "Well, it seems to me that the important thing here is that America's industrial power is brought into space in a meaningful way. The President will like that. It's about time that industry really moved into space."

He's buying it! Kinsman's heart leaped. He's bought it!

"I think you're perfectly right about that," said Ellery Marcot. "Perfectly right."

"What I'd like to know," the Secretary said, with a nod toward one of his civilians, "is why our hired geniuses and university consultants never brought the whole ball of wax together the way the Major has, here."

The aide flushed. "Well, it's one thing to be sitting out in left field . . ."

"Relax, George," the Secretary said, making a patting motion with his free hand. "Relax. I was only tweaking you."

He got up from his leather-backed chair. "A very good presentation, Major. Good thinking. I'll speak to the President about it at tomorrow morning's briefing."

Kinsman could only say, "Thank you, sir." It was so weak that he wondered if the Secretary heard him.

Turning to General Sherwood, the Secretary asked, "Jim, see that my people get copies of those slides and all the backup material, will you?"

Sherwood rose, beaming. "Certainly, Mr. Secretary. Be glad to."

They all filed out of the conference room, leaving Kinsman standing there rooted to the spot. We did it, he told himself. Then he corrected, No, *you* did it. Don't blame anyone else.

He walked slowly out of the conference room. The others had already started back toward their own offices. All except Marcot, who was standing by the window talking with Murdock. The Colonel had been waiting in the anteroom all through Kinsman's presentation. He must've walked off the soles of his shoes, pacing up and down, thought Kinsman. Murdock looked rumpled, exhausted; hands clasped behind his back, the expression on his face halfway between eager anticipation and utter dread as he talked with Marcot.

Frank Colt jounced into the anteroom, the slim pile of slides clamped under one arm. He gave Kinsman a big grin and a thumbs-up sign.

Marcot came up to Kinsman, with Colonel Murdock trailing behind him. For once there was no cigarette in the Deputy Secretary's mouth.

"Major, you've done an impressive job. For the first time since I've been here I feel we have a logical, cost-effective program that not only meets the nation's defense needs, but will promote the civilian economy in a major way, as well."

"Thank you, sir."

"You pulled it all together into a coherent whole. That's exactly what we needed." Marcot jammed both his hands into his jacket pockets.

Feeling awkward and a bit foolish, Kinsman merely repeated, "Thank you, sir."

Marcot pulled out a fresh cigarette and lit it. "But we're not out of the woods yet." He blew a cloud of smoke toward the ceiling. "Not by a long shot."

"What do you mean?" Colt asked.

"There's still the Congress. They'll have to approve an even bigger Aerospace Force appropriation than we started with, to get this larger program going. We'll still have to face McGrath and his ilk."

It still boils down to that, Kinsman said to himself. He had almost allowed himself to forget Neal in the past hectic week.

Murdock patted Kinsman on the shoulder and said, "We're on top of that situation, aren't you, Chet? You're getting to McGrath."

"I've been trying . . ."

Colt said, "But with this new program, the way it all fits together and ties Moonbase into the rest of the Defense Department's space programs, not even McGrath and the peaceniks in Congress can vote against it."

"Can't they?" Marcot's long, hound-sad face had years of bitter experience written across it. "I can just see McGrath rising on the floor of the Senate and making a very eloquent speech about the Aerospace Force's paranoid schemes for

247

extending the arms race to the Moon. I can see his cohorts telling their constituents back home about the hundreds of billions of dollars the Defense Department wants to throw away in space instead of spending down here on welfare and urban renewal."

"Bullcrap!" Colt snorted.

"But it works," Marcot answered. "It gets votes."

"Then we've got to stop McGrath," Colt said. "He's the leader of this faction. Get him to vote our way, pull his fangs, do *something* . . ."

Murdock bobbed his head. "It's up to you, Chet. It's your job."

Kinsman looked at the Colonel. Thanks. Thank you all. To Marcot he said, "Very well. I'll handle McGrath. But I want something in return."

Murdock looked shocked. Officers don't make deals; they carry out orders. But Marcot grinned wolfishly, the way a politician does when he's trading favors and expects to come out ahead.

"You want something?" he asked Kinsman.

"Yessir. The original motivation for this program was to make certain that we go ahead with Moonbase. That base will need a commanding officer. I want to be that man."

"But that'd be a colonel's slot!" Murdock blurted.

"Then I'll need a promotion to light colonel to go with it," Kinsman answered evenly.

Marcot glanced at Murdock, then said, "First we've got to get the Congress to approve the funds. Then, when we know there's going to be a Moonbase, naturally we'll want someone who's thoroughly familiar with the program and its implications to command the base."

Colt nodded. Murdock still looked bewildered.

Without a smile, without even daring to admit to himself that this was happening, that *he* was forcing it to happen, Kinsman said, "Thank you. I appreciate it."

Raising a tobacco-stained finger, Marcot emphasized, "But first we've got to get the Congress to vote the funds."

"I know," said Kinsman.

"Very well. We understand each other." Marcot glanced at his wristwatch. "I'm going to be late for a reception. Japanese embassy. Their military attaché has been pumping me about our ABM satellites."

They walked out into the corridor. Marcot headed off toward his domain; Colonel Murdock, Colt, and Kinsman took the stairs that led up to their lesser offices.

As they climbed the steps, Colt burst out, "You did it, man! You finally did it! Terrific!"

"We've all been working on this," Kinsman said.

"Naw, I don't mean that. You stood up to 'em and told 'em what you wanted. Commander of Moonbase. And he took it! Man, you got the power now."

They reached the landing and pushed through the scuffed gray metal doors into the corridor as Kinsman said, "I just want him to know that I want to be on the Moon, not down here."

"You talked yourself into a damned quick promotion," Murdock snapped.

"But, Colonel," Colt said quickly, "don't you see? If they move Chet up to light colonel they're gonna hafta give you a general's star."

Murdock blinked and almost smiled. "There's no guarantee . . ."

"You'll still be in command of the overall lunar program," Colt argued smoothly. "And the program's going to be a lot bigger than anybody had thought. You'll be running the whole operation from Vandenberg while we're up at Moonbase. They'll have to give you a star."

Breaking into a contented grin, Murdock said, "You know, you might be right. It's more responsibility, bigger budget, bigger staff. They couldn't pass me over again."

The two majors left the smiling Colonel at his office, then continued down the corridor to their own cubicles. The hallways were empty; the Pentagon had only a skeleton crew after 4:30 P.M. Their footsteps clicked against the worn floor tiles and echoed off the shabby walls.

"You finally came around," Colt said. "I never thought you'd make it."

"You make it sound like a religious conversion," Kinsman grumbled.

"Just the opposite, man. Just the opposite. You finally got it through your skull that if you want something you gotta give something. You want to be commander of Moonbase, you gotta let them have what they want. No other way."

"We're not going to put weapons on the Moon."

Colt looked at him. "Yeah, I know. But those mines and ore processors . . . long as we're using them to ship raw materials to orbital factories so they can build laser satellites, then they're part of a weapons system."

Kinsman did not break stride, but inside he stiffened.

"You're gonna be commander of a military base, *Colonel* Kinsman. Moonbase is gonna be the key to the biggest military operation the world's ever seen."

And that's the price for my soul, thought Kinsman. He left Colt and slipped into his own cramped office. The air-conditioning had been turned off at the official quitting time for the daytime staff. The paper-strewn cubicle was already muggy and stuffy.

It may be a military base, Kinsman told himself, and it may be there to supply raw materials for weapons systems, but there'll be no fighting on the Moon. Not while I'm there.

Then Marcot's cagey, cynical face appeared in his mind. "First get the Congress to vote the funds," he heard the Deputy Secretary saying.

"The Hungarian recipe for an omelet," Kinsman muttered. "First, steal some eggs."

With a sigh he sat at his desk and tapped out Neal McGrath's phone number. An answering service responded. Kinsman did not bother to leave his name on the tape. Then, out of pure routine, he tapped his own message key on the computer board. The display screen spelled out in green letters: PLS CALL MS WOODS: 291-7000 EXT 7949.

Kinsman stared at the message for a long moment. Persistent woman, he thought. As he punched the number she had left, he grinned at her use of the "Ms." Helps her forget she's married, I guess.

Jinny's face looked blander, plainer than he remembered it when she appeared on the tiny display screen.

"Oh . . . Major Kinsman! You got my call. I was in the shower. They've been touring us all around Washington all day . . ."

No makeup, he realized. That's what it is.

"You said you'd call me when we got into town," she was gushing, "but we were out all day and I never trust hotel switchboards to get messages straight and nobody down at the desk speaks English anyway so I called the Pentagon, I remembered you said you worked at the Pentagon, and asked them to look you up. All I remembered was that you were in the Air Force and you had been an astronaut. I even forgot your rank, but they found your number for me anyway!"

"I'm glad they did, Jinny," he said. The old oil. You do it automatically, don't you?

They met at a Japanese restaurant on Connecticut Avenue. Marcot's not the only one who'll nibble on sushi tonight. They had no trouble getting a tatami room for themselves, where they took off their shoes and sat on the floor. The restaurant was nearly empty. Even in the best parts of the city business disappeared once the sun went down.

"I'm sorry I wasn't able to call you earlier," Kinsman said as they sipped sake. "It's been a wild week for me."

"Me, too," Jinny said, looking at him over the rim of her tiny porcelain cup. Her hair was carefully done, her makeup properly in place. She wore a sleeveless frock with a neckline low enough to be inviting, yet still within the bounds of decorum.

Does she or doesn't she? Kinsman asked himself. As if it matters.

When they left the restaurant Jinny wound her arm around Kinsman's and said, "I'm so tired . . . they had us on the go all day long. Do you mind if we just go back to my hotel room and have a drink there?"

Like the cobra and mongoose. But which is which? Kinsman wondered.

Her hotel was a cut above standard government issue. The bed was a double, the furnishings fairly new and in reasonably good condition. The room was clean without smelling of disinfectant. Kinsman put money in the automatic liquor dispenser and bought a scotch for himself and a vodka tonic for Jinny. He poured the liquor and soda into plastic glasses, and found that the Styrofoam ice bucket was already filled with half-melted cubes.

"I've just got to get out of this dress," Jinny said, picking up her pink travel kit and heading for the bathroom. "I'll only be a minute."

Kinsman took the room's only chair and shook his head.

This game's pretty silly, you know. A voice inside him answered, Don't be scared; you're doing fine.

On an impulse he went to the phone and, sitting on the edge of the bed, tapped out the number for Walter Reed Hospital. The hospital's information display glowed on the phone screen:

MAY WE HELP YOU?

"Yes," Kinsman said. Speaking as clearly as he could for the computer, he asked, "The condition of Mr. Frederick Durban."

SPELLING OF LAST NAME?

"D-u-r-b-a-n. Frederick."

ARE YOU A FAMILY MEMBER?

"His son," he lied.

DURBAN, FREDERICK. DECEASED 1623 HRS TODAY. FUNERAL ARRANGEMENTS ARE BEING HANDLED BY . . .

Kinsman slammed a fist against the phone's OFF button. I know what the funeral arrangements are, he said to himself. Looking out the window at the darkening city, he thought, Four twenty-three this afternoon. Right in the middle of my goddamned presentation. Right in the fucking middle of it!

"What's the matter, Chet? You look awful!"

He turned to see Jinny standing a step inside the bathroom door, her hair loose and tumbling to her shoulders, an iridescent pink nightgown clinging to her.

"A friend of mine . . . died. I just called the hospital and found out."

She came to him and put both hands on his shoulders. "I'm so sorry."

"He was an old man. I expected it. But still . . ."

"I know. It's a shock." She sat beside him on the bed and slipped her arms around his neck and kissed him. He kissed back and felt her mouth open for him.

She disengaged and reclined languidly on the bed. Patting the covers, she said, "Come on, lay down beside me."

He remained sitting. "Jinny . . . I can't."

She gazed up at him, smiling. "If it's my husband you're worried about, never mind. We have an understanding about this kind . . ."

But he shook his head. The picture was forming in his mind again. He could see her floating helplessly, arms out-

252

stretched, reaching toward him, screaming silently, eyes wide and blank.

"No," he said, more to himself than to her.

She was staring at him now, looking uncertain, almost afraid.

"I've got to go." He got to his feet.

Jinny sat up on the bed. "Because of the man who died?"

"Yes."

"He was someone close to you? A relative?"

"You really don't want to know about it," he said, feeling clammy sweat on his palms. Almost pleadingly, "Please don't ask me anything more about it."

"Are you . . . a spy, or something?"

He focused on her for the first time since shutting off the phone. She was wide-eyed, lips parted, nipples erect with excitement.

"I can't tell you anything," he said, trying to make it tight-lipped. "I've got to go. I'm sorry."

"Will I ever see you again?"

"Maybe. But probably not. Where I'm going . . . probably not."

He went to the door. She rushed after him and gave him a final kiss, hard and desperate. He left her there clinging to the door, playing the role of the abandoned *femme fatale*.

Kinsman loped past a row of phones in the hotel lobby and grabbed the last remaining taxi standing at the curb. As it growled and rattled out into the sparse nighttime traffic he gave the black driver the McGraths' address in Georgetown.

Mary-Ellen let him into the apartment, a puzzled look on her face. "Chet, you look as if you're ready to take on the entire Sioux nation. What's the matter?"

"Where's Neal?"

She led him back to the parlor where the party had been. No one was there now except the two of them. The big room was filled with sofas and wingback chairs, the empty fireplace, mirrors, paintings, lamps, bookcases, end tables, the big circular Persian etched brass hanging between the French windows, a hundred pieces of bric-a-brac acquired over the years of their marriage.

"Neal's out," Mary-Ellen said. "He won't be back for a few days."

Kinsman looked at her. "The committee hearings are still running."

"He hasn't left town," she said, weariness in her voice. "He's just . . . not here."

"He's with Diane."

She nodded.

"And you're letting him do it?"

"Do you know any way I can stop him from doing it?"

"I'd think it would be pretty easy for you, if you wanted him to stop."

She dropped into the sofa nearest the dead, dark fireplace. "Chet, nothing is easy."

"Do you love him?" he asked, sitting down beside her.

"Do I breathe?"

"Hey, I'm the one who's supposed to give flip answers to hide his feelings."

Mary-Ellen's hands made a helpless flutter. "What do you expect me to say? Do I love him? What a question! We've been married nearly sixteen years. We have three children."

"Do you love him?"

"I did. I think maybe I still do . . . but it's not so easy to tell anymore."

"He said you agreed to a divorce after he's re-elected."

"Yes."

"But why?" Kinsman asked. "Why are you letting him do this to you? Why are you taking it like this?"

"What else can I do? Wreck his career? Would that bring him back to me? Threaten him? Force him to stay with me? Do you think I want that?"

"What the hell do you want?"

"I don't know!"

"You're lying," Kinsman said. "You're lying to yourself."

Tears were brimming in her eyes. "Chet, leave me alone. Just go away and leave me alone. I don't want . . ." She could not say anything more; she broke down.

Kinsman took her in his arms and held her gently. "That's better. That's better. I know what it's like to hold it all inside yourself. It's better to let it come out. Let it all out."

"I can't . . ." Her voice was muffled, but the pain came through. "I shouldn't be bothering you . . ."

"Nonsense. That's what shoulders are for. Hell, we've known each other a long, long time. It's okay. You can cry on my shoulder anytime. Maybe if I'd had the sense to cry on yours when I needed to . . ."

She pulled slightly away, but not so far that he could no longer hold her.

"We have known each other a long time, haven't we?"

"All the way back to Philadelphia," he said.

"I've known you as long as I've known Neal."

"I was jealous as hell of him," Kinsman remembered.

"He . . . he said I'm . . . he said that I couldn't give love. That I'm incapable of it."

Kinsman grimaced. "I haven't been able to give love to anyone for years."

A new look came into her eyes. "Is that what happened to you? All those rumors . . ."

He pulled her closer and kissed her. Gray-eyed Athena, goddess of wisdom and of war, I'll take you over treacherous Aphrodite every time. Their hands moved across each other's bodies, searching, opening, pulling clothes away.

Still half-dressed, he leaned her back on the couch and was on top of her, into her, before the picture of the dead cosmonaut could form in his mind. He heard her gasp and felt her clutching him, hard, furiously intense, alive, molten, burning all the old bad images out of his brain. Everything blurred together. He found himself sitting on the edge of the couch beside her, staring into those strong, wise gray eyes. Wordlessly she got to her feet and led him to the bedroom. She shut the door firmly. In silence they finished stripping and went to the bed. They made love and dozed, alternately, until the sun brightened the curtained windows.

"God," she murmured, and he could feel her breath on his cheek, "you're like a teenager."

"It's been a long time," he said. "I've got a lot of catching up to do."

He showered alone, and when he came back into the bedroom to dress she had gone. He found her in the kitchen, wrapped in a shapeless beige housecoat, munching a piece of dry toast as she sat at the counter that cut the room in half. An untouched glass of orange juice stood on the counter before her.

"Hungry?" she asked, wiping toast crumbs from her lips.

"I'll get something from the cafeteria in the Pentagon," he said.

"Have some juice, at least." She pushed the glass toward him.

"Thanks," he said.

"Thank you."

Suddenly they were both embarrassed. Kinsman felt like a sheepish kid. Mary-Ellen stared down at the toast on her plate.

He did not know what to say. "I . . . uh, guess I'd better be going now."

"It's awfully early. I don't think the buses are running this early."

He shrugged. "I'll walk for a while."

"Aren't you tired?"

And they both broke up. Kinsman lifted his head and roared. Mary-Ellen laughed with him.

"Tired? For God's sake, woman, I'm exhausted!"

"I should hope so," she said. "You had me scared for a minute, there."

She came around the counter and put an arm around his waist. He took her by the shoulders and together they walked through the parlor, toward the house's front door.

"I do thank you, Chet," Mary-Ellen said. "You've helped me to see myself—everything—in a new light."

"My pleasure."

"Not entirely yours."

"I . . . feel kind of funny about it, though," he admitted. "Christ, it's almost like incest!"

She smiled at him. "I know."

"It was a one-time thing. I mean, I don't think either one of us could . . . well, *plan* something like that."

They were at the door now. Gently she disengaged from him. "No, it was a surprise. A once-in-a-lifetime, wonderful surprise. If we tried to repeat it, it wouldn't work."

Nodding, "No, I guess it wouldn't."

"But it was good."

"Damned good. Thanks, Mary-Ellen. You've chased away a devil that's been haunting me for a long time."

"Then I'm glad."

They kissed, swiftly, almost shyly, and he left.

The door burst open as if it had been kicked and Neal McGrath's bulk filled the doorway.

Kinsman looked up from his apartment's desk. The clock at his elbow said 10 P.M. He had spent the day in the Pentagon, ignoring McGrath's committee hearings, working with the Secretary of Defense's staff on the briefings they were giving at the White House.

"You sonofabitch!" McGrath growled.

He slammed the door shut and took two strides into the shabby room. His tall, rangy body seemed to radiate fury.

"You bastard!" McGrath's fists were doubled, white-knuckled. "You screwed my wife."

"While you were screwing your girlfriend."

McGrath took another step toward him, raising his fists.

Kinsman stopped him with a pointed finger. "Hold on, Neal. You're bigger, but I've trained harder. All you're going to do is get yourself hurt."

"I'll kill you, you sonofabitch." But he stopped and let his hands fall to his sides.

"I don't blame you," Kinsman said softly. "What happened last night . . . it was completely unexpected. Hell, Neal, I came to your house looking for you. Neither of us planned it. It just happened. You ought to know about things like that."

"Don't hand me that!"

"I know, I know," Kinsman said, keeping his voice low. "Now we're talking about your wife, and that's different. Okay. But maybe now at least you know a little of what she's been going through."

McGrath said nothing. He stood in the middle of the small room panting like a bull in the arena that was confused by the noise and the light.

"It's not going to happen again," Kinsman added. "We both agreed on that."

"I thought you were my friend," McGrath said, his voice cracking with misery.

"Yeah, I thought so, too." Kinsman turned and pulled

257

the chair away from the desk. "Come on, sit down. I'll get you a beer. We've got a lot to talk about."

Numbly McGrath took the chair. Kinsman went to the refrigerator and pulled out two cold bottles of Bass ale. Fumbling in the drawer for a bottle opener, he wondered, Will the English ever come into the twentieth century and put screwtops on their beer? He found the opener, pried the tops off, then walked over and handed one bottle to McGrath.

"Hope you don't want a glass. They're both dirty."

McGrath gave a grunt that was almost a laugh. "What are we drinking to?" he asked, not looking up at Kinsman.

"To understanding," Kinsman said, stretching out on the open sofabed.

"Understanding what?"

The real world, man. The real world. "Understanding why I came over to your house last night, trying to find you. Understanding what's happening in the Pentagon and the White House, and what's going to hit the Congress in the next few days."

McGrath sat up straighter in his chair. "What the hell are you talking about?"

"I'm not authorized to tell you, Neal, but I'm going to anyway and if anybody's snooping on this conversation they can go rush their tapes to whoever they want to."

Inadvertently McGrath's eyes scanned the room, looking for microphones.

"The Aerospace Force has been working for some time," Kinsman said, "on the development of a manned interceptor spaceplane that will be used to destroy Soviet ABM satellites."

"I know that. Nobody in the Pentagon has seen fit to brief me about it, but I've got my own sources."

"Okay. You know, then, that this will mean we're going to actively pursue the objective of preventing the Soviets from deploying a Star Wars type of defensive shield in orbit."

"Yeah, and they're going to try to stop us from deploying our own," McGrath said. "That's what I've been fighting against since I came to the Senate."

"You're shoveling shit against the tide, Neal. It's going to happen whether either one of us likes it or not."

McGrath muttered something unintelligible.

"And we're going to start building our own ABM satellites," Kinsman went on, "in orbital factories, out of materials mined from the Moon."

"The hell you are."

"The hell we're not! The whole Department of Defense is behind this one, Neal. It's not just a little hospital of a Moonbase anymore. It's not just us *Luniks*. The entire military-industrial complex is in the act now. And so is the White House."

Understanding dawned in McGrath's eyes. "So that's why Dreyer's people have been huddling with the committee chairman. And the big aerospace primes are starting to give cocktail parties . . ."

"They're lining up their votes."

With a stubborn shake of his head McGrath said, "Once we start mining operations on the Moon the Russians will do exactly the same thing. Or worse: once they see that you're using lunar resources to build Star Wars hardware, they'll try to stop you. World War Three could start on the Moon and spread to Earth."

"No, it won't, Neal. There won't be any fighting on the Moon. I promise you that."

"How can you—"

"I'm going to be the commander of Moonbase."

"You want to spend a hundred billion dollars on top of everything we're already spending and bring the world to the brink of nuclear war, just so you can play soldier on the Moon."

"You know me better than that, Neal. We'll keep the Moon demilitarized. There won't be any armaments on the Moon. Just the mines. And the hospital." And a graveyard, he added silently.

McGrath shifted on the chair, making its wooden legs creak. "I'll do everything I can to stop this nonsense. I'm dead-set against it."

"The Pentagon will roll over you like a steamdriver, Neal. This isn't just a minor Aerospace Force program anymore, the kind you can nibble off the list and then go home and show the voters how much money you've saved them. This is the big time. Corporations like General Tech and the other big aerospace primes are coming in on this. It'll

259

mean employment for those half-empty shops and factories all across Pennsylvania."

"It will mean inflation . . . and war."

"No, dammitall!" Kinsman raised his voice. "The ABM satellites will protect us against missile attack. The cheaper we make them, the easier it becomes to replace damaged or defective ones, the *safer* we'll be. Right now, this minute, somebody in Russia or China or seventeen other nations can push a button and inside half an hour this whole country will be just one big mushroom cloud. There's no way to stop a missile attack! Not until the ABM satellites are deployed."

"We're going to deploy them; you're getting your Star Wars system."

"Building them from lunar resources will make them cheaper and easier to deploy. We'll be able to protect more people, more parts of the world, sooner."

"Unless you provoke the Soviets into a preemptive strike because they're afraid we'll attack them once we have all our satellites in place."

"But they'll be putting up their own ABM satellites. You said so yourself."

"And you're building your goddamned interceptor to knock them down. What happens when the two of you start fighting in orbit? You could start a nuclear war here on the ground."

Kinsman took a swig of ale. "If that's going to happen, it'll happen whether we have a Moonbase or not. Neither one of us has any control over that."

"But I'm not going to vote to help you make it easier for them to start a war," McGrath insisted.

"But war isn't the only possibility, Neal. Look at the benefits we can get."

"Such as?"

"A solid industrial base in orbit. Shipping lunar ores to orbital factories can start the ball rolling on the solar power satellites and all the other peacetime industries in space that will help people on Earth. Opening the door to all the raw materials and energy in space. New jobs. New technologies. New industries. Space is our escape hatch, Neal. If we use it wisely we can put an end to the causes for wars on Earth. We can get out of this coffin we've built for ourselves down here."

"We've been through all that before. It'll take twenty, thirty years before space industries even begin to help the poor and disadvantaged here on Earth."

"Even so," Kinsman said, "what other program do you have that can help them? Everything else is taking from Peter to pay Paul. That's what causes wars, Neal: trying to steal a bigger slice of the pie. All those welfare programs you're pushing, all they do is prolong the misery. Space operations can open up new sources of wealth, make the pie bigger."

"For the rich. For the corporations."

"For everybody! If you do it right."

"I don't believe it, Chet. And I can't vote for it. It's impossible."

"Then you'd better kiss the Minority Leadership goodbye," Kinsman said. "And maybe your seat in the Senate, too."

He stared at Kinsman for a long, silent moment. "So it boils down to that, does it?"

"You knew it would."

"All this high-flown talk about the future and the benefits to the human race . . . it all comes down to the fact that you're willing to blackmail me just to get your ass up to the Moon."

"That's right."

"You *are* a sonofabitch. And a cold-blooded one, at that."

Kinsman grinned at the angry, smoldering Senator who had been his friend. "Neal, a fanatic who's willing to sacrifice his life for his cause is perfectly willing to sacrifice *your* life for his cause."

"So you can get to the Moon. You'd wreck my career, my life, you'd wreck the whole world just to get what you want."

"You'll live through it. And the world has a way of taking care of itself. Believe me, you'll both be far better off with me on the Moon. Me, and a few thousand other *Luniks*."

McGrath drained the last of his ale, then hefted the empty bottle in his big hand. "I can't vote for it. Even if I wanted to, I couldn't switch my position on this. My own party would crucify me."

261

"Yes you can. And I'll bet those big, bad industrialists in Pennsylvania will even contribute to your re-election campaign if you do."

"No," McGrath said firmly.

"It's suicide to vote against the national defense appropriation, Neal."

"I have always voted against wasteful spending."

"But this isn't wasteful! It'll create jobs, for Chrissake. Look on it as an employment program."

"That will lead us into war."

"That will lead you into the White House someday. Sure, some of your supporters will get disenchanted and turn against you—for a while. But you'll gain more supporters than you lose. You'll end up with a much wider base of support."

"By going against everything I believe in."

Suddenly exasperated, Kinsman burst out, "What the hell do you believe in, Neal? Your opinions about space are stupid! You're just as blindly ignorant about it as my father was. All those programs you back, for helping the poor and the needy—they've squandered more goddamned money on bureaucratic bullshit than anything that's ever gone through Congress. And they don't work! You've got *more* unemployed, more welfare cases right now in your own state than you did when you first came into the Congress. Look it up, I've checked the numbers."

"That's not the fault of the welfare programs."

"But those programs aren't helping! You want to be Minority Leader, you've got ambitions to head the party, but you're turning down an offer that's guaranteed to bring you more support than you've ever had because of a stubborn ideological bias that's just plain stupidly *wrong*. Just what the hell do you want?"

"I want to be able to live with myself."

"And with who else? Diane? Mary-Ellen? Both of them? Do you want to be able to live with those unemployed workers back home? To be an unemployed worker yourself? Take your pick."

McGrath got to his feet. For a moment Kinsman thought he was going to throw the empty bottle against the wall. But

262

he let it drop from his fingers. It bounced once on the thin carpeting and rolled toward the sofabed.

Kinsman stood up, too.

"I've heard enough," McGrath said. "I'm leaving. If I ever see you near Mary-Ellen again . . ."

"You won't," Kinsman said. Then, grinning, he added, "Of course, one way to make sure of that is to send me a quarter-million miles away."

McGrath glared at him.

"You can have your Minority Leadership, Neal. All I want is the Moon."

The committee hearings were scheduled to go on for another week before the senators voted. Kinsman spent the time briefing White House staffers and key Congressional leaders, including Senator McGrath. The State Department reared its head and mewed about upsetting the delicate balance of offensive and defensive armaments that had been negotiated so painstakingly at Geneva over the past decade. But the Central Intelligence Agency cut State's legs off at the knees with evidence that the Soviets were developing a spaceplane that looked so exactly like the USAF interceptor they suspected the plans had been stolen.

Then came the critical vote on the defense budget by the Senate Appropriations Committee. The budget included a small supplemental item for Moonbase: the first year's funding, "a scant fifty million," as Marcot put it, "the nose of the camel." Everyone knew, thanks to Kinsman's briefings, that the full camel would cost twenty billion or more.

The first test came almost unnoticed, except by Kinsman and the other *Luniks*: no senator proposed an amendment to the budget that would eliminate the Moonbase program.

The second test was the roll-call vote of the committee. Kinsman sat in the rear of the ornate committee chamber, holding his breath as the roll call went down the long green-topped table. Only three senators voted nay. Two abstained. McGrath of Pennsylvania was one of the abstentions.

Moonbase passed. Kinsman leaned back in his chair and let out a year-long sigh.

You've got what you wanted, he said to himself. Now all you have to do is worry about whether it was the right thing to want.

Immediately he answered himself, No! All you have to do is to *make* it the right thing.

"So that's how Neal's going to handle it," Kinsman was telling Frank Colt that evening as they celebrated at a bar in Crystal City. "He's not going to vote in favor, but he's not going to stand in the way."

The bar was jammed. Half the Pentagon seemed to be there, clamoring for drinks. Music blared from omnispeakers set into the red plush-covered walls. The lights were glittering, splashing off the mirrored ceiling. Colt and Kinsman stood at the bar, wedged in by the frenetic crowd.

Colt hiked his eyebrows. "Politicians! They got more tricks to 'em than a forty-year-old hooker."

Grabbing his drink from the bar before the guy next to him elbowed it over, Kinsman shouted over the noise, "Who cares! We're going to the Moon, buddy!"

The guy next to him gave Kinsman a queer look.

Colt laughed, then turned to look over the crowded, throbbing room. Kinsman did the same, resting his elbows against the bar. All the tables were filled, people were milling around the dance floor, hollering in each other's ears, laughing, drinking, smoking. There was not a square foot of empty space.

Looking over the noisy crowd, Kinsman realized that he would be leaving this kind of scene far behind him. No great loss, he told himself. No real loss at all.

Then he noticed a stunning Asian woman sitting at one of the tiny tables with an almost equally good-looking blonde. The Oriental had the delicate features of a Vietnamese.

Colt spotted them, too. He nudged Kinsman in the ribs. "Now *that* looks like a scrutable Oriental."

"They do look lonely," Kinsman said.

Colt nodded. "And hungry. Probably waitin' for a couple of gentlemen to offer them a square meal."

"Or a crooked one."

They started pushing through the crowd, heading for the women's table.

264

"Seems to me," Colt yelled at Kinsman over the blaring music, "it's been a helluva long time since we tried this kinda maneuver together."

Kinsman nodded. "A helluva long time."

Colt's grin was pure happiness.

Washington lay sweltering in muggy late August heat. The air was thick and gray. The sun hung overhead like a sullen bloated enemy, sickly dull orange. Any other city in the world would be empty and quiet on a Saturday like this, Kinsman thought. But Washington was filled with tourists. Despite the heat and soaking humidity they were out in force, cameras dangling from sweaty necks, short-tempered, wet-shirted, dragging tired crying children along with them. Waiting in line to get inside the White House, swarming up the steps of the Lincoln Memorial, clumping together for guided tours of the Capitol, the Smithsonian museums, the Treasury Department's greenback printing plant.

Kinsman waited in the cool quiet of the National Art Gallery beside the soothing splashing of the fountain just inside the main entrance. Wing-footed Mercury pranced atop the fountain. Kinsman laughed at the statue's pose. Looks like he's giving us the finger.

Diane showed up a few minutes late, looking coolly beautiful in a flowered skirt and peasant blouse. Kinsman went to her and they kissed lightly, like old friends, like siblings.

"How'd you get my phone number?" she asked. "I'm only in town for a few days . . ."

"Neal's office."

"But he's back in Pennsylvania during the recess."

"Yes, but his office is still functioning."

He took her by the arm and began leading her back toward the museum's main doors.

"Where're we going?" Diane asked.

"I want to take you to dinner. This is my last day here. I'm moving out to Vandenberg tomorrow."

"I know. Neal told me."

They stepped outside into the glare and soupy heat. "He's up there in the cool Allegheny breezes mapping out his campaign for the Minority Leadership, playing family man for

Mary-Ellen and the kids and the voters down home."

"He's pretty sore at you," Diane said as they walked down the steps toward the jitney stop.

"Yeah. I guess he's got a right to be."

"He said he's going to fight against your defense programs once he's Minority Leader."

Kinsman looked at her. "That's his way of salving his conscience, Diane. Behind all the rhetoric, he's going to let us go ahead and do what needs to be done. He's got the White House on his mind now."

"You took advantage of him. And me."

"That's right. And of Mary-Ellen, and the Aerospace Force, the Pentagon, the White House—the whole human race."

She did not answer him.

Their talk through dinner was trivial at first, impersonal, almost like strangers who had nothing in common. Avoid arguments during mealtime, Chester, Kinsman could hear his mother telling him. If you can't say something pleasant, then say nothing at all.

But finally he had to ask, "How'd the tests come out?"

"The tests?" Diane seemed genuinely puzzled, then she realized what he meant. With a plaintive little smile she said, "Oh, I'm pregnant, all right. It's going to be a girl."

"You're going to have it?"

She nodded.

"And Neal?" Kinsman asked.

"I don't know." Diane's smile turned slightly sadder. "*He* doesn't know what he wants—now."

It was still hot and bright outside when they left the restaurant, but the downtown Washington streets were already emptying. The tourists were hurrying for their air-conditioned hotels and restaurants, exhausted and sweaty after a day of tramping around the city. They wanted to cool off and relax before the electrical power was shut down for the night.

"Hey, I've got an idea," Kinsman said. "Come on."

He flagged down a dilapidated taxi and helped Diane into it. She looked puzzled. "Washington Monument," he told the driver.

The line of tourists that usually circled the monument

266

was gone by the time they arrived there.

"Is it still open?" Diane asked.

"Sure. I've never been up the top. Have you?"

"No."

"Then now's the time!" Kinsman gripped Diane's hand tightly as he led her up the grassy slope to the immense obelisk that loomed before them. On either side of the path the silvery solar panels that provided electricity for the monument's night lighting looked like miniature fairy-tale castles, stretching all around the spire. As they approached the gigantic column, with the sunset sky flaming red and orange behind it, its marble flanks began to look gray and dingy.

"The world's biggest phallic symbol," Kinsman said. "Dedicated to the Father of our Country."

Diane grinned sourly. "You would look at it that way, wouldn't you?"

There were only half a dozen other people waiting inside, speaking German and another language that Kinsman could not identify. They milled around for a few minutes and then the elevator came down, opened its doors, and discharged about twenty bedraggled tourists.

As the elevator groaned and creaked its way up to the top of the monument, Diane whispered, "Is this thing safe?"

Kinsman shrugged. "I'd feel a lot better if it had wings on it."

Finally the elevator stopped and its doors wheezed open. They stepped out and went to a tiny barred window. The entire city lay sprawled below them, smothered in muggy, smoggy heat. The sun was touching the horizon now, and lights were beginning to twinkle in the buildings that stretched as far as the eye could see.

"If I have some good luck," Kinsman said, "this is the last time I'll see Washington."

Diane asked, "Why did you call me, Chet? What do you expect from me?"

Surprised, he answered quickly, "Nothing! Not a damned thing. I just wanted to . . . well, sort of apologize. To you, and to Neal. He won't even talk to me on the phone, so I sort of figured I'd tell you."

"Apologize?"

"For . . . using you both, as you put it. I think it would have happened anyway, sooner or later. Somebody else would have twisted Neal's arm the way I did. But I was his friend and now I've made him into an enemy."

"You certainly have," she said.

"And you?"

She looked out at the city, so far below. "His enemies are my enemies. Isn't that the way it's supposed to be?"

"So I've heard."

He stood beside her, gazing out at the buildings and the scurrying buses and cars, all those people down there, all the cities and nations and people of the entire planet. Suddenly, finally, the enormity of it hit him. Grasping the iron bars set into the stone window frame, Kinsman could feel himself falling, swirling out into emptiness. Good God, he thought. All those people! I've set myself up against all of them. I've forced them to do what I want, without a thought for their side of it. What if I'm wrong? What if it's not the right thing?

Almost wildly he searched for the Moon in the darkening sky but it was nowhere in sight.

"Neal says you're going to start a war in space," Diane said, her voice low but knife-edged. "He says your Moonbase is going to lead to World War Three. You're going to kill us all."

"No." The word was out of his mouth before he knew he had spoken it. "Neal and the rest of you, you just don't understand. The most important thing we'll ever do is to set up permanent habitats in space. It's time for the human race to expand its ecological niche, time we stopped restricting ourselves to just one planet. Our salvation lies out there, Diane, maybe the only chance for salvation we'll ever have."

She turned to him. "That's just a rationalization and you know it. You say it's important because it's what you want to do."

"Maybe. But that doesn't change a thing. Maybe history is the result of huge massive forces that push people around like pawns. Maybe it's the result of scared, lone individuals who're driven to pull the whole goddamned human race along with them. I don't know and I don't care. I'm going to the Moon. The rest of you will have to figure things out the best you can."

"And you're leaving all this behind?"

He looked out at the sprawling city. "What's to leave? This whole planet's turning into an overcrowded slum. If we do get into World War Three it won't be because of a few thousand people living in space. It'll be because six or seven billion people are stuck here on the ground."

"But those people are worth fighting for!" Diane said. "We have to struggle for social justice and freedom *here*, on this world. We can't run away!"

"I'm not running away, Diane. I'm helping you. I'm on your side, honest I am. I'll be sending you back all the energy and natural resources you need for your struggle. I'll be helping those poor people to become rich. And I'll send you back some new ideas about how to live in freedom, too."

She shook her head. "You're hopeless."

"I know. We both decided that a long time ago."

"You're really going to the Moon. In spite of everything."

"*Because* of everything. Want to come along?"

"Me?" She looked startled.

"Sure. Why not? You could be the first woman to give birth on another world."

"No, thanks! I'll stay right here."

"Then we'll never see each other again," Kinsman said. The sadness of it, the finality of it, left him feeling hollow, empty.

With a knowing look Diane said, "Oh, you'll be back, Chet. Don't get dramatic. You won't stay up there forever. Nobody could. You'll be back."

But his eyes were focused beyond her, on the window at her back. Through its narrow aperture he could see the full Moon topping the hazy horizon, smiling crookedly at him.

"Don't bet your life on it," he said.